The BAD BOY BILLIONAIRES
Collection I

Volumes 1 - 4

JUDY ANGELO

Author contact:
judyangelotreasure@gmail.com

For updates on new books visit:
www.judyangelo.blogspot.com

BAD BOY BILLIONAIRES
Judy Angelo

Volume 1 – Tamed by the Billionaire
Volume 2 – Maid in the USA
Volume 3 - Billionaire's Island Bride
Volume 4 - Dangerous Deception
Volume 5 - To Tame a Tycoon
Volume 6 - Sweet Seduction
Volume 7 - Daddy by December
Volume 8 - To Catch a Man (in 30 Days or Less)
Volume 9 - Bedding Her Billionaire Boss
Volume 10 - Her Indecent Proposal
Volume 11 - So Much Trouble When She Walked In
Volume 12 - Married by Midnight
Volume 13 - The Billionaire Next Door
Novella - Rome for the Holidays
Volume 14 - Rome for Always
Volume 15 - Babies for the Billionaire
BAD BOY BILLIONAIRES, Coll. I - Vols. 1 - 4
BAD BOY BILLIONAIRES, Coll. II - Vols. 5 - 8
BAD BOY BILLIONAIRES, Coll. III - Vols. 9 - 12

The NAUGHTY AND NICE Series
Volume 1 - Naughty by Nature

MEET THE BAD BOY BILLIONAIRES
FROM COLLECTION I
VOLS. 1 - 4

TAMED BY THE BILLIONAIRE - Vol. 1
Roman Steele - The business tycoon who has the daunting task of taming the spoiled princess.

MAID IN THE U.S.A. -Vol. 2
Pierce D'Amato - The software billionaire who thinks he's in control but instead finds himself at the mercy of an angelic four year old and a dark-eyed French beauty who steals his heart.

BILLIONAIRE'S ISLAND BRIDE - Vol. 3
Dare DeSouza - The owner of a line of Caribbean resorts who tries to teach our beloved heroine a lesson she'll never forget...but then ends up learning the greatest lesson of his life.

DANGEROUS DECEPTION - Vol. 4
Storm Hunter - He loves motorcycles, fast cars and now he's got to add one more item to his list of loves: Danielle Swift. Dani has a charm he tries to resist but this committed bachelor is no match for this bold and independent woman who's like none he's met before.

MEET THE BAD BOY BILLIONAIRES
FROM COLLECTION II
VOLS. 5 - 8

TO TAME A TYCOON - Vol. 5
Enrico Megalos - A shipping tycoon with a big problem but one which 'lion tamer', Asia Miller, is determined to fix.

SWEET SEDUCTION - Vol. 6
Jake McKoy - Billionaire author, philanthropist and recluse - a man with a past that is tearing him apart. Will Samantha Fox be the woman to pull him out of his shell?

DADDY BY DECEMBER - Vol. 7
Drake Duncan - Billionaire investor and a man determined to win the love of his life: a woman who is just as determined...to stay the heck out of his way.

TO CATCH A MAN (IN 30 DAYS OR LESS) - Vol. 8
Stone Hudson - Owner of Hudson Broadcasting Corporation, Stone is thrown for a loop when he meets a woman gutsy enough to laugh at him. And then she turns into a temptress. How can he resist?

Alpha males at their best - which one will you fall in love with?

MEET THE BAD BOY BILLIONAIRES FROM COLLECTION III VOLUMES 9 - 12

BEDDING HER BILLIONAIRE BOSS - Vol. 9
Rockford St. Stephens - The owner of a newly acquired luxury vacation business who finds himself boss to an executive assistant who can't stand him...but who he finds impossible to resist.

HER INDECENT PROPOSAL -Vol. 10
Sloane Quest - The media mogul who's rocked back on his heels when his top competitor, the lovely Melanie Parker, makes him an offer he can't refuse.

SO MUCH TROUBLE WHEN SHE WALKED IN - Vol. 11
Maximillian Davidoff - The cosmetics giant turned NASCAR entrepreneur who's bowled over by the most ornery woman he's ever met.

MARRIED BY MIDNIGHT – Vol. 12
Reed Davidoff – The fashion mogul who gets caught up in a fairy tale romance that makes him wish he could reverse his past. After the mistakes he's made, can he win the hand of the princess?

Table of Contents

TAMED BY THE BILLIONAIRE

JUDY ANGELO

The BAD BOY BILLIONAIRES Series
Volume 1

THE TAMING OF A PRINCESS...

Serena Van Buren, the privileged daughter of a wealthy businessman, can't wait to begin her three-month tour of Europe with her college mates. Little does she know that fate has other plans in store!

Instead of dancing with handsome Italians and dining with charming Frenchmen Serena finds herself trapped in a six-month internship with overbearing business tycoon, Roman Steele - an arrangement orchestrated by her own father.

Serena is determined to show Roman that she won't yield to the demands of any man, boss or no boss. She's a Van Buren, after all, known to wither a man with one look. But Roman Steele is like no man she's ever met before. Suave, sexy and stunningly handsome, there's something about him that she can't resist. It looks like Serena Van Buren has finally met her match.

A sweet and saucy romance that will have you smiling...

CHAPTER ONE

Roman Steele stared across the boardroom table at his long-time business associate. "So basically you're telling me she's a spoiled brat."

The older man frowned. "Since you put it so bluntly…yes, I guess that's what I'm saying." Richard Van Buren laced his fingers across his stomach and leaned back in the chair. "She's getting me worried, Roman. She's all grown up now. She can't keep behaving like this."

"Don't you think you're being melodramatic?" Roman asked, slightly amused. "You said she's grown now. I would think the realities of life would calm her."

"That's the problem. I haven't exposed her to any of those realities." Richard shook his head then sighed. "Ever since her mother died when she was six I've been spoiling Serena, letting her have her own way. Trying to make up for the loss of her mother, I guess." His eyes took on a distant look and his voice trailed away.

"But you went overboard?" Roman prompted.

Richard grimaced. "I let her run wild for years. I thought with the supervision of the housekeeper she would be all right. After all, girls are supposed to be easier to raise than boys, right? Guess I was wrong." Richard smiled ruefully. He reached into his breast pocket and pulled out a brown leather wallet from which he took a small photograph. He slid it across the table. "This is my Serena when she was nineteen." He shrugged. "It's a couple of years old."

Roman picked it up and found himself staring at the smiling face of a girl sitting on the back of a shiny black stallion. She was breathtakingly beautiful with long chestnut hair floating around her heart-shaped face and a pretty pout that drew attention to the pink petals of her lips.

Her eyes were the exquisite blue of the Pacific Ocean and in them was a bold defiance that spoke of the girl's confidence and spirit.

Roman raised his eyebrows. "So this is Serena," he said, almost to himself. "She's a beauty."

"That's the problem," Richard said grimly. "She's beautiful and she knows it. And she's also the daughter of a wealthy man who spoils her." His face turned sad. "This is not how I want things to be. I want my daughter to be prepared for the world. When I pass on she's the one who's going to take charge of the company and right now she's not prepared for any of that."

Roman tore his gaze away from the photograph and looked back at Richard. "You talk as if you plan to leave soon," he said with a chuckle. "You're as healthy as a horse."

"Yes, but you never know..." Richard tapped his silver pen on the table, his weathered face thoughtful. "Serena is finishing up college in a week. She'll be twenty-one with a Bachelor's degree in art history. She didn't even do her degree in business like I told her. How prepared can she be to take over the business?" He shook his head then smiled wryly. "I can't even rely on her to find a suitable husband. She's shown no interest in the guys who've come knocking. She'll probably keep rejecting them for years to come."

"So what are you going to do about this?"

Richard shrugged. "Short of forcing her into marriage with a man with some business sense, I have no idea." Then he grinned at the preposterous idea. "If only we were back in the nineteenth century."

Roman sat back and looked keenly at Richard. He could see that despite his attempt at humor the older man was distressed. They'd just finished up a business meeting where they'd discussed a possible collaboration between both their companies. They were considering a partnership in the development of a new line of skin care products. Out of the blue Richard started talking about his daughter. The situation was obviously weighing heavily on his mind.

"So let me get this straight," Roman said, folding his arms across his chest. "You have a daughter who likes to have her own way. She doesn't listen to you yet you give her whatever she wants. You've been doing this for the past twenty-one years and now you want her to settle down and get involved in the business?"

Richard gave a solemn nod. "I know I've been a terrible parent. And I know it's late. I should have been firm with her all those years." He gave a deep sigh. "She's not prepared, Roman. My daughter needs a crash course in real life."

Roman released his folded arms and leaned forward. "I have an idea that could help."

"Yes?" Richard raised his eyebrows, obviously curious.

"What if your daughter worked for me for a while, say for the next six months?"

"You would take her under your wing, be a mentor to her?"

"Right. I'll give her responsibilities that will equip her to help you in the management of your company. There's just so much you can learn within a six month period but I can structure her role and experiences so that they'll give her a foundation in business. You can build on that once her internship is over."

Richard looked doubtful. "You know she could easily get that experience at my office."

"True, but how seriously do you think she'd take her job knowing that she could leave work, go shopping and never get fired?"

Richard's lips tightened. "I see your point."

"Now I can't promise you that after six months your daughter will be an angel but what I do promise is that she'll leave my company with experience in the various aspects of business."

"Sounds good so far," Richard said, still with a hint of doubt in his voice. "I'm going to have to figure out the best way to break this to her. I know she had her heart set on touring Europe right after graduation but now this? She's going to have a fit."

"And you, dear Dad, are going to sit her down and let her know she starts work at Steele Industries the first week of July."

"That's just a week after she gets here."

"What better time to start? It will be before she gets used to being at home, all relaxed. She needs to jump in head first."

Richard nodded then he expelled his breath and on his face was a look of relief. He rose and stretched out a hand to his partner in crime. "Roman, as of the first week of July my daughter is in your hands. Let's shake on that." There was a twinkle in his gray eyes as he smiled. "I just hope you know what you're getting yourself into."

Roman grasped Richard's hand. "Don't you worry about that. By the time I'm done your Serena will be a new woman." He smiled, full of confidence, as he released the man's hand. "You can trust me on that."

******

Serena listened distractedly as her friends chattered away. Her mind was not with Tammy and Jan today. Graduation was just two days away and she was looking forward to her father flying from Toronto to be with her in New York for the ceremony. The day after graduation she would go back home with him where she guessed he would throw her a massive 'surprise' party. She knew what was coming so she'd have to start practicing her 'Oh, my gosh. I'm so surprised' look. Serena chuckled to herself. Her dad was so predictable.

Her smile widened as she remembered something very important. She'd had a great four years at the exclusive Alexander University and would be graduating magna cum laude. Daddy would be sure to give her a wonderful gift for that. She was dying of curiosity, wondering what it would be. The sun-yellow Porsche she'd admired on her last trip home? Diamond earrings? What if it was that Ferrari she'd pointed out at the auto show? Serena could hardly contain her excitement but she bit her lip and stayed silent. No, she wouldn't blurt her ideas out to her friends. She really didn't know what the gift would be. The only thing she was sure of was that it was going to be expensive. It always was.

"Serena," Tammy said petulantly as she pulled on her friend's arm, "you haven't heard a word I said, have you? I was asking if you wanted to go into Saks."

"That's fine," Serena said, slightly annoyed at being pulled out of her reverie.

"It's only two days before graduation," Jan said, raising her eyebrows at Serena. "Aren't you the least bit anxious since we haven't even bought our dresses yet?"

"We'll be wearing graduation robes," Serena said, rolling her eyes. "Nobody will see our dresses." Right then she wasn't interested in anything as mundane as a dress.

"We're going to take our robes off sometime, aren't we?" Jan pressed.

Serena sighed then turned her attention to her friends. She'd much rather head for the Gucci store to look at handbags or do her shopping at Prada but she felt a pang of guilt. She'd been ignoring them all day. Time to make them happy. "You're right," she conceded. "We need to get some new clothes. Let's go."

The shopping trip was pleasant and by the time Serena and her friends were finished she had six new outfits. She knew she only needed one for the graduation ceremony but the others had looked so beautiful she just couldn't resist the temptation of taking them too. And anyway, it was no big deal. She had a platinum card and her Dad took care of the bills every month. She didn't even see the statements. They were all sent straight to his office for payment.

"I'm tired," Tammy said, yawning, as they headed towards Serena's Mercedes Benz SUV. They were all loaded down with shopping bags.

"And I'm hungry," Jan piped up. "We haven't eaten since eleven o'clock and it's almost seven now."

"I heard of a new Chinese restaurant that opened up on 49th Street," Serena said. "Let's have dinner there. My treat."

The restaurant and the food were as exquisite as Serena had heard. The oriental tapestries that covered the walls were of rich black and red embroidered velvet and the wine-colored carpet was plush beneath her sandaled feet. The food was brought in ornately decorated silver bowls and, placed before each of them, were little plates that were toasty-warm to the touch. Steam rose from the various bowls, filling the air with a mélange of delectable aromas, tangy, spicy and savory. Then the server brought a small wicker basket covered with a soft white napkin and the sweet smell of fresh-baked bread wafted towards them. Tammy picked up a tiny egg roll and popped it into her mouth.

"Delicious," she said, licking her fingers delicately. "You couldn't have picked a better place."

"I told you it would be great." Serena winked at her. "But just remember that diet you're supposed to be on. No appetizers for you."

Tammy groaned. "Please. Don't remind me." She looked longingly at the basket of bread rolls in the middle of the table then sighed. "You're right. I definitely can't afford to gain back those twenty pounds I practically killed myself to take off."

Jan chuckled and leaned over and gave her shoulder a squeeze. "You'll be all right, Tammy. We'll make sure you stay on track. That's what friends are for."

After their hunger had been assuaged the friends relaxed, sipping green tea and coffee. They were in no hurry to get back to the university. After all, tomorrow was Saturday and they would have a chance to sleep in late. They were deep in conversation when a shadow fell across the table. They looked up. There standing over them was Chad Thornwell, the university jock, a guy so full of himself it was a wonder he hadn't fallen in love with...Chad Thornwell. Then again, maybe he had.

"Hey, Beautiful," he said, eyes trained on Serena, "wanna hook up before graduation?" Then he stood there, muscular arms folded, grinning down at her. He looked so smug with his spiky blonde hair and bright blue spandex top that showed off every cut of his chest muscles. The glint in his eyes and the self-satisfied curl of his lips told a girl everything she needed to know. This guy thought he was God's special gift to womankind. Period.

Tammy and Jen, forever in awe of the college stud, looked at Serena and giggled. Then they started preening for him, Jan straightening her back so her tiny breasts could finally be seen in her loose sweater and Tammy dabbing daintily at her lips with her napkin and peeking up at him with wide, worshipful eyes.

Serena rolled her eyes then looked away. Chad had been pursuing her all year…ad nauseum…no matter that he'd slept with half the women on campus. What part of 'no' didn't he understand? What could she say to get rid of him once and for ever? Then, like a whisper from an angel on her right shoulder…or more likely a devil on her left…it came to her. Just crush his inflated male ego, girl, right here right now in front of his adoring fans. Slam him when there's an audience and he'll be gone for good.

And then he did the unthinkable. In the middle of her ponderings he had the audacity to lean down and try to plant a kiss on her cheek, his face suddenly so close that, with a gasp, she drew back sharply. The nerve of him to try that. And in front of an audience.

Eyes wide, she leaned away from him then reached down and grabbed her purse. "Hold on just a minute," she gasped, feigning astonished awe. "I didn't expect that." She gave him a tremulous smile.

Quickly, she fished around in her purse then as her fingers circled the intended object she nodded. "There. Found it." She pulled out a pack of mint gum and held it up to Chad in full view of her friends and all those who had turned to watch. "Take the whole pack. Trust me, you need it."

Serena never saw a man back off so fast. He jerked back and when he straightened his face was red as tomato. His lips worked like he wanted to say something biting and couldn't find the words but he only flexed his muscled arms and glared down at her. What was he going to do? Hit her? He couldn't be that stupid.

With a flick of her head, Serena dismissed him. She turned her attention back to her sheepishly grinning friends, totaling ignoring the man glowering down at her. Then as if finally getting the message he turned and stormed out of the restaurant, almost bowling over a server carrying a tray of food.

"Ooh," Jan said, giggling out loud once he was gone. "You can be such a wicked witch sometimes."

"Sometimes a girl's got to do what a girl's got to do," Serena said, unapologetic. "I don't have time to waste on flirts."

"So how do you think you'll ever find a husband?" Tammy chimed in.

"Don't worry about her." Jan rolled her eyes. "That's how she's always been. She's a cold one. Never has time for guys."

"I'm not cold." Serena glared at her friend. "I'm just picky."

"You'll pick yourself right into spinsterhood if you're not careful." Jan grinned at her.

Serena was unperturbed. She smiled. "You never know. I may find the perfect guy in Paris."

"It's going to be great," Tammy said, her brown eyes sparkling with excitement. "Just the three of us traveling all over Europe. We're bound to run into some hotties."

"Yes, well," Serena said in her most snooty voice, looking down her nose, "I'll be going to Europe for the culture not to look for men."

"Yeah, right." Jan grinned at her.

Serena laughed then waved the server over for the bill. "You're right. I'm looking forward to this trip for more reasons than one. I can hardly wait."

CHAPTER TWO

Serena bounded down the wide staircase then walked quickly down the hallway toward her father's office. It was still very early in the morning but she liked to go riding when the dew was still on the grass and the air smelled fresh from the night. Her black stallion, Prince, would be ready and waiting for her and she would have the usual carrot in hand. He loved these tidbits and she enjoyed it when he stretched his neck and neighed in gratitude.

This morning though she would have to make a quick stop. The housekeeper had stopped by to tell her that her father wanted to see her before she headed out. It was probably going to be one of his usual lectures about being careful on her ride and not staying out too long and traveling with a cell phone. She shook her head and smiled to herself. He treated her like such a baby.

Even though she walked briskly it took her a little while to get to her father's study. The family home was massive, more like a mansion. Serena had always wondered why her father held on to it. There were only the two of them there outside of the household help. They had a housekeeper, a cook, a gardener and a chauffeur for just two of them. Not that she minded the service. But the house seemed such a waste on just two people. However, her father had insisted that it was the house he'd bought for her mother and even after her death he could not bear the thought of parting with it.

But Serena's real reason for wanting to move from her magnificent family home was that she wanted to be closer to the city, closer to all the action and her friends. Bridle Estates was no place to be when you wanted to hang out at parties and go on quick shopping trips. It was too far away from everything else. She loved the fact that she had a lot of space to do her riding. They were sitting on acres and acres of land. But sometimes she wished she had it all, the luxury plus the convenience. Like the Rosedale area. That would be perfect, an oasis of stately homes in the heart of the city. She had to start working on her dad, make him see the wisdom of moving.

Although she was wearing riding boots her feet padded along the plush carpet. When she got to the double doors of her father's office she knocked lightly then pushed them open and walked in.

"Hi, Daddy," she said brightly, even before she saw him. "Beth told me you wanted to see me?"

As she walked into the spacious office the black leather chair behind her father's desk swiveled round and she saw her father's smiling face. "Good morning, Princess," he said in his deep, gravelly voice. "You look well rested this morning."

"And you look tired." She threw herself down in the dark leather chair in front of him. "You look like you've been up all night. Have you been drinking?"

"No, I haven't." He smiled at her indulgently. "But I have been thinking. A lot."

"About what?"

"About you."

Serena frowned as she looked into her father's gentle gray eyes. "What about me?" Then her heart melted in realization. "Oh, I know what you've been thinking about." She jumped up from her chair and went quickly around the desk to put her arms around her father's shoulder. "I know you'll miss me, Dad, but it's only going to be for a few months. You can survive without me."

Her father nodded then patted her hand gently. "That's what I want to talk to you about, Princess." He

26

took her hand and pulled her around to face him. "I'm afraid the trip is off."

Serena's mouth fell open. She pulled her hand away from her father's grasp and stepped back quickly. Then she jammed her balled fists on her hips.

"What are you talking about, Daddy? How could the trip be off? I've been planning this all year."

"I know." He sighed and clasped his hands across his middle. "But I'm going to have to change that plan. There is something that I want you to do that is far more important than a trip to Europe."

"What could be more important than my trip to Europe? That's supposed to be the last part of my education. The finishing touch, remember?"

"Serena, be quiet for a moment." Richard's voice was stern.

Serena sucked in her breath. He rarely spoke to her in that tone of voice. Something serious must have happened. She walked back to the chair she had vacated and sat on the edge. She looked across at her father and his usually gentle eyes were now sharp and businesslike.

"I want you to listen very carefully, Serena." He rested his hands on the desk. "I love you very much but I have to admit that I've failed you as a parent. Now I want to make things right. I want to make sure you're well prepared for the world." He leaned back in the chair, loosened his arms and put a hand to his eyes as if in pain.

"Are you all right, Dad?" Serena got up and quickly went over to her father. "Is something wrong?"

"No, no." He shook his head and dropped his hand. His face looked grave. "I'm so ashamed of how I've handled your upbringing all these years. I have failed your mother."

"Daddy, why are you saying these things? You've been the best dad in the world. You've given me everything I've ever wanted."

"Therein lies the problem." He sat up straight and fixed her with a serious look. "Serena, I've arranged for you to work with Steele Enterprises assisting the president and CEO, Roman Steele. It will be an internship of sorts so you can gain some experience in business."

"What?" Serena jumped up from her chair and stared at her father. Had she heard right? "What are you saying, Daddy? I'm supposed to be traveling all summer. How can I be in Europe and work with this Roman person at the same time?"

"That's the thing. You won't be in Europe. You'll be working starting Monday."

Serena gasped. "That's in less than a week." She shook her head, confused. "What happened, for you to do this to me? I don't get it."

"That's what I was trying to tell you, Serena. I need to prepare you for the world. I'm not going to be with you forever. I want to know that when I leave this earth you're prepared to face the world alone."

"But I don't need to cancel my trip. I can do all of that when I get back. I'm only going away for three months."

"I'm sorry, Serena, but you have no choice in this." Her father's voice was firm. "It's time for me to put my foot down. You'll report to work on Monday and you'll be with Steele Enterprises for the next six months. You'll earn your own money, learn to budget, and your allowance will be suspended until the end of your internship period."

Serena jerked back, shocked into silence. Then she felt quick tears sting her eyes. "How could you? What have I done to deserve this? How am I going to manage without my allowance? It's not fair!"

"It's what has to be done. I can't prepare you for the world by pampering you. You're a woman now, Serena, not a child. From now on I will treat you as such."

For a long while Serena could only stare back at him, her dismay burgeoning till she felt she would burst into tears right in front of her father. That had worked for her in the past but somehow she knew it would not work for her now. With a sob of frustration Serena spun on her heels and stalked back to the door. When she got there she turned and glared at Richard.

"I'll do what you say because I have no choice but I will never forgive you for this." With that she marched out, slamming the door behind her.

******

Serena rode hard as she hit the open field. Her eyes were narrow slits and she was breathing hard as she leaned forward in the saddle but it was not because she was exerting herself. It was because she was seething. She could not believe her father was making her cancel her long awaited trip. He'd even threatened to cut off her allowance. In all her life she could not remember her father ever speaking to her in that way. And he'd said it was because he loved her. And he was showing his love by making her work for one of his old fogey business partners?

Well, she was going to make him change his mind. And she knew one way that she could do it. She would get an ally.

Within minutes she was trotting the horse up the dirt track to the back of her grandmother's house. She was lucky to have a grandparent who lived just a few miles away, someone who always had time for her and who listened to what she had to say. If Serena was upset about anything at all she knew that Grandma Sylvie would be there for her. This was one of those times.

Although it was not yet eight o'clock when Serena knocked on the kitchen door the smell of eggs and hot chocolate already wafted through the air. Within seconds the door flew open and Grandma Sylvie stood there smiling, her gray hair in rollers.

"What took you so long?" She took Serena's hand and pulled her into the kitchen.

"How did you know I was coming?" Serena stepped into the kitchen then gave the petite woman a quick hug. "Are you psychic or something?"

"No." Sylvie's eyes twinkled. "Your dad called. He knew you were going to head right here after the little talk you both had."

"He told you about that, did he?" Serena pulled out a chair and sat around the kitchen table while Sylvie bustled about doing what she loved best.

Sylvie loved cooking, especially for people who had problems. She'd often told Serena that it was her way of helping. If you came to her with your woes the least she could do was make your stomach happy. Right now she was making a cheese omelet just the way Serena liked it - with lots of onions and green papers wrapped in the middle. She quickly slid the omelet onto a plate and laid it on the table. She poured two glasses of orange juice then pulled out a chair and made herself comfortable beside her granddaughter.

"So. Tell me all about it." Sylvie put her elbow on the table and rested her chin in her palm. Her green eyes sparkled with interest. "Richard gave me his version but I know you're ready to share yours."

"He practically threw me out of the house, Grandma." Serena was pouting but she didn't care. She was so angry. "He told me I had to get a job. Can you believe it?"

Sylvie chuckled as she popped a piece of egg into her mouth. "Sure I can believe it. You just finished college so the next step would be to use those skills in the working world. Or did I get things wrong?"

"You're forgetting something. I was supposed to be in Europe a couple of weeks from now." Serena folded her arms across her chest and frowned. "That was supposed to be one of my graduation presents. You know that. Now I'm going to have to stay here and work for some old geezer." She shook her head. "I don't understand why he would do this to me."

"You'll understand in a while," Sylvie said as she reached over and patted Serena's arm. "Now eat something before you wither away. You're so skinny already."

"Oh, Grandma." Serena got up and began to pace the floor. "You just don't understand. Daddy is trying to sabotage all my plans and I don't get it. Why does he hate me?"

Sylvie burst out laughing. "You are such a drama queen. You know your father doesn't hate you. He loves you. Don't you see that's why he's doing this?"

Serena scowled. "This has nothing to do with loving me. If he did he would let me go away like I planned. My best friends are going."

"Serena." Sylvie's voice became serious. "Sit down and let me talk to you."

Serena knew when to obey. She went back to her chair and waited for the lecture she knew was coming.

"And stop fiddling with your fork." Sylvie slapped her hand and Serena pulled it back. "Now, young lady, it's time to wake up and smell the coffee." Sylvie gave her a stern look. "Your father...and I...have spoiled you rotten. You're a sweet girl and no one can deny that. But what is also true is that your dad has always given you everything you wanted, and so have I. I agree with Richard. You're a

31

woman now. We can't keep treating you like a child." She reached over to take Serena's hands in hers. "You have a lot to learn about life, Serena. And remember, you are Richard's only heir. All your father is trying to do is to get you ready for life. You must understand that."

Sylvie put her hand under Serena's chin and lifted it so that their eyes met. "Do you promise me that you'll do what your father asks? Will you do this for me?"

Serena tried to look away but her grandmother's stare was so intense that she felt transfixed. When Sylvie dropped her hand Serena heaved a sigh of resignation then nodded slowly. "All right, I'll do it." Then she set her mouth in a mutinous pout. "But if the old geezer I'm going to work for thinks I'm going to be his new gopher, he'd better think again. And he'd better be nice to me or else he'll wish he'd never met Serena Van Buren."

CHAPTER THREE

As Serena drove along Bay Street she was lost in thought. She was on her way to Steele Industries for her first day at work and she was not looking forward to it. In fact, she was busy thinking of ways to derail her father's plans to make her a 'working woman'. Yes, she'd promised her grandmother she'd give it a try but she hadn't promised she'd be a model employee. Maybe she could get herself fired on day one. She bit her lip, giving it some thought. Was that a good idea, though? Effective today she would no longer receive a monthly allowance and would need to earn her own money. And she'd have to survive that way for the next six months. She shuddered at the thought. She had never felt so trapped in her life.

She found the place easily enough and pulled off the road and into the parking lot where she slid into the last empty spot. The sign said reserved but right then she didn't have time to be choosy. She reached over for her Hermes handbag then slid out of the SUV, the slim skirt of her Chanel suit making it impossible for her to hop down. She put on her sunglasses then slammed the door and walked briskly toward the main entrance, her stilettos tapping loudly on the pavement.

Serena entered the lobby and for a moment was taken aback by the magnificence of the main entrance. The lobby was huge with a high cathedral ceiling from which a massive chandelier hung. The black marble tiles on the floor glistened and as she looked down she saw herself reflected in their sheen. The walls were covered in the same dark marble but those were accentuated with gold trim. The company logo on the wall and the handles of all the doors were in gold. She had to admit the building was impressive.

She approached the massive receptionist desk and, putting on her most formal tone, she said to the woman sitting there, "Serena Van Buren, here to see Mr. Roman Steele."

"Good morning." The woman acknowledged her with a nod. "Do you have an appointment with Mr. Steele?"

"Uhh, yes," Serena said quickly, too embarrassed to tell the woman that she was reporting for her first day at work. "He's expecting me."

"I'll have someone take you up." She directed Serena to have a seat in one of the soft black leather chairs along the side of the wall.

She'd been sitting there for less than a minute when a statuesque woman with raven-black hair exited the elevator and approached her. She was impeccably dressed in a wine-colored suit and matching pumps. She had the body and gait of a model.

"Ms. Van Buren?" The woman's voice was husky, almost as deep as a man's. Serena tried to hide her surprise behind a bright smile. She stood up and took the woman's outstretched hand.

"Yes, I'm Serena Van Buren."

"Welcome," the woman said then released her hand. "My name is Theresa Lederman. I'm Mr. Steele's personal assistant." Then her brows knitted. "Did you have a problem getting here? We were expecting you some fifteen minutes ago." The disapproval was evident in her tone.

Serena immediately bristled and straightened to her full height, not that it made much difference since Theresa Lederman had a good four or five inches on her. She gave the woman a frosty look. "I'm not used to driving on Bay Street at this time of morning. I had no idea the traffic was so heavy." Then she frowned, angry at herself for even responding. She'd never had to explain herself to anyone before. And who did this woman think she was to ask her about being late? She was nothing but a glorified secretary, after all.

The woman looked down at her and nodded. "Well, this is your first day so I can understand. But you will have to head out earlier tomorrow. Mr. Steele postponed a meeting specifically in order to meet you this morning and he's already lost fifteen minutes." She beckoned Serena toward the elevator. "Unfortunately, he'd wanted to spend at least an half an hour with you to get you started but now he'll only have a few minutes."

"I'm…sorry," Serena said grudgingly, suddenly feeling guilty for her previous display. She was going to have to check her attitude. She gave an inaudible sigh. Being an employee was not going to be easy.

At the tenth floor Theresa punched in a code and the glass doors automatically slid open. They entered another beautiful lobby, a smaller, more intimate version of the one below. She strode down a hallway then stopped in front of a door and knocked. Serena heard nothing but apparently the woman did because she pushed it open then stepped aside to allow her to enter. "Ms. Van Buren," was all she said by way of presentation then as Serena stepped into the room she pulled the door shut behind her.

Stepping hesitantly into the middle of the room Serena looked around at the expansive office, impressed with the elegance of its décor and the wide bay window with its impressive view of the city. A quick survey revealed that the long anticipated Roman Steele, the man who would hereafter control eight hours out of each of her weekdays, was nowhere to be seen.

Okay, now what? Stand here like an idiot or plop self into one of the chairs and wait? Where the heck was he, anyway?

As if in answer she heard the rustle of paper then a deep voice behind her. "Welcome, Miss Van Buren."

Serena jumped. She turned toward the voice then stared in wide-eyed surprise at the startlingly handsome man who filled her vision. Tall and broad-shouldered, he towered over her five foot three inch frame in an immaculate suit the color of midnight. Ink-black hair framed a tanned, rugged face that spoke of strength, power and pride. Eyes the color of black diamonds bored into her, making her flush under his intense scrutiny. When his firm lips curled in what could only be amusement, she dropped her gaze and her eyes sought refuge in the rich crimson of his tie.

She'd been staring like a doe caught in headlights but she couldn't help it. Roman Steele was so shockingly different from the middle-aged balding man she'd expected. Who could have known he'd look like he belonged on the cover of GQ? And why in heaven's name was her heart racing like she'd just done a hundred-meter sprint?

Serena took a quick breath, trying desperately to steady her pulse. She lifted her face again. "Where did you come from?" she asked, then cursed herself for sounding so breathless.

He cocked an eyebrow then giving her a crooked smile he waved his hand in the direction of a door which stood slightly ajar. "I was pulling a file from the vault." He seemed amused at having taken her by surprise. "Please. Have a seat." He waved her to a chair then went and sat behind his massive desk of deep mahogany. "I'm glad you could finally join us."

Serena felt her face redden at his sardonic tone. "I got caught in traffic," she began then bit her lip, realizing how easily the man had intimidated her.

She'd had a plan to come into this office and, through either intimidation or charm, get herself out of this predicament. She'd planned to get her new employer on her side, get him to talk to her father, reason with him about how unnecessary the internship was. She could see that intimidation was not going to work here. This man was too bold, too sure of himself...and too darned handsome. Risky as it might be she would just have to try charm instead.

She looked at him with wide eyes. "I'm so sorry I was late this morning, I really tried to be on time. It won't..." She paused, lowered her lashes and looked down at her hands. "It won't happen again," she said in a soft whisper.

Through the thickness of her lashes she peeped up at Roman and saw that he was taken aback by her response. She had to bite her lip to keep from smiling her satisfaction. Then his eyes narrowed and she quickly dropped her glance. She could not afford for him to read the true Serena. Not yet, anyway. Not if her plan was going to work.

"Good. I will appreciate punctuality in future." Roman's voice was firm.

Serena looked back at him, frowning slightly. She had not expected this. Normally, as soon as she started playing "defenseless maiden" all the men in her presence would jump to protect her and her feelings. She had expected Roman to tell her that it was okay, that she didn't have to worry about being late. So charm had not worked with him. Not yet, anyway. She was not going to give up.

"I wanted to give you a proper introduction to Steele Industries, tell you about what we do here and what you will be expected to do in your new position. That won't be possible seeing that we're having this conversation twenty minutes later than planned." He looked at her sternly.

She glared back at him, unable to stop herself. Her plan to charm this man seemed useless. He was much too overbearing. She could feel her face grow hot again but this time it wasn't from embarrassment. She was too angry to be embarrassed. The man was frowning at her as if she were a wayward child.

"According to what your assistant told me you still have about ten minutes before your next meeting. Wouldn't it make sense for you to make use of those minutes?" She gave him her haughty Serena Van Buren glare, the one she'd used to shrivel many a man who'd sought her attention.

Roman's eyes narrowed. He seemed unimpressed. "I would appreciate your remembering your position here."

"And what, exactly, is that position, Mr. Steele?" she said in challenge. "If you realize, you still haven't told me what I'm supposed to be doing here."

"As I'm sure your father already told you, you'll be working closely with me. You'll be my special project coordinator, assisting me in the launch of a new line of hair care products. You'll be involved in all aspects of the launch – product development, consumer research, marketing, sales and finance. "

Serena was silent for a moment, absorbing it all. Then she said slowly, "My father never told me any of this. It sounds like you plan to work me into the ground."

"The job will require you to work with various departments. This is what people do, Miss Van Buren. They work for their compensation." Roman's voice was unyielding. "You will be expected to carry your weight around here just like everyone else."

Serena bristled at his tone. "Mr. Steele, I want you to understand something. I don't need to be here. I'm only here to please my dad so if you think I'm going let you-"

"As my employee you will do as I instruct," he said coldly. "You may have thought you were coming here on holiday but you're here to work. And make no mistake, you will deliver."

"And if I don't?"

"Then be prepared to face the consequences."

CHAPTER FOUR

"Hello." Serena's voice was husky with sleep. She rubbed her eyes and peered at the clock radio on her night stand. Six o'clock. Now who in the world would be calling her at this hour?

"Wake up, sleepy head." Tammy's shrill voice was jarring.

Serena put the phone receiver away from her ear and glared at it. She could still hear Tammy's giggles from afar and she was not amused. She was still frowning as she put the receiver back to her ear.

"Tammy, why are you calling me so early in the morning? This had better be important." She sighed and shook her head. "Although I have a feeling it's not."

"I have Jan on the phone, too," Tammy said cheerfully, totally ignoring Serena's annoyed tone. "We're doing a three way so we can give you the good news together."

Serena yawned and stretched luxuriously under the down comforter. "What good news?"

"Tammy and I are leaving for Paris next week." Jan's voice was breathless.

"What? You're still going? Without me? We were supposed to do that as a group, as friends." Serena sat up in the bed, fully awake and peeved at this turn of events. She'd been planning this trip with Tammy and Jan all year and now they were planning to run off without her.

"But Serena, you won't be free for months. You're stuck in that job thing you're doing and we still want to go." Tammy could not hide the eagerness from her voice.

"We got another girl to join with us," Jan chimed in. "Remember Kelly Snow? We told her about the trip and she's crazy about the idea. You know we needed a third person to split the hotel costs."

"I was supposed to be that third person to help you guys out," Serena said bitterly. "And now all you do is stab me in the back."

"There's no need to be nasty about it," Jan scolded her. "You're not available right now and we still want to go. When we get back we can do lots of things together but this might be our last chance to fulfill our dream of exploring Europe. You can go any time you want. All you have to do is ask Daddy. But Tammy and I have to grab this opportunity while we can."

"I know," Serena said softly, "and I'm sorry. It's just that I was so looking forward to doing this with you guys. If I go by myself it won't be any fun. I just thought you would wait for me."

"You know we would if we could," Jan said soothingly. "We'll make it up to you, Serena. Promise."

"Just do your best on this job of yours and maybe your dad will be so impressed he'll give you an even better gift than a trip to Europe." Tammy's voice was softer and a little less shrill than usual as she tried to comfort her friend.

"Yeah, that job," Serena said with a sigh. "It's only my second day and I hate it already. The personal assistant is bossy and my boss...well, let's just say he's definitely not what I expected."

"I bet he has a paunch and a bald head and gives you googly eyes across the desk." Tammy had begun to giggle again.

"Not exactly," Serena said slowly, suddenly not sure she wanted to share everything with her friends. She had boasted so much about how she would 'wrap the old geezer around her little finger'. Roman Steele was definitely not an old geezer and wrapping him around her little finger was probably going to be as easy as wrapping cold steel around that digit.

Jan's voice broke into her thoughts. "Just let them know you're a Van Buren. Once you fix them with that cold stare they'll wither."

"Uhh, guys, I've got to go now." Serena cut in before Jan could say more. "I have to get ready for work."

"Doesn't that sound weird?" A chuckle followed Tammy's question. "I've never heard you say anything like that."

"Come off it, Tammy," Jan said, sounding annoyed. Then she said in a voice that was quiet and almost apologetic, "We understand, Serena. We'll let you go now. Call you later, okay?"

"Okay." She hoped they didn't hear the sob in her voice.

Serena hung up the phone and for the next few moments she just lay there, staring at the wall as the thought sank in. They were going to Europe without her. While they were touring famous museums, meeting charming Frenchmen and handsome Italians, she would be slaving away at a boring office job.

She shook her head, dispelling the awful thought, then slid out of bed and headed for the bathroom feeling abandoned and alone. Her friends had betrayed her and were heading off to have fun without her, with boring Kelly Snow to boot. Her father had shipped her out of the house, cut off her allowance and put her in this apartment in the city. Okay, it was a nice apartment but it wasn't home and she missed her dogs and her horse. Her father had turned out to be a cruel, cruel man. What was worse her grandmother who had always defended her now seemed to be on his side. She just could not understand why her friends, her family, the whole world had turned against her. It was not fair.

Then as she stared at her frowning face in the bathroom mirror her mind tiptoed back to Roman Steele. Gorgeous, heart-stopping Roman Steele. She had to admit, he was one of the most attractive men she had ever seen, with his deep dark eyes and glossy black hair that curled sexily at his nape. Olive-skinned with a strong, square jaw, he could give any of the Italian hunks a run for their money. The man oozed sex appeal.

But he was also a serious man. She'd seen that very clearly on day one. He was not one to mess around with. But still, she couldn't just bow her head and play meek, mild-mannered assistant like he probably wanted. No way. That was definitely not her style.

She glanced at the clock on the wall. A quarter to seven already? Had she been daydreaming so long? She began to strip. If she wanted to get to the office on time she'd have to be on the highway in the next forty-five minutes. Today she was not in the mood to be chewed out by Roman Steele.

Or was she? Serena lifted her face to the mirror again and this time a look of mischief was reflected there. Did she want to be a good girl or did she want to get fired? To be good or not to be good, that was the question. And she had the answer.

Today she would make Roman Steele so angry that he would be happy to see the back of her. Salary be damned. Today was the day she was going to get fired.

CHAPTER FIVE

After a two hour stop at Holt Renfrew where she lounged in the cosmetics department and got a free makeover Serena pulled into the parking lot of Steele Enterprises at exactly eleven-fourteen a.m.. As she shoved the shopping bags aside and reached for her purse her heartbeat accelerated and her palms grew damp. This was it, the showdown she'd been waiting for.

She signed in at the front desk then rode the elevator to the sixth floor where she headed straight for the cubicle to which she'd been assigned. Dropping her bag and cell phone onto the desk she slid into her chair and breathed a sigh of relief. So far so good. She knew a bombshell was about to fall but not just yet. When it did, she wanted to be ready.

Serena unzipped her handbag and reached for her lipstick and compact. She needed to fortify herself for the battle ahead. There was nothing like looking your best to boost your confidence. She flipped the compact open and was peering into the tiny mirror, tracing her lips with ruby red, when she felt eyes on her. She turned quickly and found herself staring into the flashing dark eyes of Theresa Lederman.

Snapping the compact shut Serena lifted her face to the woman and gave her a look laced with challenge. For a moment neither of them spoke. Theresa was obviously trying to intimidate her but it wasn't going to happen. What? Did she think her icy stare could browbeat a Van Buren? She'd have a long wait.

Finally, the woman spoke. "Mr. Steele asked for you over two hours ago."

Serena cocked an eyebrow. "Oh?" She did not offer an apology.

"He had a meeting with the advertising agency this morning. He wanted you to participate." When Serena just stared back at her Theresa pursed her lips, obviously put out by her lack of response at the announcement. "He asked me to take you to see him as soon as you got in."

"No problem," Serena said, her tone light as she rose to face Theresa. Little did the woman know that inside she was shaking. "Let's go."

Theresa looked surprised at her boldness but she held her tongue, turned on her heel and headed toward the elevator. Serena followed some distance behind, not wanting to seem like a wayward child being escorted to the principal's office. She felt the weight of curious eyes from the nearby cubicles but she held her head high, refusing to look to the right or the left. She desired no distraction. She needed her wits about her to face the imminent wrath of Roman Steele.

The two women rode the elevator in silence. At the tenth floor Theresa strode down the hallway, knocked on the heavy oak door and, just like the day before, opened it and stepped aside. On her face was a look of something close to...sympathy?

Serena blinked. That did not make sense. The woman had no reason to feel sorry for her. But then the door was pulled shut behind her and there was no more time to think about it, no more time to prepare. She'd been thrown into the den with the lion.

Serena's eyes snapped over to Roman's desk and there he sat, face rigid, dark eyes flashing with an anger she could feel clear across the room. She stood stock-still, heart pounding in trepidation. Her fingers curled into fists as she fought to steady her nerves. *Come on, Serena, what's the worst he can do to you? He certainly can't kill you.* Still, she did not budge, opting to stay close to the door...just in case.

She was still contemplating her next move when, in one fluid movement, Roman got up from behind the desk and began to walk toward her.

Serena gasped and took an involuntary step back. When her bottom smacked the door she realized there was nowhere to go, nowhere to hide. What the heck had she gotten herself into?

But then, to her relief, he stopped in front of the desk and pulled out a chair. "Are you going to stand there all day, Miss Van Buren?" He held out his hand, directing her gaze to the empty chair. "Have a seat." Then without so much as another glance in her direction he went back around the desk and sat down.

Serena expelled her breath. The man wasn't coming to get her, he was simply offering her a chair. What was she thinking? She'd been so wired up, expecting his rage, that she'd imagined his anger. Her sudden fear had been unfounded. She was not out of the woods yet. She'd be stupid to think that. But at least it seemed that he would be calm and collected about things.

Before she could lose her courage Serena walked over to the chair and perched on the edge, hands clasped tightly in her lap. *Okay, Roman Steele. Do your worst. I'm ready for you.* She was preparing herself for the fight she knew was coming.

He did not cut corners. Folding his arms across his broad chest he gave her a cold stare. "So what's your excuse today? More traffic on the road?"

Serena shrugged in as casual a manner as she could muster. "No. I just didn't feel like coming in early today."

Roman stared at her in stunned silence. Then his brows fell and he glared at her. "You seem to misunderstand your position here. As an employee of this company it is your responsibility to get to work on time-"

"And what do you do with employees who don't follow the rules?" Serena cut him off before he could launch into the lecture she knew was coming. "You fire them, right? Well, I would suggest you give me my walking papers because you and I know this is not going to work out."

"Oh, so that's it. You're working to get fired. Well, don't hold your breath. It's not going to happen."

Her shock at his response made Serena hop to her feet. "What? What do you mean, it's not going to happen? You have to fire me."

Roman's lips curled in a sardonic smile. "Oh, do I? Sorry to disappoint you but you're stuck here with me. You'll leave in six months and not a day sooner."

"You can't do this to me." Serena's voice cracked with frustration. "I'll never fit in here. I'll never do what you want. You need to fire me. Now."

Roman leaned forward in his chair, his face as hard as rock. "Never."

Serena gasped. What kind of game was this man playing? Why couldn't he see reason? "I don't want to be here and you don't want me here. Why don't you fire me? You know you want to, so what's stopping you?"

Roman's nostrils flared. "You don't know what I want to do right now."

"Of course I do," Serena retorted. "You want to take your perverse pleasure in torturing me. You know I can't quit because of my father's conditions. The only way I can get out of this is if you fire me. So why don't you just do it? You want me to beg? Is that what you want?"

"You don't know what I want," he said through gritted teeth, his scowl as black as night.

"I do know, you sadist. You want to make me suffer-" Serena gasped as Roman got up and in two strides was right in front of her, his large frame towering over her. "What-"

"This is what I want. I've wanted it ever since I laid eyes on you." His arm snaked round her waist and he pulled her body into his, so close that she could feel the powerful muscles of his suit-clad legs and the hard ripples of his chest through the cotton of his shirt. His other hand cupped her head as he pulled her even closer, bringing her face up to his, forcing her to stand on tiptoe.

She put her hands up, clinging to his broad shoulders for balance, and he pressed firm lips to her gasping ones, taking full control, kissing her until she melted in his embrace. As his tongue explored her she responded willingly, eagerly, wanting this too, more than anything in the world. Had he known she wanted his kiss from the very first day they met? Had he seen the desire in her eyes? She would not ponder any of that. For the moment she would wipe everything from her mind and revel in his kiss.

Too soon he lifted his head, withdrawing his lips from hers, leaving her panting. Slowly, he withdrew his arm and set her back on her feet.

Still feeling like she was floating on air Serena opened her eyes and peered up into Roman's face. What she saw there made her step back in dismay. The scowl on his face was even darker than before. Was he totally unmoved by the kiss?

Roman gripped her upper arms and set her away from him. "I suggest you leave my office now," he said, his voice a harsh growl, "or else I won't be responsible for my actions." Then, with a look of disgust he released her arms and turned back towards his desk.

Serena did not wait to see what he would do next. Smarting from the blow of his rejection she turned and marched to the door. When she went through it she pulled it shut none too gently. She was fuming. She was mortified. She was…she didn't know what she was. She'd never been so humiliated in her life. So she disgusted him, did she? And yet he refused to release her from her bondage? Well, she would just see about that.

******

Roman dropped into his chair and let his breath out in a whoosh. He shook his head, hardly believing what had just happened. What the hell had he done? Serena Van Buren was an employee, for Christ's sake. On the job for all of two days. The daughter of his associate, a girl entrusted to his care. And what did he do? He'd done a damned good job of playing the pervert, taking advantage of the girl right there in the middle of his office. Jesus, what was he thinking? He was so disgusted with himself he could not sit still. He got up and began to pace the room.

What had he gotten himself into, offering to mentor and train Serena Van Buren for six months? He could not even keep his hands off her. Damn! He was in big trouble.

CHAPTER SIX

It was almost a week since the incident in Roman's office and Serena was finally getting over the shock of his kiss. Thank goodness he'd left for California the next day so she hadn't had to face him again. After the incident she'd felt ashamed and somewhat bewildered. The man had practically thrown her out of his office. She couldn't understand his reaction after what she thought had been a passionate, earth-shaking kiss. She'd spent days reliving every moment of that kiss and each time her heart would thump and her breath would catch in her throat. It had been absolutely magical.

Today, though, she would have to get her emotions under control. Roman was scheduled to be back in office this morning and, as much as she thought she was not ready to see him again, she knew the meeting was inevitable. How would she handle their first encounter after that kiss? Maybe for him the whole thing meant nothing but it had practically devastated her defenses. This was the first man she'd ever met who'd knocked her barriers down with just one blow.

The clock on her desk said nine thirty when there was a knock on her door and Theresa entered the room. "Mr. Steele needs you in his office. Make sure you take your notepad with you." She was formal, as usual, but this time there was more of an edge to the woman's voice.

"Is something wrong?"

"No, nothing. Just get down to Mr. Steele's office right away." Without another word she turned and left the room.

Serena lifted her eyebrows, surprised at Theresa's terseness, then she sank back into her chair. Her heartbeat had accelerated at the announcement and she took a couple of deep breaths to calm her nerves. "Well, here goes," she murmured and grabbed her pen and pad.

When Serena entered the office Roman was sitting at his desk holding a bottle of what looked like shampoo and a small gold jar which she guessed contained face cream.

"Have a seat, Miss Van Buren." His voice sounded pleasant enough but his stare was intense. She slid into the chair in front of him and kept her eyes downcast.

For a moment there was silence then Roman spoke in a low voice. "Serena, look at me."

Surprised at his change of tone, she lifted her head and looked into his eyes. She was taken aback by what she saw there. He actually looked ashamed.

"Serena," he said, "I owe you an apology."

Serena held her breath and stared back at him, incredulous. Roman was apologizing to her? He'd seemed like the kind of man who would apologize to no-one. Now that she was seeing a new side of him it confused her all the more. Was he apologizing for the kiss or for kicking her out of his office?

"I behaved inappropriately and for that I'm sorry. I assure you, it will never happen again."

It will never happen again. It will never happen again. The words reverberated in her head and for some reason her spirits sank. It will never happen again? Dear God, she wanted it to happen again. More than anything.

Swallowing her disappointment Serena looked back at Roman and gave him a small smile, accepting his apology with a quick nod.

"For the next few weeks you'll be working closely with the marketing team," he said, his voice professional and cool. "I'll make sure you participate in meetings that are relevant to your development. What I want is that at the end of your time with Steele Industries you should have a good handle on project management, marketing, and promotions. For today, though, you'll sit in on my meeting with the ad agency."

He leaned forward and placed the bottle and the jar in front of her. "These are two products from the Enchanted line we'll be launching next quarter. I want you to get involved in every aspect of the launch, starting with this meeting. The ad execs will be here in about ten minutes so I'll give you a quick briefing to prepare you."

Roman spoke quickly, filling her in on the consumer research that had been done and the reason why the company thought the line had great potential. Serena scribbled feverishly, trying to keep up with him, and was relieved when he finally told her it was time to head for the main conference room.

The agency executives arrived moments later and as soon as Roman introduced her to Martha Foxworth and Herman Moore the meeting began. Martha presented storyboards of television commercials with the first one depicting a woman shampooing then drying her hair and a man coming in and sliding his fingers sexily through her long brown tresses. On a second storyboard a woman applied Enchanted face cream to a wrinkled face followed by a close up shot of the crow's feet by the side of her eyes. The next shot showed a close up of the same eye but this time the skin was smoother and softer. The tagline for this commercial was "Your face never looked so good".

Last in her set Martha presented a print advertisement featuring the moisturizing face cream. The model was a beautiful dark haired woman, seeming to be in her late thirties, and she held a young child in a close embrace. The little girl had her hand on the woman's cheek, as if stroking it, and the tagline for the product said, "I just love your baby face."

After the initial presentation Martha reviewed each campaign in detail, giving Roman and Serena a chance to understand the reasoning behind each and soliciting their input. Serena was impressed by Roman's knowledge and understanding of the advertising business and, for the most part, she kept silent, absorbing as much as she could. She did make some suggestions on the clothing worn by the models but she kept her comments to a bare minimum, leaving the meatier comments to her boss.

Roman expressed concern about how the message was relayed while Serena's few comments were focused on the visual impact of the ads. Being the daughter of a wealthy man, she had lived for years in the public eye and knew how to make a good first impression. She was an expert in haute couture, make-up and styling.

Because of that she looked at the advertisements with discerning eyes and was able to find flaws where she knew the average woman might not. She felt a little guilty for involving herself too much but she knew she would feel even guiltier if she kept silent. After all, Roman had invited her into this meeting, not to be a statue but to participate. She knew she was here to learn but she also knew she had a lot to share, regardless of her lack of experience in business.

With that conviction she began to speak her mind. She made recommendations for the wardrobe for the models, and for the television commercial she even suggested changing the model all together. From what Roman had told her about the Enchanted line of products she knew it was targeted toward young, professional women. The model selected by the agency was in her late thirties. She reasoned that they needed to use a model to whom the target market would relate. Both Martha and Herman were looking at Serena with an air of surprise but Roman had a satisfied smile on his face.

"I guess we'll have to go back to the drawing board," Martha said, a hint of annoyance in her voice.

"We want this campaign to be perfect," Serena said calmly, "so it doesn't make sense for us to rush to put out something substandard."

Martha sucked in her breath but said nothing. She began packing up her storyboards and papers and sat back down beside Herman.

"I guess this is a good time for me to take over," the man said, pulling out two folders and sliding one to Roman and the other to Serena. "I had put together a budget for the campaign but seeing that we're going to make changes, some of these figures will change as well. Still, I wanted to give you an idea of what the budget will look like."

"No problem," Roman said, nodding. "Let's see what you have."

Roman and Herman began to discuss the budget line by line. Serena tried to listen but felt totally distracted. There was something about that print ad campaign that was bothering her. She just couldn't put her finger on it. She was itching to ask Martha to let her see it again but felt she'd be rubbing salt in the wound. The woman already probably hated her for making all those comments and changes to her campaign.

She became so distracted that she began to fiddle with her pen and more than once Roman glanced over at her. Finally he said, "Is something wrong, Serena?"

"Aah, yes," Serena said, deciding to take the opening he'd given her. "I just want to see that print ad again."

He raised his eyebrows but said nothing and turned to Martha. The woman shrugged and pulled out the ad then slid it over to Serena who studied it for a few seconds. "There's just something about this tag line...I don't know. I just love your baby face...can we change it?"

"Why would we want to do that?" Martha's voice was sharp but she hurried to change her tone. "I mean, it's just perfect for the print campaign. The little girl is stroking her mother's face and telling her she loves her baby face."

Serena shook her head slowly. "It sounds a bit corny to me. What about, caress your face with love?" She looked across at the woman as she spoke and saw to her surprise that Martha's eyes lit up and a smile spread across her face.

"That's perfect. I can build a whole campaign around that tagline."

Serena looked at Roman and he, too, was smiling. He gave her a nod and an enigmatic smile. For some reason it made her think of his touch and a shiver ran down her spine.

For the rest of the meeting Serena remained silent but a warm glow suffused her body. She knew she was being silly but Roman was pleased with her and she was happy.

The meeting wrapped up shortly thereafter and Theresa came in to escort the visitors out. Serena picked up her notepad and pen and was heading out of the conference room when Roman spoke.

"Just a moment, Serena."

She stopped in her tracks, her heart thumping loudly in her ears. She turned and saw that he was smiling at her. Goodness, he was so handsome when he smiled. She remained standing, her notepad clutched tightly in front of her, and waited.

"You did well today." His voice was soft and as he took the four steps that brought him within inches of her she shuddered in reaction to his nearness. She struggled to keep her face calm, not wanting him to know the effect he was having on her.

"You've got an inborn talent that came out in the meeting today. You have an eye for beauty." He smiled down at her then took her elbow and turned her toward the door. "You may go now but rest assured you'll be in many more of these meetings from here on."

Serena simply nodded, held her back straight and walked out. For the second time in a week he was showing her the door. She was glad for the praise but she would have preferred it if he'd swept her into his arms again and kissed her passionately like he'd done at their last meeting. Was she the only one who'd gotten drunk on that kiss? She bit her lip and kept on walking, her face as placid as Lake Ontario. She would never let him know how much she craved his touch.

******

That night Serena could not sleep. She'd climbed into bed at ten thirty then tossed and turned for hours with no sleep in sight. She'd had a wonderful day. No, a terrible day. She sighed in frustration. It had been a totally confusing day. First, she'd been defiant, preparing to challenge Roman next time she saw him. Then she'd tingled with the anticipation of seeing him again after their kiss. When he made the declaration that he'd never touch her again she felt deflated. When he praised her after the meeting she felt all gooey. Then he'd shown her the door. Back to depression.

What made it worse, despite her resolve to hate her job and do everything in her power to get fired she'd actually enjoyed the meeting with the ad agency. She'd learned so much in the space of just a couple of hours and, she had to admit, she was looking forward to learning even more. She groaned. That was going totally against her plan. What was she going to do now?

She looked at the clock. One thirty-five, which meant it would only be six thirty-five in the morning in Paris. She was sure that neither Jan nor Tammy would be up at this hour but she didn't care. Right now she needed someone to talk to. She picked up the phone and dialed Jan's cell number, praying that the roaming feature would work. It did. Jan answered the phone on the fifth ring.

"Hello." Her voice sounded groggy and far away.

"Wake up, sleepy head," Serena said, trying to sound cheerful. "What are you doing in bed at this hour? Do you know what time it is?"

There was a pause then Jan said dryly, "Of course I know what time it is. It's an ungodly hour of the morning . You know I never get up this early. I'm on vacation, for heaven's sake." There was a hint of annoyance in her voice.

Serena sighed. "I know I shouldn't have called you so early but I just need to talk. I'm all alone over here and I'm going crazy."

"What's going on, Serena? Are you all right?" Jan sounded fully awake now. Her voice was sharp with concern.

"I'm fine," Serena said with another heavy sigh. "It's just that you guys are over there having all the fun and I'm here working so hard. And to make things worse I have a devil of a boss who's driving me mad."

"What on earth do you mean? Didn't we discuss the plan for your boss? You were going to go in there and show him that you're a Van Buren. So what happened?"

Serena could not help smiling to herself. They had been so naïve. "Let's just say, he's not exactly the boss I expected."

"Is he nice?"

"I wouldn't describe him as…nice." Serena bit her lip and wondered how much she should tell her friend. Then she continued, "He's probably the most gorgeous man I've met in my entire life."

"What? You never told me this."

"How could I? You're halfway across the world. You and Tammy abandoned me when I needed you most."

"Come off it, Serena," Jan said, sounding exasperated. "I'm not going to feel guilty about that. We had a plan and you backed out. Mind you, I know it wasn't your fault but you certainly didn't expect your father's rules to apply to Tammy and me. Now let's get back to the real issue here. Tell me about this hunk."

"What's going on?" Serena heard Tammy faintly in the background.

"Serena's found a man and he's handsome," she heard Jan say.

"No, I haven't," she retorted. "The man is my boss, for goodness sake."

"Really? She's finally fallen for a guy?" It was Tammy's voice again, closer this time.

"Yeah, and she's going to tell me all about it," Jan said excitedly.

"Will you guys stop that?" Serena yelled into the phone. They hadn't even waited to hear her story but had jumped to all kinds of conclusions. Trust her crazy friends to be so…crazy.

"Okay, okay." Jan laughed into the phone. "I'm listening."

"Thank you," Serena said in a huff then she drew in a deep breath and began. "As I was saying, my boss is nothing like I expected. He's over six feet tall and he has jet black hair and such startling dark eyes. And his skin is dark, like…I think he's part Italian or something."

"Sounds like a movie star," Jan said, dreamily.

"Hey, I'm not hearing any of this," Tammy whined in the background.

"Shh, I'll tell you all about it when we're done," Jan hissed, quieting her. Then she said to Serena, "So have you gone out with him yet?"

"What do you think I am? I just met the man last week. Anyway, his name is Roman Steele and he's the CEO of Steele Industries-"

"Roman Steele? I know him. I mean, I've seen him in the papers before. You're right, he's a real hunk. You're so lucky…"

"No, I'm not. He acts like he doesn't even notice me." There was a sudden hitch in her voice and Serena sat up and cleared her throat.

"It sounds like there's something going on, something you're not telling me."

"No, there's nothing," she said quickly, "It's just that…he's…" Serena bit her lip as a sudden tear stung her eye. She didn't know how to go on, she didn't know what to say.

"Serena," Jan said in a schoolmarm voice, "be careful what you're doing over there. Sounds like you've gotten yourself into something deep. But whatever you do, don't fall for him."

Too late. Serena put her left index finger to her lips and began to nibble at the nail. It had only been a week since she'd met the man but that advice had come way too late to save her heart.

CHAPTER SEVEN

It was after five o'clock but Roman had no plans to leave the office any time soon. He'd been working on a report for the past three hours and, looking down at the papers in front of him, he realized that he didn't have very much to show for all that time. He'd been distracted all afternoon and, as important as this report was, for the life of him he just could not put his mind to it.

And it was all Serena Van Buren's fault. The witch was driving him crazy. He'd avoided her most of the week but this morning they'd spent over two hours together poring over the files of old ad campaigns, discussing those that had been successful and restacking those that had not had much impact. They'd sat together around the conference table, so close that he could smell the light fragrance of her perfume. The closeness had made him aware of her every move and he'd been hard put not to pull her into his arms and kiss her breathless.

Today Serena was wearing a tailored navy blue suit that clung to the soft curves of her hips and bust. The soft waves of her hair floated around her heart shaped face, giving her the look of an angel. Her full lips were rose pink and there was a slight flush to her face that made her look vibrant. Once when they both reached for the same sheet of paper their hands touched and she jumped as if she'd been shocked. He'd felt it, too. A jolt of electricity rushed through his body, making him suck in his breath. He'd tried hard not to react to her closeness but it became almost difficult to breathe and he couldn't help glancing at her every now and again. He shook his head as he remembered how his physical reaction to her had been so strong that at one point he'd had to get up and go over to the table to pour himself a glass of water just to get away from her.

What in the blazes was happening to him? He, a thirty year old man, was acting like a lovesick schoolboy. He sighed and rubbed his eyes. Somehow he had to fight this attraction to her. Richard Van Buren had trusted him with his daughter and he could not afford to jeopardize their relationship.

Roman was still sitting at his desk, staring out the window, when there was a knock at the door. Serena peeped in and he felt his heart tighten in his chest.

"What are you doing here?" His voice was sharper than he'd intended.

"It's almost six o'clock. I thought you were gone already." She stepped inside the room and pulled the door shut behind her. She looked just as fresh as she had first thing in the morning. If anything, she looked even more fetching right at this moment. She stood there looking so beautiful it was annoying. "I'm still here because of the work you gave me which you said you absolutely had to have first thing in the morning. I was going to leave it on your desk. " She held out a folder as she approached.

He reached out and took it from her but did not bother to open it. Instead, he continued to stare at her in silence until she began to look uncomfortable and averted her eyes.

"It doesn't matter that I stayed behind to finish it," she continued, seeming to want to fill the silence. "It's not like I'm rushing home to do anything special. I'll probably just go home and watch TV."

"What? No shopping at the mall? No partying in the evenings? I thought girls like you spent the evenings partying or hanging out with friends."

"I don't go out partying." Her tone was cold and he could see the anger flash in her eyes but then her shoulders drooped almost imperceptibly. "And my best friends have both gone to Europe for the summer so I'm alone."

"They can't be all gone to Europe. Don't you have other friends around here?"

She shook her head. "No, I don't have many friends."

"Why am I not surprised?" Roman said dryly.

Serena glared at him then said, "Well, you have your report. If you don't need me for anything else I'll be leaving." Without waiting for his reply she turned and stalked out of the office, closing the door smartly behind her.

******

When Serena got home she flung herself into the sofa and turned on the television. She was still smarting from Roman's comment about not being surprised that she didn't have lots of friends. How dare he insinuate that she was unlikable? She gritted her teeth and frowned at the television screen, her mind racing to find ways to make him pay for that comment.

Maybe she could kidnap him and torture him by pulling out the hairs on his chest. Strand by strand. She smiled with mischief at the thought of watching him squirm then her heart jerked as she pictured her fingers caressing his torso. She had no idea whether or not Roman had hair on his chest but he just seemed like the type of man who would. She bit her lip and tried to concentrate on the news report of some flooding in Florida but her mind would not let go of the dark haired Adonis who made her heart thump.

Her mood finally lightened when America's Funniest Videos came on. She laughed out loud when a minister's robe caught on fire and he had to rip it off in front of the congregation. She was still chuckling when the television show went to a commercial break and she used the opportunity to get a drink of water from the kitchen. She took a bottle from the fridge and was turning to head back to the living room when she saw the stack of mail she'd left on the counter. She'd forgotten about that. She picked them up and took them back to the couch with her then sat back down just in time to see a toddler swing a baseball bat at his father's groin. She shook her head and groaned in sympathy. That must have hurt.

She began opening mail as she watched the show, separating them into two piles. The one with junk mail was a lot bigger than the one with her real mail. In fact, she'd received only two real pieces of mail, both of which were bills. The first was for her cell phone. Four hundred and ninety-two dollars. She sighed. Not exactly what she needed now that she was on a limited budget.

She sat up straight, however, when she opened the second envelope. It was her credit card bill and it was a whole lot higher than she'd anticipated. She was only two hundred and sixty-five dollars away from reaching her twenty thousand dollar limit. Now where in the world was she going to get the money to pay off all of that? With the allowance her father used to give her it had never been a problem. In fact, she'd never had to worry about paying her own credit card bills before now. This time, though, she had nothing to fall back on except for the measly salary that she would receive a whole two weeks from now. Her credit card payment was due by the end of the month. And she couldn't get money from her other credit cards to pay this one. The other two were all maxed out.

Her mood swung back to depression. There was no way she was going to survive for six months like this on the salary of an entry level management trainee. The fact that her father was paying for this apartment was a big help but it still left her in a hole because, by the time she paid her phone bill, bought food and gas, visited a few restaurants and put away money for miscellaneous spending, she'd be broke. And, of course, she had to do some shopping. It was her only emotional outlet.

Serena looked at the phone then back at the television. She was itching to call her father and plead with him to just forget this whole thing about her working. She wanted her old life back. She reached for the phone then pulled back her hand. It irked her to have to go crawling back to him but she didn't know what else to do. Finally she decided to call. Desperate times called for desperate measures, they said. There was no way she was going to survive without any credit cards at all so she had no choice but to call.

But the conversation didn't go as well as Serena had hoped. In fact, it was a disaster.

"Why haven't you returned my calls," was her father's first response to her greeting. "I was planning to come over there just to see if you were all right. The least you could do is call your dad once in a while." He sounded both annoyed and relieved.

"I've just been busy, Dad. I don't get home till late evening and by the time I get here, I'm beat. I always plan to call you but then I fall asleep before I get a chance."

"That's no excuse. You have a cell phone. You can call me during the daytime. And I'm sure Roman wouldn't kill you if you called me from the office."

"Okay," she said with a sigh, "I'll do that." She paused then before she could change her mind she blurted out, "Dad, why don't we call this whole thing off? It's not working out for me. I've got bills piling up and I don't get paid for another two weeks."

"What kinds of bills? I pay for your apartment and that includes your utilities. All you have to worry about is your food."

"Yes," she said slowly, "and my credit card bills."

"I paid off all your credit card bills two months ago. Even though you maxed them all out at the same time I made sure all your balances were paid up. That's almost thirty thousand dollars. Have you maxed them out again in such a short time?"

Serena bit her lip. "I guess I have," she said, her voice soft and defeated. Then she added quickly, "But it's just because it was graduation time and I had to do a lot of shopping. I had to go to the graduation ball and the ceremony looking good, didn't I?"

"I guess so," her father said, "but you didn't have to shop at Prada for all your stuff."

"But I didn't," she began to protest then stopped. She decided to change her tone. "Daddy, seeing that things are so tight for me, do you think I can start getting my allowance again? I need to pay off some of these bills."

"Serena," he began in the tone he used when scolding, "you know our agreement. No allowance for six months. You have to learn to live on a budget and manage on your salary. How do you expect to run this business when I'm gone if you can't even run your own life? This pampering has got to stop. Spoiling you with hefty allowances and clearing off your credit card balance from shopping sprees is no way to prepare you for the world." He sighed heavily. "I know it's hard on you and I hate doing this but it's for your own good."

"So you're not going to give me my allowance back?"

"No, I'm not."

"Well, will you at least pay part of the credit card bills?"

"I'm sorry. I can't."

"This is so not fair," Serena said bitterly. "You're my dad. Why are you treating me like this?"

"You're no longer a child, Serena. You need to start accepting responsibility and taking charge of your own life."

"But all I asked for was-"

"That's enough. I'm already helping you by paying for the apartment. Your monthly salary is all you have to work with so start working on a budget."

Serena slammed the phone down and slumped back in the couch in a huff. She'd never been rude to her father before but this situation called for it. She sat with her arms folded tightly across her chest, teeth biting into her bottom lip. What did she know about budgets? Where would she even start? Her father was putting her through hell. She would never forgive him.

CHAPTER EIGHT

Serena bit her lower lip and frowned as she stared down at the framed portrait. She lifted her index finger to her lips and began to nibble absently at the nail then, realizing what she was doing, she dropped her hand guiltily and slid it into the back pocket of her jeans. When was she going to get rid of that awful childhood habit? Whenever she was nervous or deep in thought she always reverted to that one habit she found so hard to break. She was twenty-one, for goodness sake. Time to put down such childish behavior.

She sighed and walked away from the bed then went to stare out the bedroom window of the apartment. It was a hell of a thing, being broke. For the first time in her life she knew what it was like to want something badly and not have the money to get it. She'd seen an exquisite gold watch at Diamante's and had wanted it for her grandmother's seventy-fifth birthday but with a little over two hundred dollars available on her credit card how could she? And there was that small matter of her personal expenses. The little that was left on the card would have to serve her till pay day. With gasoline prices skyrocketing she had no idea how she would make the money serve that long.

The long and short of it was she had no money to buy Grandma Sylvie a birthday present. And so she'd turned to her long-time hobby. Instead of buying a gift she'd dug through a box of old photos and found one of her grandmother when she was ten years younger, laughing and happy with her husband of over forty years. Serena's grandfather, still handsome in his senior years, was holding her in a tender embrace and he was smiling down at her with a love that was undeniable.

Serena stared at that photo for a long time. She knew the grief Grandma Sylvie had suffered when Grandpa Harris died of pneumonia at the age of sixty-seven. She'd married her childhood sweetheart and had never returned the interest of any other man. She missed him immensely, and she missed the love they shared. Serena wanted to recapture that love for her grandma, even if only on paper. And so she began to draw.

It took most of her Saturday morning but she didn't mind. Serena sketched the photo, creating an eighteen by twenty-four inch replica in charcoal, and then she pulled out the elegant gilt-edged picture frame she'd found at the discount store. Gently, she placed the picture inside and as it lay on the bed in its frame she ran loving fingers over the faces of her grandparents. Then she went to the closet to get wrapping paper and a bow.

After she'd wrapped the gift she propped it against the side of her mahogany chest of drawers then headed out to the kitchen to tackle the second half of her project. Today she was going to bake a cake. No matter that she'd never baked a thing in her life, she was going to do this for her beloved grandmother and nothing was going to stop her. Now that she'd created one project with her own hands she was eager to do more. She'd downloaded the recipe from the internet and it looked as easy as ever.

Smiling and humming to herself Serena laid the printed page on the kitchen counter and checked the list of items she'd need. She opened the fridge and the cupboards and started gathering all the ingredients. When everything was laid out she put on her frilly white apron and giggled. She looked like Betty Crocker. Now if only the look would enhance her skills as a baker. No matter, she was ready to take the plunge. Yellow sponge cake, here we come.

******

Roman shuffled through the papers on his desk. Where the hell was it? He could have sworn he'd left it on the pile in the middle of his desk. He sat back in the chair and frowned, trying to remember. Serena had handed him the file then slipped back out, spending less than ten seconds in his office. After he'd stopped admiring her cute little tush in tailored black pants he'd dropped the file back onto the desk and he'd gone back to what he'd been working on. Now where had it gone since then?

He got up and went over to the file cabinet, checked on top, checked inside. All clear. He walked over to the credenza and opened it to check all the files inside. Had Serena come in later that day and taken the file back? Beginning to get annoyed he walked out of his office and headed down to the sixth floor. There he checked her desk and the cabinet in her cubicle. No file. And there was no one to ask. It was Saturday and he was the only one working in the building. He normally encouraged his employees to use weekends for family and relaxation. He frowned on people working overtime unless absolutely necessary. As far as he was concerned if you weren't a good enough time manager to get your work done during the weekdays then some improvement was needed.

Just thinking about it made him smile to himself. Today he was the guilty party. He had a good excuse, though. This week he had been back and forth between New York and Toronto and so he just hadn't had the time to sit still long enough to review the file. But now he needed it in order to get ready for his meeting on Monday morning. Now how the heck was he going to prepare without that file?

He had no alternative. He had to call Serena. He felt a twinge of discomfort at having to disturb her on the weekend but he knew she would understand. Back at his office he flipped through the employee directory then dialed Serena's home number. She picked up on the fifth ring.

"Hello?" Her voice sounded breathless as if she'd been running.

"Serena, this is Roman. I'm sorry to disturb you but I need the MacGyver file. Did you take it back from my office?"

"No, I didn't," she began then she paused. "I remember Theresa saying she wanted to add a couple of documents to the file, though. Maybe you could check her office?"

"Thanks a lot, Serena. And again, I apologize for disturbing you on a Saturday."

"That's okay," she said then she gasped. "Oh, my God. Smoke!"

Roman heard the clatter of the phone as she dropped the receiver and then he heard what sounded like the banging of pots and pans. What in the blazes was going on? "Serena. Are you okay?" He was shouting into the phone but obviously she couldn't hear him. All he could do was clutch the receiver and wait. Something was going on, he had no idea what, and he hated feeling helpless. But what else could he do? He was too far away to do anything.

Finally, after what seemed like ages, Serena came back to the phone. "I'm sorry, it was…I burned my cake," she wailed into the phone.

"Your what?"

"My cake," she yelled, her voice full of frustration. "I was trying to bake a cake for my grandmother and the whole thing burned. It's all black and hard and it's still smoking."

Roman almost had to bite his lip to keep from laughing out loud. Serena Van Buren baking a cake? He was having a hard time picturing it. The high society girl in apron and oven mitts looking like the picture-perfect housewife from the magazines of the nineteen sixties. No way, not this spoiled rich girl.

"What am I going to do now? Today is my grandma's birthday and I was planning to go over and take her a cake. Now I messed up everything."

To Roman's surprise Serena began to sob. It was like a dam of frustration had broken inside her. The sobbing got louder and was punctuated with hiccups.

Roman would not have believed it if he hadn't been on the phone with the girl. Fiery Serena breaking down over a cake? She could easily order a hundred cakes. What was making her so emotional? "It's not the end of the world," he said, trying to soothe her. "It's only a cake."

"It's not only a cake," she retorted. "It's my cake, the cake I was making for my grandmother. It was supposed to be special." She sniffed and took a couple of deep breaths, apparently trying to calm herself. "I followed the recipe to the letter. I don't know what went wrong. I didn't exceed the time on the packaging. The cake was only in the oven like twenty minutes."

"And what was the temperature setting on the oven?"

"The temperature what?"

"Okay. I think we've found the key to your problem." Roman shook his head then chuckled. "You probably had the temperature setting way too high and that's why you burned your cake."

Serena heaved a sigh. "Why can't I do anything right? What am I going to do now? I wish somebody had taught me about these things."

For a moment there was silence and Roman could just imagine her biting her bottom lip as she seemed to do when she was deep in thought. She was obviously at a loss when it came to domestic matters and why shouldn't she be? He was sure she hadn't had to cook anything in her life. And now she had taken it up on herself to bake a cake for her grandmother by herself. He could only admire her for that.

On an impulse he said, "This cake of yours, how soon do you need to have it ready?"

"I told my grandma I wanted to come by around four o'clock this afternoon. I wanted to surprise her with something homemade but who am I kidding? I'll never be able to do this by myself."

"I may be able to help."

"You? How?"

Roman chuckled into the phone. "I'm an excellent chef, if I may say so myself. I learned at the hands of the best."

"Would you...show me?" Serena's voice sounded hesitant but hopeful.

"It's only a little after eleven right now so if you can hang in there while I locate this file and finish what I'm doing I'll help you bake your cake. Do you have all the ingredients or do I need to pick up something on the way?"

"N...no, I have what I need. Do you know where I live?"

"Sure. I had to check your file to get your home number and I see you listed at one of the apartments just a few miles east of the office. I don't mind swinging by. In fact, I'd love to get my hands full of flour again. It's been a while." Roman smiled to himself as he remembered the last time he'd done any cooking. It had been at the family Thanksgiving gathering three years earlier at his parents' house. He'd been appointed chef for the day. Since then, though, he hadn't had a chance to do any real cooking since he was always traveling and his housekeeper took care of his meals when he was at home.

But then he thought of something and his smile disappeared. Was he being presumptuous to invite himself over to the girl's apartment? It was stupid of him to even make the offer.

"On second thought, maybe it's not such a good idea," he said, his tone apologetic. "I'm sure you want to do this on your own-"

"No way. I'm not going to let you back out of this. You made the offer and I'm taking you up on it. You'll come over...won't you?"

It was that hesitation in her voice, that soft hint of pleading, that got him. Serena had always played tough but she was vulnerable in so many ways. How could he say no?

"All right, I'll be there in an hour or so. That is, assuming I find the file. I'll give you a call before I head out."

"Great," she said with a happy laugh. "I'll have everything ready and waiting. Promise."

After Roman hung up he sat for a moment tapping his fingers on the desk. He liked the sound of that. Ready and waiting. Maybe he liked it a bit too much. Was he making a mistake in seeing Serena outside of the office, even if just to help her?

Roman sighed. Maybe he was overreacting. He'd been busy with traveling and the office for so long he could do with some down time. Amusing himself with cake baking would certainly be different. And with Serena nearby it would definitely not be boring. It might even end up being fun. He was looking forward to it.

CHAPTER NINE

Serena could not believe that she had just invited her boss over to help her bake a cake. Which employee dared do something like that? An employee like her, it seemed, one who was desperate. It was not like her friends were anywhere near and could come over to help and the birthday celebration was this afternoon. She'd grabbed at his offer and, nervous as it made her, she did not regret it. If she had a delicious cake to take to her Grandma Sylvie's house it would all be worth it.

She busied herself tidying up the kitchen, getting rid of the burned cake and setting out the ingredients for the next one. Then it was time to tidy herself. With a grimace she got rid of the apron. There was no way she wanted him to see her looking like a housewife. A girl had her image to think about. She got rid of the gray sweat pants and the oversized white T-shirt and changed into a primrose yellow shirt and jeans. She wanted to apply some make-up but then thought better of it. She didn't want him to think she was getting all dolled up because of him. Instead, all she did was apply a little lip gloss and put her hair up in a ponytail.

The hour flew by and all too soon Serena heard the buzzer. Ready or not, Roman was here. She pressed the button to let him in then glanced in the mirror to make sure everything was in the right place. Then, with a deliberately nonchalant air, she sauntered to the front door. Perfect timing. As she rested her hand on the knob there was a knock. She pulled it open and when she saw Roman Steele standing in the doorway her heart did a backflip.

She'd thought he was sexy in his business suit but today the sight before her eyes made her mouth water. Roman was dressed casually in a navy blue polo shirt and jeans. The light material of the shirt stretched across his broad chest, accentuating his muscled torso. This was the first time she'd seen his arms exposed and those, too, were well muscled. It looked like he worked out a lot. She could just imagine those arms around her, pulling her close.

"Aren't you going to invite me in?" Roman smiled down at her and chuckled.

"Oh. Yes, come in." Serena stepped back and held the door open so that Roman could enter. "Sorry about my bad manners."

"No problem," Roman responded, his eyes resting on her, and she could swear she saw something close to admiration in his expression. But for what?

"So, where do I start? Point me to the kitchen."

Serena gave him a quick smile. She had no problem getting started right away because it was almost one o'clock and she needed everything to be ready by at least three thirty. "Just follow me," she said and led the way.

Serena could sense that working in the tiny kitchen with Roman was going to be quite an experience. The fragrance of his woodsy cologne filled her nostrils and the nearness of him made her constantly conscious of the virile man in her tiny apartment. She'd never worked this closely with a man before. The fact that the man was Roman did not make anything easier.

"I see you have everything prepared," Roman said as he eyed all the items laid out on the counter. "Let me wash my hands and we'll get right to work."

Serena nodded and stepped back so that he could prepare himself then as he worked she stood over in the corner and watched. Never in a million years would she have imagined Roman as being an expert in the kitchen but he did everything with such competence that she could only stare in admiration.

"Were you formally trained in cooking?" she asked.

Roman laughed. "No, not this kind of cooking. I can cook up a good business deal but this is something I learned at the hand of my mother. I've always enjoyed it." He beckoned to her with a nod. "Now come on over. It's time for you to get your hands dirty."

Slowly, Serena walked over to stand by Roman's side. She almost felt intimidated by his size. Even more disconcerting was his nearness. His male presence filled the tiny room, making every inch of her body aware of him.

Roman turned with the bag of flour and held it out to Serena. "Here. Take this and measure out one cup." Serena reached out to take the bag from him and their fingers touched. She jumped back and stared up at him.

"Are you all right?" Roman cocked an eyebrow as he looked down at her.

"I'm…I'm fine," Serena said then took a step away from him. She'd felt it, a shock that ran through her the moment his fingertips touched hers. Had he felt it, too? She couldn't tell but she knew that having him so close was driving her crazy. She had to put some distance between the two of them.

She rested the bag on the counter. "I'll be right back. I just need to check something." Before he could stop her she exited the kitchen and made a beeline for her room.

Serena knew she was being crazy but how was she going to handle being so close to this man to whom she was so attracted? She had to get a hold of herself. She had to stop acting like an idiot before the man thought something was wrong with her. She took two deep breaths then headed back to the kitchen.

She'd only been gone three minutes but already Roman had all the ingredients in the bowl and had turned on the mixer. When she walked in he turned and smiled at her.

"I know what you're up to," he said and his grin widened.

"You do?"

"You had no intention of helping me with this cake, did you? You slipped out so that I'd get started and I'd be done by the time you got back. I know your trick."

"Oh, that. You…you got me. Guilty as charged."

The rest of the baking project went without incident and soon the cake was in the oven, scheduled to sit there for thirty minutes. Now what were they going to do? "Would you like to watch some television?" Serena asked. "There's a basketball game on."

Roman nodded. "Sounds good to me."

And so it was that Roman ended up sprawling comfortably on her sofa watching the big screen TV while she perched on a bar stool watching him. He was so absorbed in the game, the Knicks versus the Lakers, that she wondered if he even remembered she was there. But she could never forget his presence. His aura filled the room. She needed to get out and away from him. He was having too much of an effect on her.

"I'm going to check on the cake." She slid off the stool and was heading for the kitchen when his voice stopped her.

"Don't you dare. If you keep opening that oven my cake is going to go flat."

"Your cake? I thought it was mine."

Roman cocked an eyebrow. "And who did all the work? Certainly not you."

Serena turned on her heel and gave him a threatening look. "You'd better not tell my grandmother that."

Roman laughed and lifted his hands in surrender. "Okay, okay, you're the boss. It's your cake and I had nothing to do with it."

"I'll give you some of the credit," she conceded with a smile. "Just a little."

The light banter eased the tension for Serena and the rest of the waiting time flew by quickly. Before she realized it, it was time to get the cake out and get ready to go to her grandmother's. "You're coming, right?" When he seemed to hesitate she continued. "You can't back out now. You promised."

"If you want me to," Roman said, staring at her intently, no longer seeming interested in the basketball game. One hundred percent of his attention was focused on her.

Serena squirmed a little under his gaze but she knew she wanted to spend the rest of the afternoon with him. A very pleasant hour had already passed and she did not want it to end that quickly even if she would have to share him with her grandmother.

In the office they'd had to be very professional, almost formal, but here on a Saturday afternoon she began to see a more relaxed side to Roman. He was absorbed in the basketball game, cheering on the Knicks while she rooted for the Lakers and soon they had a good rivalry going. She loved it. She'd never been a fan of sports but with Roman there to share the game with her it was fun.

"I do want you to come." Serena gave Roman a smile. "Grandma Sylvie would love to meet you and I think you'd like her, too."

He nodded. "I need no further convincing."

"Okay, let me get changed and we'll get going." As she hurried to her bedroom she hoped he did not see the silly grin on her face.

CHAPTER TEN

Roman held the door open as Serena slid from the passenger seat of his black Mercedes Benz. From the city it had taken them a little over thirty minutes to get to her grandmother's house. Throughout the journey Serena sat in the passenger seat with the cake cradled on her lap. You would think it was the most precious thing in the world. But he wasn't knocking her. He could see that this gift, small as it was, meant a lot to her and that her grandmother was a very important person in her life.

With Serena on her feet Roman opened the back door and carefully took out the large gift-wrapped object that Serena had placed in his hands. He could guess that it was a picture of some sort because he could feel the pattern of the engraved frame.

As they walked up the winding gravel driveway Roman looked around, admiring the surroundings. They were out in the country and it was beautiful, with wide open fields and woods that formed a backdrop to the sprawling ranch house.

Serena must have seen him staring because she said, "My house is not far from here. I often ride over to visit Grandma Sylvie. It's so exhilarating, galloping across the fields."

"I can imagine," Roman said. In his mind's eye he could see her on the back of a horse, her hair a dark curtain flying behind her as she rode. He had no doubt that she was an expert horsewoman. He wondered if one day he would have the privilege of riding with her.

They climbed the steps and crossed the wide porch that circled the house. Serena rang the bell and within seconds the door swung open and a petite white-haired woman was smiling up at them.

"Serena, darling." The woman tilted her head and gave her a kiss on the cheek then her eyes left her granddaughter's face and rose to meet Roman's. Her smile widened. "And who do we have here?"

For some reason, maybe because of the twinkle in her grandmother's eyes, Serena blushed. "This is Roman Steele, my boss."

Sylvie gave a polite nod. "Welcome, Roman. I'm pleased to meet you. Won't you come in?"

When they got inside Serena handed over her prized possession, the birthday cake.

"Oh, my," Sylvie exclaimed. "What a wonderful surprise. I'll take it to the kitchen and we can have some in a little while." As she headed down the hallway she called out, "Make yourselves comfortable. I'll be right back."

Serena directed Roman to an elegantly furnished living room filled with family portraits.

"Please have a seat," she said, indicating the couch. Instead of sitting, she went to stand by the mantelpiece.

This drew Roman's attention to the painted portrait above the fireplace. It was the picture of a beautiful blonde-haired woman on horseback. "Was that your mother?"

Serena nodded. "She loved riding."

"As you do," Roman said, seeing the wistful look in her eyes.

At that moment Sylvie walked into the room. She smiled at them. "That's my Patricia," she said then tilted her chin towards Serena. "Serena looks just like she did when she was this age." Sylvie gave Roman a sad smile. "We lost her when Serena was six years old, still just a baby. Richard has been both mother and father to her since then."

"And you too, Grandma."

"Yes, I've been there, but the job of raising you has always been your dad's. And outside of spoiling you rotten I think he's done a wonderful job." Sylvie's laugh was like the tinkle of bells. "She's got him wrapped around her little finger," she said to Roman, "but it's only because he's had to endure two major scares in his life. One of them left him without his wife and me without my daughter."

Roman frowned. "Two major scares?"

Sylvie nodded. "Yes, he almost lost Serena, too."

"Grandma, you don't have to-"

"It's okay, Serena," Sylvie said as she walked over and put her arm around her granddaughter's shoulder. "We need to speak about these things. It's not healthy for us to bury our pain. This is the only way we can find healing." Sylvie's eyes grew misty. "Serena had leukemia when she was eight years old. She spent quite a bit of time in hospital and Richard almost went crazy with worry. He couldn't bear to lose this one part of Patricia that she'd left behind." Sylvie wrapped her arms around Serena's waist and pulled her close and there was a tremulous smile on her lips. "But my Serena pulled through. She was a fighter, this girl. There was nothing that would keep her down."

Roman nodded and looked at the two women, so very different in ages but so much alike. Both were petite and although Sylvie's hair was white and the signs of age were on her face, the sparkle in her blue eyes told him that she had been just as feisty as the young woman who stood beside her. He could now understand, too, why Richard had gone overboard in satisfying the desires of his daughter. It seemed he was trying to make up for all that she'd gone through, the loss of her mother and the threat to her own life.

But still, the pampering had to stop somewhere. Serena was a woman now. And what a woman. As he stared at her all he wanted to do was bury his face in the valley between her luscious breasts.

Roman's thoughts were cut short when Sylvie released Serena and clapped her hands smartly. "Okay, let's get something to eat. You both must be starving."

They all headed for the kitchen where she'd already placed a basket of fried chicken in the middle of the table, a bowl of salad, a tray with corn on the cob and a steaming bowl of mashed potatoes.

"Mmm, looks good," Serena, said rubbing her stomach. "I could eat a horse."

"You know what the sad thing is, Roman? She really could eat a horse and she wouldn't gain a single pound." Sylvie shook her head and feigned a look of indignation.

"What are you complaining about? You're not fat." Serena laughed.

"That's because I watch my diet. You don't have to. With your youth and high metabolism you can eat anything. It's just not fair."

Roman laughed, enjoying the banter. "You're like me, Sylvie. I have to eat right and exercise."

"You? You don't have a spare ounce of flesh on your body," Sylvie said with a touch of exasperation. "I'm sure you don't have to work too hard to keep that body in shape. It sure looks good to me."

"Grandma." Serena frowned at the older woman but Sylvie only laughed.

Then it was Serena who was looking at him with what seemed like admiration. Was she checking him out? Roman could only hope so.

They had a pleasant meal with conversation that left Roman feeling relaxed and at home. He could not tell the last time he'd enjoyed himself so much. Here he was having dinner with his employee and her grandmother and he felt like he'd known them for years. From time to time his eyes would wander over to Serena and as she chatted comfortably with Sylvie he could not help but see her with new eyes. She was still the feisty young woman who walked into his office a few weeks earlier but now he could see another side of her. It was obvious that she loved her grandmother dearly. Maybe the woman didn't replace her mother but there was a love and understanding between the two that could not be denied. And from their interaction he could see that underneath the strong and independent façade that Serena showed the world she was still young and vulnerable.

When they'd finished the meal Sylvie gathered up the dishes and placed them in the sink. She began to rinse them off when Roman got up. "I'll do it."

"Roman, you're a guest. Sit down and relax. Chat with Serena." Sylvie continued to rinse the dishes.

By this time Roman was almost by Sylvie's side. "You're being too good to me, Sylvie. I never get a chance to do household chores so give me this one opportunity. I like being domesticated from time to time."

Sylvie laughed and stepped aside. "Okay, if that's what you want. Who am I to fight a man who wants to do housework?"

Roman rinsed the food from the dishes and set them in the dishwashing machine and turned it on. While he was drying his hands Serena went to the counter for the cake and rested it on the table. "Time for the birthday girl to have some cake."

Sylvie was beaming, obviously pleased with the attention. Serena got a knife and handed it to her. "Cut the cake while I take a picture." She pulled out her cell phone from the back pocket of her jeans and held it up. "Go ahead."

Sylvie stuck the knife in the middle of the cake and then slowly pressed down, cutting a huge slice which she laid on the plate. "Roman, you get the first bite."

"No way," he said with a chuckle. "You're the birthday girl."

"No, you're the guest. You go first."

"If you guys are going to fight about it I'll go first." Serena reached out to take the plate but her grandmother pulled it back.

"Oh, no, you don't. It's my birthday and I'll go first."

Roman laughed. "That's what I thought."

Roman and Serena sat down with Sylvie and they all munched on the cake.

"Mmm, this is good." Sylvie said, obviously enjoying herself.

"Sorry I didn't get to put icing on it, Grandma. We couldn't figure out that part, not so quickly anyway."

"We? Did you help her make this, Roman?"

Roman nodded. "I couldn't let her do it all by herself."

"I was wondering about that. When my Serena told me she was going to bake me a cake I was doubtful. I never knew of that girl ever going into a kitchen to make anything. But she came through. With your help, of course."

"I'm sorry I didn't get you the usual from Michael's Bakery this year," Serena said. "I know you love their cakes but…I just wanted to do something different."

"Child, are you apologizing for making me a cake? You'd better not, because I love it. Who cares about Michael's cake when I can get one from the hands of my own granddaughter? And you too, Roman." She beamed at him. "It's delicious."

"Now, for your present," Serena said and got up. She hurried out of the kitchen.

Roman was left in the kitchen with Sylvie. She had just popped the last bit of her cake into her mouth and was smiling at him with knowing eyes. "So what do you think of my Serena?"

Taken aback by the directness of the question Roman did not answer right away. Then he spoke. "She's an admirable young woman. Despite her lack of experience she has an eye for beauty and I can see her doing very well in marketing. I'm sure her father will have a great asset when she joins the company."

Sylvie laughed. "That's not what I meant and you know it. I can see that you like her very much."

The comment almost floored Roman. Was it so obvious?

"Here it is." Serena came back just in time, the wrapped gift in her hand. Gently, she laid the large flat rectangle on the table. "Time to open your gift."

Sylvie stared at it eagerly. "I think I know what it is. It's shaped like...it's the picture I saw at the Royal Ontario Museum. The one that featured the skyline. I know that's it. You saw me admiring it and you got it, didn't you?"

Serena shook her head. "I'm sorry but that's not what it is. I hope you still like this one, though."

Sylvie chuckled. "I'm sure I will." She slid her finger under the paper at the back and quickly peeled off the tape then she slid the frame out of the wrapping. What came out of the package was the gold-framed charcoal portrait of Sylvie and a handsome man smiling down at her. Sylvie's eyes widened in surprise and then her lips trembled and tears filled her eyes. "Oh Serena, it's beautiful."

"Grandma, you're crying. Are you sure you like it?"

"I love it, I absolutely love it. You captured the moment beautifully." Sylvie gently caressed the face of the man with her weathered hands. Then she put her fingers to her lips. "This was a moment I will always remember.

And now you've captured it for me with your own hands. Thank you."

"I…I couldn't think of what to give you and I couldn't buy you a nice gift like I usually do so I thought maybe this would be a good substitute."

"This is the best gift you could have ever given me. I don't need perfume or expensive jewelry. I want memories. I want something that's from you. You've given me both with this gift." She laid the portrait gently back down on the table then got up and opened her arms. Serena stepped right into them and, with tears in their eyes, the two women embraced.

CHAPTER ELEVEN

Serena sighed as she slid out of Roman's car. She felt happy, even contented. She'd had a wonderful evening with her grandmother and with Roman there it had been even more fun. They'd ended up playing board games with Sylvie and when Roman started having a winning streak Sylvie and Serena had had to gang up on him to beat him. Serena could not tell when she'd had so much simple, satisfying fun.

It was almost nine o'clock but she didn't want her day with Roman to end. As he took her hand to help her out of the car she looked up at him. Then she smiled hesitantly. "Would you like to come up for a drink?"

Roman looked down at her, his face partially hidden in the shadows, and for a moment he was silent. Then he said, "Are you sure? You're not tired?"

"No, I'm fine. Are you tired?"

Roman let her fingers slide from his hand then he shrugged. "Not at all."

"Okay, then. It's settled." Serena walked ahead of him into the lobby, wondering where she had found the courage to invite her boss back upstairs. It wasn't like earlier in the day when he'd come specifically to help her with the cake. Now it was more like…a date.

Once they were back in the apartment Serena felt at a loss for words. She'd invited Roman up because she'd enjoyed his company and wanted more of it but now she felt nervous. She decided to escape to the kitchen. "Would you like a drink? I have wine."

"A drink would be nice," he said with a nod. "White wine if you have it."

Serena hurried to the kitchen where she poured two glasses of wine and laid them on a silver tray. Taking a deep breath she headed back to the living room. *Come on,*

Serena, what are you afraid of? She was the one who'd invited him. Deep down, though, she knew what she feared most. It was herself.

When she got back to the living room Roman was still lounging in the sofa as he'd been when she left but this time there was a big book in his hand. He was deeply engrossed and as she got closer Serena saw that the book in his hand was her old photo album.

She almost dropped the tray. Goodness, where had he found that old thing? And then she remembered. Earlier that week she'd been looking for an old school photo and had dug it out of her trunk. She must have left it on the lower tier of the coffee table. And now it was in his hands.

She could feel her face grow warm with embarrassment. She'd been somewhat of a nerd in her younger days, her constant reading forcing her into thick glasses at the age of ten. Sometimes it was hard being an only child and after her mother's death and her own bout with cancer she'd drawn more and more into her shell. She'd been a loner with books as her only friends. When she got into her teens she'd breathed a sigh of relief when she was finally allowed to wear contact lenses. And thank God for laser correction which she'd done as soon as she'd gone off to college.

Now Serena stared at Roman in horror. Had he seen her at her worst? She cringed inside. Quickly, she walked into the room and set the tray down on the coffee table with a smart bang.

"What have you got there?" she said casually, wondering how to get the album away from him as fast as possible without seeming rude.

Roman looked up at her, a big grin on his face.

Not a good sign. He'd probably gone through the whole lot of photos already.

"Interesting," he said, his look enigmatic. His face gave nothing away but his smile said it all. She'd been discovered and not in a flattering way.

Serena leaned over and reached for the album. Rude or not, it was time to get that thing away from him. "I'll put that away. I'm sure there are a lot more interesting things for you to do with your time."

"Oh no, you don't," he said with a chuckle and held tight, refusing to let her take it from his hands.

"But those are just old pictures. Nothing you'd like to see." She stepped around the table, determined to retrieve the source of her embarrassment. Some of the photos in there were so terrible the man could blackmail her with them if he wanted.

"Oh, but I do," he said in a teasing tone and slid the book away from her and onto the seat beside him. Clearly, he was determined to keep flipping through the pages, leaving her open to more and more humiliation. Well, it wasn't going to happen.

Before he could guess her intention Serena dove for the album and snatched it up into her arms. She was turning away, determined to get the book as far away from him as possible, when she felt hands like bands of steel wrap around her waist. With one tug he pulled her off balance then she was falling backwards, unable to stop herself from landing squarely on his lap.

Roman laughed out loud as her bottom landed on the hardness of his jean-clad legs. "Where are you going, little girl?"

She gasped, still hugging the photo album close to her chest. "I...I just wanted to..." She stopped, not able to go on. The words fled from her mind and all she could think about was the feel of his hardness through the fabric of her jeans. It wasn't just the firm muscles of his legs that had her squirming. Right where the curve of her hip rested on his groin she could feel the solid rock of his arousal.

Now Roman's smile was gone and in its place was a look of passion so deep, so intense that Serena clutched the album, her shield, even tighter. But he was having none of that. With strong fingers Roman pulled the book from her hands and laid it on the table. Then he turned his attention back to her.

Dear Lord, what was he going to do now? It was a stupid question. The thumping of her heart and the tightness in her lungs told her she already knew. Roman was going to kiss her and she wanted it so bad. Her nipples hardened in anticipation.

As Roman lowered his head Serena closed her eyes and when his lips touched hers she sighed. She'd been waiting for this for so long. God, how she wanted him.

As she melted in his embrace Serena felt Roman's hand slide up to cup the back of her head and then he was in total control, his masterful kiss making her gasp in response. Soon she was kissing back, giving him as much as he gave, all her caution thrown out the window.

He slid his lips away and she gave a soft moan which became a mewl when he began to nibble her ear. Christ, when his lips moved lower to tickle her neck she had no power to resist. Eyes closed, she tilted her head back all the better to give him access.

Roman needed no further encouragement. His lips feathered over her skin then paused at the valley between her breasts, warming her already heated flesh. Serena slid trembling fingers through the silky thickness of his hair, pressing him into her, wanting the sweetness of his lips on her body.

Roman seemed to sense her desperate need because, with one hand, he began to loosen the buttons on her blouse. Within seconds he had it wide open and only the lace of her bra separated his skin from hers. Without hesitation he moved the cups away, pushing them down until they lay under her breasts which now thrust upward to meet his gaze.

He dipped his head and captured her right nipple between his lips then sucked it deep into his mouth, making her gasp out loud. He nipped at the bud then soothed it with the silky smoothness of his tongue until her toes curled from the sensuous caress. When she felt she would swoon from the pleasure he switched to the left breast and there he continued his sweet assault.

By the time Roman lifted his head Serena was lost in the passion of the moment. She slid her hands around his waist and pulled till she got the fabric of his polo shirt out of his pants. She lifted it up, exposing his muscled torso to her gaze. Fascinated, she ran her hands over his stunningly beautiful body.

Encouraged by an involuntary groan from his lips she slid both hands up until her fingers grazed his nipple. They hardened in response. Now she wanted to give him the same pleasure he had given her. She lowered her head and pressed her lips to his chest, covering one nipple with her mouth while she rolled the other between her fingers. And just like he'd done to her she sucked on the sensitive part of him, nipping then caressing, until another groan escaped his lips.

Serena shifted in his lap, intent on driving him over the edge. She slid her hands down his sides, never once releasing his nipple from her lips, then moved her hands across and down to the buckle of his belt. There was a boldness that surged through her, one that she had never felt before, and she wanted more of him...to see him, to caress him, to know every inch of this man who had captured her mind and her soul.

She was pushing at the belt strap, trying to get it through the buckle, when Roman's big hands covered hers. Her hands stilled and she lifted her head and looked into his eyes, so dark and intense.

"No, Serena. We can't."

"W…what?" Was she hearing right? Did he want her to stop? He could not mean that. Not when she was weak from wanting him.

He gripped her upper arms and shifted, sliding her off his lap and on to the seat beside him. He dragged his shirt back into place then leaned over and, as cool as you please, began to button her blouse.

Mortified, Serena ripped her shirt from his hands. "I can do it," she said, her voice sharp with humiliation. Then more softly, in a dejected whisper, "It's okay. I can do it myself." She turned her back to him and quickly straightened her bra then redid the buttons on the blouse. She could not believe he was rejecting her yet again. What was it about her that turned him off? She gave an involuntary sniff, the pain of his dismissal like a knife in her chest.

"Are you all right?" Roman reached out a hand to her.

She shrugged him off then got up and crossed the room. She wanted to get as far away from him as she possibly could. She wanted him but he did not feel the same. That much was very clear.

Roman got up and finished tucking his shirt into his trousers. Then he looked over at her and sighed. "I'm sorry, Serena. That should never have happened. I think it's time for me to go."

Serena shrugged, feigning nonchalance, but inside her heart was crumbling like a sand castle in the rain.

Without another word Roman walked to the door and opened it. For just a moment he glanced back at her. Then he was gone.

When the door clicked shut behind him Serena went back to the sofa and collapsed in a dejected heap. What an awful way to end a beautiful day.

CHAPTER TWELVE

Going to work that Monday was one of the hardest things Serena ever had to do. How could she face the man who had made her feel so low? Ever since she had joined the company weeks before her life had been turned upside down. Where had her Van Buren swagger gone? She didn't even feel like herself anymore.

She heaved a sigh as she switched on her computer and pulled out her chair. Thank God she had more than enough work to keep her busy and her mind off her awkward situation. She had the agency file to go through and several spreadsheets to prepare for a meeting with the budget manager. Now all she had to do was keep her nose to the grindstone and stay out of Roman Steele's way.

It was almost lunchtime when Serena was interrupted by a low voice. It was Theresa.

What now? Had the woman come to summon her to Roman's office? Would this be the dismissal she'd been working so hard to get? Instead of filling her with elation the thought made her heart slow with anguish. Her spirit fell at the thought of never seeing Roman again. She did not think she could bear it. Despite her distress Serena put on a brave face and gave Theresa a tight smile.

"I just stopped by to let you know that Mr. Steele left this morning for New York."

"New York?" Serena stared up at her, stunned. He'd spent most of Saturday with her and he hadn't mentioned a trip to New York. Was this something he'd come up with at the last minute to avoid her? "I see," she said, her voice low and controlled. "Did he say when he would be back?"

"The meetings go until Thursday but he'll probably be out all week," Theresa said. "We might not see him till next week." She laid a folder on Serena's desk. "He asked me to make sure you got this. While he's meeting with the

Consumer Research Company he wanted you to get started on the work with the local focus groups. Apparently this project has a tight timeline."

Serena nodded and opened the folder. It was thick, full of what looked like response sheets from hundreds of surveys. It would take her days to tabulate and analyze this information to create a meaningful report. Still, there was nothing like work to take your mind off your troubles. She didn't even flinch when Theresa produced a second file.

"There's this, too, but if you like I could hold on to it till you're done with the first project." The woman actually looked guilty.

"No, not at all. I prefer if you give me everything all at once." She took the second file and gave Theresa a confident smile. "I guess I'd better get started." Theresa took the hint and departed, leaving Serena staring at her sad and lonely computer screen. Or maybe it was she who was sad and lonely. She shook her head. *Come on, Serena. Roman or no Roman you have a job to do.* And no man was worth pining over. Certainly not one who felt he was too good for her.

Despite her troubles the week flew by for Serena. Work was a great salve for her wounds and the perfect source of distraction. Eventually she found she was beginning to enjoy what she was doing. She'd been consulting with the heads of various departments and working closely with the product development team. She was learning so much that she almost felt grateful to Roman for teaming up with her father to make her do the internship.

Almost. She was still a bit peeved at having been forced into it but even she had to admit that if she ever were to work in her father's business this was just about the best preparation she could have had. Working with cross-functional teams was a true learning experience and one which opened her understanding of team dynamics and collaboration.

Before she knew where the week had gone, Friday came and she still had not completed project number two. Theresa told her that Roman had called every day to check on the progress of the assignment but he'd never spoken to her. Even though she was disappointed maybe that was a good thing. After all, what would she say to him? Or him to her? It would only create awkwardness on both sides. Besides, the next time she spoke to him she wanted to be able to say she'd completed all her projects.

That evening when everyone was calling TGIF to one another and packing to go Serena still sat at her desk plugging away. She was determined to finish the assignment before shutting down for the weekend. When Roman stepped in on Monday morning her finished reports would be sitting on his desk. What was more, they would exceed his expectations because she'd gone out of her way to commission professionally produced illustrations and charts. She'd even included a presentation on a new campaign idea she had, one that would take greater advantage of social media opportunities. That was the part that still needed fleshing out. It would take her a few more hours but she wasn't complaining. It wasn't like she was rushing home to family and friends. She was on her own now in many senses of the word.

Serena glanced at the clock. Six twenty-one in the evening. If she had any hope of leaving the place by nine she'd better get cracking.

*****

Roman relaxed into the plush leather seat of the limousine that was taking him from the airport back to his office. It was late, he knew, and everyone would have already left for home. After all, it was Friday. Which of his employees would give up their Friday night to work overtime? That would be a rare occurrence. In fact, he discouraged that sort of thing. For him, balance was important and the weekend was the time for relaxation, family and friends.

Unfortunately for him there was no family to run home to. All he'd be rushing to was a huge and empty penthouse suite freshly cleaned in anticipation of his return. His housekeeper would have made sure everything was spotless and a warm meal would be waiting for him. But what joy was that when you were eating alone?

So instead of heading for home he went straight to the office. He had no intention of staying there late. He'd retrieve a few files and then he'd be on his way.

He was surprised when he met the head of security in the lobby and learned that the building was not as empty as he had anticipated. One eager beaver, as the man put it, was still plugging away on the sixth floor at almost nine o'clock at night. That eager beaver was Serena Van Buren.

At the man's words, Roman frowned. Serena? She was the last person he would expect to be working until this hour on a Friday night. He knew he'd left quite a bit for her to do in his absence but not so much that she'd have to give up her weekend. He would have to check on her. He'd deliberately avoided speaking to her while he'd been away on his business trip. He wanted to give her space, time to recover from that unhappy incident at her apartment. But now there was no avoiding it.

Roman was surprised when he got to a sixth floor that was totally silent. He'd expected to at least hear the hum of computers, the tapping of fingers on a keyboard or a printer in motion. But there was nothing except the eerie silence of a deserted office. The security guard must have been mistaken. Either that or she'd already left.

Roman decided to continue on his way to his office on the tenth floor. The door was slightly ajar and he nudged it open with foot as he began to loosen his tie. He was just about to throw his briefcase onto the sofa when he froze. There Serena lay, fast asleep, her head resting on the arm of the couch, her long, dark hair cascading almost to the floor. Her face, unguarded and innocent, was flushed in sleep and her long lashes formed crescents that fanned out on her smooth skin. On her lap was a folder and he could guess what had happened. She'd probably gone to his office to leave the reports he'd requested and had found the sofa too hard to resist and then sleep had come to claim her.

For a long while Roman stood staring down at the vision of beauty before him. He wanted her so badly he could taste it. Finally, unable to resist, he reached out a hand and touched the soft fineness of her hair. He lifted a tendril from off her face and that was when she woke up.

Serena's eyelids fluttered then slowly her eyes opened. "Roman? What? Where?" Clearly disoriented, she tried to raise her head then sat back down and groaned. She lifted a hand and rubbed the back of her neck. Then she blinked up at him like a very sleepy kitten.

Roman chuckled then reached out and gently helped her to her feet. She stifled a yawn then stretched, almost involuntarily, and her body swayed. He could see that she was still half asleep. He reached out to steady her and before he could stop her she was relaxing into him, her soft curves molding into him. God, that felt good.

His arms circled her waist as he held her so she would not fall and then she was pressing her body into his. She laid her head on his chest and gave a soft sigh then began to move her lips against the fabric of his shirt as if searching for the hardened nub of his nipple. His groin tightened in response. The little minx was driving him crazy.

He knew he should stop her but when she slid her hands up his body and began to loosen the buttons on his shirt he did not. All week he'd been dying for this, for the heat of her body, the softness of her fingers, the caress of her lips. All week he'd been reliving those precious moments when she'd responded to him with a seductive innocence that he'd found so hard to resist. And now she was in his arms again.

Serena had opened five of the buttons and was tugging on his tie to loosen it. He reached up to help her. In one quick move he slipped it off and threw it on top of the desk.

Then she dipped her head, and like she'd done days before, she pressed her lips to his chest and captured his sensitive bud between sharp white teeth, sending shockwaves ripping through his body. Roman cupped her head with his big hand, reveling in the pleasure she was giving him with her lips, turned on by her soft sighs and moans. In a final effort at resistance he groaned then kissed the top of her head and captured the hands that worried his belt.

"Serena," he whispered, his voice hoarse and strained, even to his own ears, "are you sure you want this?"

In response, she kissed the middle of his chest then sighed. "Roman," she whispered, her voice breathless, "I've wanted this ever since the day I met you." She wrapped her arms around his bare waist and pressed her body against his. "Please don't reject me again."

Reject her? What the hell was she talking about? How could he reject such a delicate but wickedly tempting flower? He'd been trying his best to resist her precocious charms but it was no use. She was offering herself up to him and his body was clamoring for her. He had to have her.

Roman shrugged out of his jacket and popped open the rest of the buttons on his shirt. He threw it onto the floor.

Then he turned his attention to the little witch who lay back on the sofa, smiling dreamingly up at him. There was no hesitation in her eyes, no fear, no uncertainty. Instead, what he saw was the intensity of her desire, a desire that seemed to match the craving he was feeling. Dear God, he could see it. She wanted him as much as he wanted her.

Before he could move to help her, Serena began to undress. Her jacket and top were off in seconds and then she was sliding her skirt down her legs. Then she lay back dressed only in lacy black bra and matching panties. She was beautiful.

Roman sat on the couch and lowered his head to the fullness of her breasts. He kissed the tops of the soft mounds and licked at the heated flesh till Serena moaned and arched her back, gasping for more. This time Roman wanted nothing between them. He slid his hands under her back and snapped the bra open then slid it from her arms and dropped it on the floor beside them. Her breasts, so full and round, creamy mounds of delectable flesh, fell open to his gaze. The delicious pink cherries on their tips made his mouth water.

Serena did not show an ounce of shyness. She seemed to revel in his look of admiration. Her lips curved up in a sweet smile of satisfaction and then she took the next step, raising her hips and hooking her fingers into the sides of her panties. She slid them down her long, lean legs, never once taking her eyes off his face. Now, totally naked she lay back on the sofa and looked up at him expectantly.

Roman needed no further invitation. Quickly, he unbuckled the belt and shucked trousers, socks and shoes then he was standing, naked and aroused in front of her.

For one quick moment he saw what looked like fear in her eyes. Her eyes widened when they fell on his manhood, swollen and ready, but then she looked back up at him, deep into his eyes, and there was no more anxiety there. All Roman could see was desire that burned with an intensity that fueled his own want. He moved quickly, sliding a condom from his wallet and preparing himself for their lovemaking.

Roman went to her then, covering her soft, yielding body with his. He pressed his lips to hers and when she opened like a flower unfolding he captured her lips, her tongue, kissing her with a passion he hadn't felt in years. What was it about this little witch that made him lose all control? The taste of her mouth, the feel of her soft breasts against his chest, the caress of her arms as they wrapped around him, the smoothness of her legs as they raised up and wrapped around his waist. It was all too much. All he wanted to do was bury himself inside this sweet, seductive siren and ride her till she took him to the brink and over the edge.

As the kiss deepened, Roman positioned his hips over hers and as she opened to receive him he entered her, pressing his manhood into her core.

Suddenly, she stiffened and moaned into his mouth. Then she was clinging to him as if she would never let go.

Roman pressed forward and then he felt it…a resistance that told him this girl was a virgin. What the hell? Too late, Roman realized that this was no siren in his arms but an innocent girl playing 'woman'.

Too late. It was his body that was in charge now. There was no turning back. His quick thrusts hauled him over the edge and then he was exploding deep inside the writhing, moaning girl in his arms.

And then she was there too, riding the waves of ecstasy to her own peak, crying his name as her flower blossomed and pulsated around that part of him that pressed deep within her core.

It took a few minutes for their rapid breathing to slow and their bodies to return to calm. During that time Roman held Serena in his arms, his body still but his mind racing.

Dear God, what had he just done?

CHAPTER THIRTEEN

Slowly, Roman released Serena from his arms and got up from the sofa, frowning in self-disgust. He'd just deflowered a virgin, the daughter of a man who had entrusted her to his care. He shook his head, feeling lower than a snake crawling in the dirt. She'd been so assertive, had seemed so sure of herself. He'd thought she'd had some experience.

With a curse he picked up her bra and panties from the floor and dropped them on her belly. Then, still not looking at her, he pulled on his boxers and pants and hurriedly dragged on the rest of his clothing. The tie, he stuffed into his pocket.

He looked over at Serena. She had not moved. She simply lay there, naked and flushed, staring up at him with huge eyes. She looked so forlorn, so innocent, that the self-recrimination he felt was like a knife ripping into his gut.

"Why didn't you tell me?" he barked, scowling down at her. He clenched his fists at his side. Right then he felt like shaking her, he was so angry. Why would she keep something like that from him? If he'd known he would never have come within a million miles of her. "Why didn't you tell me you were a virgin?"

Only then did Serena move. Her mouth was set in her classic pout, the one he'd found so alluring the first day they met, the one that had been his downfall.

In one fluid movement she slid off the sofa and slipped on her panties. Then she was snapping her bra closed then straightening to her full height, just shy of the nipples on his chest. She glared up at him then still not saying a word, she turned round and bent to gather up her blouse and skirt, giving him a delicious view of her pert behind. His manhood stirred in his pants. He groaned. Even now his body was betraying him.

Serena dressed quickly and only then did she look him full in the face, her blue eyes flashing with anger. "Why should I tell you? So that you could reject me again? That's what you love doing, isn't it?"

"What are you talking about?" Roman shook his head in frustration. The girl was not making sense. Or was she? At her apartment and tonight she was the one who had made the first move. She was a virgin and yet she'd played the part of temptress so well. He frowned as a new thought came to him. Did she have an ulterior motive? He had to know.

"Did you...want to get pregnant? Did you think I wouldn't have protection?"

Serena looked stunned. "Is that what you think? That I want to get pregnant? You think I want to trap you with a baby?"

Roman gave a harsh laugh, unfazed by her look of outrage. "Isn't that what you women do all the time?"

Serena gasped and before he knew her intention she slapped him across the jaw. Hard.

*****

Serena stumbled back, her palm stinging from the sharp blow she'd just given Roman. Heart pounding, she could only stare back at his thunderous face with wide eyes. Oh, Lord, what had she done? Her violent reaction was an obvious shock to him but it was even more of a shock to her. She'd never hit anyone in her life.

Roman stood there, hands balled into fists at his sides, his face drawn in a dangerous scowl. He looked ready to wring her neck.

Serena trembled in anticipation of his wrath. Palms wet with nervous perspiration, heart thumping loudly in her ears, she bit her trembling lip and waited for the axe to fall.

Then suddenly, and to her utter confusion, Roman's scowl gave way to a strange look. Was it regret? Pain? She could not tell. She never got the chance to figure it out. Without a word he picked up his jacket from the floor and strode toward the door, leaving her standing there gaping in the middle of the room. When he slammed the door shut behind him it was with a bang of finality that left her dejected and drained.

All the tension left Serena then. Her body sagged and she slumped down onto the sofa, feeling the strength leave her body. Roman was gone. And this time she knew it was not just from the room, it was from her life.

CHAPTER FOURTEEN

After Roman left Serena sat for a long time, totally disgusted with herself. She'd been stupid to think that a man like Roman Steele could have any interest in her. Of course he would want a worldly woman. Of course he would want someone who matched his level of experience. To him, she must seem like such a novice. Why would he have time for someone like her?

Serena heaved a sigh and propped her chin in her cupped hands. Why had she stayed back at the office working so late on a Friday night? If she hadn't, none of this would ever have happened. But deep down inside, she realized, she'd known what she was doing. She'd worked late into the night because she wanted to impress Roman. She wanted to have the report finished and perfect and sitting on his desk when he got back from his trip. And, she now realized, she'd hoped that maybe, just maybe, he'd come to the office that night and find her there.

Serena lifted her face from her hands. The revelation hit her like a slap to the cheek. She'd always known she wanted this man but now she knew without a doubt that she was in love with him.

The thought made Serena even more depressed. She was in love with a man who did not love her back. He did not even want her the way she wanted him. That much was clear from how he'd been so quick to walk away.

She groaned. How could she have fallen for the one man she'd met who wasn't falling over himself to impress her? How could she be in love with the one man who had ever looked at her with an expression of disgust?

She didn't know how she could have fallen for the worst man in the world she could ever have chosen. One thing she knew for certain, though: Roman Steele must never know what she felt for him.

*****

"Serena, you've been there all of six weeks and you're telling me that you've learned all you can?" Richard's voice was sharp with annoyance. "The plan was for you to be there for six months not weeks."

"I know, Dad," Serena replied, trying to keep her voice calm and soothing, "but I've learned so much in the time I've been there. I think it's time I join you and learn about the family business."

"I'll have to talk to Roman about that." Richard sounded unconvinced. "Is this something you both agreed on?"

"Not exactly," she said, her voice hesitant, "but I'm sure he'll agree that it's time for me to move on."

For a moment there was silence. Then Richard spoke. "Okay, I'll give him a call. But I want you to understand that if you decide to break the internship and start working with me the same rules apply. You'll be here to work, not play around."

"I understand," Serena replied, her voice subdued. She felt a little hurt at her father's statement but how could she blame him? Her history had not exactly been one of dedication and interest in anything to do with the family business.

Now, though, things had changed. She really had learned a lot from Roman and she'd also learned a lot about herself. To her surprise she'd enjoyed the world of business, coming up with new product concepts, taking them from the seed of an idea to birth into the marketplace. Roman had opened her eyes to her abilities and given her newfound confidence in herself. He'd never once expressed doubt because of her lack of experience. Instead, he supported her every step of the way, offering her diverse opportunities to utilize her talents, making her feel she belonged. Too bad he hadn't found it in his heart to love her, too.

She shook her head. It was no use thinking about Roman anymore. It was time to move out and move on. "I'm ready to join you, Dad," she said, her voice strong with determination. "I'll come right away if you'll have me."

Serena was not surprised when her father called her late that afternoon to tell her that Roman had agreed that she'd learned enough from him and she was ready to move on to the family business. No, she wasn't surprised, but she could not help feeling hurt that he'd made no attempt to keep her. Her father made it sound as if Roman had not even questioned her decision to move on. She sighed. He was probably glad to see the back of her.

The day she packed up her things and left the offices of Steele Industries, Roman was nowhere to be seen. He hadn't even had the courtesy to come and wish her well. Obviously, she was of so little importance to him that he could not even spare the time to bid her goodbye. Well, if he wasn't thinking about her, then she certainly wouldn't think about him. At least, that was what she told herself. Easier said than done.

Serena started at Van Buren and Associates the following Monday morning. There was no fanfare at her arrival and she didn't expect it. She was treated like a regular employee, assigned to her task, and instructed to execute them according to deadline just like everyone else.

Eventually, as she learned more about the business she began to take more initiative. She asked her father to allow her to work more closely with the heads of each department so she could learn as much as possible in the shortest amount of time. She spent a few days in the manufacturing plant working with the operations manager, then with the sales manager working in the field, then with the marketing director meeting with the advertising agency.

Every evening she went home feeling satisfied with a day well spent, knowing that soon she would become a valuable asset to her father. She would be one of the few people in the company with such a broad knowledge base, covering all aspects of the company's operations.

Despite all that her nights ended with a feeling of dejection. She could not get Roman Steele off her mind. He was always in her thoughts but was he thinking about her, too? She doubted it.

Sometimes she wondered if she'd made a mistake in declining her father's offer for her to move back home. No, she told him. She needed this feeling of independence. It was part of growing up. She'd even reminded him of the speech he'd given her about budgeting. How would she ever learn if she didn't have to live within her means? And so they'd agreed that, at least for one year, she would remain a salaried employee and she'd be responsible for her own bills. She'd be leading the corporation one day. This was just another part of her preparation for that day.

The drawback was that she was left all alone each evening with no one to talk to, no one to reign in her mind that constantly wandered to a man who could not care less about her.

And what was the use of having friends who were halfway across the world? Serena sighed and picked up the phone. She'd call the one person in the world she knew she could always talk to, no matter what the time of day.

Sylvie picked up the phone on the third ring. "Hello?" Her voice was bright and cheerful, no matter that it was almost eleven o'clock at night.

"Grandma, can you talk?" Serena tried to keep her voice light and happy but there was a tremble to it that must have given her away.

"Are you all right?" There was a world of concern in Sylvie's voice.

"I'm fine," she replied with a soft sigh. "I just need to talk."

"It's about Roman, isn't it?"

Serena bit her lip. "How did you know?"

Sylvie chuckled softly into the phone. "I know you, Serena. Your father told me about your sudden departure from Steele Industries. That could only mean one thing. You had a falling out with Roman. And it had nothing to do with work."

"But how could you know?"

"Child, I'm a woman with several decades head start on you. I know when a man's involved." Then her voice turned serious. "I wanted to ask you about this but I didn't want to be a nosy mother hen. It's your life and I have to let you learn at your own pace. I knew you'd reach out to me when you were ready." For a moment Sylvie was silent. Then she said, "Do you want to talk?"

The question opened the floodgates for Serena. Without telling her grandmother everything she revealed that for the first time in her life she'd fallen head over heels for a man who, ironically, did not feel the same way about her.

Sylvie gave a soft laugh. "Now you know how those young men felt, the ones you dismissed so easily."

Serena sighed. It wasn't much fun when the shoe was on the other foot.

"But how do you know he doesn't love you, too?" Sylvie asked.

"How could he? He rejected me."

"Did he? Or did you walk away?"

Now what kind of question was that? She'd walked away because he'd rejected her. What was her grandmother getting at? "He was the one who-"

"How badly do you want this, Serena?" Sylvie asked, cutting her off. "What have you done to let him know how you feel?"

What had she done? Hadn't she done enough? She was about to say just as much to her grandmother when the words sank in. She, more than most, knew how fleeting life was. She'd only had her mother the first six years of her life. She'd almost lost her own life two years later. If she wanted anything in life she needed to act decisively and act now. Life flew by a lot faster than generally thought.

Could she afford to deny herself whatever happiness life could offer? No, she couldn't. She wouldn't. Even at the risk of being rebuffed she needed to know for sure. She had to see Roman one more time.

*****

Roman lifted the glass to his lips and took a sip of Bacardi as his eyes skimmed the room. There were beautiful women everywhere, all in attendance at the agency's launch of the Enchanted product line. Members of the press milled around with cameras hanging from straps around their necks. Models preened in front of them, posing for pictures.

But as his eyes scoured the room there was one woman, only one who he wished would fill his vision. But she was nowhere to be found.

He'd had Theresa send invitations to both Richard and Serena. Richard was there but he'd come alone. The disappointment of Serena's absence was bitter on Roman's tongue.

He could not believe that he, a calm and collected man at the mature age of thirty, had been floored by a slip of a girl. Try as he might, he could not get her out of his mind. Serena had come into his life, grabbed hold of his heart then walked away…taking his heart with her.   But whatever the cost - his friendship with Richard, his pride or her scorn - he had to see her again.

CHAPTER FIFTEEN

The next morning did not come fast enough for Roman. Now that he'd made up his mind to take action he wanted to move right away. He'd beat himself up over the past few weeks since Serena left. He knew he was the one who had driven her away and he felt like a heel for treating her that way. Still, he justified it with the thought that it was all for the best.

The guilt was eating him up. How could he explain his actions to Richard? Would the man accept that he'd fallen in love with his daughter? Hell, he hadn't believed it himself. He'd never believed in love at first sight but here he was, the victim of the very thing he'd derided.

And then there was the matter of the difference in their ages. Would Serena, fresh out of college, really be interested in him?

These were the questions that swirled around in his mind, immobilizing him when all he wanted to do was find her and make crazy love to her.

Now he pushed those questions to the back of his mind. He was going to swallow his pride and self-doubt and seek her out. If she slammed him and told him never to contact her again then he would have to honor that. But he had to know how she truly felt.

He leaned forward and reached across his desk then picked up the phone receiver. Before he could change his mind he dialed the number for Van Buren and Associates.

It took just a few seconds for someone to answer the phone and advise him that Ms. Van Buren was not in office. Damn. He didn't want to wait till tomorrow to talk to her. He scrolled through his phone and found her cell phone number. He dialed. It went straight to voicemail. Now what?

He stared at the phone, deep in thought. Maybe this was just not meant to be. Then he shook his head. No, he would not give up so easily. He got up, reached for his jacket and grabbed his car keys. He had to find her.

******

Serena hopped into her yellow Porsche, a belated graduation gift from her father, and sped out of the parking lot of her apartment complex. Now that she'd made up her mind nothing was going to stop her.

She was on her way to Roman's office. She had no appointment but she was determined to see him today. She had to hear from his own lips what he felt about her.

Serena rode the elevator to the tenth floor where she was met, as expected, by Theresa. She was shocked when the woman greeted her with a smile.

"Good to see you again," she said warmly, then gave her a look of curiosity. "You're here to see Mr. Steele?"

"Yes, how did you guess?" Serena said cheekily then smiled back at her, genuinely relieved at the woman's pleasant demeanor. Maybe, now that she was out of the picture, Theresa had let her guard down. "Is he in?"

Theresa shook her head. "I'm sorry. He rushed out of here about half an hour ago. Said there was something urgent he had to do."

Serena's heart sank. She'd spent several minutes preparing for this meeting Roman, coaching herself on what she would say. Now that she was all psyched up Roman was missing. She wanted to get it out while she had the courage. After today would her fear keep her away?

Hiding her disappointment behind a bright smile, Serena thanked Theresa. "Please let him know I came by," she said as she headed back to the elevator.

Downstairs in the parking lot Serena sat in her car for a full five minutes, fighting the urge to cry. She'd wanted resolution. She just couldn't go on like this. But he was not here so no matter what she wanted there was nothing she could do.

Taking a deep breath, she turned the key in the ignition. She had to get out of there before she broke down altogether. She put the car in reverse and began to back out of her spot beside a big black Dodge Ram pick-up truck.

There was a loud bang. Serena screamed and slammed on the brakes. Then she whipped her head around. She'd run into a sleek black car.

"Oh, no," she whispered. Where the heck had that come from?

She hadn't seen or heard anything. Oh Lord, she'd probably been too distracted. And now she'd gone and destroyed somebody's car. What if someone was hurt?

Serena flung open the door and hopped out then dashed toward the car. She didn't even glance at the damaged vehicles. Instead, she flew to the driver's seat. All she could think was, dear God please don't let anyone be hurt.

As she got to the door of the black Mercedes Benz it opened and a tall, dark haired man in a navy blue suit got out. Serena gasped.

"Roman?"

"Serena."

"What are you doing here?" They both came out with the words, each taking a step toward the other then they stopped just two feet apart.

"I came to see you," Serena said, her heart thumping wildly. Just the sight of him, the way a stray black curl had fallen onto his forehead, made her body tingle in response. The memory of his hands, his lips on her body, the images came flooding in, making the heat rush to her face. Even in the confusion of the accident he looked gorgeous.

"And I went to see you," he said, his lips curving in a crooked smile. At her look of confusion, he continued, "I thought you'd be at your apartment. When I didn't find you there I decided to come back to the office and then try calling you later."

"You were looking for me?" Serena's voice was a breathless whisper. Dared she even think it? Had Roman missed her even half as much as she missed him?

"I was," he said, and this time as he looked down at her the smile was gone and there was a serious look on his face. "Serena, this is neither the time nor the place but there is something I have to tell you."

"Yes?" She held her breath as she stared up at him. For the first time she saw uncertainty in his eyes. Roman reached out and took both of her hands in his. He pulled her into the shadow of the truck. "I know I've been a jerk these last few weeks-"

"These last few weeks?"

He chuckled. "Okay, ever since we met. But it was for a good reason. Or what I thought was a good reason at the time." He took a deep breath. "From the first day we met...I fell in love with you."

Serena's heart soared. She took a step closer. "But...why did you keep pushing me away?"

"There was so much standing between us. I was your boss-"

"So?"

"Come on, Serena. How do you think that would have looked?" Roman gave her his signature smile, crooked and captivating. "And remember your father left you in my care. I still don't know how I'm going to break this to him."

Serena took a step closer until they were only a hair's breadth apart. "Trust me," she whispered, "he already knows. When I went running back to Daddy I know he guessed there was a man involved. He knows me. That man could only be you."

Roman chuckled then shook his head. "And then there's that thing about our ages."

Serena frowned. "What thing about our ages?"

"I'm nine years old than you."

Serena laughed. "That's it? I thought you were in your forties."

Roman glared down at her but there was a huge grin on his face. "You don't mind my age?"

Serena snaked her arms around his waist. "I absolutely love it. Why do you think I never got involved with a man my age? Too immature. Now you? You're just old enough to match my maturity."

At that Roman laughed out loud. "So, have I done a good job of taming the princess?"

"You've done an excellent job," she whispered, smiling up at him, "a job I hope will never end."

"Never fear, little one," Roman said softly as he looked deep into her eyes, "you have me for life."

And there in the parking lot, in the full view of anyone who wished to see, Roman wrapped his arms around Serena and gave her a kiss that told her without a doubt that he meant every word.

EPILOGUE

Serena woke to the most beautiful day of spring she'd ever seen. It was also the happiest day of her life. Today she would marry the man who had captured her mind, her heart and soul.

She hopped out of bed and ran over to the window to breathe in the fragrance of the flowers under her window. Simply delicious.

Serena smiled as she stared out her bedroom window. She'd moved back home to spend time with her father before the wedding but last night was the last she'd spend under this roof as Serena Van Buren. By the end of the day she would be Serena Steele.

She leaned out of the window to get a better view of the south lawn. The decorators were already bustling about, making sure the trellis and its trimmings were in order. It would be a garden wedding right on the lawn where she used to play with her mother. Maybe her mother would look down on her today and send her wedding blessings on the breeze.

There was a knock at her door and Serena spun around to see her father peeping in. "Ready for your big day, Princess?"

"Oh, Daddy, it's like I've been ready all my life." She went to him and stepped into his arms. When he released her from the hug she saw that his eyes were shiny with unshed tears.

"Your mother would be so happy," he said, looking down at her with a smile. "You made an excellent choice for a husband."

Serena's eyes widened. "I did? You sure you're not upset?"

"Upset?" Richard laughed. "I couldn't have made a better choice myself. In fact, there's something I must tell you." His eyes sparkled with mischief. "I was hoping for this outcome all along. I knew if there was one man who could bring the woman out of my little girl, it was Roman Steele."

"Daddy, did you set me up?" Serena pouted but a smile tickled her lips, making her mirth obvious.

"No, but I'd like to think your mother had a hand in this. Today more than ever I feel her presence and I think she's smiling."

Serena smiled up at her father and now it was her turn to blink back happy tears. "I feel her, too, Daddy. And I know today in the garden she'll be right there with me as I take my big step."

Then, as the birds whistled in the tree outside her window, Serena turned and looked out at the sun rising in the brilliant blue sky. "Thanks, Mom," she whispered, "for finding me the best man I could ever want."

THE END

MAID IN THE USA

JUDY ANGELO

The BAD BOY BILLIONAIRES Series
Volume 2

WHO EVER SAID BILLIONAIRE BACHELORS AND MODEST MAIDS DON'T MIX?

Celine Santini couldn't have been more shocked when billionaire bachelor Pierce D'Amato offers her a job as nanny to his four-year-old charge. After all, he hardly even knows her. But after finding herself thrown into an unexpectedly intimate encounter with him, are they really strangers? Celine is captivated by the green-eyed heartthrob who takes her heart ransom but how can she give in to her feelings when they're from two totally different worlds?

From the first day he lays eyes on the dark-eyed beauty, Pierce D'Amato knows he is lost. He immediately devises a plan to get her under his roof...and it works. But the more he gets to know the sweetly seductive Celine Santini the more he realizes there's a lot more to this woman than he could ever have imagined. Her intriguing combination of sophistication and innocence keeps him forever off-balance and, before he knows it, his bachelor heart turns traitor. The heart knows what the heart wants and it wants Celine Santini...whatever the cost.

A thrilling romance with twists and turns that will keep you turning the pages...

CHAPTER ONE

Celine hummed a love song as she pushed the housekeeping trolley down the carpeted hallway. Today was going to be a great day she'd told herself, no matter that she was stuck in Cambridge for yet another summer when she'd much rather be back home in France with her mother and two rowdy little brothers.

She smiled as she thought about Marc and Sylvan. The ten and twelve year olds were probably driving her *maman* crazy at this very moment with their constant pranks and rough play. If only she could be home with them. She was the only one who could keep those two in check.

She stopped at the door to suite 1206. No time to dwell on that now. She had twelve suites to clean in the next few hours and she wanted to make a good impression. For the last two summers she'd worked at small hotels where the pay was minimal and the hours long. This summer she'd been lucky to land a job at one of the largest hotels on Main Street. She'd be earning almost fifty percent more than she'd made at her previous job. It was still a far cry from adequate but if she kept to a tight budget she might just be able to save enough to go home for Christmas.

Celine knocked on the door. No answer. She knocked again just to be sure then stuck her keycard in the slot and pushed it open. Gathering up a handful of towels and tiny bottles of toiletries she tucked them in the crook of her arm, grabbed the handle of the vacuum cleaner then backed into the room.

The presidential suite was magnificent with a spacious living room filled with antique furniture and ornate carpeting. A sparkling crystal chandelier hung from the ceiling. Celine paused to admire the elegant room. Oh, to be able to live like this. She chuckled to herself. It would probably take a month's salary for her to pay for one night in this suite.

Now where to start? She had an armful of towels so the bathroom it was. Still humming she pushed the door and walked into the bedroom.

At that moment she heard a click and the bathroom door opened. She gasped and the towels fell from her hands. Standing in front of her, his face hidden by a thick towel, was a tall, muscular and very naked man.

Celine screamed.

"What the…" The man dropped the towel and stared back at her in obvious shock. "Where did you come from?"

"I…I'm sorry," Celine said as she backed away. "I thought the suite was empty. I'm so sorry."

The man was staring at her with eyes that were shockingly green. "I was in the shower," he said, raking his fingers through his dark brown hair, "so if you knocked I wouldn't have heard a thing."

Mon Dieu. He was standing there, tall and lean and every inch a man, and he was making no move to cover himself. Celine dropped her eyes, her face hot with embarrassment. She turned to flee.

"Wait. I want to talk to you."

Was he serious? She would not turn back to talk to a naked man no matter how handsome. She was back in the living room and had already grabbed hold of her vacuum cleaner when his voice stopped her.

"Don't leave," he said, his voice imperious and bold. He sounded like the kind of man who expected to be obeyed. He was standing in the bedroom doorway and this time, thankfully, he had the towel wrapped around his waist. "Wait for me in the living room. I'll get dressed."

Without bothering to wait for a reply he turned and went back into the bedroom, leaving Celine staring at the empty doorway. Who did this man think he was, to be ordering her around like that? She frowned as her thoughts raced wildly. Come to think of it, that was a good question. Who was he, really? He had to be a very important person or else a very rich one to be staying in the presidential suite of one of the most expensive hotels in town. Her heart pounded as a new thought crowded her mind. Was he going to come back and reprimand her for violating his privacy? Was he going to report her, or worse, get her fired? Her palms grew damp and she slid them down the sides of her uniform. She couldn't afford to lose this job, she just couldn't. When he came she would have to plead her case.

In less than a minute the man was walking out of the bedroom in dark slacks and a white shirt which he buttoned casually as he approached. His long, lean feet were bare.

"Have a seat," he said and beckoned to the couch by the window.

"Excuse me?" Celine stood stock-still, her hand on the vacuum cleaner, her eyes wide as she stared back at him. Why was he offering her a seat? If he was going to reprimand her why not do it quickly and let her go? He must really plan to lecture her. She decided to speak up, maybe appease him before he got the chance to blast her.

"I'm very sorry for barging in on you like this," she said, her voice earnest. "It won't ever happen again. I'll be back later to clean your room." With that she started toward the door, pushing the vacuum cleaner before her. Maybe if she made a quick exit nothing more would come of this. At least, that was what she hoped.

She was halfway to the door when he laughed, a deep husky laugh that sent a little shiver up her back. It stopped her in her tracks. She turned to stare at him.

"No need to fly so fast," he said, tucking the ends of his shirt into his trousers. "I'm not going to bite. I just want to talk to you about something."

He wanted to talk to her? About what? Her curiosity got the better of her and when he waved her over to the couch again she released her hold on the vacuum cleaner and went to sit demurely on the edge of the chair.

"My name is Pierce D'Amato," he said and plucked a business card from the desk. He reached over and handed it to her. "And you are?"

"Celine Santini."

"Pleased to meet you, Ms. Santini," he said with a smile then cocked an eyebrow. "You're Italian? Your accent sounds French."

She nodded and smiled. "Good guess. I'm from France but my dad was an Italian American serviceman. I speak all three languages."

He gave her quick bow of the head and looked impressed. "Now that we know each other we can talk." He leaned against the desk and folded his arms across his chest. His face grew serious. "I'm in a dilemma, Ms. Santini, and I wonder if you can help me?"

Celine frowned. What in the world could she do to help a man like him? He was obviously a powerful, wealthy man and she was nothing but a PhD student moonlighting as a hotel maid.

"I'm a busy man," he said, deftly buttoning his cuffs as he spoke, never once taking his eyes off her, "but I suddenly find myself in a difficult situation. I've got my business to run and now I've got a four year old. I need the services of a nanny."

Celine could only stare at Pierce D'Amato, convinced that the man had gone mad. He didn't know a thing about her. What was he thinking?

"I know this sounds crazy," he said, giving her a smile that told her he'd seen the confusion on her face, "but I was just appointed guardian for my cousin's little girl and...I'm a bit lost, to say the least." He shrugged. "What do I know about children?"

"So you're looking for someone to take care of her."

"Yes, a nanny, companion, helper. Whatever you call it. I already have a housekeeper but she's got her hands full and I don't think she's up to the challenge of a four year old. Mrs. Simpson is almost sixty."

"But what about the agencies? They can help you find lots of people who would be happy to take care of a child."

"I went that route already. Hated it." He grunted as if in disgust. "They sent me young, old, fat, thin. Kylie hated all of them. She's really picky, that little one."

"And you think...she'd like me?"

He chuckled. "I'm sure of it. From the second I laid eyes on you I knew you were the girl for Kylie."

The second he laid eyes on her? How could he form an opinion that fast? And then she remembered she'd formed an opinion of him in that split second, too. And as she remembered their encounter her face grew warm. Celine shook her head. "I don't understand."

He laughed then stood up and walked over to the window. He looked down at the street below then turned to look at her. "As funny as it sounds when my eyes met yours something clicked. You have a freshness about you that I think will appeal to Kylie. And you look like a girl who isn't afraid to have fun."

Now what did he mean by that? Celine frowned and rose to her feet. "I'm sorry, Mr. D'Amato. I don't think that would be a good idea. I've got a good job here and-"

He laughed. "Working at what? Minimum wage? I could give you many times that without blinking."

Celine sucked in her breath. The nerve of him. "Money isn't everything. I don't know you. How can I leave my job to go to a man I don't know?"

"Is that all?" He waved his hand dismissively. "I've got great references, starting with the man who owns this hotel. He's one of my clients."

"Mr. Pierrefond?" she asked, her voice a reverent whisper. "You know him?" Every one of the hotel employees knew and respected John Pierrefond. He was one of the few billionaire businessmen in the area who took a personal interest in his employees. He was in his seventies but he remained as involved in the operations of his businesses as when he'd started out. The veteran employees never stopped talking about him.

Pierce shrugged. "We've been doing business for years. Ask him." Then he gave her a grin that revealed a charming dimple in his right cheek. "He'll stand by my character. I don't go around ravishing innocent maidens, if that's what you're worried about."

The smile disappeared as quickly as it had come. He glanced at the heavy gold watch on his wrist then back at her. "Listen, I have to go. Keep the card and call me. You have until tomorrow. I'm heading back to Springfield and I need an answer before I go."

Celine nodded and slid the card into her pocket. "Of course," she said, hurrying to retrieve the vacuum cleaner. "I'll think about it and let you know."

"Good." He nodded and before she was even out the door he was heading back to the bedroom.

Celine closed the door behind her, leaned her back against it and closed her eyes. Talk about an interesting start to the day. She'd just met the most seductively handsome man and her heart still raced at the memory of Pierce D'Amato with his broad shoulders, narrow waist and the silky strands of black hair that nestled around his...

Mon Dieu. She had to get a hold of herself. But the image of Pierce was burned into her mind and she knew that, like it or not, it would haunt her for a very long time.

She pushed her trolley on to the next suite. She had no intention of still being in sight when Pierce exited his room. The next time she saw him, if there ever was a next time, it would be on very different terms.

CHAPTER TWO

Heart thumping, Celine drove up the long and winding driveway that led to Pierce D'Amato's house. Actually, house was an understatement. What she was looking at was a mansion. The place looked big enough to house five families and still have room to spare. She pulled her Toyota Corolla into the space between a sleek black Jaguar and a candy-red Porsche. She couldn't help but grimace. Beside the other vehicles her ten-year old car looked so out of place. Oh, well. The other cars would just have to get used to working-class company.

She slid her damp palms down the sides of her jeans, shaking her head in annoyance. She hated how they perspired when she was nervous. There was no need to be, she knew, but her body was saying otherwise.

After almost an entire day of vacillation Celine had decided to call Pierce D'Amato. After all, how could she throw away the chance to possibly double her salary? With such an increase in fortune she would be able to afford two, maybe even three trips back to Europe each year to visit her family. Her eyes grew misty at the thought of Christmas at home in France.

She'd confided in Bridgette, a friend she'd made on her first day of work, and received a glowing report from the older woman. Bridgette had met Pierce many times and she described him as a true gentleman known for giving generous tips to hotel staff who served him. Still, there was a sparkle in the woman's eyes that told Celine she was smitten by him. And who wouldn't be? With his sleek, dark looks and intense green eyes, Pierce D'Amato looked like he had the power to charm any woman he desired.

That evening Celine called Pierce and he invited her to meet with him in his home office so she could be introduced to his little charge. They'd talk further, he'd said, and then she could make her final decision.

And so it was that she found herself walking toward the magnificent steps of Pierce D'Amato's residence. She clutched the strap of her bag tighter, gave her palms one last swipe on the seat of her jeans and climbed the steps to the expansive marble-tiled entrance.

She rang the bell then stood there plucking at the buckle on her bag, trying to steel her nerves for her next meeting with Pierce. Try as she might she could not wipe from her mind the memory of his strong toned body and she wondered how she'd react when he opened the door. She took a deep breath, trying to slow her racing heart. It would not do to let this man see her sweat.

The door opened and a plump gray haired woman smiled up at her. "Miss Santini. Welcome. I was expecting you. I am Elizabeth Simpson. Come in."

Celine released her breath, thankful that it was the housekeeper who opened the door. That would buy her some time to get her wits together. She gave the woman a smile and a whispered "thank you" then entered the house.

Celine was in awe. The foyer was huge with a high cathedral ceiling graced with a sparkling chandelier that looked like a host of tiny stars floating in mid-air. The white columns reached gracefully up to the ceiling and multicolored tiles of marble glistened beneath her feet. She was almost afraid to step on them. This wasn't the entrance to a private home. It was more like the lobby to a grand hotel.

"I'll take you to the office and let Mr. D'Amato know you've arrived," Mrs. Simpson said as she led the way down a hallway that seemed to run along the length of the house. "You're a bit early so he's not quite ready but he won't keep you waiting."

"Thank you," Celine said again but she was hardly listening to the woman. She was too distracted by the splendid paintings that lined the walls. She loved art and paintings in particular. She could live for days in a museum and not miss life in the outside world. Pierce's collection fascinated her. She caught her breath at the sixth one. Was that a Picasso? No, it couldn't be. She stared at it, almost bumping into Mrs. Simpson as she walked. She would have to come back and check that out later.

They were walking past wide French doors now, and through them Celine saw a huge swimming pool, its water glistening brilliant blue in the bright sunshine. And there in the pool, his back to her, was the man who had occupied her thoughts since the day they met. Pierce was standing in the shallow end of the pool, the skin of his shoulders and back deeply tanned by the rays of the hot sun. His hair, wet and slicked back, gleamed in the sunlight.

Celine almost stopped walking. Her eyes fixed on the broad shoulders she remembered, the narrow waist, and those lean hips now encased in black hip-hugging swim trunks. She could see the outline of firm cheeks through the wet material that clung to his body. For the second time in two days she was seeing this man without his clothes on.

Celine bit her lip to keep from smiling. If she were totally honest she would admit that neither experience had been painful.

She caught a glimpse of a little blonde head just by Pierce's hand and realized that he was in the water with the little girl she'd heard about. He was probably giving her a swimming lesson. For a man who made it clear how busy he was it came as a surprise to Celine that he was spending a weekday afternoon entertaining a child. She admired that. She smiled and kept on walking.

Mrs. Simpson was right. Pierce did not take long to appear at the office door. She'd been sitting there less than five minutes, just enough time for Mrs. Simpson to bring her a cup of herbal tea, when Pierce arrived fully dressed in white button down shirt and navy trousers.

"You're early," he said as he walked over and gave her a nod of greeting. "I didn't expect you for another half hour."

"I'm sorry," Celine said. "I wasn't sure what the traffic would be like so I decided to give myself ample time." She laid the cup and saucer on the table beside her. Pierce sounded quite formal. This was a job interview, of course, and she would be as professional as he was.

He turned those intense green eyes on her. "Thank you," he said with a smile. "I appreciate punctuality. Now let's bring you up to speed on what this job requires." Pierce gave Celine the details on Kylie's situation and the kind of help he was looking for. Kylie's mother, a cousin of his and a widow, had been in a serious motor vehicle accident and had sustained severe head injuries. Now she lay in a coma with only a fifty percent chance of recovery. The little girl had been at the daycare center when it happened. Not having any close relatives, Kylie's mother had listed Pierce's name as the emergency contact person. And so it was that he became an overnight surrogate parent.

"What about Kylie's father?" Celine asked, her heart going out to the little girl who was now without her mother. "Why doesn't he help?"

Pierce shook his head, his face solemn. "Sadly, he died when Kylie was only two. He had congenital heart disease. Had a heart attack and died when he was only twenty-seven."

"Oh, no," Celine whispered. What a tragedy for a child to experience. First, the loss of her father and now a mother who was barely clinging to life. What must the little one be going through?

At that moment Mrs. Simpson came in holding the hand of the little girl who'd been the subject of their conversation. She was dressed in a white puff sleeve summer dress with a yellow bow. She looked like a delicate little daisy.

"Here she is, Mr. D'Amato. Kylie is ready to meet your guest." Mrs. Simpson smiled at Kylie and gave her a little push toward Pierce. The child walked slowly up to him and with a serious little face she rested her tiny hand in his outstretched one.

Pierce gave her a gentle smile then said softly, "There's someone I'd like you to meet, Kylie. This is Celine who came all the way from Cambridge to meet you." He turned the child to face Celine. "Why don't you go over and say hello?"

Kylie hesitated and turned wide blue eyes up to Pierce as if seeking reassurance. Then, at his smile and nod, she looked at Celine for the first time. She took a quick breath then walked over.

Celine felt her heart melt instantly. There was a world of sadness in Kylie's eyes but she did not flinch and she did not cry. She went to Celine and took her hand and did not utter a word of protest. What a brave little soldier she was. Celine felt like pulling her into her arms and hugging her till she felt only love and peace. It was so heartbreaking to see grief in the eyes of one so young.

Celine slid off her chair and kneeled in front of the child so their eyes were level. "I'd like to be your friend, Kylie," she said, making her voice as soft and comforting as she could. "May I?"

The girl remained silent, staring back at Celine with eyes filled with uncertainty. Then slowly she nodded her curly blonde head and lifted her thumb to her mouth.

"May I have a hug?" Celine tilted her head and smiled.

Kylie didn't wait for Celine to open her arms. She simply popped the thumb out of her mouth, took the two steps she needed to get to Celine, and wrapped her arms tight around her neck. No words were spoken but Kylie buried her face in Celine's neck and began to cry softly.

"It's okay, *ma cherie*, it's okay," Celine soothed as she rubbed the child's back and held her close. "I'm here for you."

For almost a minute Kylie clung to her until finally she quieted and lifted her face. "I'm glad you're my friend," she said in a tiny whisper then rested against Celine with a sigh.

Celine lifted her head, her eyes pricking with tears of sympathy, and when she looked at Mrs. Simpson the woman was dabbing at her face with a dainty handkerchief. When her eyes wandered over to where Pierce stood, his hands shoved deep into his pockets, his face was somber and dark with emotion. They'd all been affected by Kylie's innocent plea for comfort.

When Mrs. Simpson left the room taking Kylie with her Celine looked directly at Pierce. After meeting the child there was no way she would say no to this job. How could she deny her the attention, sympathy and love that she so desperately craved?

"I want this job," she said and her voice cracked on the last word. She cleared her throat, trying hopelessly to hide the depth of her emotions. "I want to be here for Kylie. When can I start?"

Pierce nodded and although he did not smile his eyes told her he was pleased with her decision. Still, he asked, "Are you sure?"

"I want to help Kylie," she said, her voice earnest. "I can't explain it but I feel a connection between us."

Pierce nodded again and this time the smile reached his lips. "I could tell. Don't ask me how, but the moment my eyes landed on you I knew you were the one. I knew you'd be perfect for Kylie."

Celine sat back in her chair, surprised at the strength of his confidence in her. How could he have known that? He hadn't even known a thing about her before that day. And even though she'd emailed him her resume and references after they spoke on the phone he still didn't know that much about her.

And what about him? Was she perfect for him, too?

Celine's breath caught in her throat and she stole a guilty glance at Pierce. Where had that thought come from? Why in the world had she even gone there? She meant nothing to this man, absolutely nothing except someone who'd make a great nanny for his charge. If she was going to survive at this job she'd better reign in her unruly emotions.

If it was one thing she knew it was that she and Pierce D'Amato were in two totally different classes and unless she suddenly won a few hundred million dollars in the Super Lotto never would their two worlds meet.

CHAPTER THREE

Pierce watched as Celine climbed into her car and drove away. He thanked the stars he'd found her when he did. Kylie needed someone like Celine in her life. And then there was him. What was it about the girl that drew him to her, made him determined to get her under his roof? It had been weird. That first day they met he'd heard the scream, dropped the towel and found himself staring into the liquid brown eyes of a startled and stunningly beautiful woman. No matter that she was in a maid's uniform and had her sleek black hair pulled into an old fashioned bun. He'd felt a jolt of electricity run through him, a shock that made him freeze. What the hell, he'd thought. He'd never reacted to a woman like that before.

And she'd appeared just when he was praying for a miracle, just when he'd almost given up hope of finding the perfect nanny for Kylie.

He remembered seeing her fright and saying something or other to reassure her but he'd been so startled that seconds passed before he remembered that he was still standing stark naked in front of her. By that time she was already turning to flee. Good thing he'd stopped her from leaving the suite altogether. Now because of his quick action she would be working for him under this very roof. He couldn't help but smile at the turn of events. He was looking forward to getting to know Miss Celine Santini.

When Celine's tail lights disappeared Pierce went inside in search of Kylie. He found her watching cartoons.

"Uncle, can I have ice cream?"

Pierce went over and tousled her hair. "Of course, Kylie. And it's 'may I have ice cream', okay?"

"Okay," she said as she stuck her thumb in her mouth and looked up at him with big blue eyes, her little face as solemn as a priest. Pierce knew what that meant and his chest tightened in sympathy. The thumb in the mouth meant that Kylie was really missing her mother right then. Her thumb was her source of comfort in a world that had turned upside down.

"Come on, sweetie," he said and lifted her up in his arms. "Let's both go get some ice cream."

***

A week had passed since Celine arrived at Pierce's house with her suitcases and few possessions piled into her car. Thankfully, she would be able to spend the next five months or so focusing on Kylie and her needs since she didn't need to check in at the university until October. Since her arrival Kylie had spent every waking moment with her and slowly, tentatively, the little girl began to open up like a tender flower in the morning dew.

The first three nights were difficult. Kylie had cried herself to sleep each night, refusing Celine's attempts to comfort her. On the fourth night, instead of trying to read a bedtime story, Celine pulled toys from the box and acted out the story of Snow White and the Seven Dwarfs right there on top of the little girl's blanket. Kylie laughed so hard she had to wipe happy tears away with the back of her hand.

After that she insisted that Celine pile the toys onto the bed each night so they could act out Cinderella, the Bremen Traveling Musicians and all her other favorite bedtime tales. Celine was happy to oblige and when Kylie asked her to climb into the bed with her she pulled the child close and they cuddled until the little head dipped onto her shoulder and Kylie slipped softly into sleep.

Next day Celine woke to the sound of birds whistling outside her window. It was going to be a great day, she knew, because it was sunny and bright, it was Saturday, and Pierce would return home.

She knew it was stupid of her to feel the way she did but she couldn't help it. She was actually looking forward to seeing Pierce D'Amato again. She was sure that a man like him would have women flitting around like moths to a flame. He probably had myriads of female admirers in every city he visited. He certainly wouldn't notice her, a simple nanny working to make a living.

Even though she knew there was no way she could compete for his attention Celine could not stop herself from feeling a jolt of excitement at the thought of seeing him again. With a smile on her face she hopped out of bed and padded across the hallway to Kylie's room. She tapped on the door and went in then leaned over to tickle the little girl's cheeks.

"Wake up, sleepyhead," she said with a laugh as Kylie stretched and opened her tiny mouth in a yawn that could swallow an elephant. "Time to get ready for a fun day."

Half an hour later Celine and Kylie were in the kitchen having a breakfast of pancakes, eggs, strawberries and yogurt. They were racing to see who would finish first. They had a full day scheduled. First, Celine would review letters and numbers with Kylie then they would take a dip in the pool then do lunch and then gardening.

Celine knew that working in the garden, planting seeds and nurturing the flowers were all excellent therapy for her little charge. She was in her second year of the PhD program in Psychology and much of her research involved child development, motivation and counseling. There was something about working with your hands that calmed the nerves, and working outdoors in the fresh air surrounded by the beauty of nature were like magic to soothe the spirit and comfort the soul. This was what Kylie needed in her life right now - structure, physical activity and a feeling of accomplishment.

After lunch Celine plopped a wide-brimmed straw hat onto Kylie's head and they went out to the garden that circled the back patio. The little girl was armed with a miniature garden fork and shovel while Celine followed with a watering can.

"Race you," Kylie yelled and took off across the grass, laughing as she ran.

Celine ran after her, laughing too, happy to see that she was in a cheerful mood.

When they got to the far end of the garden Celine flopped down onto the grass, panting and laughing, then she slid a finger across her brow, pretending to wipe sweat away. "Wow, you're a really fast runner," she said, opening her eyes wide as if in amazement. "I couldn't catch you in a million years."

"Really?" Kylie asked, eyes wide with wonder. "Did I run that fast?"

"Yes, you did," Celine said and reached over to tickle her. "You're my Olympic champion."

After that they settled down to some serious gardening, with Celine digging the holes and Kylie dropping the seeds in and covering them with earth. Then it was Kylie's job to water the seeds while Celine weeded out that section of the garden to make sure they didn't choke the seedlings when they popped out of ground.

They were so absorbed in their task, working together in comfortable companionship, that they both jumped at the snap of a twig behind them. They whirled around to see a tall, blonde and exquisitely beautiful in woman in a cloud-white summer dress staring down at them. Celine put up a hand to shade her eyes from the sun and that was when she saw the woman's face, perfectly made-up with crimson lips that curled in what looked like disdain.

Celine, taken aback by the sudden appearance of the stranger, took off her garden gloves and rose to her feet. She was at least a couple of inches taller than the unexpected visitor but somehow she felt almost intimidated in her presence. The woman was looking at them with such an unfriendly expression that it was as if they were the intruders and not her.

"Hello," Celine said, still feeling a little off balance. "May I help you?" She felt Kylie move closer to her and she put a reassuring hand on the child's shoulder.

"So you're the new maid," the woman said, her eyes flashing with something akin to dislike. "I heard about you but nobody told me you were beautiful."

"Excuse me?" Celine said, unnerved by her statement.

"Pierce told me he got a nanny for his new…responsibility." She turned her eyes on Kylie and from her look Celine could tell that, for some reason, the child was a source of annoyance to her. Then she trained her flashing blue eyes on Celine again. "But I thought it would be somebody like Mrs. Simpson. He never told me you were young." Her brows settled into a frown that made it obvious that this was a major problem.

Celine raised her eyebrows, unable to hide her surprise. "And you are?"

The woman's eyes widened as if shocked that she would ask. Or maybe she was shocked that she didn't already know of her. Celine didn't know which.

"I am Sophia Redgrave and I own the home next door. Pierce and I have been friends for several years." The woman said the words with a haughty sniff.

Celine did not miss her deliberate emphasis on the word 'friends'. Sophia Redgrave was obviously sending her a message. Her relationship with Pierce was a whole lot more than just friendship.

Celine didn't know what deflated her more, the thought that Pierce was involved with the woman or the thought that there was any possibility of Sophia Redgrave getting involved in Kylie's life. The woman obviously had a problem with the child's presence at the house. Heavens, what if Kylie became Pierce's charge permanently? And what if Sophia became his wife? What would happen to poor little Kylie? She shook her head, trying to dispel the horrible thought. She gave the woman a cold stare, as chilly as the one that had been directed at them. "Is there anything I can help you with, Ms. Redgrave?"

"No, there's nothing you can do for me," she said and raised a delicate hand to brush away the wisps of hair that the soft breeze had blown into her eyes. "But I'll speak to Pierce about the activities of this child. Why do you have her out here digging in the dirt? Shouldn't she be in school?"

"There's no school on Saturdays. Besides, she's only four. Whatever she needs to learn I teach her at home."

Sophia frowned. "You? Teach her? What would a maid know about what's best for a child? She needs structure in her life. The best thing that Pierce could do for her is to get her into a good boarding school."

Celine gasped. "Boarding school? Are you mad?" The words were out before she could stop herself. She could not believe the woman would suggest such a thing.

Sophia's lips tightened and she glared at Celine. "I would ask you to remember your position." Then with a look full of scorn she said, "I went to boarding school in Europe all of my young life and it did me a world of good."

Celine could just imagine the good it had done her. That was probably what had turned her into the world-class bitch she was now. The nerve of her to even think of putting dear little Kylie into boarding school.

"Celine, am I going away?"

She looked down to see Kylie gazing up at her with huge, scared eyes, the hint of tears already appearing in the corners.

Celine felt like someone was squeezing her heart. How could she have been so thoughtless? She'd been discussing Kylie's future with this woman right in front of the child as if she weren't there.

She dropped to her knees in the dirt and pulled Kylie into her arms. "No, *cherie*, you're not going anywhere. Your home is right here with Uncle Pierce."

"And you?" Kylie asked, searching Celine's eyes as if for even more reassurance.

But how could she promise Kylie that, too? She was only an employee, after all. Pierce could terminate her employment at any time. And if this meddler Sophia Redgrave had any say in it that day could come sooner rather than later. Still, she had to say something to appease the child. She'd already experienced enough confusion for one day.

"*Oui, cherie* , and me too."

Kylie smiled and Celine's heart sang. The little girl was going to be all right. Pulling her close, she gave her a quick kiss on the forehead.

"Oh, so you're a foreigner, are you?"

Sophia's words broke into their communion of friendship, making them turn their attention back to her again.

"You called her 'cherie'. Lots of foreigners come to this country and then decide they're never going home. Are you an illegal immigrant or something?"

Of all the backwards things she could have said, for Celine this was one of the worst. As wealthy and sophisticated as she might be Sophia Redgrave was obviously living in a world of stereotypical perceptions. She was a bigot who needed a curt response.

But then she remembered. Not in front of Kylie. As much as she itched to put Sophia Redgrave in her place she would not do it at the expense of Kylie's happiness.

Taking a deep breath, she counted to ten in her mind then slowly expelled the air. In a calm voice she said, "If you'll excuse me I have to take Kylie inside now." Then she quickly gathered up the tools, took Kylie's hand and walked away leaving the grand Ms. Sophia Redgrave staring after them.

***

Pierce groaned and shook his head. Yet another delay and two more hours this time. He looked across at his pilot and the man gave him a shrug and an apologetic grin. There was nothing he could do. If air traffic controllers said they had to sit out the windstorm then that was what they would do.

Pierce checked his watch. After eight o'clock. Mrs. Simpson would be gone by now and Kylie would already be in bed. He'd spoken to her earlier that day and promised he'd be home to read her a story. He grimaced. He'd broken a promise to a child who was very sensitive right now and needed stability and reassurance. Breaking a promise was definitely not the way to give her that.

Then his mind went to the woman who had crowded his thoughts for the whole week he'd been away. He shifted in his seat as his loins tightened at the very thought of her. What was it about Celine Santini that turned him on every time? He couldn't think about her without imagining kissing her till she was breathless, his hands sliding down to cradle her soft, full breasts.

He shook his head and stood up then he went over to the plate glass windows of the lounge and began to pace. He had to rein in his thoughts. Celine was an employee and he'd better remember that. But, damn, why did she have to be so sexy?

And there was more. There was something about her that drew him like a magnet. It wasn't just her physical beauty. Maybe it was her infectious smile or her obvious love for children. There was something good and calm and nurturing about her that made him trust her completely. He'd trusted her with Kylie and even though he'd done his duty and checked all her references he'd known from the first time they met - brief as it had been - that she was genuine.

He smiled to himself as he thought about getting back home and seeing her again. Of course he wouldn't see her tonight. It would be too late for that. But he'd be home all day Sunday in the company of his two 'girls'. He chuckled at that thought. He, the dedicated bachelor, had become a family man in the space of just a couple of weeks. The thought of the responsibility of a family had scared him for years but now he was looking forward to seeing his pretend one. He must be getting old.

Pierce did not get home till almost two o'clock in the morning. Tired and grimy from his travels he dumped his suitcase in the hallway and climbed the stairs to the master bedroom where he stripped and went straight into the shower. It was only when he was clean and refreshed that he felt the weight of weariness lift from his shoulders. God, it felt good to be clean.

He pulled on his boxers then grabbed his robe from the hook and shrugged it on and secured it with the sash. Then, barefoot, he headed over to the wing that Celine and Kylie occupied. He wanted to check on them quickly before retiring for the night.

First, he peeped in on Kylie. In the room was a dim light cast by the softly glowing nightlight by Kylie's bed. Quietly he padded over to look down at the sleeping child.

She was resting peacefully as she clutched her teddy bear, her blonde hair curling softly around her face which was slightly pink from sleep.

He left the room and returned to the hallway then glanced at the door to Celine's room. He thought of checking in on her too but quickly dashed the idea. What was he, a Peeping Tom? He couldn't invade her privacy like that. No, he'd have to be patient and wait till morning to see her again.

He was just about to turn away when he noticed that the door was ajar. Had she done that deliberately, probably so she could hear if Kylie cried out in the night? Or was she still up? He could see a dim light through the thin slice between the door and the jamb. She might be up reading.

For a moment he paused then his curiosity got the better of him and he approached the door. He gave a soft tap. Hearing no response he slowly pushed the door just wide enough for his head to go around.

The bedside lamp was on but Celine's bed was empty. The covers were neatly spread and the bed looked like it hadn't been slept in.

Pierce frowned. Where in the blazes was she? His eyes swung over to the bathroom door but it stood open and the bathroom was in total darkness. Now he was really concerned. Celine wouldn't have left Kylie in the house all by herself, would she? No. He was certain she would never do such a thing.

He backed out of the room then took the few steps to the other door down the hallway. Before he even pushed it open he could tell this was where he'd find Celine. As he stood at the door the fragrance of her perfume wafted toward him. He followed the flowery scent, stepping into the sitting room Celine shared with Kylie, and walked over to the loveseat by the window.

And there she lay, curled up in the seat like a little cat, a book of fairy tales resting on her hip. She must have come into the sitting room after putting Kylie to bed and had fallen asleep with the book still in her lap.

Pierce contemplated getting a blanket and covering her where she lay. She was wearing a nightdress of white silk and the coolness of the night would certainly give her a chill. But then he realized that wouldn't be enough. The love seat hadn't been made to accommodate a sleeper and the steep arm had her neck positioned at what looked like an extremely uncomfortable angle. She'd be sure to have a strain by morning.

He had no choice but to wake her.

"Celine," Pierce whispered softly, not wanting to startle her out of sleep.

She didn't budge. Her breathing remained deep and peaceful.

"Celine," he said again and this time he touched her arm. It was smooth and cool to the touch. He frowned. The girl needed to be in her bed under a warm blanket. At Pierce's second try her eyes fluttered but she did not wake.

He sat on the loveseat, his hip touching the curve of her waist, and leaned over her. "Celine, wake up," he whispered. "You need to go to bed." He put his hand on her shoulder and gave her a slight shake.

Her eyelids fluttered again and this time they opened. She looked up at him sleepily. "Pierce," she whispered, her brown eyes cloudy with confusion, "what is it?" Then her eyes widened and she struggled to sit up. "Kylie. Is something wrong with her?"

"Kylie's fine," he soothed, putting out an arm to steady her. "You need to get to bed."

"Oh," she sighed and relaxed against his arm. "You scared me. I thought something happened."

"Nothing at all," Pierce said but this time his voice was strained and he was finding it difficult to breathe. Celine had slumped against him and he could now feel the weight of one of her delicious breasts. He immediately hardened in response. Christ, what was this woman doing to him?

The soft silk of Celine's nightgown slid over the hairs on his arm, sending shockwaves rocketing through his body. His mouth went dry with want. He wanted so badly to kiss her, to taste those lips, to consume her. He wanted to kiss the tops of those beautiful breasts. He gazed into her eyes then he dipped his head, the intensity of his desire making him groan, and pressed his lips to hers.

Celine gasped and then to his great relief she was responding, tentatively at first then with a passion which almost matched his own. Stirred by her ardor he teased and explored then he took possession of her mouth, kissing her till she was breathless in his arms.

"Celine, where are you? I'm thirsty." The tiny voice cut through the sizzling tension.

Pierce froze. Then he jerked back and jumped up off the loveseat.

"Can I get some water?" The door creaked open and Kylie stood there sleepily rubbing her eyes. Then the little girl's eyes widened as she stared up at Pierce. "Uncle Pierce, you're home." She ran into his arms and he picked her up in a huge bear hug.

"Yes, little one, I'm home. I got in late but I made it. Did you miss me?"

Kylie nodded, her eyes huge and earnest. "Uh huh. I wanted you to come home before my bedtime."

"I'm sorry I got in late, sweetie," he said softly, "but I'm here now. Do you forgive me for being late?"

She nodded again. "Uh huh."

"Thank you." Pierce smiled and gave her a soft kiss on the cheek. "Now let's go get you some water."

As Kylie rested her head on his shoulder Pierce turned around to glance back at Celine. She sat on the loveseat staring up at them, or more accurately up at him, as if in shock.

"Go to bed." Pierce mouthed the words soundlessly then before Kylie could start asking questions he took her out of the room and down the hall.

After Pierce had settled Kylie back in her bed and returned to his room he lay back in the pillows for a long time reliving every second he'd spent with Celine. He ached, thinking of what could have been. He knew without a doubt that if Kylie hadn't walked in when she did they'd have found ecstasy in each other's arms. But it was not meant to be. Not this night, anyway.

He folded his arms behind his head as he stared up at the ceiling. His brain was telling him to stay away from her, that he'd acted out of line and should back off. She was his employee, after all.

But then there was another part of him that wanted to possess her, body and soul. He'd gotten just a taste of sweet Miss Celine Santini and he desperately wanted more…

CHAPTER FOUR

Celine sat up in the bed and twisted the blankets in her hands. She stared at the curtains blowing softly by her window. After that episode last night how was she going to face Pierce?

She could hardly recall how it started. All she remembered was finding herself in Pierce's arms then he was kissing her and then she was lost. Pierce had expertly awakened her body to a sensual symphony played by his hands, his lips, his body, so powerful and vibrant to her touch. He'd kissed her lips till she melted in his embrace. Thank God Kylie walked in when she did. Somehow deep in her heart Celine knew that if the spell had not been broken she would have been powerless to resist him.

Taking a deep breath Celine summoned her courage and climbed out of bed. It was Sunday and there would be no Mrs. Simpson to fix breakfast for Kylie so she needed to be up and ready to face the day. Like it or not, she would have to face Pierce D'Amato.

When Celine went downstairs with Kylie the man who dominated her thoughts was already sitting at the table, cup in hand, reading what looked like the New York Times on his iPad. He turned around as they walked in.

" Hello, Miss Bright Eyes," he said with a smile then set the cup down and opened his arms to give Kylie a Good morning hug. He kissed the top of her head then still smiling, he raised his eyes to Celine who hung back, keeping a few feet of distance between them. His smile seemed innocent enough but in them was a look that made Celine squirm.

So he was remembering, too. That much was obvious from his look. But where she felt shame at her behavior, at how easily she'd fallen under the spell of his seductive caress, he seemed pleased. There was not a hint of regret in his eyes.

Celine didn't know whether to feel angry at his lack of shame or flattered. This was all so confusing. She dropped her eyes and walked over to the stove, anxious to find something to do, anything to keep her from having to meet his eyes again.

"Good morning, Celine."

With his greeting Pierce forced her to turn her attention back to him. She pasted a smile on her lips. "Good morning," she said and glanced at him then quickly turned back to her task, painfully aware of his eyes trained on her. Furtively she took a quick breath then exhaled slowly, trying to calm her jangling nerves. How was she going to survive a day in his company?

Celine breathed a sigh of relief when Pierce engaged Kylie in conversation. They began a serious discussion about the merits of each of her toys and which would make the best friend of all, Barbie or Elmo or The Little Mermaid. Celine fixed Kylie's oatmeal and within minutes she'd set her cereal, orange juice and banana on the table.

Only then did she turn her eyes to Pierce. "What would you like?" she asked, her voice a lot more controlled and calm than she felt.

Pierce stared back at her, his look enigmatic, but there was a curl to his lips that told her he was reading far more into her question than she'd meant.

She felt the heat rise to her face and she was turning away, trying to hide her distress, when he spoke.

"I'll have whatever you're having," he said then gave a soft chuckle which was not lost on her.

Celine struggled through a breakfast of scrambled eggs and toast with Pierce. It was difficult sitting right across from him, trying all that time to avoid his eyes. Thank goodness Kylie was there to entertain them.

When she'd collected the dishes and she stacked them in the machine then sighed with relief. Breakfast was over. Now she could escape.

"So what would you like to do today, Princess?" Pierce's words broke into her thoughts. "I'm all yours."

"Swimming," Kylie yelled and clapped her hands in delight. "I love swimming."

Pierce chuckled. "I would never have guessed." He looked over at Celine as she stood by the sink. "What say we meet at the pool in about forty-five minutes?"

Celine nodded. "I'll have her ready. That would be more than enough time for her breakfast to settle."

Pierce cocked an eyebrow. "What do you mean, you'll have her ready? You mean you'll both be ready."

Celine stared at him. He wanted her in the pool with them, he in nothing but swim trunks and she in bathing suit exposed to his gaze? How would she keep her eyes off him? After last night, knowing what it felt like to have those broad shoulders beneath her palms, his warm skin pressed against hers, how would she stay calm so close to his near naked body?

No, not a good idea. "I…was thinking of catching up on some…reading." She floundered for an excuse. Lying had never come easy to her. "Maybe you and Kylie could spend some quality time together?"

Pierce gave her a look that told her he knew she was doing her best to avoid him. Then he shrugged and looked down at Kylie. "Sorry, Princess, Celine doesn't want to go swimming today. I guess we'll just have to call it off."

"No," Kylie wailed. "I want to swim."

Pierce shook his head and on his face was an exaggerated look of regret. "No can do. Not unless Celine is going to be here to help me with you."

"Celine, you have to come," Kylie cried tugging at her hand. "Please?"

Celine patted her head and with the little girl distracted she got her chance to glare at Pierce. She grew even more peeved when she saw the wide grin on his face. The snake. He'd used Kylie to force her hand. He knew she'd never refuse the little girl. How could he be so low?

Apparently he could go that low and quite easily, too. Without any sign that he felt guilty he smiled and said, "Okay, ladies, meet you here in forty-five. Don't be late."

When Celine and Kylie arrived at the pool Pierce was already in the water. His body, sleek and strong, cut through the water as he did laps up and down the pool. When he looked up and saw them he rolled over onto his back and waved.

"Come on in," he called to them. "The water feels good." Kylie was the first to respond. Slipping her hand from Celine's grasp she ran to the edge of the pool and jumped, almost landing on top of Pierce's head. He laughed and caught her then waved to Celine. "Your turn."

She grimaced and shook her head. Did he really think she was going to jump into his arms? Not likely.

"Don't let me come get you," he said with a grin and hoisting Kylie onto his shoulders he began to swim toward the lip of the pool.

Celine knew not to play around then. Quickly she let the towel fall from where she'd wrapped it tightly under her armpits, exposing her bikini clad-body to his gaze. Pierce stopped paddling and his appreciative stare told Celine he liked what he saw. She could feel her body go pink all over. Wanting to hide herself as quickly as possible she hurried to sit on the edge of the pool then slid into the water, relieved when it flowed over her body. Of course the water hid nothing from his view but it gave her some small comfort knowing that something, though transparent, was covering her.

It took all of fifteen minutes before Celine began to relax. Maybe it was Kylie's shrieks of laughter when Pierce bobbed her up and down or maybe it was this other side of Pierce that she was seeing - so carefree, playful and even mischievous. He thought nothing of playing tricks on poor Kylie, sinking to the bottom of the pool, making her think he'd disappeared, or swimming up behind to tickle her ear. It was like Celine was seeing the little boy he used to be. She could just picture him - active and naughty and loads of fun. Soon Celine was caught up in the horseplay, too. When Pierce almost drowned her with a tidal wave of water she swung after him, trying to give him a taste of his own wicked medicine. But he was too strong and too fast. As hard as she swam she couldn't catch up to Pierce and finally she gave up and swam back to Kylie who was giggling uncontrollably as she watched from the shallow end of the pool.

Celine ducked down and whispered in her ear. "Just watch," she said. "I'll get him." Then she put up her right hand, Kylie did the same, and they did a high five.

Celine turned to check out Pierce's location. He was still on the far end of the pool but now he was lounging, doing the backstroke, leisurely floating back towards them. Obviously, he felt there was no more threat. He'd probably thought she'd given up and gone back to sit with Kylie and lick her wounds. Well, he had grossly under estimated her and he was about to get the shock of his life.

With the slippery stealth of a snake Celine slid back into the water but this time she took a huge breath and went under, traveling swiftly along the bottom of the pool. As she moved she watched Pierce float toward her, totally oblivious to the danger lurking below. Then when he was right above she crouched and, using the bottom of the pool for leverage, she vaulted straight up and shot toward him.

Celine grabbed Pierce around the waist and dragged him under and as he kicked in surprise she shot away from his reach.

She was laughing as she got back to Kylie's side. Why had she done that? For the life of her she couldn't tell what made her as to dunk her own boss. Dear God, she must be losing her mind.

He'd been so close, he'd been so warm when she grabbed him around the waist, he'd been so firm to the touch. And she'd been so turned on. The horseplay was supposed to have been pure innocent fun but tell that to her body. Every time Pierce came near her nipples turned into hard pebbles she was sure he could see through the fabric of her bikini top. And every time she saw his lean muscled body cut through the water her breath caught in her throat. She was dying to slide her hands over his muscled chest and tight abs. She was craving to slide her lips down his back. She'd never had such bold thoughts in her life. What was this man doing to her?

By now Pierce had swum back to the surface and still sputtering, was staring at her through the water streaming down his face. The glitter in his eyes told her he wasn't about to take that without a response. He shook the strands of wet hair from his face and fixing his dark eyes on Celine, ducked down into the water, his body, mouth and nose below the surface. Like a crocodile stalking its prey, with only his eyes and the top of his head above the surface, Pierce streaked toward her.

Although she knew it was in fun, and although she was fully aware that this was a man and not a beast, an unreasonable fright filled Celine and she shrieked. The game was becoming too real. She scooped Kylie up and swam quickly toward the steps, intent on getting out of the pool and escaping her stalker's clutches.

She was almost out when a woman's high-pitched voice cut through the air. "Well, what have we here?" As one, they spun in the direction of the voice. And there stood Sophia Redgrave looking cool and crisp in a pant suit of white linen. In her arms she gingerly held a tray on which lay a colorful cake cover.

She gave them a tight little smile. "I was ringing the doorbell but when there was no answer I decided to come around. Did I break up a party?"

Her eyes flashed with something akin to anger as they swept over Celine and Kylie. But then her face softened as she turned her attention to Pierce. "I brought you something special," she said, her face softening into a smile. "I'll take it to the kitchen. Come see."

Pierce raised his eyebrows then he smiled and swam to the side of the pool where she now stood looking down at him.

"What do you have there?" he asked, his voice full of amusement.

Sophia shook her head and gave him a teasing frown. "I'm not telling. Only if you're a good boy and follow me." Without waiting for a reply she minced her way up the path in her high heeled gold sandals, her bottom swaying seductively as she went.

Pierce watched her go then he turned to Celine and Kylie who had not moved from the edge of the pool where Sophia found them. He raised his eyebrows and grinned. "Who doesn't like a surprise?" he said with a shrug. Then he put his hands on the side, hauled himself out of the water and loped up the cobbled path to the house.

With each step Pierce took up that path Celine's heart slid lower and lower. When he finally disappeared into the house she felt like her heart was a rock that had rolled to the bottom of her belly.

How could she have been so stupid? How could she have forgotten about Sophia Redgrave?

She'd had her doubts when the woman implied that she and Pierce were more than just friends. She hadn't heard Mrs. Simpson mention her so then she'd thought the woman was probably exaggerating. Maybe she just wanted Celine to think they had something going on.

But if she'd had any doubts about the veracity of the woman's statement she didn't have any such doubts now. The way Pierce's face lit up, the way he'd run off after the woman told her all she needed to know. Pierce D'Amato was taken and if she knew what was good for her she'd stay as far away from him as possible.

CHAPTER FIVE

Next day Pierce flew out to Texas and it was another four days before Celine saw him again. Not that she minded. She needed time without him near, time to build up her defenses and accept that Pierce was her employer and that was all.

Who was she kidding? The man was a billionaire. Why would he want her? Women like her were just playthings for men like him, toys to be used and discarded when you got bored. Sophia, on the other hand was in his class. She had lots of money, Celine was sure, and she certainly had the attitude.

She, on the other hand, had nothing. How could she compete?

That evening when Pierce got home Celine was prepared for him. Her heart was encased in a steel vault and nothing he said or did would have any impact on her. She would keep her face neutral and she would greet him with a professional smile. As hard as it was, for the sake of Kylie and for the sake of her own sanity she would divorce herself from her emotions. She would be as cool as you please and she would be the perfect employee. Nothing more, nothing less.

That was her plan.

But when Pierce walked in the door the look of dejection and sadness on his face dashed all her well-made plans.

Shocked, she rushed to his side. "Are you all right?" she asked, searching his face. What in the world could have happened for him to look so terrible?

"I need a minute," he said and dropped his bags on the floor. His eyes swung past her to Kylie who seemed to have sensed that something was wrong. She hadn't come running to jump into her Uncle Pierce's arms. She just stood there, her fingers twisting the sash that hung from her dress, her blue eyes huge in her pixie face.

Pierce straightened and as he did so he took a deep breath and looked at Celine.

In that moment she knew. No words were exchanged between them but the anguish in his eyes, the extreme exhaustion on his face, were all she needed. The worst had happened. Sweet, gentle Kylie had lost her mother.

Celine's lips trembled and even though she'd never met the woman she felt like she would burst into tears. When she felt her face begin to crumble she bit down on her lip and inhaled slowly. No, she would not break down. This was not her moment. This was Pierce's loss and more than anyone, it was Kylie's.

"What do you want me to do?" Celine whispered as she looked up into Pierce's grief stricken face.

"Take her," he said. "I need a few minutes. Just take her to her room and I'll be up soon."

Celine nodded and went over to Kylie and took her hand. "Come, Sweetie," she said in a soft, soothing voice. "Uncle Pierce will come visit you in your room. Let's just give him some time to rest for a bit."

Kylie said nothing. For a moment she continued to stare up at Pierce then she nodded, her face now looking far older than her four years, and turned with Celine and walked away.

Kylie Nichols was the bravest little girl Celine knew. Like a miniature soldier she sat quietly, her hands in her lap as Pierce told her how he had gone away to visit her mother after receiving an urgent call from the hospital. Unfortunately, she'd slipped away before he arrived. But the nurses told him she'd passed peacefully, just like falling asleep for a very long time.

"Is Mommy in heaven now?" Kylie asked in a barely audible whisper.

"Yes," Pierce said, his eyes shiny with emotion. "The angels are taking care of her now."

Only then did Kylie's tears begin to flow. As Pierce kneeled on the floor in front of her he opened his arms. She walked into the hug and laid her head on his shoulders. Then her tiny body shook with her sobs.

Pierce let her cry and as she did he rubbed her back soothingly and crooned soft words of comfort into her ear. It took several moments before the crying stilled and Kylie lifted her face to look into Pierce's eyes. "I wish Mommy could have stayed with me," she said with a sigh, "but I think Daddy needed her more. I know they're together now."

When Celine heard her utter those words she felt like pulling her into her arms and bawling. What a stoic little four year old. She was acting with a maturity far beyond her years, handling her tragedy with a courage that many adults would not have been able to muster.

That night Kylie slept in Celine's bed, in her arms. There was no way she would have let her sleep alone. As the child slept she stroked her hair until she, too, drifted off into a dreamless sleep.

Days later Pierce flew them out to New Haven in his private jet where Kylie said her final goodbye. For her sake it was kept a quiet affair with only close relatives and friends attending. She spent the entire ceremony sitting on Celine's lap, wrapped in her arms.

When they returned home they were especially nice to Kylie, never letting her spend much time alone but allowing her enough space to grieve. Even Sophia went out of her way to be nice, bringing her toys and a book about angels. Still, it took a few days before the first smile appeared on Kylie's face and even more days before they heard her laugh. It would take a long time for her to heal but Celine knew that her little soldier would pull through.

***

"I want a change of environment for Kylie. Since the funeral she hasn't left the house. She needs to get out, to breathe again." Pierce folded his arms across his chest and leaned back against the marble top island in the middle of the kitchen.

He'd been thinking about it for some time now. He wanted to take her to a place where she could play and laugh again, somewhere that didn't remind her of her loss.

"Disney World?" Celine rested her chin in her palm as she stared up at him. Today she'd forgone the ponytail and let her dark hair fall gently onto her shoulder.

Pierce gave it some thought then shook his head. "No, a bit too much for her I think. Sort of from one extreme to the other, you know?"

"What about a Caribbean cruise? One of those that caters to children?" Celine asked with a slight tilt of her head. She looked so cute when she did that.

He wrinkled his forehead. "Hmm, no. That's just more of the same." He released his arms and stretched them wide to loosen the kinks in his back. "I want to take her somewhere different but I want it to be a more gentle change of environment. Not so fast paced."

Then a thought came to him. Celine had spoken with such animation each time she'd mentioned her kid brothers and her mother. Would a week or two in the company of a loving family be the change that Kylie needed?

"What about a trip to Europe?"

At his words Celine's brows lifted and she looked up at him with just a hint of excitement in her eyes. "Europe?" she asked. "So far away?"

Pierce chuckled. "A seven hour flight? That's not bad. Try fourteen or eighteen hours. I've done lots of those. Now that's far."

There was a faraway look in Celine's eyes. It was clear that she was thinking of home.

Pierce decided to press home his point, get her on board while she seemed to be in a nostalgic mood. "How would you like to go see your family?"

Celine turned wide expressive eyes to him. "Do you mean it?" Her voice was a breathless whisper, almost as if she were afraid to utter the words.

"Of course. You've talked so much about Marc and Sylvan that I feel I almost know them. I'd love to meet them." He was smiling as he walked over to the table and pulled out a chair. He sat down across from Celine. "More importantly, it would be great for Kylie. Being around other children is probably what she needs right now."

Celine began to worry her bottom lip with her teeth. "I don't know. I would absolutely love to go home for a visit but...the boys and Kylie? I'm not too sure. They can be a bit rough."

"Don't underestimate the depth of understanding that kids can show. And even though they're boys," he said with a chuckle, "they can be compassionate. Hey, boys aren't that bad. I know. I used to be one."

At that comment her face relaxed and her lips curved in a smile. Her liquid brown eyes sparkled as she looked back at him. "You've convinced me. I would love to take Kylie to meet my family."

He put on a mock frown. "What about me?"

Celine burst out laughing. "And you, too, Pierce. I'm sure they'll all love you."

***

"So this is Mr. Pierce D'Amato. *Bienvenue, Monsieur.*"

Claire Santini took his hands in hers then stood on tiptoe to kiss him on both cheeks. She was a diminutive woman with raven black hair caught up in a bun on the crown of her head. Her dark eyes shone in her rosy face and her lips told of much laughter and mirth. She reminded Pierce of a sprightly little sparrow, full a lively energy that could never be extinguished.

She was something of a contrast to her daughter. Where she was tiny and slightly plump with eyes as black as night, Celine was of slender build with deep brown eyes a man could lose himself in. Even though she was of medium height she was at least four or five inches taller than her mother.

When Claire released his hands Pierce looked over at Celine as she stood in the middle of the modest living room. "So where are the young men I've heard so much about?"

She rolled her eyes. "Hiding I'm sure, just waiting to play a prank on us." But then she smiled broadly and her eyes flashed with eager anticipation. She put her fingers to her lips and tiptoed to the door that led into the kitchen. It was slightly ajar and, without warning, she reached an arm around and came back with a boy, now howling with laughter.

"Marc, what do you have there?" She demanded as she pulled a huge water gun from his hands. "You were going to soak us, you naughty boy. *Tu es si mechant.*" She deposited the toy on the floor. "Come, you naughty boy. Give your sister a hug." She wrapped her arms around him and kissed the top of his head.

"Ugh, kissing. Gross. *C'est pas bon.*" Marc struggled out of her arms but his flashing dark eyes showed that he was loving the attention.

"Marc, not like that, *mon petit*. Behave." Claire shook her head and gave him a stern look. "Now go and get your brother. Tell him enough with this hiding."

Sylvan had obviously been listening to everything because at his mother's words he peeped round the door then stepped out into the living room. With his huge brown eyes and dark hair he was like a male version of Celine. More subdued than his brother, or maybe wishing to seem more mature, he approached his sister with a small smile which widened into a huge grin. Obviously he was unable to contain his joy at seeing his sister again.

"Sylvan," Celine cried. "You've grown so tall." She gave him the same treatment she'd given Marc, hugging him close, but he was almost as tall as she was so she ended up kissing him on the cheek. Unlike his brother, he showed no objections.

Then Celine went over to where Kylie stood hiding behind Pierce. "Come, *cherie*. Don't be shy." She took the little girls hand. Gently, she pulled her forward. "Guys, this is Kylie. Come on over and say hi."

Kylie clung to Celine with one hand then stuck the thumb of her free hand in her mouth. She stared up at the boys with huge, tired eyes.

Marc grinned and gave her a quick wave. "Hi," he said then shoved his hands into his pockets.

Sylvan, though, took a different approach. He must have seen Kylie's uncertainty at being in a strange house with three strangers who talked funny. He crouched low and looked into her eyes. With a smile he extended his hand. "Pleased to meet you, Mademoiselle Kylie."

For a moment she hesitated then, not letting go of Celine with her left hand, she popped her thumb out of her mouth and extended her right hand to Sylvan. He took it, wet thumb and all, and shook her hand. "I know we'll be good friends," he said.

Kylie said nothing but she nodded slowly and slipped the thumb back into her mouth.

Claire must have seen how exhausted the child was because she patted her hands together and proceeded to shoo the boys out of the room. "Time to rest now. The travelers are very tired."

Her words triggered a feeling of weariness in Pierce and if he felt so tired he could imagine how the others felt, and especially Kylie who was not used to flights several hours long. Although she'd slept through most of the journey she would not have slept as soundly as when she was in her own bed.

What made it worse, where it would now be the middle of the night back in Massachusetts it was bright daylight in France. It would take at least twenty-four hours for their body clocks to adjust.

After a light meal Claire bundled them off to bed, Celine and Kylie sharing Celine's bedroom and Pierce occupying Marc's room.

Celine's home was a small, neat bungalow in the tiny village of Thomery-By just outside of Avon, the nearest town of any significant size. As for Paris, they'd traveled almost an hour from Charles De Gaulle Airport to get here. It had been a long journey but as far as Pierce was concerned it had been worth it.

Here in this village, far away from the bustle of the city, he knew Kylie would find healing. As he lay back in the bed listening to the birds whistling in the branches that hung by the window he could imagine her running across the grassy meadows with the boys or picking the flowers that lined the winding pathways they'd seen on the way here. Everywhere you looked there were flowers. Gardens bloomed in front of the little houses and Pierce could sense the pride of the inhabitants in their beautiful little town.

He smiled in contentment. He was looking forward to a relaxing, peaceful stay in this sleepy village.

Next afternoon when they had fully recovered from the plane ride Celine decided to introduce Pierce and Kylie to her hometown. They embarked on a walking tour of the village which took all of two hours. They stopped to meet the butcher who was hanging a string of sausages in the window then they moved on to the shop of a seamstress who sat by the window humming as she worked on what looked like a wedding gown. When she saw Celine she dropped the fabric, clapped her hands together then ran outdoors to greet her. Celine got the same response at the post office, the pharmacy and the tiny library she told him had been like her second home. It was obvious that she was known and loved in her community.

They continued on, enjoying the crisp air and bright sunlight, until they got to the local grocery store now operated by Celine's old piano teacher. Tall, thin and reedy, he looked like a bespectacled stick insect. He kissed both Celine and Kylie on their cheeks. When he turned toward him Pierce took an involuntary step back but the man only extended his hand in greeting.

"*Bonjour,*" he said, eyeing Pierce suspiciously.

"*Bonjour,*" Pierce replied and but with cool reservation. Where did this guy come off looking at him like that?

The man turned back to Celine and began an animated conversation in French of which Pierce understood only two words, *fiancé* and *mariage*.

When the words left the man's mouth a strange look passed over Celine's face. She bit her lip and looked down at the ground. It was obvious that whatever he'd said had upset her. When she finally looked up her serene expression had fled and her brown eyes flashed with unmistakable anger.

She replied to the man's comment, her tone curt. She nodded and said her goodbye then she pasted a smile on her face and turned to Kylie and Pierce.

"I guess you two must be hungry now. Why don't we head home?"

They'd been walking in silence for a few minutes, Celine seeming lost in thought, when Pierce decided to question her change in demeanor. She'd gone from cheerful and bubbly to quiet and somber in the space of minutes, all because of a conversation she'd had with her old teacher. There was obviously something worrying her because she kept biting her lower lip and frowning. She probably didn't even realize she was doing that.

"What's up?" he asked. "That guy obviously pissed you off. Want to talk about it?" She looked up at him then, a startled expression on her face. His question must have jerked her out of her reverie. "I…" She shook her head and looked away and Pierce could swear he saw the glint of tears in her eyes.

What the hell had the man said to her to upset her so much? "Celine, tell me," he urged. "Is there anything I can do?"

She took a deep breath and gave him a brave little smile. Then she shook her head. "Thanks for asking but no…there's nothing you can do."

Not wanting to push, he continued walking by her side. Then he felt a soft hand on his arm.

"Maybe…if I talk to someone about it, it might help." Her voice was soft, hesitant, and there was a hint of pleading in her eyes. "Can we talk…later?"

"Of course," he said, searching her eyes for a hint of what could have caused her such distress. Could it be something to do with her family? Was it something that money could fix? If so, he had lots of it. For some reason that he couldn't quite explain he felt protective of her, almost as if she were…his.

Later that evening after a meal of salad, baked fish, bread and Camembert cheese, Pierce left Kylie with the boys and walked down to a nearby stream with Celine. They sat on the soft grass of the bank and Celine, her voice low and subdued, began to speak.

"It's very difficult to speak about this and I'm sorry to burden you," she said with a rueful smile, "but I think my behavior earlier requires some explanation."

She looked down at her hands then back at him. "I was engaged once, to the son of the gentleman you just met. The grocer."

Pierce felt his heart lurch in his chest. It was like she'd told him she was about to die, his reaction was that violent. Why had her words affected him like that? Hell, he'd known her less than two months. Still, her words had given him a real jolt.

"We'd gone to high school together and then when we ended up going to the same university in Paris. In senior year we got involved." She seemed to be deliberately avoiding his eyes, looking down at the ground where she pulled distractedly at the blades of grass. "We planned to get married right after graduation but then he said we should wait until after graduate school."

She heaved a sigh then lifted her face, the strain showing in the tightness of her lips. She swallowed. "I waited. He wanted to get his MBA at INSEAD. He knew that a degree from the top business school in France would open doors for him. He didn't want to start a family just then so I supported his decision." She shrugged. "I wanted to do my Master's too so I thought I'd do my graduate degree while he did his, and then we'd get married afterwards. Another year or so shouldn't matter, right?"

Pierce said nothing, sensing that all she wanted to do just then was talk. She needed to get whatever was bothering her off her chest.

She gave a bitter laugh. "The problem was, he went back to Paris but I went to the United States. I wanted to be part of an excellent Psychology program so I applied to Harvard and was accepted. That was the beginning of the end." She slid her legs up, wrapped her arms around them and rested her chin on her knees. "I came home at Christmas, still wearing my engagement ring," she said her voice cracking, "to learn that he was going to be a father in two months."

So that was it. The bastard had cheated on her. No wonder she didn't want to talk about it. Then Pierce frowned. So why was his father talking to Celine in a tone that made it seem like she was the one at fault? Something was not adding up.

His confusion must have been obvious because Celine began to speak again and this time she was offering an explanation.

"*Monsieur* Girard, he knows that after my Master's I went back to America to do my PhD because I didn't want to be around Giles, the memories and the thought of what could have been." She began to worry her lip again. "He's upset because…" she paused and drew in a long breath, "because Giles wants me back and I won't say yes."

What in the blazes?

"Hold up. You lost me." Pierce held up his hand. "He wants you back? What about the other woman? What about the child?"

Celine shook her head. "That's the thing. He keeps saying it was an accident." She gave a laugh full of disbelief. "Yet he married her and they settled down right here in Thomery."

"And so you left."

182

Celine nodded. "I had to."

Pierce got up and brushed the grass from the seat of his trousers. This story was getting even more confusing. "I still don't get it. You said he wanted you back."

She laughed dryly. "Yes. Funny, isn't it?" Then she shook her head. "He and his wife were divorced a year ago and he's been hounding me ever since."

Son-of-a-gun. "Now he wants you back?"

She nodded. "Now he wants me back."

For a moment Pierce was silent. The nerve of the jerk. He felt like if he had the chance he'd punch this Giles guy in the gut. As much as it was none of his business he was pissed at the situation.

More than that, he realized with shock, he was alarmed. What if Celine still had feelings for the guy? What if he tried to weasel his way back in? Where the heck would that leave him?

He raked his fingers through his hair and stared out over the water. Things were getting really complicated. Here he'd thought he was making things better by choosing Celine's hometown as their vacation spot but he'd dropped her right into a hornet's nest.

He turned to face her. "So what does this guy's father have to do with all this? Where does he come off tackling you about this?"

"Monsieur Girard always wanted us to get married. I was his favorite pupil. He still wants me to consider renewing my relationship with Giles." She shrugged. "He means well."

"Yeah, right." Pierce response was cold. "He needs to mind his own business and not pressure you into something you don't want to do." He looked at her as he said the words. Was it really something she didn't want to do? Or did she still have a soft spot for her ex?

As if sensing the direction of his thoughts Celine got up and threw her handful of ripped up grass blades into the bubbling water. "It's getting cool out here. I guess we'd better go back to the house."

Well, that was an effective end to the conversation. It seemed he'd touched a very sensitive nerve. Pierce looked at Celine, trying to gauge her feelings but she'd already turned, effectively shielding her face from his gaze. She was heading up the bank, leaving him to follow.

Celine's reaction was not a good sign and now he was worried. Very worried.

CHAPTER SIX

Days passed and neither Pierce nor Celine brought up the subject of their conversation. Without words both of them seemed to have agreed to focus on Kylie and her amusement.

When Pierce saw the rosy cheeks of the child as she raced about outdoors with Sylvan, Marc and a little puppy they'd acquired he knew he'd made the right choice in taking her here. No trip to Disney World could have done for Kylie what her new friendships had done for her. Without pampering her the boys took full charge of her, taking her on long walks from which she returned exhausted but brimming with stories of the birds she'd seen in the woods, the flowers she'd picked and the bugs she'd caught.

"Bugs?" Celine wrinkled her nose when Kylie first told her about her new found interest. "Yucky."

Kylie only giggled and ran off to find the boys she now seemed to view as her big brothers. Obviously she wanted to be like them and if collecting bugs was what they loved to do then she'd do it, too.

A whole week passed and Pierce's life settled into a comfortable rhythm that had him wondering how he would adjust to the fast paced world of business when he got back to the United States.

He had competent managers at his software development firm so he was not worried. Still, he knew he couldn't stay away for too long. He'd get rusty and when it came to business and negotiations you didn't want to do that. Still, he was enjoying the down time and he knew Mrs. Simpson was glad for the time off to visit her grandkids.

One evening after picking up a steak from the butcher shop Pierce returned to find that the magic bubble he'd been living in had suddenly burst.

As he rounded the corner and strolled toward the cul-de-sac where Celine's house was nestled he realized that she was standing at the bottom of the gravel driveway and she was not alone.

Standing mere inches away from her was a man, tall and blonde and what you'd call handsome in a 'Brad Pitt' sort of way. He was deep in conversation with Celine and as he spoke he moved his hands expressively as if trying to make a point. At one point he even reached out and put his hand on her shoulder. She seemed to flinch and he pulled it away.

Pierce slowed his pace as he approached, taking his time so that he could observe Celine's reaction to the man he assumed was her ex-fiancé. Her head was down and her shoulders drooped as if she carried the weight of a nation on them. When she lifted her face to respond to a comment Giles made her eyes flashed with anger. Or was that the gleam of unshed tears?

Pierce felt like a hand encircled his heart, squeezing hard, making him feel almost physical pain. Were they going to kiss and make up?

He was almost upon them now and as one they turned and looked at him. Now he could see it. Yes, those were tears in Celine's eyes. What the hell had the jerk said to make her cry? Pierce turned to him and he knew his face was set in a dark scowl but he didn't give a damn. If the man was harassing Celine he'd better be prepared for a fight.

He walked up to them and mere feet away. His eyes skimmed Celine's flushed face and came to rest on the long lean face of the man he now considered her tormentor. He glared at him.

The man took a quick step away from Celine. He frowned as he stared back at the newcomer. He looked back at Celine, his eyes uncertain.

Before Pierce had a chance to think what to do next he felt slender arms sliding round his waist and looked down to see Celine smiling up at him. In her eyes was a look of relief. "*Mon amour*, what took you so long? I've been waiting for you," she said, her voice sweet and low and seductive.

Pierce almost sucked in his breath but caught himself just in time. God, she sounded sexy when she talked like that. And the look she was giving him. This must be what they called 'bedroom eyes'. Whatever they called it, it was having a hell of an effect on him. He could feel himself harden in his trousers.

"I came back as soon as I could," he said and returned the smile. "You know I can't stay away from you for too long." Okay, so that was corny but she'd caught him off guard. No time to think of sophisticated lines. But no matter, their act was working. A pink flush began to creep up the neck of Gyles whatever-his- name-was and soon his face was totally red.

"*Ex....Excusez-moi*," he spluttered then backed away and as Pierce held Celine close with one arm and cradled his package of meat with the other the man turned and practically fled down the road back toward his father's house. As soon as he was out of hearing distance Celine released her breath in a whoosh and pulled her arms from around Pierce's waist, then she stepped back and out of his reach.

He felt the loss. He'd enjoyed having her warm body, her sensuous curves, pressed against his torso and he wanted more. But short of reaching for her and hauling her back into his arms like he wanted, he had no choice but to abide by the distance that she'd created between them.

"Thank you so much," she said with a smile. "You came just in time."

"For what exactly?" he asked, searching her face. What was she feeling at this moment? And what had caused her to put on that act?

"I'm sure you know who that was."

"Yeah, I guessed," Pierce replied. "Your ex."

"Yes. He's been here for the past hour trying to get back on *Maman's* good side. He was so persistent that I could see he was getting on her nerves." She gave a little laugh. "I thought I'd make things better by suggesting I'd walk him out to the road. That's when he started bringing up old memories, all the good times, trying to convince me to take him back."

"Remembering… was that what made you cry?"

She chuckled softly. "How did you guess? I kept telling him not to bring them up but he kept going on and on. My tears were partly out of sadness at what we'd lost but also out of sheer frustration. I couldn't get him to shut up. I just wanted to smack him."

Pierce laughed at that. "You? Smack someone? I'd love to see that."

"Oh, I'm quite capable," she said with a laugh which told him her cheerful spirit was back. "Don't try and test me."

Pierce smiled but said nothing. Oh, he was tempted to test her. He wanted nothing more. He wanted to test those lips so soft and pink and pliable. He wanted to nibble his way down her neck then down lower to those delicious breasts-

"I'm glad I came on this trip."

Celine's words jerked Pierce out of his reverie.

"In spite of the stress?" he asked. Then he said, "Of course, seeing your family makes it worthwhile."

"Yes, that goes without saying but that's not I meant." She gave him a smile, obviously amused when he frowned at her in confusion. "I'm glad I got to see Giles again."

Pierce felt like she'd kicked him in the stomach. Now what the hell kind of game was she playing? Hadn't she just said that she didn't want to talk to him?

"I'm glad because all this time I've been blaming myself for our break up. I've been so wracked with guilt that half of the time I couldn't stand myself."

Pierce gave her a sharp look. What was she talking about now? She was like a pendulum that kept swinging from one confusing side to the other. "Okay, I can see this is going to take some explaining because right now you have me confused as hell. "What say we drop off this meat in the kitchen and head down to the stream?"

She seemed to like that idea. She was smiling as they walked up the pathway to the house and her step was light. It looked like she dropped a ton of troubles off her shoulders.

Pierce couldn't wait to get down to the stream to hear what Celine had to say. She was the most baffling woman he'd ever met. A soon as he got there he flopped down in the grass. "Now put me out of my misery," he said, looking up at her as she stood above him in her sexy pink halter top and even sexier skinny jeans. "Spill it."

She dropped into the grass beside him and wrapped her arms around her legs then dropped her chin on her knees. It seemed to be a favorite position of hers. "What I was saying was, I don't feel guilty anymore. For the first time I feel as if I've been set free."

"And what, pray tell, were you feeling guilty about?" Pierce pulled up a blade of grass and used it to tickle her shoulder.

She laughed and shrugged it off. Then her laughter died away and a more serious look settled on her face.

"I've never shared this with anyone but somehow I feel as if I can trust you." She turned her face away and looked out at the water.

That statement got his attention. He wiped the grin off his face and sat up, the better to give her one hundred percent of his attention.

"Giles and I were in a relationship for all of senior year in college and throughout a whole year of graduate school. During that time he'd asked me…many times if we could…make love. I told him no. I wanted to wait till marriage."

Pierce frowned, almost not believing what he was hearing. Was she saying what he thought she was saying?

"When he got Amelie pregnant I was devastated. I was hurt and confused but I also felt it was all my fault. Maybe if I hadn't denied him he would still be with me, maybe even be my husband right now." She turned to Pierce, her eyes earnest. "But you know what? It wasn't until this trip back home that I realize what a jerk he really is. I'm glad he didn't wait for me.'

For a moment Pierce was silent, letting it all sink in. So what she was saying was, for the whole two years of her relationship with this man she'd remained a virgin? In the twenty-first century? Was that even possible?

He shook his head knowing that he was the one being the jerk right now. Good thing he wasn't stupid enough to blurt his thoughts out loud.

"So what was it that made you realize he's a jerk? You've known him for years."

"Pierce, do you know what that man said to me? When I asked why he wanted me back, why he hadn't stayed with his wife, he said he'd never wanted her in the first place. He'd only married her because he got her pregnant."

Pierce nodded. That was a stupid and insensitive thing to say. Still, he wouldn't be the first man who said something like that. Lots of men got women pregnant and married them just to save face. There had to be something more to make Celine so incensed.

"And when I asked him about his son, the poor little one caught in the middle of this, he said he can always get other children. He wants to have children with me." Eyes flashing with outrage she released her legs and stood up, apparently too agitated to stay still. "I couldn't believe he would say something like that. If he can talk like that about his own flesh and blood can you imagine what he'd do with me when he got tired of having me around? The pig." She spat the words out, not hiding her disgust.

Pierce nodded. Now that was low. For a man to deny his child he'd have to be lower than a snake crawling on its belly.

"Anyway," Celine said with a sigh, "I finally realized how lucky I was for not having slime like that in my life. I wouldn't want him to rub off on me." She shuddered as if the thought repulsed her. "And when you saw me with those tears in my eyes they weren't for me they were for that child who has such a heartless bastard for a father."

Pierce got up then. He could see the emotions as they played across her face. Yes, she was angry but she was also in pain. She might not know it but he was reading every emotion that flashed across her face.

Before he realized what he was doing he reached for her and wrapped her in his arms and this time she did not step back or pull out of his embrace. Instead, she rested her cheek on his chest, right against his beating heart, and she cried.

She cried, he knew, for many things. She didn't have to tell him. She'd bottled up her emotions for so many years and now it was time to let them flow free. She cried for what could have been, for what never was, for the guilt she'd borne and now for the relief of knowing she'd made the right decision. She cried because now she was free.

Pierce let her cry and when, after long moments her hiccups softened into sighs, he put his finger beneath her chin and tilted her face up to his. She was vulnerable but he wanted to kiss her so bad he stifled his better self, lowered his head and pressed his lips to her soft, willing mouth. She responded to him eagerly, almost desperately, and when her arms slipped round his waist he felt a thrill run through him. He pressed her closer and his kiss grew urgent, the hunger he'd felt for her intensifying with the taste of her lips. God, how he wanted this woman.

Too soon he had to release her lips. He heard Kylie in the distance and knew that in minutes they'd be set upon by a yelling four-year-old girl, two gangly boys and a barking dog.

For a long while he looked deep into those liquid brown eyes, trying to read their depths. This woman, so seductive and sultry yet so vulnerable and innocent, what was she thinking right now? Was she wanting him as much as he wanted her?

He didn't have the chance to find out. As the shouts of the children came closer and closer he slid his hands down her arms to her hand then slowly let go and stepped back.

Celine stared, wide eyed, back at him.

He could see that he'd shocked her with that kiss but that was the least of his problems. They were heading back to the United States in a few days and when she was again his roof he'd have a hell of a time keeping his hands off her. God help him.

CHAPTER SEVEN

Celine arrived in the United States feeling like a new woman. The unexpected all expense paid trip to see her family had been like a miracle, and having both Pierce and Kylie with her made the visit even more special. And to top it off she'd found resolution to that part of her life that had haunted her for so long. Giles St. Juste was not and had never been the man for her. Now she had closure.

She soon settled into her old routine with Kylie, reviewing letters and numbers and reading stories in the morning then spending the afternoons at play on the lawn, swimming in the pool or working in the garden. She'd been nanny to the little one two months now and she almost saw her as her own daughter. At times her mind would fast forward to the day when she would have to go, return to her life as a student, leaving behind a child who had become so special to her. And Pierce. To think that there would come a day when she would never see him again. It did not bear thinking about.

She still remembered his kiss that day by the stream in Thomery-By. She'd relived it so many times in her mind. She hadn't wanted that moment to end.

But it did. And it was a good thing, too, because she was losing her heart and soul to Pierce D'Amato.

What was she going to do? She'd just overcome one hurdle by expunging Giles from her heart and now she'd gone and created another problem? The man was her employer which was bad enough but on top of that he was involved.

Or was he? Sophia had been over several times since their return but most times it was when Pierce wasn't around. Each time she'd come she'd made it clear that she was dying for both her and Kylie to disappear. She continued to hint at a long-standing relationship with Pierce but then Celine hardly saw them together. Was their relationship a secret? Was Pierce engaging in love trysts at her house rather than his, seeing that she and Kylie were there? It made her heart ache just thinking about it.

There was something Celine had to do, something that was against her nature but totally necessary under the circumstances. She was going to have to meddle in somebody else's business.

That night after she'd put Kylie to bed she went downstairs to find Pierce. He was lounging in the comfy couch in that room he called his 'man cave'. Fitted out with a huge television that covered half of one wall it had surround sound that made the room sound like a movie theatre when the TV was on.

Tonight he didn't have it on. Instead he lay in the semi-dark room, seeming to be lost in thought.

"Pierce," she said as she stood in the doorway, "can we talk?"

He jumped, clearly startled at the sound of her voice. Then he propped himself on one elbow and looked over at her. "Sure, come on in," he said.

She stepped into the room but she didn't go near the couch where he lay. It would not do to get so close to a man who looked so sexy in an A-shirt and faded jeans that hung low on his hips.

She went to perch on the edge of an easy chair and folded her hands in her lap. She was deliberately trying to look subdued. What she was about to say was something that might rile Pierce up so she didn't want to come across as aggressive in any way.

"I want to talk to you about Kylie," she said quietly.

Pierce frowned and sat up. He planted his bare feet on the floor and rested his elbows on his knees. He trained his green-eyed gaze on her. "What is it?"

Celine took a breath. How to begin? She decided to plunge right in. "I'm concerned about Kylie. What's going to happen to her when I leave in the fall?"

Pierce expelled his breath and a look of relief passed over his face. "I thought you were going to tell me something was wrong with her."

"No, not at all," she replied quickly. "I'm sorry I scared you and I really don't mean to pry but...I just need to know what plans you have for Kylie after I'm gone."

His eyebrows lifted. He seemed taken aback by her question and for a moment there was silence.

Had she upset him with her question? She held her breath. She knew she'd taken a risk in digging into his personal business but she had a very good reason for asking.

"I've been giving it some thought," he said finally then he shook his head, "but to tell the truth, I haven't made a final decision."

"Do you have any ideas, any plans?" Her voice came out breathless with relief. He was actually having a conversation with her about the matter. Thank goodness he hadn't slammed her for being nosy.

"I've had a few suggestions thrown my way," he said with a thoughtful look. "A distant relative to come in, a matronly lady who can be like a mother to her, boarding school-."

"What did you say?" Celine's words shot out in a vehement whisper. " How could you even consider it?"

"What? The caretaker or the-"

"The boarding school." She cut him off before he could even finish the sentence. "Pierce, you are not sending that little girl to a boarding school."

"I never said-"

Celine hopped to her feet, unable to sit still a moment longer. "Yes, you did. You said you were considering it."

"Will you calm down?" Pierce straightened his back and glared up at her. "Sit down so we can have a sensible discussion."

Celine sucked in her breath. Was he ordering her around?

"Please," he said, his tone softer, almost apologetic. But not quite. "Have a seat so we can talk."

She sat back down on the chair and waited for him to speak. She'd better get control of her emotions or else she'd be out of Kylie's life even earlier than scheduled. She couldn't afford for that to happen. She would cling to her little charge as long as she could.

"Now," Pierce began, his tone firm, "I said I got suggestions but that doesn't mean I was planning to implement any of them. I need to evaluate all the options and then I'll decide what's best for Kylie."

"And when are you going to decide?" Celine shot back.

"Soon," he said, frowning again.

Celine didn't know if it was out of annoyance at her questions or simply because he was thinking. She decided to assume he was thinking. Now would be the best time to air her major concern. "I know who made those suggestions. It was Sophia, wasn't it?"

He nodded.

"And did you ever stop to think that she might have an ulterior motive?"

Pierce cocked an eyebrow and stared back at her. He said nothing. He was obviously waiting on her to explain herself.

"Sophia has made it very clear that she doesn't want Kylie…or me…around." She shook her head as the anger rose in her. "I don't care what she thinks about me but how could she dislike Kylie?"

Pierce frowned. "What makes you think that?"

Men were so dense. How could he not know what the woman was really like? "Pierce, haven't you noticed how cool her interaction is with Kylie? It was only after the death of Kylie's mother that she acted with any kind of warmth... if you can call giving a few stuffed toys being warm."

Celine got up, unable to stay seated any longer. She needed to express herself and she needed her hands, her whole body in order to do that. She was wound too tight sit still. And she had to make him understand.

She wrung her hands together then she blurted it out, that thing that had been worrying her all this time. "What's going to happen to Kylie when you and Sophia get married? How is she going to live with a woman like that?"

"What?" Pierce looked at her as if she'd gone mad. "What are you talking about?"

"You and Sophia," Celine said exasperated. Why was he pretending? "She said you've been seeing each other for years and that it was only because of your business and frequent travels that you decided to delay marriage." When Pierce still looked dumbstruck she waved her hand in an expression of frustration. "Think about it. Now that there's a child in your home there's no reason to delay the marriage. In fact, it's a very good reason to settle down. But then who's going to protect Kylie from...her?"

Her voice cracked and she felt the sting of a tear in the corner of her eye. She turned away. The last thing she wanted was for him to see how this was affecting her. Let him think this was only about Kylie because Kylie was, in truth, her greatest concern. But deep down inside she had to admit it was about her, too. How could she bear the pain of knowing that she didn't have a chance in this world of being with the man who had stolen her heart?

Pierce burst out laughing.

Celine whirled round to face him. What in the world did he find so funny? Before she could move he was on his feet and walking toward her. Then he was close enough that she breathed in the fragrance of what must have been the bath gel he showered with. It was a fresh, masculine scent that had her reeling.

He put his hand on her shoulder. "Rest assured, Sophia and I are not getting married."

She looked up into his eyes, her heart pounding loudly in her ears. "You're not?"

"No," he said, "we're not." He let his hand slid from her shoulder but he did not step away. Instead, he took her hands in his. "I've known Sophia for many years. I met her through her husband." When Celine frowned he smiled. "They're divorced. She got the house." Then he shook his head. "Trust me, whatever Sophia led you to believe, there is nothing going on between us. We're just friends."

"Then why would she..." Celine's voice trailed away.

"Who knows? Maybe she just enjoyed leading you astray." Pierce shrugged. "Maybe she thinks you're a threat to our friendship."

Now Celine was really confused. "Me? How? I'm just the nanny."

"Oh, but a very beautiful, extremely seductive nanny."

Celine's heart lurched at his words. She looked up quickly, her eyes searching his. Was he toying with her? But no, his green eyes had clouded over with a passion that could not be mistaken.

"Let me kiss you, Celine," he whispered, his voice hoarse with emotion. "I've been dying to taste your lips again and it's driving me crazy."

Celine looked deep into his eyes. She should resist him. Dear God, she knew she should. But how could she when her body was reacting so strongly to his? Her breath caught in her throat as her nipples pebbled in response to his closeness and, oh Lord, she was growing moist. Down there. She ducked her head as a wave of embarrassment washed over her.

But, just as he'd done by the stream, Pierce took control. He would not let her flee. With a gentle hand under her chin he tilted her head up. Then he dipped his head and covered her mouth with his.

The kiss by the stream had been gentle and sweet. This kiss was nothing of the sort. Pierce kissed her with a fervor that spoke of pent-up passion and desire and this time it seemed he was holding nothing back.

His tongue slipped past her lips to plunder her mouth till she was gasping. Her hands slid up to his shoulders, so solid and strong, and there she clung. Her legs, like jelly, could no longer support her. She'd turned to chocolate and had melted in his heated hands.

Pierce released her lips just long enough to bend and lift her off her feet and into his arms.

"Pierce," she gasped. "What are you doing?"

"Just making you more comfortable." He grinned wickedly, his green eyes glinting in the light cast by the lamp in the corner of the room. "Just relax," he whispered. "I'm not going to hurt you."

He took her over to the long black couch and laid her gently in the cushions then he was leaning over her, blocking out the light and all she could see was his handsome face - his strong forehead, firm lips and his rugged jaw with the captivating cleft in his chin.

Celine shivered, suddenly feeling out of her depth. *Reste tranquile, Celine. Calm down. He's only a man after all.* But that was the problem. Pierce D'Amato was all man and he wanted her. She could see it in the flash of his eyes. She could hear it in the rasping of his breath as he dipped his head to kiss her neck. She could feel it in the pounding of his heart as she pressed her hand against his chest. And even worse, she could feel the intensity of his passion in the hardness that now pressed against her leg.

If Celine had any fear it fled when Pierce began to nibble on her ear lobe. She sighed and arched her back in response. He must have seen her reaction as a signal to go farther because his lips shifted from her neck and slid down to the shadow between her breasts. His hands came up to cup them and then his thumbs were circling her nipples through the fabric of her blouse, making them pucker into deliciously painful pebbles, sending jolts of lightning coursing through her body.

"So beautiful," he whispered then with a groan he pushed away the blouse and the top of her bra and took the distended rosebud into his mouth.

She gasped and writhed under the expert teasing of his lips. Oh God, he was driving her crazy with want. He released the nub then moved his lips to its twin, administering the same sweet torture till she cried out and arched her back, forcing the nipple deeper into his mouth.

It was when his hands slid lower to caress her belly that she froze. Her eyes opened wide as she realized what was happening. Pierce had bewitched her with his caresses and now he was moving in for the kill. How could she have been so easily seduced? How could she have been so stupid?

Pierce was a man of the world and he must have been with many women. He knew exactly how to turn a woman on. He was certainly doing a good job on her. But was he using his seductive charms to get her into his bed? And to what end? So he could give her the last paycheck and send her packing at the end of the summer?

The thought was like a bucketful of ice-cold water in her face.

She wanted Pierce, there was no doubt in her mind about that. But not like this. She would gladly give him her all if only he had half the love for her that she felt for him. But why would he? He could have any woman in the world. Why in heaven's name would he settle for her?

"No,'" she said, her voice coming out in a moan. "Please. Stop."

Pierce went completely still. Even his chest froze, as if he'd stopped breathing. Slowly he lifted his head and in the hazy green of his eyes was a mix of desire and confusion.

He pulled back from her then and raised himself up to sit on the seat beside her. He looked down at her, his eyes boring into her with an intensity that made her look away. "What's wrong?" he asked, his voice quiet and low.

She refused to look at him, could not meet his eyes. What was she going to say? That she didn't want to go farther because he hadn't told her that he loved her? He would laugh in her face if she said something as stupid as that. Instead, she just shook her head. "I…can't," she said, her voice a broken whisper.

Pierce sucked in his breath. Then he reached out and took her chin in his hand and turned her face toward him.

She kept her eyes lowered, not wanting him to read the expression there.

"Celine," he said softly, "don't tell me you're…still a virgin?"

She bit her lip, not trusting herself to speak. Instead, she simply nodded.

She knew she was misleading him, making him think that was why she had stopped him. But that hadn't been the main reason. She'd stopped him because she was afraid. She didn't want to be used, to give up her body to a man after waiting so long, and then to be discarded like a dirty old rag.

Her mother had taught her well. Not until marriage, she'd told her, or else as soon as they get what they want they move on to someone prettier or better. Don't let them use you for practice. She'd never forgotten those words and she'd held fast to that principle in her one and only relationship with Giles.

But now with Pierce it was different. What she felt for Pierce went far beyond what she'd ever felt for Giles. With Pierce she would have thrown her mother's advice out the window without another thought...if only he could love her.

Pierce stared at her in silence and shook his head. "I'm sorry, Celine. I didn't mean to come on so strong but I had no idea..." His voice trailed away and he seemed to be searching for words. "I know you told me about waiting for marriage but I thought...since you and Giles broke up and you came to America, I just assumed you had a relationship here."

She looked at him askance.

"I'm sorry, that's not quite what I meant," he said back-pedaling. "I'm making a mess of this, aren't I?" He broke off and stood up then raked his hand through his hair in an obvious sign of frustration. "Listen, forget what I said. I'm just ...sorry."

Oh, Pierce, you just don't get it. I love you but how can I make you love me too? She thought it but she didn't dare say the words out loud.

Instead, she simply straightened her blouse and in a voice that was surprisingly calm she said, "That's okay, no apology necessary." She lowered her legs to the floor. "I think I'd better go now." She got up and took the few steps toward the door then she stopped. She turned back to look at Pierce. "Please think about what will make Kylie happy." Then she turned and walked out the door.

***

Pierce stared at Celine's retreating back then with a soft curse under his breath he walked over to the couch. Instead of sitting in it he leaned against the back of the big chair and crossed his arms. He was pissed but it was at himself that he directed his anger. After Celine had confided in him, told him about her decision regarding her sexuality, he'd still gone ahead and made the wrong assumption.

Now she probably thought he was a jerk and with good reason. He couldn't blame her if she decided to stay a million miles away from his reach. But he wished she wouldn't. He wanted this woman in his life. He'd be the first to admit that sex had something to do with it. There was no denying his attraction to her. But it was more than that. There was some sort of spiritual connection he could not explain. With each passing day she seemed to be growing on him and in him, becoming part of his soul. It was almost as if he couldn't imagine waking up and not seeing her in their home. His and Celine's and Kylie's. This was how he'd begun to think of home.

And then there was her connection with Kylie. From day one he'd observed her interaction with the little girl, how she'd pulled her out of her shell to bloom like a tiny little flower in the sun. How could he separate Kylie from that?

He shook his head. He didn't know what he'd do in the fall when it was time for Celine to return to the university. Kylie would be devastated. And he? He didn't even want to go there.

Celine had asked about his options and pleaded with him to do what was best for Kylie. There was one option he'd not mentioned, one that would be ideal, at least for him and for Kylie. But for Celine? He didn't know.

There were so many things he didn't know. Like Celine... she was such an enigma. Did she have feelings for him? Did she crave him as much as he craved her?

He knew he wanted Celine to a degree he'd never felt for any woman. She was different from anyone he'd ever known. But he, confirmed bachelor, was he ready to give up his fast paced life to become a father and husband in one jump? More importantly, if he asked her to marry him, would she say yes?

His lips tightened and he stared with blind eyes at the space in front of him. Somehow, after the way he had behaved tonight, he doubted it.

CHAPTER EIGHT

That weekend Pierce took Kylie and Celine to the zoo where, for the first time, the little girl saw real live elephants, lions, tigers and zebras. As the adults expected, her favorites were the monkeys who entertained them with their antics. One of them punched his brother then took off, running smack into the patriarch of the clan who gave him a whack for his troubles. They all laughed out loud at that.

Next they went to the small amusement park where they went on all the rides - the merry-go-round, the haunted train, the bumper cars and the kiddies' roller coaster.

Last and scariest of all was the Ferris wheel. All three of them sat in the chair and when they went up, up into the air, so high they could see the tops of trees and buildings, Celine was the only one who screamed to get down. Even after they got home Kylie would not let her forget it. Both she and Pierce teased her relentlessly that night until she feigned a pout and marched off to bed.

Next day, Sunday, was another day of wonderful weather. And again, Celine decided that she and Kylie would spend most of the afternoon outdoors. To Celine's shock and near horror Pierce had decided to try his hand in the kitchen. She decided she'd made the right decision in taking Kylie outside just in case he blew up the house experimenting with the stove.

They had been playing tag on the lawn for a while when Celine put a hand on Kylie's shoulder and stopped her. She'd heard a sound coming from the copse of trees that lined the garden path. She stood still listening. There it was again, the soft cry of what sounded like a cat.

"Kylie, wait over by that rock," she said. "I just want to check on something."

Walking stealthily across the grass she ducked under a branch then pushed through some bushes until she entered the cool shadows of the alcove created by the trees.

"Celine, where're you going?" Kylie's call was plaintive.

Celine realized that she'd probably become scared when she disappeared but, not wanting to scare the animal, she remained silent. She had a soft spot for cats. They were her favorite animals and she'd had several as pets when she was growing up.

The tiny cry came again then Celine saw it, a black and white kitten curled up in the root of a tree. "Hi, baby," she crooned, "What are you doing here? Are you all alone?" She looked around but the kitty's mommy was nowhere in sight.

She went closer, slowly, fearing that the little cat would flee in fright. To Celine's surprise it did the exact opposite. When its big green eyes came to rest on her it got up from its cradle at the foot of the tree and walked over to her. The cat looked like it was about three or four months old, still quite young but old enough to survive and thrive without its mother. Not shy at all, it yawned and stretched its neck up as if to invite Celine to scratch its head.

"Aw, you're so cute." She took the invitation and tickled the little head. Then she straightened. So. What was she going to do now? She couldn't leave the cat in the woods to starve. On the other hand, this was not her home. If she'd been in France the cat would be installed at her house, no question about it. But here? She didn't have that right. The only option, it seemed, was to take the cat and ask Pierce to take it to the shelter.

She stretched out her hand and the cat immediately came to her. It must have strayed from someone's house, it was so tame. Then, cradling it to her chest, she headed back to the lawn.

"Celine," Kylie cried her voice full of relief. "Where were you? Why did you go into the woods?"

"Look what I found," Celine said with a laugh. She shifted her little bundle so that Kylie could see.

"A kitty," she exclaimed in wonder. "You found a kitty."

"Yes, and I'm going to give her some milk and find a nice box to make a bed for her."

"And then we get to keep her?" The child's eyes were wide and full of hope.

"I don't know, *cherie*." Celine shook her head. "That all depends on what Pierce says. I was thinking of taking her to the shelter."

"The shelter? Oh, no. I want to keep her. I want her for my friend." Kylie almost looked like she was going to cry.

Celine's heart went out to her. A pet was just what she needed, something to hug, to love, to call her friend. She could suggest it to Pierce. They could take the cat to the vet, have her checked and vaccinated, and then Kylie could have a pet of her own. At the end of the day, though, it would be Pierce's decision.

"Can I touch her?" Kylie stretched out a hand but Celine turned, keeping the cat out of reach.

"No, not yet. I have to make sure she's safe before I let you play with her." She saw Kylie's face fall. "There's something you can do to help me, though. Why don't you help me make a carrier box for her so we can take her safely to the vet? You can help me make air holes in the box."

That seemed to cheer her up. Her face brightened and she skipped ahead of Celine up the path toward the house.

"Uncle Pierce, guess what? We have a surprise," she yelled as they entered the kitchen.

He turned toward them, a head of lettuce in his hand. "What kind of surprise?" He said with a smile that matched hers. "Is it something delicious?"

"No, you can't eat it," she said with a laugh. "You can hug it and kiss it."

Pierce frowned as if in deep concentration. "Is it a baby? Maybe a dolly baby?"

"No," Kylie crowed and shook her head.

Celine laughed and still cradling the very comfortable cat, she turned to Pierce so that he could see.

He looked at the bundle in her arms and blinked. Then his face turned ashen.

Pierce let the lettuce fall to the ground and began to back away, his eyes trained on the cat in Celine's arms. Then to her horror he began to sweat and shake then he was hyperventilating. He backed away into a corner of the room and slid his back down the wall to crouch on the floor. Wrapping his hands around his knees, he began shaking uncontrollably.

What in the world...it had something to do with the cat. Pierce had taken one look and had simply fallen apart.

Celine rushed back outside and deposited the cat on the grass. Then she dashed back inside where Kylie stood staring at Pierce, her eyes wide with distress. He still crouched on the floor, his body shaking.

Celine ran over to kneel beside him. "Pierce," she cried out, touching his back. "What's wrong?"

He didn't respond and curled even tighter as if to get away from her hands.

Celine hopped up and reached for the phone. She needed help. She began to dial 911.

It didn't take much for Celine to realize that Pierce had a severe phobia to cats. With the help of a paramedic on the phone she was able to calm him so the violent shudders ceased and his gasping breath grew deep and steady again.

She'd grabbed the kitchen towel and with it she dabbed at the perspiration that had settled on his brow then she wrapped her arm around his shoulder.

It was only when Pierce was back to normal that Celine removed her arm. He lifted his head and looked at her with a mixture of gratitude and embarrassment. Then he asked for Kylie but Celine had whisked her away to the den and switched on the Disney channel, effectively removing her from the scene of Pierce's distress.

"Thanks," he said, his voice hoarse and strained.

Celine shook her head, still reeling from what had just happened. "No, Pierce. Don't thank me. I almost killed you by bringing that cat into the house." She felt so full of guilt her heart hurt.

He shook his head and gave her a reassuring smile. "No, you didn't. And anyway, how could you have known?"

They were silent for a while. Then she asked the question uppermost in her mind. "Why are you so afraid of cats?"

"I think it had to do with an incident when I was an infant. My mother told me she had a pet cat before I was born and when she gave birth and took me home the cat seemed to go crazy." He chuckled. "It must have pissed her off that she wasn't the center of attention any more. Mom said she used to hiss at me all the time as I lay in my crib and once she even took a swipe at me. Scratched me on the arm."

"What?" Celine said, indignant. "Didn't your parents get rid of her?"

"Eventually they did but not before she did lasting damage. Since then I haven't been able to look a cat in the eye without seizing up."

"Oh, Pierce. I can't imagine what that must be like."

"Hey, it's not that bad," he said with a shrug. "I just stay away from them and all is well with the world."

"Until today," she said.

"Until today." But he was smiling at her now, back to his old self, the confident green-eyed Pierce that she loved.

And after what had happened today she felt she loved him even more. She'd always seen him as so bold, powerful and invincible - the billionaire businessman, always in control. Now she'd seen another side to him, a side that was vulnerable, a side that needed her. She'd been able to take him in her arms and comfort him and her strength had been his. For once she'd felt that she'd been the one giving, not receiving.

A half hour later the three of them sat down to Pierce's meal of macaroni and cheese from the box, fried chicken made by his own hands and a salad. He couldn't take credit for the salad since Celine had been the one to rescue the lettuce, wash it and prepare it. After his ordeal Pierce had not been up to any more challenges in the kitchen.

After a surprisingly delicious meal considering that it had been made by a near novice, Celine found the kitten and boxed her up while still outdoors then she drove to the shelter where she handed her over to the care of the staff there.

That night after putting Kylie to bed Celine went back downstairs to check on Pierce. She was being something of a mother hen but she couldn't help it. Today the protective instinct in her had been triggered and now it was working overtime.

She found him in his usual place of refuge, the den. "All is well?" she asked peeping in.

He was leaning back in the sofa, feet up on the ottoman and when he saw her he smiled. "All is well. Well in my world, at least." When she hesitated in the doorway he waved her over. "Come. Sit."

Celine smiled to herself. Giving orders, as usual.

Last time she'd been in this room alone with Pierce she'd sat on the seat farthest away from him. Tonight she went and sat on the sofa. He raised his eyebrows but said nothing. He simply scooted over to give her more room.

She relaxed in the couch and looked at him. He was dressed casually in gray sweatpants and a light cotton shirt. When decked out in his suits Pierce was immaculate but at home he was totally relaxed and casual. She liked that.

"Pierce, do you mind if I ask you something?" she asked.

"Sure. Go ahead."

"Earlier today you mentioned your mother. Why doesn't she come over to visit?"

"I wish she could," Pierce said. "My parents decided to retire in Hawaii. I talk to them every few days but as you can imagine visits take some advance planning, particularly with my busy schedule."

"And your brothers and sisters. What about them?"

"No brothers, one sister. Happily married, living in San Diego with her husband and two kids." He gave her a smile of amusement. "Anything else you want to know?"

She groaned inwardly. She'd been Miss Nosy Parker again.

"Don't worry, I'm not offended. Flattered, actually. What makes you want to know about my family?"

She glanced at him then looked away again, a sudden shyness seizing her. "I just want to know more about you."

He seemed pleased at that and her heart soared. She really did want to get to know Pierce and she had so little time. The end of the summer was fast approaching. When she left his home she wanted to take all these memories of him with her. "What were you like as a boy?"

He chuckled. "Very much a geek. I was the kid with the glasses who was always hanging around the computer lab begging to be allowed to create new programs."

"Aw, that's so sweet," she said, laughing.

"No, it wasn't." He shook his head. "I can laugh about it now and I can be grateful for all those hours in the lab. I started my software company back in high school."

"You did?" Celine could have guessed he was the genius type but he'd far exceeded her expectations.

"Your parents must have been so proud."

"They were, but at the time I almost wished I could have been a normal kid. It wasn't easy being the school geek." He shrugged but there was a pain in his eyes that he could not hide.

"You were bullied?"

"Yeah," he said casually. "Like most nerdy kids I was the brunt of jokes. Got beat up a fair number of times."

"Oh, no," she whispered. Her heart went out to the kid he'd been. He must have suffered so much.

"But, hey," he continued, "it all worked out great. It was all those hours spent hiding in the computer lab that made me the man I am today."

And what a man that was. He was as far from geek as could be. He had a sophistication about him, an aura of self-assurance that made him compelling. And it didn't hurt that he was extraordinarily handsome. No wonder she found him irresistible.

As if thinking similar thoughts Celine and Pierce turned to each other at the same time. When their eyes met she knew he was thinking exactly what she was thinking. She wanted him so much her mouth went dry.

There was nothing she wanted more right now than to have his arms around her, his lips on hers. But as she gazed back at him she knew he would not make that move.

So she did.

With newfound boldness Celine slid across the sofa, closing the few inches that separated their bodies. Then before she could change her mind she reached her hand up to touch his cheek.

He stared down at her, his green eyes sparkling with emotion, but still he made no move. He was waiting for her to take the lead.

Sliding her hand to the back of his head she tilted it down until his lips touched hers. She moaned as her body tingled in anticipation.

Only then did he move. Sliding his arms around her he leaned into the kiss, taking full control as she knew he would. She gasped as his tongue slid past her lips to taste her, tease her then plunder her till she felt like her very bones had turned to liquid.

As they kissed, Celine slid her hands inside the neck of his T-shirt to caress his shoulders and then as the passion of his kiss intensified she clung to him as if for dear life.

The moment he lifted his mouth from hers she dipped her head and caught his ear lobe between her teeth. She felt a thrill of satisfaction when she heard him groan. She pressed her advantage, sliding her lips down his neck. Then she was lifting his T-shirt to feather soft kisses across the broad muscles of his chest now bare to her gaze.

She did not meet his eyes. She refused to look at him, knowing there'd be questions there. This time she wanted nothing to get in the way. Just as he'd done to her she moved her lips lower, lower until she'd caught a taut flat nipple between her teeth. When he moaned she smiled and she did not stop. She covered that sensitive part of him with her lips and sucked and nibbled until his chest heaved and his heart pounded in his ears.

Next, she slid her hands down his taut, muscled belly and stopped just shy of the top of his sweatpants. Dared she go farther?

Yes, she dared. She loved this man. She knew that without a doubt. And now, whatever the consequences, she was ready.

She was sliding her hands under the waistband of his sweatpants when she felt firm hands on hers.

"Celine, stop now or else I won't be responsible for my actions." His voice was hoarse, his breathing labored. She knew he was trying hard to resist her.

But she wouldn't let him get away. Not this time.

"You won't be responsible," she whispered. "I will."

With a groan he reached for her and hauled her up so he could capture her mouth. He gave her a searing kiss that told of pent-up passion and want.

And then, ever so gently, he pushed her away, sat up and shoved his T-shirt back down.

Celine stared at him in shocked silence. It took several seconds before she could speak. "What are you doing?" she asked, totally bewildered. "Why did you stop me?"

Tucking the T-shirt into his sweatpants, almost as if to shield himself from her, he looked at her with an expression she could not figure out. "I had to stop you. I didn't want you doing something you would regret."

"But I wanted it," she said. "I'm ready, Pierce. I really want this."

He stared back at her, his face a reflection of the battle raging inside him. But then he shook his head. "No. You don't. Not yet." He got up and when he looked back at her his face was serious and his lips tight. "I'm going to turn in now. I suggest you go to bed."

Then he turned and walked to the door and just like that he was gone.

Celine sat on the couch, unable to move. Tonight had turned out to be one of the worst nights of her life. She'd come to Pierce ready to give him everything, and he refused the one thing she had to give. What else could she give a man that had it all? What else but herself?

But he'd rejected her most precious gift and now she knew it was no use trying. She'd never be good enough for Pierce D'Amato.

CHAPTER NINE

The days that followed were difficult for Celine. It was hard having to put on a cheerful face, laughing and playing with Kylie, when inside she was dying. Each time she was in the same room with Pierce she felt the heat of embarrassment rise in her face as the memory of his rejection came rushing back. Each time he spoke to her she avoided his eyes, not wanting to see amusement or scorn reflected there. She would not be able to live with that. When she left she wanted to remember the good times she'd had in this house. She did not want to spoil those memories any more than they'd already been blemished by that night.

By the following week, though, things began to improve. She'd finally accepted the fact that outside of their working relationship there would never be anything between her and Pierce. Of course, she'd known that from the beginning. Still, she'd been stupid enough to let herself fall under the spell of their situation living under his roof, spending so much time together. She'd forgotten her role. Now, though, things were back in perspective. She knew where she stood and she would never let herself forget it.

After that talk with herself things got a whole lot better. She began to laugh again and Kylie, who'd had to put up with her distraction, looked relieved that her old Celine was back. As for her interactions with Pierce, she kept them light and amicable. She did not seek out his company but she no longer avoided being in the same room with him as long as Kylie was there, too.

Being alone with him was another matter altogether. Her body seemed intent on betraying her, her breath growing shallow and her nipples puckering anytime he came near. But she did her best to hide her response to him. She only hoped he could not sense the depth of her inner turmoil.

Then one morning something happened that made Celine realize that she wasn't the only one who was suffering. She woke up to the sound of soft sobbing and sat up to find Kylie curled up in the bed beside her.

"What's wrong, *cherie*?" Celine's heart lurched. Had Kylie been hurt? She threw back the covers so she could see the child's body. No, she looked fine. She pulled away the hands that covered the little face. "Are you hurt?"

Kylie shook her head and began to sob louder.

Celine gathered her in her arms and hugged her close. The child's tears soaked through the top of her nightgown. "Hush, hush," she soothed as she rocked her in her arms.

"I miss my mommy," Kylie wailed then began to cry anew, the force of her sobs making her whole body shake.

Celine felt like a knife pierced her heart. Poor Kylie. She'd been so absorbed in her own problems that she hadn't been there for the child as she should have, keeping her so busy she would have less time to dwell on her loss. She cursed herself for being so thoughtless. "Oh, Kylie, I know you do," she said softly, tears filling her eyes. "Just cry, *cherie*, let it out. I'll take it all. Just cry."

It was like Celine's words burst a dam of sorrow inside the little girl in her arms. She clung to Celine and bawled. For several minutes they stayed like that, woman and child, hugging each other like they'd never let go.

When Kylie's shaking finally stilled and her sobs died away Celine gently stroked her hair and hummed a lullaby, one she'd loved as a child. She hoped the soft sounds would provide some soothing comfort.

It took a long time for them to get out of bed that morning. For a while they lay there, quiet and thoughtful, not needing any words at that moment, just resting after an emotional cleansing.

The release of that flood was an obvious source of relief for Kylie. Celine could see it in the way she relaxed against her and began playing with her fingers.

For Celine, though, it had the opposite effect. It reminded her how much Kylie would still need a shoulder to cry on. There would be more emotional outbursts and who would she turn to? She wanted to be there to comfort her but how could she?

Celine's heart lay in a painful place right then. She'd resolved to live the rest of her life without Pierce but how could she stifle her love for Kylie?

***

Pierce watched from his bedroom window as Celine and Kylie sat on the bench in the shade of the old oak tree in the backyard. Both heads were bent, one sleek and raven black, the other curly and golden. They were busy with Kylie's morning lesson, going through the story of the day. Celine had told him they'd be reviewing simple two and three letter words. Now Kylie was deep in concentration as Celine guided her through her world list for the day.

Every time he saw them together he thanked his lucky stars for the day she walked into his hotel room. While he'd been in the hotel shower that day Kylie had been on his mind and he'd been up to his ears in frustration, tired of the long list of candidates the agency had sent him, none of whom could connect with Kylie. He'd walked out of that bathroom praying for a miracle. The thought hadn't even had time to lodge in his mind when there she stood in front of him, an angel in maid's uniform.

He chuckled as he thought back to that day. His first memory of Celine was of her screaming and backing away from him, her eyes wide with fright. And yet he'd known the moment his eyes landed on her that she was the answer to his prayers. Strange as it now seemed, at the moment he'd had absolutely no doubt in his mind. And that was why he'd made sure she didn't escape before he made her an offer she would find hard to refuse.

Now as he watched his 'girls' together he had absolutely no regret at his spur-of-the-moment decision. Celine had been a Godsend in more ways than one.

And that was why he'd decided to take it slow with her. She'd told him she didn't take sex lightly so when she'd come to him he knew it had been in a moment of weakness. He wouldn't be able to live with himself if he'd taken advantage of that moment. Even though it had taken a hell of a lot of willpower he'd saved her from herself that night and he did not regret it. She probably hated him for it but it was the right thing to do.

And although she was annoyed with him right now he would make it all worth the wait. He smiled as he thought about it. That day would be soon.

Next day Pierce left for the office early as usual to avoid peak hour traffic. He had a full day ahead of him as he was expecting a cadre of programmers from Japan who would be consulting with him on a special project. It was a big deal for his firm, one that could lead to an explosion of growth in the international marketplace.

He was in the middle of his meeting when his administrative assistant knocked on the door of the conference room. He frowned. Lynette had been with him for years and she knew better than to interrupt such an important session.

She hurried over and leaned down to whisper in his ear. At her words his blood ran cold. Kylie. Pool. Hospital. Ambulance.

At that instant all thought fled his mind except for one. Kylie. He had to get to Kylie.

He shoved the chair back and with the briefest of apologies he was up and out the door. Lynette would have to do the explanation. He had no time to spare.

He jumped into his car and tore out of the parking lot, tires screeching as he went. Within fifteen minutes he was pulling up in front of St. Mary's Hospital. He'd parked the car in the tow zone but he didn't give a damn. They could have it. All he wanted was to see his little girl.

He dashed up to the reception desk and almost reached out and throttled the nurse when she calmly told him to take a number and sit down. When he growled at her and demanded to see Kylie immediately she jumped and looked like she was about to call security but she must have seen the desperation in his eyes because she called for an orderly who escorted him to the intensive care ward.

There Pierce saw Celine. She was sitting all alone on a long bench and she was twisting her hands in her lap, tears streaming down her face.

He dashed over to her. "Celine. What happened? Where is she? Is she…" He could not say the word.

Celine hopped up and turned red, puffy eyes toward him. "Pierce. *Mon Dieu*, Pierce. I'm so sorry. So sorry."

That stopped him in his tracks. It was a stake hammered right into his heart. The words were a confirmation of his worst fear. Kylie was gone.

The words sucked his strength, the very life out of him. He collapsed onto the bench and stared at Celine in shock. His Kylie, his sweet little Kylie, was dead.

He'd meant to make life so good for her, give her a family, and now it was too late. Too late, too late. The words rang in his head. Oh God, he was too late.

He dropped his face in his hands and the tears seeped through his fingers.

Celine came to him then. He felt when she sat on the bench beside him and then her arms were around him, hugging, comforting him like she'd done once before.

"We have to pray," she whispered. "Pray for Kylie, Pierce. Just pray."

Pray? What was the use of praying? Praying wouldn't bring her back so he could hold her in his arms again, so he could feel that bundle of energy, his little girl, so full of life. Celine could pray all she wanted but he just wanted Kylie.

"We have to be strong for her, Pierce. Help her pull through."

It took a moment for the words to sink in. What was she saying? Kylie was...alive?

He lifted his head and stared into Celine's eyes, willing her to say the words. "Kylie?" he said.

"They're working on her right now," she said.

Pierce's shoulders sagged with relief. Thank God.

The gigantic rock that had landed squarely in the middle of his chest began to crumble, leaving pebbles of fear behind.

"What did they say? Will she be all right?"

Celine shook her head and her eyes were full of sadness. "I don't know."

Pierce looked at her and then away. Had he been given hope just to have it dashed? No, God would not be so cruel. He clung to that thought, that hope, and only then was he able to breathe freely.

Pierce took Celine's hand in his. Her palm was damp. He could only imagine what she must have gone through, dealing with all of this without him. He stroked the back of her hand, trying to give her some small comfort. They sat like that in silence.

Finally he asked, "Celine, what happened?" He knew it would be traumatic for her to relive the experience but he had to know.

Celine's hands gripped his tightly and then she pulled it away. She drew in a trembling breath.

"Kylie and I...we did some gardening this morning and we got all muddy so...I took her upstairs and gave her a bath." She drew a deep breath then let it out in a heavy sigh. "There was still mud splattered on my leg so I fixed a quick snack for Kylie and set her at the kitchen table to eat. I told her I'd be down in five minutes. I just wanted to take a quick shower."

"Why didn't you leave her with Mrs. Simpson?"

"She called a little after you left this morning. Her grandson was sick and her daughter called on her suddenly to babysit while she went to work." Celine bit her lip. "I was alone with Kylie."

She was silent then and Pierce could imagine she must be blaming herself for that one slot of time when she'd let Kylie out of her sight. He spoke then. "But how did Kylie get over the fence around the pool?" He'd had that fence installed the same week Kylie moved into the house.

Celine sucked in her breath. "That's what I don't understand. I know I locked the gate last night and we didn't go anywhere near it all morning. I know Kylie's way too short to get anywhere near that latch so the gate must have been left open." She shook her head, her eyes distressed, her face dark with confusion. "I know I locked that gate. I'm sure of it. I did, Pierce, I did." She covered her face with her hands and began to cry.

"Hush," he said and put his arm around her shoulder. "I know."

It took several minutes for Celine to calm down and then they sat together in silence, the moments ticking by. Each time the door leading to the operating room opened both turned as one but each time it was a nurse or an orderly going about their various duties.

Finally, after an exhausting two hours a doctor dressed in green scrubs stepped through the door. "Miss Santini," he said as he approached, "and Mr...."

"D'Amato. Pierce D'Amato," Pierce said, rising to his feet.

The doctor nodded. "You're Kylie's guardian, correct?"

"Yes," he said quickly, wishing the doctor would just come out with the words. The suspense was torture.

"As you know, we've been working on Kylie for some time. She ingested quite a bit of water but the good thing is," he turned to Celine, "you got her out quickly and started CPR right away. If it hadn't been for that we wouldn't have been able to save her. The paramedics would have come too late. Your quick action saved her life."

"So she's going to be all right?"

The doctor smiled. "Your little girl is a real fighter. We'll have to keep her for at least a week for observation but it looks like she's out of the woods."

Pierce could have kissed him, his relief was so great. Kylie was going to be all right.

He turned and grabbed Celine and hugged her tight, expressing all his relief and gladness in that embrace.

Then he released her and stretched out his hand. "Thank you, Doctor," he said and shook the hand of the man who had saved his daughter's life.

There, he'd said it. His daughter. And that was what Kylie had come to be for him - a member of his family, his child. He'd been thinking about her like that for some time now and he knew that whatever the future held for him, Kylie would always be a part of it. He would make it official. She would be his daughter.

"Can we see her?" he asked.

"Yes, but one at a time." He nodded to Pierce. "You go first, Mr. D'Amato."

Pierce looked at Celine and she nodded, her face flushed with relief. "Go to her."

When Pierce disappeared through the swinging doors Celine sat back down and stared at the floor. Thank God Kylie was going to be all right. She didn't know what she would do if she hadn't pulled through. She was dying to run to her and hug her close but she would have to wait her turn.

Then she thought of the role she'd played in Kylie's near tragedy. Why had she left her alone? She'd moved quickly in the bathroom and had returned downstairs to find the kitchen empty and Kylie gone. She'd gone into the garden, thinking she'd wandered out there but there was no Kylie. Then she ran back to the pool and that was when she saw the open gate. She dashed through and there was Kylie floating face down the water.

She screamed then dove into the water and dragged her out. She immediately started with the life-saving techniques she'd learned as a teenage babysitter. She only stopped long enough to call the ambulance and then she kept working on her until the paramedics took over.

All that had taken mere minutes but to Celine it seemed like a lifetime.

She got up, too agitated to sit still any longer, and began to pace the floor. Then she came to a standstill and leaned her forehead on the cold concrete wall. Her shoulders shook but there were no tears. She was crying again because she knew what she had to do. For the sake of Kylie's safety it would be best for her to go.

CHAPTER TEN

Kylie came home six days later. Pierce installed her in her bedroom with lots of picture books, toys and games. He spent almost the entire day with her, playing with the dolls on her bed and acting out plays with sock puppets he'd made himself. Celine could see that he was trying to make it up to Kylie for the trauma of the past week, even to the point of overdoing it. It was only when her eyelids drooped that he decided to leave her alone.

Now that Kylie was home Celine decided it was time to broach the subject of her departure. She asked Pierce to meet with her in the kitchen and then she sat down and laid out her plan. She would stay another week so he could find a replacement but then she would be leaving.

Pierce was none too pleased with her announcement. "You're leaving in a week? That's a whole five weeks earlier than planned."

"I know, and that's why I'll stay the week to give you time to find my replacement. You and I know it's for the best."

"Best for you? It's certainly not best for Kylie."

"Especially for Kylie," she cried. "Look what happened to her in my care? I'd never be able to forgive myself if things had been…worse."

"Celine," he said, his face a study in exasperation, "it wasn't your fault. It could have happened under anybody's watch."

"But it happened under mine. Don't you understand what that means for me? I almost got Kylie killed." The guilt swept through her and she felt like her heart would crack right open.

"Celine, will you stop it?" Pierce's voice was harsh. "What happened was an accident. It could have happened to any one of us, to forget to lock the gate. I know it wasn't deliberate."

Celine sucked in her breath, her eyes wide with shock. "You don't believe me. You do think it was my fault."

"I'm not saying that." Pierce was glaring back at her now. "Any one of us - you, me, Mrs. Simpson - could have left the gate open. I'm not trying to cast blame. I'm just saying even if it had been you I would not condemn you for what happened."

Now he was changing his story. In Celine's mind Pierce did blame her. This discussion was only confirming that she'd made the right decision. She needed to go as soon as possible.

"Pierce," she said quietly, "I've made up my mind. I know you don't trust me with Kylie anymore so it's best for all of us if I leave. Please start looking for my replacement."

Pierce was scowling at her now. "Is that your final word on this?"

"It's my final word," she said, keeping her face blank even though she felt hollow inside.

If only she didn't have to go. She would miss Kylie so much. And Pierce. And even though he'd said she didn't have to go, even though he said he still trusted her, it was the big question that made her want to flee. How did she know she could trust herself?

She'd left the gate open, it seemed, even though she could distinctly remember locking it. Pierce seemed to think so although he wouldn't admit it. She'd been so sure and look what happened. How could she be sure it wouldn't happen again?

No, for the sake of Kylie's safety it was best if she stayed far away…no matter that her heart was breaking at the thought.

***

Sixteen days. It was sixteen days since Celine had last seen Kylie and Pierce. She'd thought things would get better with time, that the pain would eventually go away, but it had gotten worse. She was far away from Kylie and it was like being separated from her own daughter.

This summer she'd had a family, a family very different from the one in France, but a family just the same. And she missed them as she would her own flesh and blood.

She'd tried hard not to intrude in their lives but she hadn't been able to resist calling Kylie and had done so almost every day since leaving. But calling was not the same as seeing her, holding her, smelling the cherry blossom fragrance of her hair.

Celine had made sure to call the house during the daytime when she knew Pierce would not be around. She didn't know if her heart could take the deep timbre of his voice without breaking down in tears. She missed him too much for words. She'd been afraid that if she ever saw him she would break down and blurt out how she truly felt about him. And what would that achieve? He'd probably be speechless with embarrassment or bolt for the nearest exit.

Today, though, she didn't care. She had to see Kylie again. She picked up the phone and dialed Pierce's cell phone number. At the sound of his voice a tremor ran through her.

"Pierce, it's Celine," she said softly. "Do you have a minute?' She would hate to know that she'd disturbed a meeting.

"Yes, go ahead." Pierce sounded formal, clipped.

"I was wondering if you'd let me visit Kylie. I'd love to go today if that's okay with you." She'd said it all in a rush, wanting to get the words out before she lost the courage.

Silence. That was the response on the other end of the line. Total silence.

"Hello?" Celine said into the phone. Had he hung up on her?

"Celine." Pierce was speaking again. Finally. "At what point did I tell you not to see Kylie?"

"Well…never," she said, feeling stupid.

"Exactly. So why do you think you need my permission? You spoke as if you expected me to say no." Pierce's voice was cool. It seemed that she had offended him.

"I'm sorry, I didn't want to impose-."

"What time would you like to visit Celine?" He cut her off mid-sentence.

"I was thinking two o'clock in the afternoon." She'd specifically chosen that time because she knew he would not be home.

"Fine. I'll let them know to expect you." And then he hung up.

He hadn't given her a chance to say goodbye. Well, so much for him wanting to see her again. He hadn't even asked how she was doing. It was obvious that any feelings between them were all on her end. Feeling deflated, she gently laid the receiver back in the cradle and got up to dress for her trip.

Almost two hours later Celine was pulling into the long circular driveway of the house that had been like her home for most of that summer. Her heart quickened in anticipation. She hopped out of the car, opened the back door and grabbed the huge gift bag with the Molly Dolly Set with its twenty-five fashion outfits. She knew Kylie would love dressing her up.

She bounded up the stairs and rang the doorbell, a bright smile on her face. She was looking forward to seeing Mrs. Simpson, too. She'd always found her to be pleasant company.

The door opened and Celine found herself staring into the thin, well made-up face of Sophia Redgrave.

Celine's smile fled. What was Sophia doing there? Had she used her departure as an opportunity to worm her way into Pierce's life?

"Good afternoon, Sophia," she said when her wits returned. "I'm here to see Kylie."

Sophia nodded but as usual there was no smile of greeting. "We were expecting you."

She opened the door wider so Celine could enter then led the way across the foyer and down the hallway. "Kylie," she called. "Celine is here."

Out of nowhere a bundle of pink and yellow came flying toward her and Celine had just enough time to drop the gift bag and catch Kylie as she leaped into her arms.

"Celine, I missed you so much," she cried and wrapped her arms around Celine's neck.

"I missed you, too, *cherie*. So much." Celine closed her eyes and reveled in the feel of the little body in her arms. She smelled of strawberries and peaches.

They were still hugging when they heard the roar of an engine out front.

"Daddy," Kylie yelled and wriggled so much Celine had to set her down on the floor.

Daddy? It had to be Pierce Kylie was calling Daddy but when had she started doing that?

Then at the thought of Pierce her heart began to accelerate. Despite her efforts, today she would see Pierce again. Thank you, God.

Slowly, trying to seem casual, she followed Kylie back out to the front porch. Her heart did a somersault when she saw him.

Pierce was climbing out of a jet black Porsche, sunshades still on his face. The sun glinted on his dark chocolate hair. He looked super-sexy in his black business suit and red power tie.

Kylie was running to him now. He scooped her up and gave her a big fat kiss on the cheek.

How Celine wished that could be her.

Then he looked up and ever so slowly he removed the sunglasses from his eyes. And there they were, those beautiful green eyes that looked like they could see into her soul. He was looking at her and on his lips was the hint of a smile.

Still holding Kylie with one arm Pierce walked up the driveway and up the steps until he was standing in front of her.

"Hello, Celine," he said, looking down at her as she stood staring up at him.

"Hello, Pierce." She cleared her throat. "I thought you'd be at work today."

"I was," he said. "I decided to come home early."

"Because of me?" *Dieu*, had she said it out loud?

"Because of you," he said and there was such feeling in his voice that Celine blinked.

"Daddy, Celine's come home to stay," Kylie chirped up. "I am sooo happy."

Eyes wide, Celine stared at Kylie. Now where did the child get that from? She didn't want to mislead her. "No, *cherie*, I'm only here for a visit."

"No, you're not. You came back to be with me," the child insisted. She began to wriggle in Pierce's arms. "I want to go to Mommy." And she reached out both arms towards Celine.

Celine gasped and quick tears stung her eyes. Then her face crumpled and the tears spilled onto her cheeks. "Kylie, dear sweet Kylie," was all she could manage, her throat constricted with emotions. She reached out and took her from Pierce and buried her face in the child's neck.

"I still love my old mommy," Kylie whispered, "but I want you as my new mommy now."

"I..." How could she tell her that she'd love that more than anything in the world but that it couldn't happen? "I..." She tried again but could go no further.

Pierce came to her then. As she held Kylie in her arms he stood looking down into her eyes. "Celine, as you can see Kylie... and I...are having a hard time living without you. When you left you took a part of us with you. We need you."

Celine looked up at him, not believing what she was hearing. "Kylie needs me," she whispered, "but do you?"

He gave her a smile that told her all she needed to know. "I can't live without you, Celine. Won't you come back home, but this time as my wife?"

Celine had been waiting with bated breath for that question, all her life she'd been waiting and now the man of her dreams was waiting for her answer. Was this all a dream?

"Are you sure?" Celine whispered. "You're not still angry with me?"

"I was never angry with you. I love you. You've been my miracle angel since the day we met."

"Yaay," Kylie chortled. "Mommy and Daddy are getting married."

"Hold on, Kylie," Pierce said, laughing. "Celine still hasn't said yes."

"Yes, yes, yes," Celine said through her tears and walked into the arms Pierce held open wide.

And so they hugged - Pierce, Celine and Kylie, all three - happy in knowing they were now a family.

EPILOGUE

Kylie was the prettiest flower girl in the world. Slowly and carefully, her face beaming with pride, she left the church vestibule and walked up the aisle with her basket of red rose petals, sprinkling the flowers along the path ahead of her.

She followed a very nervous ring bearer, a little friend she'd made on her first day in junior kindergarten. In his black suit the little gentleman walked ahead of Kylie, stopping every few minutes to check that she was still there.

The church was full of friends and family including Claire, Sylvan and Marc. Pierce's family was there, too - Elizabeth and Carlos from Hawaii and Sharon, her husband and two children from San Diego.

Mrs. Simpson beamed as she looked toward the back of the church and saw Celine standing there, waiting on the organist to start the bridal march.

Sophia was in the congregation, too, looking more stylish and elegant than anyone in the church. She'd been Celine's greatest surprise. At the news that Pierce had proposed to her the woman seemed to have changed her whole demeanor as if she accepted that it no longer made sense to pretend. She did not become warm and inviting but she became a great source of advice to Celine as she prepared for her big day.

To Celine's even greater surprise and relief she solved the mystery of the pool gate. It was Sophia who had left the gate open and not Celine. She'd come by early that morning to borrow the long net to give to her pool cleaner. It had been too early in the morning to wake anyone. It was only when she heard Mrs. Simpson speaking about the mystery of the gate that she realized her role in Kylie's near death experience. She apologized in tears and since then had become Kylie's greatest ally, even at times when she deserved to go to the naughty corner.

Now it was time for Celine to walk up the aisle. As the bridal march began she lifted her head. Her heart soared as she smiled at the man who waited for her at the other end. Tall, dark and deliciously handsome in his suit and bowtie, Pierce was smiling at her and in his eyes was a light that told her never to doubt his love again.

And so, as the strains of the march filled the church she stepped forward proudly, ready to start her new life as mommy to an angel and wife to her beloved, Pierce D'Amato.

THE END

BILLIONAIRE'S ISLAND BRIDE

JUDY ANGELO

The BAD BOY BILLIONAIRES Series
Volume 3

BAD BOY BILLIONAIRE VERSUS REBEL ISLAND
BRIDE - AND THE WINNER IS...

Normally shy and reserved, college student Erin Samuels
goes to the island of Santa Marta where she breaks out of
her shell and does things that shock even her. And, as if
that weren't bad enough, she ends up trapped in a marriage
by blackmail!

Dare DeSouza is used to women throwing themselves at
him and he lumps Erin Samuels in the same category.
Gold-diggers, that's what they all are, but this time he has a
plan. He sets out to teach Erin a lesson she'll never
forget...and ends up learning the greatest lesson of his life.

An island romance that will keep readers guessing every
step of the way...

CHAPTER ONE

"Come on, Erin. Just get it over with."

She shook her head and bit her lip. That was easy for Robyn to say. Robyn was the daring one but she'd never done anything like this in her life.

"Go for it," Maria said in support.

Erin could have happily smacked her. Perspiration settled on her brow but it was not from the Caribbean sun that bore down from a cloudless sky. Erin was nervous as hell.

Inhaling deeply she floated her palms on top of the sparkling water of the swimming pool and stared across its length to the knot of men sitting at the pool bar. They were drinking, talking and laughing, their backs to the pool and the swimmers, their lower bodies submerged in water. The pool bar was a popular location and all the concrete stools were taken with a few of the men resorting to standing in the waist high water and leaning on the counter.

"Just do it and get it over with, Erin." That was Tisha talking.

Erin turned to look back at the group and not for the first time since they'd arrived on the island of Santa Marta she wondered what in heaven's name she was doing here with them.

They were like a rainbow coalition – Robyn with her pale freckled skin and copper red hair, Maria with her waist length black hair and Latin features, Tisha with her shoulder-length braids and mahogany skin. And then there was her, with her creamy skin and chestnut-brown hair.

But they were not a coalition by any means. She was the odd one out. They were all from wealthy families, privileged girls who thought nothing of making trips to the islands for sun, sea and sand. She, on the other hand, had only made it here through the generosity of Robyn's parents and their strong suggestion that Erin take a well-deserved break from on-campus work. She'd spent several months with them while in foster care and they'd been very kind. Now, even though years had passed since she'd left, they still insisted on reaching out to her from time to time with small surprises. This trip was a huge surprise.

Robyn had not been pleased at the sudden addition to her travel party but she finally conceded at her parents' insistence. Erin suspected that she'd given in only because she thought she'd found a readymade gopher for the trip.

Now here she was, caught in a stupid dare, one that her sense of fairness would not let her get out of. The other girls had all performed their assigned tasks which ranged from flirting with strangers to kissing the bartender. And although she'd told them she was not interested she'd been roped into the game. Now it was her turn. She refused to kiss anyone but they'd demanded that she meet them halfway – so she'd agreed to the task: select a man, strike up a conversation, and if he asked her out within two minutes of meeting her she'd win the bet. Stupid? Sure, but she was tired of the harassment and the accusation of being a wet blanket. She'd do it and then tell them to leave her the heck alone.

Tisha swam up to her. "I see a real cutie. Check out the blond-haired guy."

Following the girl's finger she stared at the back of a tall, well-built man with spiky hair. As she watched he turned to the man beside him and, laughing out loud, gave him a slap on the back. The blond-haired man seemed friendly enough and probably would not take offense but still, for some reason she had reservations about approaching him. He might like the attention too much.

Surveying the backs of her potential victims Erin's eyes fell on the strong, lean torso of a dark-haired man. He sat with his back straight although he seemed relaxed in every other way. He was sipping a martini and though he often smiled at the jokes of the other men he seemed more reserved, even aloof. This man, clad in hip-hugging black swim trunks, exuded a power which seemed to draw her to him.

Immediately she knew he would be her target. He looked like a serious kind of guy who would just have a normal conversation with her and then let her go. She didn't care if he asked her out or not. She just wanted her task to be over.

And that would be the end of that.

Sucking in a deep breath, Erin began a slow wade through the waist-high water. She never took her eyes off the back of her now chosen prey.

She was halfway across the pool when she heard giggling behind her. Turning, she gave the girls a scathing look. They held their hands over their mouths, still sniggering, but thankfully they quieted down. The last thing she needed right now was distraction.

Slowly, Erin turned and continued her slow march through the water. All right, she was scared but she'd never backed away from a challenge and she certainly wasn't going to start now. More than that, at all costs she wanted to avoid Robyn's sulking. The girl was a whiner and a bully and tonight Erin did not want to deal with the drama.

She was almost there now. She could see the damp hair curling at the nape of her victim's neck. He was laughing, a deep rumble that emphasized his masculinity. Was this a man she could flirt with? She bit her lip and kept walking. Too late to turn back now.

So focused was she on getting to her target that she forgot the curved metal bar that ran underwater behind the stools. She bumped her foot, lost her balance and began to pitch forward toward the man.

She panicked.

Flinging her arms up Erin grabbed for the nearest support, anything to keep herself from falling. That happened to be the dark stranger's shoulder. She pulled him off his stool, throwing him backwards into the liquid blue of the pool. There was a shout and a huge splash and, to her horror, he disappeared beneath the surface.

"Oh, my God, I'm so sorry." Her hands flew to her mouth and she stared wide-eyed as her victim jumped up, coughing, black hair pasted down on his head, water streaming down his face.

Her eyes rose to his face and she took an involuntary step back, suddenly overwhelmed by the sheer height of him. While sitting he had looked tall but now, face to face, he towered over her five feet four inches.

He was still coughing and by now his friends at the pool bar were laughing heartily at his demise. Even her friends' giggles had turned to peals of laughter.

But Erin did not take her eyes off the man in front of her. His black hair curled wetly around his tanned face and the set of his jaw emphasized his square chin. But it was his gray eyes, so unusual in his dark face, that held her gaze. She could not look away. Like a wild cat he was watching her. Now she was the prey. The look on his face made it clear she was in deep trouble.

He took a step toward her and she backed away.

"You want to play, do you?"

Before she could move another inch he caught her wrist and pulled her up against his hard body. She was pressed so close that she could feel the ripples of his stomach muscles against her chest.

When he dipped his head she jerked back and clamped her lips shut. What in the world? Was he trying to kiss her? Was he crazy?

Suddenly Erin felt herself falling backward and as she hit the water she shrieked. It was cut short when she went under but in seconds she was up, coughing and spluttering, glaring at the now laughing man who stood before her.

"You beast," she yelled. "What are you trying to do? Kill me?"

"Two can play, my dear."

His smug expression, his laughing mouth, the amusement in his eyes so incensed Erin that, before she knew what she was doing, her hand flew up to shove him in the chest.

But he was quick, too quick for her. As it went up he grabbed her wrist. Then, staring deep into her eyes, he turned her hand slowly and bent his head to plant a searing kiss in the middle of her palm.

The touch of his lips sent an electric jolt shooting up her arm and through her body.

She snatched her hand from his. With all the haughtiness she could muster she held her head high, turned and pushed through the water and away from the laughing man.

"I'm leaving," she said to the girls, her voice clipped and cold.

To her surprise and relief they followed her out of the pool without protest, saving her the indignity of listening to the man's mocking laughter.

**

Dare watched the curvy brunette leave the pool, her posse of giggling friends in tow. She'd looked very young but she was obviously in charge. Although the smallest in the group, she held herself like a queen and the three girls tripped after her.

"You're getting old, man." His attorney, Ed, slapped him on the back, still laughing. "Normally you don't let them get away that easily. Are you losing your touch?"

He shook his head, still watching the girl's delectable tush in her hot pink bikini as it disappeared around the corner of the pool hut and out of his view. Only then did he turn to Ed.

"No, still on the ball, but you've got to know how far to go with girls like her."

"Girls like her?" Ed raised his eyebrows. "You know her?"

"Don't need to. I know those kinds of girls and that's all that counts."

"Meaning?"

"Didn't you see that was a set up? That was no accident. That girl and her friends were after something."

"Meaning...you."

"I've had enough of them throwing themselves at me to know when there's just another groupie around."

"Somehow she didn't seem that way to me." It was the first time Roger had spoken. He'd done his share of laughing but had made no comment throughout the whole episode. Now Dare's accountant sounded amused but mildly protective.

"Hold up." Dare gave him a hard look. "Don't tell me you're falling for that game. Don't you see it was all a ruse to get my attention?"

"What makes you think-"

Dare held up his hand, effectively silencing the balding man. "I don't think. I know. I heard them giggling back there long before she attacked. I knew they were up to something. I just didn't expect a near drowning."

"I think you have it wrong, senor."

246

All three men turned back to the counter to a smiling bartender. He was busy wiping glasses but it was obvious he'd been listening and had formed his own opinion, one he was more than willing to share.

"How's that, Danny?" Dare had to hear this one.

"Been observing those girls for the last couple of days and that tiny one who jumped you is as harmless as a kitten."

Dare stared at Danny's wide smile, incredulous. "That kitten almost drowned me."

"Nah, she just tripped. I think she was trying to flirt with you."

"And is that any better, trying to come on to me? I'm sick of being stalked."

"Aw, senor, I should have your problem."

All the men at the bar laughed at Danny's comment and he laughed too, but he was not done.

"It's those other girls you should worry about. For the last two days they've been in the pool daring one another to do all kinds of crazy things." He slid a fresh martini in front of Dare. "Today is the first time I saw the little one get involved. I guess they must have goaded her into it."

Dare was silent for a moment, thinking. He delayed his response by sipping at the drink. Somehow he was not convinced by Danny's defense. But still, he was intrigued.

He could still feel the petite girl's luscious breasts pressed into his chest even though he'd held her for less than two seconds. She was appealing, no doubt about that, and there was something about her that made him want to see her again. But he'd better let go of that feeling, and fast. He wouldn't fall for that trick – again.

"Danny boy, you have a lot to learn." He laughed good-naturedly at the bartender. "Gold-diggers come in all shapes and sizes."

"Dare, I am shocked. This is not like you," Ed said, imitating the voice of an elderly schoolmarm.

Dare couldn't help laughing out loud. But then he got serious. "I have lots of reasons to be like this and it comes from not so pleasant experiences." One in particular, but he wasn't going to go into that with them.

"Let's forget about them and get back to a more interesting topic. Like basketball."

The men got back to their previous conversation and in no time were engrossed in Roger's account of the most exciting basketball final of all time – the Chicago Bulls against Utah Jazz in 1998 when Michael Jordon scored the winning basket in the last minute of the game, locking Utah out and winning 87-86. He'd been there and never tired of recounting his experience.

Dare joined in the conversation at all the appropriate moments but his mind was far away, wondering if he would see that pixie again. After the way his body had reacted to her it would be best if he never did.

CHAPTER TWO

"I can't believe you did it." Robyn's voice was tinged with disbelief.

Erin bit her lip, wanting to shout that it was a stupid thing to do. Instead she shook her head and walked over to the villa's wide bay window that faced the white sandy beach and the brilliant blue sea. The island was beautiful, a paradise on earth, but here she was in the middle of all this beauty and all she was feeling was miserable.

She'd almost drowned a man and had embarrassed herself in the process all in the name of fitting in. Somehow it didn't seem like it had been worth it. And what a man she'd picked. He was obviously not like the fun-loving guys who had fallen prey to her friends' pranks. This one obviously did not appreciate being jumped. She should have known that from his posture. He was no college kid, that was for sure. More like some big shot businessman. A really hot businessman.

Her mind rushed back to the feel of his muscled torso pressed against her breasts and her breath quickened. Even now, just at the memory of it, a delicious shiver coursed through her body.

But the man was a jerk for dunking her like that. Attraction or no attraction, he was the kind of man to stay far away from. She just prayed that for the rest of her week on the island she would not run into him again.

"Come on, Erin. Get out of that funk. Let's take a dip in the ocean." Maria took her by the shoulders and began steering her toward the French doors. "The day is young. We're bound to find some hunks lounging on the beach."

That did it for Erin. She'd had enough of hunks for one day. "You guys go on ahead. I'll just catch up on some reading."

"On spring break?" Tisha huffed in disgust. "You never know when to quit, do you?"

Erin smiled ruefully, not wanting to dampen their high spirit. "Yeah, that's me. Got to get my daily fix or I'll have withdrawal symptoms. You guys go on and have fun. I'll see you later." And before they could object she turned and headed for her bedroom, closing the door firmly behind her.

That evening Erin woke to the sounds of the girls returning from what must have been an exhilarating day at the beach. They were even louder than usual, giggling and screaming as they burst into the villa. Could she survive another three days of this? She wished Robyn's parents hadn't bought the airline ticket for her. She would have gladly remained behind at the college, locked away in the library, absorbed in a stack of books.

She sighed in relief when they didn't bother to knock on her door but instead showered and dressed to go down to the garden for the buffet style dinner that was usually served there. She wasn't hungry and worse, she didn't want to take the chance of running into that man again.

Erin was deep into the history of medieval European art when the girls returned.

"Give it a break, Erin." Robyn walked over to the sofa and grabbed the tome out of her hands. "You do know how to kill a party. Why do you have to study all the time?"

"I'm not studying. For me that's fun reading." Erin forced a smile, not wanting to dampen their mood. "So how was dinner?"

"Good food, like always." Tisha kicked off her sandals and walked over to turn on the TV. Then she flopped down onto the couch across from Erin. "I ate so much fried fish and tacos I feel like I'm going to pop."

"I've got the perfect way to work off all this food." Robyn's eyes sparkled.

Erin's heart sank. What weird scheme was she cooking up now?

"There's a new DJ coming to the resort nightclub. He's from Japan and word is he's really good. Keeps the dance floor hopping, is what I hear."

"Does he play salsa?" Maria swayed her hips to imaginary music.

"He can play anything. All you have to do is request it."

"So what time do we hit the dance floor?" Tisha looked more than interested. She was always one for a good dance party. She could dance all night and not break a sweat.

"What time can you be ready, Erin?" Robyn gave her a pointed look.

"Me? I didn't say I was going."

"You've been hiding out in your room all afternoon and you've been studying on spring break, only heaven knows why. I'm not leaving you in here to take the color of the walls."

"It's okay, I'm fine…"

"No, it's not fine. My dad didn't fly you down here so you can be a drag and spoil all the fun. We're all supposed to be having fun together."

Erin's smile froze and she stared back at Robyn's determined face. She hadn't just thrown that in her face, had she? But one look at the girl's unapologetic glare said that she had, and she was not taking it back.

So that was it. Because Robyn's father had paid for her trip to Santa Marta Erin was beholden to her and was supposed to follow her every command. She was here to make sure Robyn had fun.

Obviously that was what the redhead thought or else she would not be staring back at her so smugly after making a comment like that.

Okay, now she knew where she stood and she could not wait for the week to pass. In the meanwhile she would play along with Robyn's game, humor her if that was what she wanted, then when they got back to Vancouver she would go back to her life on the college campus, far away from Robyn and her demands.

By the time they were ready to leave at about nine o'clock that night Erin felt a little better. She might as well try to have some fun. After all, she might never have the opportunity to have an island vacation again. She'd spent a lot of time trying to look good. Her normally curly hair had been brushed straight and swept up in a chignon high on top of her head. The new look made her feel sophisticated, confident. She'd picked a black dress with a flared skirt that fell just above the knees and she was wearing her favorite high heeled sandals, the one with the rhinestones on the straps. She might not be the best dressed in the group but she could stand beside any of them.

As they walked along the cobbled pathway leading from their villa to the main building of the tropical resort Erin breathed in deeply, savoring the fruity smell of the flowers that lined the path. It was a balmy, tropical night. The gentle breeze from the ocean wafted over her skin and the sound of the rolling waves was soothing in her ears. Despite the problems, she'd been enjoying her stay on the island and didn't want to think about leaving all this to go back to cold Vancouver just yet.

They knew they were close to the nightclub when they heard the horns, trumpets and steel pans of the island music.

"Hey, I don't know how to dance to that kind of music," Tisha said with a pout.

Maria laughed. "You? You can dance to anything, girl. I've seen you on the dance floor."

Tisha looked pleased and started to sway her hips to the liquid sounds, her gold dress floating around her athletic legs.

"That's not how you do it," Robyn chimed in, obviously determined to turn the spotlight back on herself. "When you do these island dances you have to be real sexy and twist your hips like this."

She started to gyrate in tight circles and soon had her friends dissolving into helpless laughter. Dancing was definitely not one of Robyn's talents.

By the time they entered the nightclub Erin's mood was much lighter, even carefree. The enthusiasm of the girls was rubbing off on her and she was ready to dance.

At first they all four danced as a group, forming a tight little circle in the crowd of people. When the DJ switched from merengue to the steady rhythms of reggae they kept on dancing, bobbing to the sounds of Bob Marley's "We Jammin'".

Tisha really showed her moves when the DJ began to play dancehall music. The deep, gravelly sound of Sean Paul's lyrics filled the room and she began a slow, sexy movement of the hips that had Erin staring in fascination.

The people dancing closest to their group were watching Tisha too and soon they were cheering her on, clapping to the tune of the music while she danced. When the song ended they all clapped and she curtsied cutely in appreciation.

Erin was not surprised when a handsome, honey-colored man approached her friend and asked her for a dance. Tisha gave him a brilliant smile, obviously flattered by his attention, and sauntered off to the other end of the dance floor.

Maria, who loved attention, began a sexy Latin dance, no matter that the music had no Latin flavor at all. She was not used to Tisha usurping her position as the most visible and most attractive member of the group. She wanted to win her position back.

As she danced, her body-hugging red dress glittered under the strobe lights, emphasizing her voluptuous hips and ample curves. Her long hair swayed, tickling her bottom like a scarf of jet black silk.

Maria now began to get the attention she craved, with the crowd giving her the cheers and claps they'd just showered on Tisha. This only spurred her on to more risque moves and Erin stared in surprise as the Latin beauty suddenly dipped to the floor and came back up, sliding her body up the length of a thin, brown-haired man who'd been watching her in fascination. She began dancing close to the man, rubbing against him, teasing him then pulling back only to press into him again.

He was obviously loving it. He slid a tentative arm around her and then as she pressed into him he became bolder, matching her dips and sways with jerky movements of his own.

Soon the crowd closed around the dancing couple. And then there were two. Erin rocked to the beat of the music and smiled over at Robyn, wondering how soon it would be before she found a partner and disappeared, too.

She did not have to wait long. Apparently getting bored with Erin as her dance partner, Robyn gave her a little wave and pushed through the crowd toward the bar. Robyn could never go too long without a drink.

Now Erin was alone. She pasted a fake smile on her face and continued to bob to the music that had suddenly become tedious.

But she couldn't go running off the dance floor like a frightened doe so she stayed there, alone in a sea of people, rocking to the steady rhythm of the music.

When the DJ switched to slow music it gave her the perfect excuse to finally exit the dance floor. She slid through the mass of dancing couples and headed in the direction of the bar. At least Robyn would be there.

But she was not.

Erin's eyes skimmed the bar, searching for the emerald green dress, but it was nowhere in sight. She sighed. Robyn must have found a guy and gone back to the dance floor. She would just have to entertain herself for a while.

"Hey, baby, you look hot."

Erin turned and came face to face with a bespectacled man, probably in his late forties, with receding brown hair and a wide grin.

"Want to dance?"

"I...no, thank you. I'm taking a break right now." Erin smiled as she spoke the words, not wanting to hurt the man's feelings.

"Aw, come on. I saw you on the dance floor. You're a great dancer. Come show me some of your moves."

The man reached out and put a hand on her shoulder and she felt a shudder go through her. He had some nerve. She jerked away from his touch.

"I really don't feel like dancing right now," she said, her voice firm. "I'm thirsty." As she spoke she was sidling away, trying to get closer to the bar and away from the man.

"Oh, so it's a drink you want. No problem, honey. That's what I'm here for. Then we can have some fun." The man reached out again and this time he grasped her upper arm.

"Let go of me." Wrenching her arm from his grasp, Erin lurched backward and came up hard against a man's solid back.

Now look what the idiot made her do. She gave him a withering glare.

"I'm so sorry," she said, turning around to face the person she had stumbled into, and her words of apology died on her lips. The man from the pool. She was staring up into his cool gray eyes and she could see he was not amused.

"Still at it?" he began, brows drawing together in a frown. "Why don't you-"

"Darling, there you are," she gushed, cutting him off.

His frown deepened but before he could say another word she put her arm around his shoulder in a quick hug.

"I'll have that drink now," she said loudly, with a little giggle as she took his arm and tried to turn him back to face the bar.

He did not budge.

Her heart skipped. He was going to blow her cover.

She stole a glance up at his face and his eyes bored into her. She could not read his expression but she knew he was angry.

She made one last try. "A pina colada would be lovely." Erin gave him her best flirtatious smile and her heart melted with relief as a slow if cynical smile spread across his lips.

In one fluid movement he slid off the bar stool and stood before her and for that moment she was very close to him, so close that she could smell the spicy fragrance of his cologne.

She breathed in then gasped as his big hands spanned her waist.

He lifted her effortlessly and set her down on top of the stool he had just vacated. He spun it around so that she was facing the bar then leaned in beside her.

"A pina colada for the lady."

"Coming right up." The bartender gave him a nod and within seconds was sliding a frothy glass in front of her.

Not knowing what to say next, she dipped her head and took the straw between her lips. She sucked the sweet, foamy liquid into her mouth, glad for the way it soothed her parched throat.

Finally, she looked at him. His face was so close she could see the faint shadow on his chin. The slight stubble gave him a rakish air and, for some reason, her breathing became ragged.

"Th...thank you," she said then licked her lips that suddenly felt so dry. She glanced back into the crowd for the man who had made her flee but he was nowhere in sight.

She glanced back at the man from the pool and he was watching her, so intently that she dropped her eyes back to her glass. Her fingers trembled as she cooled her palms on the cold glass. Bending her head, she took another sip of her drink, glad for the excuse to break eye contact with him while her mind raced to find a way to get out of this mess.

"Let's dance."

Relief flooded through her as she realized she would not have to make conversation with this man who probably thought she'd been stalking him. They could dance for a minute and then she would thank him and disappear into the crowd. Then hopefully she would never have to see him again.

Now why did that thought make her heart slide down to her toes?

She slipped off the stool and took the hand he offered. A quiver went through her and she bit her lip.

His was a large hand, warm and strong, and she could imagine such a hand sliding up her body, cupping her breasts in a bold caress.

Erin, stop it. She gave her head a quick shake and focused on her new dance partner as he led her toward the dance floor.

Once she was safely hidden in the crowd Erin gently pulled on her hand, wanting to break contact as soon as possible. To her dismay, instead of releasing her the man pulled her closer to him and began to sway to the sounds of Boyz II Men's 'I'll Make Love To You'.

Erin wanted to resist. She really did. But his hard body felt so good against hers as he held her close, and the music was so sensual that she felt her reserve melt like the ice in her pina colada. She relaxed as the music pulsated around them. She closed her eyes and let him lead, swaying her hips and matching his every move.

His hand slid to the small of her back and a delicious tingle ran all the way up her spine.

Now was the time to thank him for the dance and make a hasty exit but her tongue felt heavy in her mouth. She closed her eyes. She could not speak.

"What's your name?"

Erin jumped. The man had bent his head and his lips were close to her ear, so close that his warm breath tickled the fine hairs on her skin.

"I'm Erin. And…and you?"

"I'm Dare," he said softly into her ear, and the way he said it made her shiver.

Dare. What an unusual name. But it certainly seemed appropriate for this man holding her close on the dance floor, so bold and unapologetic.

The strains of the song died away and Erin took a deep breath. This was her chance. She cleared her throat.

"Thank you for the dance," she began then gasped as the man, Dare whatever his name was, grasped her hand and started walking off the dance floor, pulling her along with him.

She looked around frantically. Where were the girls? She needed to be rescued. Now. Her eyes skimmed the sea of people but in that mass of bodies there was hardly any chance she would find her suite mates.

Tugging her arm, Erin blurted, "Where are you taking me?"

Dare spared her a backward glance. "This place is getting too crowded for me. Let's get out of here."

Get out of here? To where? He was forgetting that they hadn't arrived at the nightclub together.

"Excuse me," she tugged again, "but I'm not going anywhere with a stranger."

The man ignored her.

By this time they were out a side door and onto a terrace surrounded by an abundant tropical garden. Dare let go of her wrist and leaned his shoulder against a cast iron trellis through which flowered vines twisted and coiled. As he lounged he folded his arms across his chest, watching her.

"So what was that about us being strangers?" He gave a dry chuckle. "After all we've shared – a hug, a dance, a dunk in the pool. I thought we were more than that?"

She bit her lip and looked away. She could understand how it all looked. As far as he was concerned she'd been the one doing the pursuing. She could only guess what he must think of her.

She took a deep breath, thinking fast. Should she tell him the truth about the stupid dare or would he think her a crazy college student who would do anything for kicks? Maybe that wouldn't paint her in such a good light but she could at least tell him about the stalker in the nightclub. He would surely understand her actions then.

She opened her mouth to speak and the man chose that moment to reach out and pull her to him. Caught off guard, she tilted into him. He took the opportunity to turn with her then backed her up against the trellis, pressing her into the flowery metal frame.

Dare raised one arm and rested it on the metal bar above her head, effectively trapping her between himself and the wall. His eyes glinted in the moonlight as he stared down at her.

Erin's heart thumped and she swallowed hard. Goodness. How was she going to get out of this predicament in a dignified manner?

"Kiss me."

"Wh…what?"

"That's what you want, isn't it? Now's your chance."

"I don't know what you're talking about." She glared up at him, shocked by his audacity.

"You threw yourself at me twice in one day. I have to reward all that effort. Now kiss me." Dare's tone was commanding. He put a finger under her chin and tilted her face toward his.

Erin's heart pounded. He was going to kiss her. And she wanted it, dear God she wanted it. But she'd always been "the good girl". Did she dare?

She did. When his lips touched hers she did not stop him. She did not pull away. Erin closed her eyes tight and clung to his muscled arms. His lips were hard, unyielding. His arm snaked around her and he pulled her tight against his body, so close that she could feel the rippling muscles of his torso against her breasts.

She kept her eyes closed, not daring to look into those enigmatic gray eyes, not wanting to read what lay in their depths.

Then all coherent thought flew from her mind as Dare softened his kiss, his lips moving sensually over hers, stealing her breath away. Erin leaned into him, her nipples as hard as pebbles, and then she was kissing him back, answering his passion with a fervor that was alien to her. She moaned under the caress of his lips.

Erin trembled in Dare's arms. Her body was responding to him like she'd done with no man before.

And as she stood there wrapped in his arms Erin knew she was in deep trouble.

CHAPTER THREE

Slowly, Dare lifted his head and stared down into the dazed eyes of the girl in his arms. What was she doing to him? He'd meant to dominate her, knock her off balance with his kiss. After all, she'd been pursuing him all day. It was time to take her up on what on what she was offering, maybe even teach her a lesson in the process.

But, to his chagrin, it was he who was caught off guard. The kiss had left him breathless. Damn, was he getting soft?

He released her and put her away from him. Only then did he speak. "I want to see you again. Let's have dinner tomorrow."

Her eyes widened in apparent shock. "Dinner? But...I don't know you."

Dare almost laughed out loud. What kind of game was she playing? Did she take him for a fool? Why else would she have been coming on to him, twice in one day, if she didn't know who he was? He would have respected her more if she'd just been honest.

"Listen, I know enough about you to know that I want to see you again."

"But..."

"No buts. Do you want to see me again?" He knew he was bullying the girl but that was the whole idea. She'd decided to play with fire so it was no fault of his if she got burned.

"Yes." Her voice was a mere whisper, her eyes huge pools of iridescent hazel. On her face was a look of uncertainty tinged with just a hint of anticipation.

Dare chuckled inwardly. The girl was playing temptress but she had a lot to learn. First lesson - don't make your feelings so obvious. With an expressive face like hers she was going to have a hard task succeeding in her chosen role as seductress.

"It's settled then. We'll have dinner tomorrow at Michelangelo's. They have a private lounge where we can eat and talk undisturbed. Seven o'clock. Meet me there."

She opened her mouth then, those soft lips still swollen from his kiss, but he cut her off before she even had a chance to utter the first word. There was no way he was giving her a chance to back out. He'd had a taste of her lips and, deceiver though she may be, he wanted more.

He took her by the elbow and turned her toward the pathway. "Come. Let me walk you back to your villa."

"N…no," she said quickly. "No, thank you. I'm fine. I can get back on my own."

He shrugged. "Until tomorrow then. Seven o'clock." He watched her hurry away, heels clicking on the cobbled stones along the lighted path. He had no concern for her safety. He'd made sure security was at its highest level at his resort, with plain clothes security guards patrolling the grounds twenty four hours a day. In his five years operating the resort he'd never had a visitor fall victim to a crime on his grounds. He was determined to keep that record spotless.

Dare DeSouza was an entrepreneur and had been since as long as he could remember. He'd grown up in Michigan and while in elementary school he'd run a candy business, buying bags of candy for a dollar and selling the sweets to his classmates for a quarter a piece. When his home room teacher found out about it he'd had to abandon his enterprise but by high school he'd graduated to selling soda pop and comic books and was raking in a few hundred dollars a week. By the time he started his engineering degree at MIT he was running an online trading company specializing in collectable items, a business which he sold in his senior year for over a million dollars. With this seed money he started yet another business, another trading company that far surpassed the success of the first, and was soon the head of a multi-million dollar operation.

Then he attended a wedding on the island of Santa Marta and was hooked for life. He loved the richness of the island, the verdant pastures and the vibrant green of the tropical foliage. The brilliant blue of the sea and the sky, the cotton white of the clouds, the rich reds of the flora - everything seemed to practically glow with life. He spent a week there and vowed that he would be back.

Next time he visited the island it was for a site visit and on his third trip he signed the documents for the purchase of Sunsational Resort on the northern coast where the best beaches lay. It was family owned but had been neglected due to lack of funds. The couple's children were less than enthusiastic about the hotel business so they were all too happy when Dare offered them over one hundred million for the place.

And then the rebuilding began - renovating, refurbishing and advertising to let the public know the resort was under new management. Sunsational Resort burst back onto the scene and outshone its rivals, soon placing among the top ten resorts in the Caribbean. He expanded to other islands until he had resorts in four additional Caribbean locations. He'd found a winning enterprise and he was loving it.

But that brought with it a host of challenges, fighting off gold-diggers being one of the annoying things he had to deal with. Just a year ago he'd almost been fooled by an expert who tried to convince him to invest millions in a venture that turned out to be phony. Good thing his accountants and attorneys had done their job and reviewed the proposal before letting him sign on the dotted line. If he'd signed he'd have had to hand over millions to a woman whose greatest asset had been her prowess in bed.

And now soon after he'd gotten rid of that one, here was another. A more innocent-looking package, to be sure, but a deceiver just the same. That was the worst part about being a billionaire. Would he ever be able to find a woman who loved him and not his money? The likelihood of that seemed very slim.

He shoved his fists into his pockets, brows furrowed in thought, and headed back toward his own villa. That other gold-digger, Chantalle Marsden, had escaped his wrath but he had absolutely no qualms about taking out his revenge on this one.

***

By the time Erin pushed open the door and entered the villa she was shaking and it was not from the light breeze that cooled her shoulders. She was shocked and she was scared. Had she just promised to go out on a date with a man she hardly knew? No, correct that. Didn't know at all. She'd met him all of two times, once in a pool, and the other time by a bar. And he'd ended up kissing her! Her heart flipped in her chest at the horror of it all. She, staid and boring Erin Samuels, had been kissed by a total stranger.

What was worse, she had kissed him back. And she had loved every second of it.

Goodness, what had she become? Was it the romantic atmosphere? Was it the fact that she was miles and miles away from Vancouver, ensconced on an island? She'd heard about girls who'd gone wild on spring break but she wasn't like that. She was Erin Samuels, bookworm, student librarian, Miss Boring. How had she gone from that to this?

Still deep in thought she walked into the bathroom, unzipped her dress and let it fall to the floor. Her underwear followed. She stepped into the shower and turned the spray on her body, letting the water wash over her. She grimaced as the realization came to her. As much as this was against her norm, she knew there was no way she would miss her date with Dare.

It wasn't until late the next day that Erin mentioned her date to the other girls.

"You, Erin?" Tisha squealed. "I can't believe it. Where'd you find a guy to invite you on a date?"

"Tisha." Maria frowned at the laughing girl. "What? Don't you think men notice Erin? She's a pretty girl."

"Yeah, but she's boring. She never wants to do anything fun." Tisha shrieked and jumped out of reach as Maria tried to pinch her.

Robyn was the only one who wasn't smiling. She seemed deep in thought. Finally she spoke. "What did you say his name was?"

"Dare."

"Check out the name," Tisha said. "Dare. If that's anything to go by, he's my kind of guy."

"But not Erin's," Robyn said with a frown. "So you met him at the bar? And you're going out with him just like that?"

"No…I mean, yes." Erin took a deep breath and began again. "He wasn't the one who came on to me. I bumped into him and anyway I'd met him before. At the pool. Remember the guy I almost drowned?"

The three girls gasped as one. "That's the guy you're going out with?" Tisha's voice was high with excitement.

Erin nodded.

"Wow, that's quite a catch," Maria said, her voice low with obvious respect. "You can see that guy's loaded."

Robyn frowned. "How do you know? All he was wearing were swim trunks and a gold chain. I didn't see anything that spelled money."

"No, but it was the way he carried himself." Maria raised her eyebrows. "Even half-naked the man exuded power. Didn't you notice how the men sitting around him practically bowed in respect? The man's big. I just know it."

"And he asked you out..." Robyn's voice trailed off as she stared at Erin. Her face had that distant look again as if there was something on her mind.

Erin frowned, almost sorry she'd brought up the subject. Her suite-mates were acting like it was impossible for a man to want to go out with her. Well, not so much Maria, but the others. Tisha had practically laughed at the idea and Robyn looked none too pleased. Was she jealous? Erin sighed. Anything was possible where Robyn was concerned. If she wasn't the center of attention she was not happy.

"Well, I just wanted you guys to know where I am tonight," she said with false cheerfulness. "Michelangelo's, seven o'clock. If I'm not home by eleven send in the marines."

Tisha chuckled. "Just keep your cell phone on. We're not going to spoil your fun. Just check in with us if you're running...late." She lifted her eyebrows and gave Erin a naughty grin. "You only live once, right?"

Erin felt the heat rise to her face. Abruptly she got up and walked toward the French doors that opened onto the back patio and the pathway to the beach. "I...need some fresh air. I'm going for a walk."

She could hear the chuckles as she slipped outside. They must think her so pathetic. The ugly duckling, finally asked out on a date when they'd been out every night since they got to the island. While the girls made friends she would return to her room each night and curl up in the sofa with a good book. Not that she'd minded. Now, though, she had her chance to prove to them that she was just as desirable as they were.

The day flew by and before Erin knew it the sun had begun to slide down toward the horizon. Her heart did a bunny hop in her chest. This was it. Her first date while on spring break.

She dressed carefully, picking out a simple yet elegant black dress. She accessorized with a pearl necklace and matching earrings then slipped her feet into high heeled sandals. Now it was time for her hair and face. As she usually did when trying to look sophisticated she took a firm brush to her curls then pinned her hair up into a neat bun. The face was more challenging. She wanted to look good but doing makeup had never been her strong point. She tried some eye shadow and hated it. She had no clue what she was doing and didn't want to ask any of the girls. She'd been humiliated enough for one day. In the end she gave up and settled for foundation, lip gloss and eyeliner. If her date didn't like her that way then that was his problem.

Then it was time to go. She'd been finding all sorts of excuses to dawdle - she couldn't find her purse, she needed another glass of water, she had to redo her lip gloss - until it was ten minutes before the hour. Now she'd have to hurry to make it to Michelangelo's on time. She could see that Dare was not the sort of man who'd take kindly to being kept waiting.

When Erin stepped into the lobby of Michelangelo's she took a deep breath and clutched her purse tightly in her hands. She peered down the dimly lit hallway toward the salon then breathed a sigh of relief. He wasn't here yet. Her racing pulse began to decelerate toward normal.

"Good evening, Erin."

She jumped then whipped round to peer into the darkness of the hallway. And there he stood, tall and imposing in an elegant dinner jacket of dark gray. Those piercing gray eyes glittered in the dim light and she felt as if his gaze stripped her bare.

"Dare," she said, her voice breathless, "I didn't see you over there."

"I know you didn't. Come." He gave her his arm. "A table is reserved for us."

She rested her hand on his arm and as she did so a shiver ran through her. Furtively, she glanced up at him through her lashes. Had he felt it, her body's reaction to his? She hoped he hadn't. That was just what she would need - her body making its response to him unmistakably clear. She breathed a soft sigh of relief when he gave no indication that he'd felt it. He simply kept on walking, her hand tucked into the crook of his arm.

The maitre d' bowed low, showing extreme deference to Dare, then directed them to a private room adjoining the restaurant, an elegantly decorated room aglow with the soft light of a dozen candles shining through stained glass shades that lined the walls. In the middle of the table was what looked like a bouquet of flowers but turned out to be flower shaped candles from which an almost heavenly fragrance wafted.

Dare released her arm and pulled out her chair then he went to sit across from her, his eyes never once leaving her face. It was if he was seeing her for the first time, so intense was his stare. Or was there something more? There was a gleam in his eyes, one that she could not decipher. The only word that came to mind was 'wicked'. She could feel her breathing grow shallow. Goodness, had she made a mistake in coming?

But then inexplicably his demeanor changed. Gone were the frown that had darkened his face, gone was the intense stare that was almost a glare, and in their place was a half-smile that, while not totally reassuring, made her breathing just a little bit easier.

Dare took charge, placing the order for both of them. He seemed familiar with everything on the menu so there was no need to question his recommendation.

In fact, just then Erin was feeling so out of her depth she doubted she would have been able to order anyway. She wasn't even sure she'd be able to eat when the meal arrived. Dropping her hands to her lap she twisted her napkin with shaking fingers and pasted a bright smile on her face.

"Are you all right?" Dare's frown was back. He was watching her intently, his gray eyes glittering like shards of glass in the candlelight.

"I'm...fine, thank you." The words came out stilted and strained. She swallowed and tried again, hiding desperately behind her fake smile. "This is a really nice place. It seems to be the nicest restaurant at the resort."

"I like it." His voice was brusque and cool. It was almost as if he had no interest in conversation.

Confused, Erin bit her lip. Why had he asked her to dinner? He was acting like she was an annoyance.

She dropped the napkin onto her lap, lifted her head and looked him squarely in the eyes. Enough was enough. "You didn't really want to invite me out, did you?"

"Excuse me?" He straightened, obviously caught off guard by her direct question.

"This...date, if you can call it that. Clearly, you don't want to be here so why did you invite me out?" Erin gave him her coldest stare.

"I'm...sorry," he said, his voice low. He had the decency to look contrite. "I've had a rough day and was a bit...distracted." He leaned forward and for the first time that evening he gave her a smile that could be described as warm. "That's no excuse for my behavior and I'm sorry.

Forgive me?" He gave her a puppy dog look that melted her heart.

How could she say no? She smiled back at him. "Of course," she said with a slight nod of her head and when he reached out and took her hand she did not pull it away.

After that the rest of the date went smoothly and soon Erin began to relax in Dare's company. He was charming and witty, and she found herself laughing at his insightful and satirical observations on life. She was seeing another side to this man she'd branded as too domineering and too bold. He actually had a sense of humor.

She'd just finished her second glass of wine when the server approached the table, bottle at ready. This time she quickly covered her glass with her hand.

"I'm fine, thank you," she told him with a smile.

"Are you sure?" Dare asked and a mischievous smile played on his lips. "You're on vacation, remember? No time like the present to let your hair down."

She thought about it. He was right. It was not like she had to drive a car afterwards so no fear of DUI. And she didn't have to get up next day to head out to work or classes. What harm could one more glass of wine do? Besides, she liked wine.

She began to slide her fingers away, her lips slightly pursed in anticipation of the tangy liquid, but then her better self, good old cautious Erin, came to the rescue. "No," she said, shaking her head. "I rarely drink so two glasses of wine is enough, I think. I'll have to walk back to the villa, remember?" She was looking at Dare and gave a little laugh as he gave her an exaggerated look of disappointment. Then when he gave her a pout and wiped away a fake tear she laughed out loud. Dare DeSouza was actually a funny guy.

Seeming satisfied that he'd made her laugh, Dare turned to the server. "Just one glass, please. We'll share it."

At his words Erin's eyes widened and she felt the warmth of a blush rise to her face. We'll share it? Whoa, hold on. Wasn't that much too intimate for two people who hardly knew each other? She continued to stare at Dare, trying to look composed, but she could feel her smile faltering.

Within an instant a fresh glass of white wine was placed on the table between them and the server slipped discreetly away. Erin tore her eyes from Dare's face and looked instead at the sparkling liquid.

He chuckled and reached out a hand to slide the glass closer to her. "You first," he said and the way he said it was both commanding and seductive at the same time.

For a moment Erin hesitated. Then the tension in her dissipated. She relaxed and reached for the glass. She wasn't going to have all of it, after all. She picked it up by its delicate stem and lifted it to her mouth, her eyes never leaving Dare's sharp gray ones. She took a small sip then another and another until Dare stopped her with a laugh.

"Hey, leave some for me. We're supposed to be sharing, remember?"

She laughed too, and lowered the glass to the table then slid it across to him. She was staring at him, she knew, but she couldn't help it. His smile so transformed his face that she could hardly believe he was the same man, the cold, hard brute she'd met the day before. He now looked something very close to a naughty boy planning some devious trick.

This time it was Dare's turn to put the glass to his lips. He gave it a slight turn with his fingers, seeming to deliberately position it so that his mouth would fall precisely where hers had been just moments before. Then, before Erin could guess what he was about to do, his tongue darted out to taste the memory of her lips.

Erin's breath caught in her throat. A simple gesture was all it had been but never had she seen anything more erotic. He'd sent her a clear and unmistakable message without saying a single word. Dare DeSouza wanted her in no uncertain terms.

Her pulse racing Erin watched, mesmerized, as Dare took a sip and another, then his tongue slipped out again this time to catch a stray drop of wine from his lips. But he did it so slowly, so sensually, she knew it was all for her.

He was obviously intent on seducing her and it was working. She drew in a deep breath, trying her best to calm her racing heart, but it was difficult to stay serene when the sexiest man on the island was coming on to her. Goodness, nothing she'd experienced in the past had prepared her for this.

Another sip and Dare had finished the glass of wine. Now he turned all his attention on her. He leaned forward and took her hands in his big strong ones.

When he looked down at them she closed her eyes, willing her hands not to tremble. *Come on, Erin, you're a big girl. You can handle this.* The best way to handle it was to distract him in some way.

"Umm, why don't we go for a walk? It's a nice balmy night." She glanced at him, hopeful that he would take the bait. She needed to get away, out of this intimate space where they were all alone and he could seduce her wickedly without prying eyes. Out in the open he would have to behave. She hoped.

He did not object. "We might as well walk off some of this food. Come." He quickly signed the bill and rose, and as he'd done before he gave her his arm.

Erin stifled a smile. The consummate gentleman when he wished to be. But she was not fooled. Underneath that polished exterior was a man who could be as hard as iron. She'd seen it in his unforgiving response to her blunder in the pool. She'd felt it in his punishing grip when he'd thought she was about to flee. And she could sense it now, as he stood tall and imposing, looking down at her with those steel-gray eyes. She took his arm, thankful to be leaving the romantic atmosphere behind. She needed all her wits about her when dealing with this man and the combination of the fragrant candlelit room and two and a half glasses of wine were not helping.

She sighed with relief as they left the restaurant behind and set off along the cobbled pathway. For a while they walked in silence under the moonlight, breathing in the perfume of the frangipanis that lined the pathway and listening to the sounds of music and laughter in the distance. It was a romantic night, with stars winking in the deep velvet of the sky, and Erin could almost imagine they were lovers enjoying the night and each other's company. If only it were true.

They'd been walking almost aimlessly for some time before Erin realized they'd left the cobblestones and were now on sandy soil. Her stiletto heels had begun to sink into the soft earth and she suddenly found herself toppling over.

With a laugh Dare caught her to him and then without warning his mouth descended and he was kissing her with a passion that left her clinging to him, breathless. Before she could recover Dare bent and swept her legs from under her, lifting her up into his arms.

Erin squealed in shock and then in delight as he swung her round then strode purposefully along the dirt path. When she looked over his shoulder she realized he'd taken her down to the beach where the waves were rolling in to break against the shore.

"Dare," she whispered, almost afraid she would disturb the steady rhythm of the ocean, "what are you doing? We can't be down here."

He chuckled, a low throaty rumble that echoed in her ear as her cheek pressed against his chest. "We can, my precious, and we are. It's the perfect night to be on the beach."

They got to a long, low palm that stretched toward the ocean and in its shadow Dare laid her on a soft bed of grass.

And there he began his sweet, sensual assault.

He started with a kiss that made her tingle all the way down to her toes. Then his lips were sliding down her neck to the valley between her breasts.

"Dare," she gasped and she could say nothing more, her nipples so eager for his lips that they ached. What was this man doing to her? He was being deliberate and slow, teasing her to a degree of desire she had never felt before.

As his breath warmed her flesh Erin moaned and shifted on her bed of grass, wanting to give him more access to her body.

Dare needed no further invitation. To Erin's relief and delight he slipped his arm behind her arched back and as her breasts thrust upward he slid her top away and captured a turgid nipple between his teeth.

Shockwaves of ecstasy rippled through her and an involuntary moan escaped her lips. She reached up with trembling hands and slid her fingers into the dark thickness of his hair then she was clinging to him, pulling his head down, and begging him for release from his slow, sweet, torture of her breast.

Dare took pity on her when he released her tingling nipple and replaced his teeth with his lips, suckling and soothing until she writhed with want.

Under his expert hands Erin felt like her very bones had melted. She was without the power to resist his hands, his lips, and his tongue. There on the warm sand under a sky filled with perfect stars she was lost to him.

"Come. Let's head back to the villas."

His words jerked her out of her heavenly trance. What? Was he stopping? Now? Her eyes fluttered open. She stared up at him, confused, but with his face hidden in the shadows she could find no answers there.

Then he was reaching out his hands to her and helping her to her feet, and as she was rising to stand beside him her heart was sinking down to the sand.

She kept her head down, unable to meet his eyes. For some reason she could not understand he'd changed his mind. He didn't want her anymore. He would walk her back to her villa and that would be that.

Maybe it would all be for the best. She'd been out of her depth, anyway. Then why did she feel so devastated?

Even though Dare continued to hold her hand for the entire walk back to the villas Erin kept her face averted, determined not to let him see her disappointment. She was so caught up in her own feelings that she was surprised when they came to a halt. Were they at her villa already? She looked up then lifted her brows in surprise. This wasn't her villa at all. This one was huge, the largest she'd seen at the resort, and it was magnificent with tiles of black marble gleaming in the light cast by the lamps at the entrance.

Erin hung back, hesitant. "Where...are we?" she whispered, looking around.

"Come," Dare, said with a reassuring smile. "We'll be more comfortable here."

He slid his card into the slot and pushed the door open. Then right there in the open doorway he pulled her into his arms and kissed her with an ardor that left her panting.

His kiss wiped all thoughts, all concerns from her mind. All she wanted was to lose herself in the powerful arms of this man whose charm had swept her off her feet. Then, just like he'd done before, he lifted her off her feet, slammed the door shut with his foot and headed across the foyer and down the hallway.

Erin's heart pounded in her chest. She was no idiot. She knew what Dare wanted and God help her, she wanted it, too. She bit her lip and pressed her face to the soft fabric of his shirt. She could feel the blood rush to her face, she could almost taste the fear, but she would not stop him. Tonight she might be making the biggest mistake of her life but she wanted this too badly to care.

Still holding her close, Dare reached down and opened the door to a massive bedroom lit by a lone lamp standing in the far corner. He strode across the room and laid her on the bed then before she even had a chance to move he'd caught hold of the hem of her dress and was sliding it over her hips and up till she had to shift so he could pull it over her head. Left in only black lace bra, matching panties and stilettos Erin could only shiver under his heated gaze.

To her shock and her body's delight Dare leaned over to plant a kiss on the softness of her belly then he was sliding his lips down, down until she gasped in anticipation.

He lifted his lips then, and there was a smile on his face and a twinkle in his eyes. "Not yet, my sweet," he whispered. "Patience."

He straightened and, with deft fingers, he unbuttoned his shirt, never once taking his eyes off her. His bare chest, so broad and muscled, gleamed golden in the light of the lamp. Next to go was his belt then his shoes, socks, and trousers until the only thing hiding his nakedness from her was thigh-length briefs that did little to conceal his straining bulge.

A wave of embarrassment washed over Erin and she was just about to turn her face away when he hooked his thumbs into the waistband and pushed the garment off his hips and down his legs. Too late. No time to avert her eyes. She could not have looked away if her life depended on it, so mesmerized was she by the sight of his nakedness, his manhood so rigid with want.

He came to her then, sliding onto the bed with her, covering her lips with a kiss that stole her breath from her. And while he kissed her senseless his hands slid down to unhook her bra and free her tingling breasts to the caress of his hands. He released her lips just long enough to divest her of panties and high heels and then he was sliding the solid length of his body up her nakedness and back to her waiting lips.

***

After he'd had his fill Dare broke the kiss and slid off the bed to grab his trousers. He pulled a condom from his wallet and ripped the packet open with his teeth. As he sheathed himself he stared down at the girl lying on his sofa, her eyes tightly closed, her teeth biting down on her lower lip. What the hell kind of game was she playing?

She'd rolled with him every step of the way, flirting with him in the restaurant, coming back to his villa, kissing him with an eagerness that was ample evidence of her desire. And she'd said she wanted this.

Now she was acting like some sort of vestal virgin who'd never done this before. Maybe it was an act. Did she think ravishing inexperienced maidens was his fetish? He almost laughed out loud. He knew girls like her. Tease - that was what they called them. Well, she'd better get ready for the teasing of her life.

Dare returned to the bed where he slid his hand along her thigh then up to her mound where he began to stroke and tease. He was getting her ready for him.

She moaned and her legs began to part for him but still she kept her eyes closed.

It was only when he moved up and over her that her eyes flew open and as he stared into those brown eyes so cloudy with passion he positioned his hips over hers and sank deep inside her.

Erin stiffened and there was a momentary flash of something akin to panic but then she closed her eyes again, shutting him out, hiding from him the depth of her soul.

Unfazed, Dare dipped his head and brushed her ear with his lips. He smiled when she moaned in response. He had supreme confidence in his ability to stoke the embers of passion in this woman. She would not be passive in his arms.

For a whisper of a moment he lay still, giving her time to adjust to his entry, and then he was moving, thrusting slowly at first then more forcefully as she writhed in his arms. When she gasped and clung to him the fire inside him flared up and trapped his breath in his lungs, making him gasp for air.

Soon it was his body that was in control and he was thrusting toward his peak, driving into her until all his lust, passion and desire exploded inside her, leaving him panting and drained.

He looked at her then and what he saw made his breath catch in his throat. She was staring up at him, her eyes misty with tears, and she was smiling. Had it been as good for her as it had been for him? It had been sweet, too sweet in fact. He'd peaked a lot quicker than normal. There was something about this girl that drove him to distraction, made him lose his cool. But not to worry. The night was still young and he planned to drink his fill of her, get her out of his system then purge her for good. By the end of the night Miss Erin Samuels would know not to mess with the big boys.

***

The sun was just peeping out on the world and the birds were beginning the morning's serenade when Erin woke to feel warm hands on her breasts. Eyes still closed, she sighed and turned to give Dare greater access to her and when he replaced his hands with his lips she moaned beneath his caress.

They made sweet love that morning and although her body ached from the vigor of Dare's attention, it was a pleasing ache that came with a feeling of total satisfaction. She'd never experienced anything like this in her life.

When he turned his head on the pillow and looked over at her she felt the blush rise in her face. She'd actually spent the entire night in this man's bed. Who would have thought that she'd have had the courage? She, who had avoided men like the plague? She felt a giggle rise in her throat as her thoughts went to her roommates. They would rib her mercilessly when she got back. Her first 'sleep over' with a man. She could hardly believe it herself. She would just have to put this down to 'island fever'.

But it was more than 'island fever'. Since the day they met there was something about Dare that had drawn her to him. Maybe that was why she'd picked him out of all the men at the bar. It was almost as if she'd had no choice in the matter. And then they'd had this night together. This wonderful, wonderful night. At first she'd been scared but then she'd relaxed in his care, feeling that for the first time in her life she'd found a man she could trust.

She was still curled up beside him in the bed, lost in her thoughts, when Dare's voice pulled her out of her reverie.

"Well, you've served your purpose. Time to go."

At Dare's words Erin's eyes snapped back into focus and she stared up at him. "Excuse me?"

"Time to go," he said again. He leaned back on his pillow and locked his arms behind his head in a gesture of relaxation. "You wanted a taste of a billionaire and I wanted a taste of you. We both got what we wanted so now it's time for you to get out."

Dear God, what was he saying? Eyes wide, Erin clutched the sheet to her breasts and sat up. "Are...are you throwing me out?" She held her breath, praying he would burst out laughing and tell her he'd been pulling her leg. But no, to her horror he was nodding, a smug expression on his face.

"Yep," he said and this time he did laugh but it was a bitter laugh that sounded mean and ugly to her ears.

"I know girls like you," he said, his voice harsh and brittle as brass, "gold-diggers on the lookout for the richest man they can find. You get him to sleep with you, get him to fall for you and then you take him for all he's got." He chuckled. "I'm on to your game, babe. This is one rich dude you're not going to take for a ride."

The blood turned to ice in Erin's veins. If he'd hauled off and slapped her across the face she could not have been more shocked. Or hurt. Or devastated.

She now realized the truth. Dare, this man she thought she had come to know, had never been attracted to her. He'd never felt anything for her. All he had wanted was to get her into his bed, use her, and then toss her away like disposable dinnerware.

Heat rushed to her face then drained away leaving her cold and shivering and dazed. Then as the chill of his words encircled her heart, turning it into a solid block of ice, she dropped the covers, no longer caring, and stumbled out of the bed. Almost blindly, she fumbled around on the floor reaching for her bra under the chair, her panties under the bed and her dress, now a crumpled mass of black silk on the floor. It looked like exactly how she felt – trampled, damaged and discarded.

With a sob she kneeled on the floor and put on her panties and bra then pulled the dress over her head. Her purse and her shoes were nowhere to be seen.

Slowly she got up and walked on unsteady feet across the room. She wanted to cry. She wanted to throw herself on the floor and bawl. But she would not. She would never give this man the satisfaction of knowing how much he had hurt her. Even though she was dying inside she lifted her chin and without a backward glance she walked out of the room.

She found her shoes and purse in the living room. She retrieved them and then she walked out of Dare's villa and out of his life.

***

A heel. That was what Dare felt like as he lay on the bed staring up at the ceiling. It had been over twenty minutes since Erin left his villa and still he had not moved. The look on the girl's face, the sight of her dejection had floored him.

Had he made a mistake? Had he been wrong in how he'd judged her? It couldn't be. She'd come on to him at the pool and just like he'd expected she'd found a way to conveniently bump into him again, this time at the bar. She'd even jumped at his invitation to dinner. And even more telling, she'd had no objection when he had taken her to his place. She'd given him every indication that she was after something and he'd been right to cut her loose.

Then why did he feel so low? Was it because of the panic he'd seen in her eyes? Was it the way she'd clung to him each time they made love? Was it the hurt he'd seen in her eyes?

Dare shook his head. No, she couldn't be feeling hurt at his rejection. Anger, maybe. Disappointment. But not hurt. She'd gone into this with her eyes wide open, knowing the risk of trying to seduce a man. She must have been prepared for either outcome.

This was what his brain was telling him. He just wished that other side of him, that weaker part that dealt with his emotions, would just shut up and accept. He'd been right in doing what he did. The girl needed to pay.

So why did he feel like such a jerk?

CHAPTER FOUR

It was just after six in the morning when Erin sneaked into the villa, quiet as a cat, and hid herself in her bedroom. Thank God the girls were still fast asleep.

She went into the bathroom and locked the door and there, in the privacy of that space, she slid down to the rug on the floor, hid her face in her hands, and wept.

She had never been so humiliated in her life. To think that she had trusted this man, had felt an emotional connection with him, and then he'd turned out to be the same as the jerks she'd known all her life. She would never trust a man again. Life was infinitely better when she was alone.

With a sniff, Erin got up from the floor. She stepped out of her shoes then stripped off her dress and underwear, removing from her body all memories of the night before. From here on Dare would be a distant memory, just someone stored away in her collection of experiences. That was all. She stepped into the tub, turned on the shower and submerged herself in the cleansing flow.

Erin was relieved when the girls got up later that morning and seemed to have forgotten about her date. They must have come in late last night, half drunk as usual. They seem to have totally forgotten that she'd even gone out. Only Robyn seemed to be regarding her with some interest. Finally, as Erin was packing the plates back onto the room service trolley, she spoke.

"So," she said, dragging out the word as she eyed Erin from across the room, "how did it go with lover boy last night?"

"L…lover boy?" Erin's heart sank as she realized she hadn't escaped. Robyn wanted answers and what Robyn wanted Robyn got.

"Yeah, your date. What? Did it bomb?" The girl looked almost eager to hear bad news.

"Yes. Yes, it did." Erin seized on the direction the conversation had taken. All Robyn wanted to know was that she'd had a terrible time and then she'd leave her alone.

"Aww, that's too bad." Tammy went over and put her arm around Erin's shoulder. "Don't let it get you down, though. We can still have some fun tonight."

Tonight. For her there would be no fun. It would be their last night on the island before heading back to Vancouver and she planned to spend it hidden away in her room.

If she'd spent her time as she normally did, alone and lost in an art history text, she would not have fallen into the trap set by the devil himself. She'd learned her lesson. Home was the safest place to be.

She said none of this out loud, though. She kept her thoughts to herself and pasted a brave smile on her face. "Sure," she said brightly. "There's always tonight."

After breakfast Maria, Tammy and Robyn went down to the beach to take advantage of their last opportunity to tan under the hot Caribbean sun and dip in the ocean. It was also their last chance to preen in front of the many available college guys who had come to the island looking for fun. When they'd hounded Erin to come along she had flatly refused. She would not risk running into Dare again.

As long as she stayed in the villa she would be safe. Thank goodness she'd never told him her last name. He would have no way of finding her. Not that she thought he'd be looking. She had absolutely no desire for him to even consider looking for her. That was what she told herself but the puddle of pain at the pit of her stomach was testament to the lie she'd been feeding herself. She was hurting and there was no denying that.

After a night of packing and contemplation Erin left the Island of Santa Marta early the next morning relieved that she would never lay eyes on this confounded place again.

**

From her seat in the crowd of black-gowned students Erin looked over at the sea of faces - friends, family and well-wishers who had come from far and near to celebrate the special occasion. Within less than an hour the ceremony would be over and each graduate would leave, ready to move on to the next stage in life.

Erin was smiling as she watched the happy faces but even as she celebrated with her batch mates she couldn't help feeling a twinge of sadness. How she wished she had someone, anyone, to celebrate with her.

There'd been a day when she'd had a mother and a father who loved her dearly. They would have been here today to share in this rite of passage but it had been nine years since they'd been torn from her life, the victims of a motor vehicle accident caused by a drunk driver.

With her only living relative being an aunt who lived and worked in South America as a missionary Erin had ended up in foster care, moving from family to family from the age of twelve until she was eighteen.

She'd won her freedom then. By working hard throughout high school she'd won a tuition scholarship to a college of her choice and now, four years later and with thousands of hours of part-time work under her belt, she'd made it. Now to face the real world. She was eager to step over that threshold and start making some real money.

Armed with her degree in liberal arts Erin sent out resume after resume to museums, government agencies, schools and non-profit organizations, hopeful that she would land a job within a few weeks. She had enough money to last her about a month and a half. So this was what it felt like to be just one paycheck away from the homeless shelter. She had to find a job and fast.

But things did not go as Erin planned. Three weeks into her job search she still had not been called for a single interview. It was all due to the recession, the career office told her, coupled with the fact that the market had just been flooded with thousands of new graduates competing for the few limited job openings. Erin acknowledged that might all be true but that knowledge didn't help her situation, now only about three weeks away from starvation. And how was she going to pay next month's rent?

And if that weren't bad enough she'd suddenly been attacked by a stomach virus. Two days in a row she'd woken up to a bout of nausea and had had to rush to the bathroom where she'd emptied the contents of her stomach. When the third day turned out to be more of the same Erin knew she had to make the sacrifice and dip into her meager savings to get the money to visit a doctor. Her college health insurance coverage had expired so all medical costs were now her responsibility.

At the medical clinic she grudgingly handed over the eighty-dollar fee then went to sit in the waiting lounge. She picked up the latest copy of Cosmopolitan then put it down again, unable to concentrate. There was just too much on her mind. There were so many things she needed to do. She needed to start pounding the pavement, she had to find a job. Dear God, how was she going to survive?

She glanced at her watch for the fifth time. Why hadn't the doctor called her yet? She couldn't afford to waste all this time just sitting around. She had to get back to her job hunting. Unable to sit still any longer she got up and went over to stare at the goldfish swimming serenely in their colorfully decorated house of glass. She envied them.

"Ms. Samuels?"

At the sound of her name Erin turned to see the medical assistant standing in the doorway, smiling at her. She gave a sigh of relief. Finally.

Dr. Saunders greeted Erin warmly and listened attentively as she described her ailment. After a quick check of her blood pressure, heart and lungs he gave a nod. "Everything seems to be in order. Will you have a seat, please?"

She slid off the examination table and went back to sit in the chair across from the doctor's desk.

"Ms. Samuels," he said with a gentle smile, "is there any possibility that you are pregnant?"

"Preg...pregnant?" The words came out in a shocked whisper.

"Yes, pregnant," the doctor said patiently. "Are you sexually active?"

"N...no. I mean, yes. I..." she could not go on. Pregnant? The thought hadn't even crossed her mind.

"So which is it?" the doctor chuckled but there was no sign of judgment on his face. "I need you to do a pregnancy test today. If it's negative we'll run some other tests but let's start there."

In a daze Erin took the lab requisition from the doctor then with a nod of thanks she turned toward the door. Could she really be pregnant?

As she sat in the waiting room she relived the night she'd spent in Dare's arms. Three times they'd made love and all three times he'd used a condom. They'd been careful. Pregnancy could not be the cause of her problems. She began to breathe a little easier at the thought. Then she thought back to the last few months since she'd left the island. She hadn't had a period since her return but that was normal for her. She was one of the lucky souls who only had a period three or four times a year. Her gynecologist had told her it would in no way affect her ability to have children so she hadn't been concerned. Until now.

The gravity of the situation was like a slap to the face. If she were really pregnant how in heaven's name was she going to manage? She could barely feed herself let alone a baby. And where would they live?

She covered her face with her hands, trying to control her emotions. It would not do to burst into tears right there in the middle of the waiting room. But, dear God, what was she going to do?

It took only thirty minutes for Erin to receive the verdict. She was indeed pregnant. And she was expected to give birth in twenty-four weeks. With that news her world crumbled around her.

Erin spent the rest of the afternoon feeling sorry for herself. Then, as she always did when facing a crisis, she began to plan her course of action.

First, she had to find a way to start earning money immediately. Looking for jobs in her field of study was not working and it didn't make sense to continue down that path. She would set her sights lower, take anything she could get, just as long as it was available now and provided a steady income. Next, she would move to a smaller place, probably somewhere farther away from the college since apartments in that area tended to be more expensive due to the high demand. She would probably even have to seek a roommate. She wasn't thrilled at the idea but under the circumstances she had no choice.

Then she would start checking out the thrift stores. As much as she hated the idea of dressing her baby in recycled clothing it was better than no clothes at all. She sighed and sat down to write her list. A crib, bedding, clothes and a stroller. At minimum she would have to have those. Oh, and a baby car seat. She'd need that the day she took him…or her…from the hospital. Even if she told them she'd be taking a taxi home the hospital staff would never let her leave without a car seat for the baby.

Her plan in place, Erin began to pound the pavement. Literally. Next day she was up with the sun. She'd dressed carefully, applied a little make-up, and with her resume adjusted to suit the marketplace she took the bus to the heart of the city and began to walk. She'd printed one hundred copies of her resume and before the week was out she planned to have dropped off every one of them.

By the end of the first day Erin had submitted applications at twenty-one establishments including Subway, Mc Donald's, Whole Foods and Tim Horton's, the most popular coffee shop chain in the country. She knew that if she was lucky enough to get a call from one of them the pay would be small, probably little more than minimum wage, but at least most of the restaurants offered employees free meals. Food was one thing she wouldn't have to worry about.

Next day Erin was out again by seven in the morning. She didn't get back home until the sun had already set. Still, she was satisfied she'd beat the previous day's record, submitting twenty-five applications that day. By the end of the third day she'd reached sixty-six in total. Completely exhausted, she only had the energy to shower and climb into bed with a prayer that her hard work would soon bear fruit.

The fourth day dawned and despite the feeling of nausea that attacked her Erin pulled on her walking shoes and headed out to begin her daily trek. She didn't feel as energetic and her spirit had begun to flag. Still, she pressed on, knocking on every door where she felt there was any possibility of her finding work.

She was speaking with a receptionist at a small family restaurant when her phone rang.

"Excuse me." She gave the woman an apologetic smile and turned away to take the call. "Ms. Samuels?" It was a male voice, deep and gravelly and very formal.

"Yes, this is Erin Samuels." Her heart leaped in anticipation. Was this the good news she'd been praying for before?

"This is Mike Mason from Benny's Restaurant. You dropped off an application on Monday." There was the sound of papers shuffling in the background. Then he continued. "I was wondering if you could come in to meet with me tomorrow?"

"Yes, of course," she said, breathless. "What time would you like me to come in?"

They made the arrangements then Erin slid the phone shut. Her first interview. At the thought her face broke into a wide smile. She couldn't help it. Thank you, God.

Then, remembering where she was, she quickly composed herself and walked back to the reception desk where she proceeded to enquire about job openings. She had to keep searching. Who knew what tomorrow would bring? She was keeping her fingers crossed that she'd nail it. But until then she would keep on looking.

Next day Erin arrived ten minutes early for her first interview. She'd worn her navy blue power suit and her curly hair was pulled back into a neat bun. She announced herself to the greeter who invited her to a small office where she could wait for Mr. Mason.

Perched on the edge of her chair with her purse clutched tightly on her lap Erin surveyed the room. It was a small, neat office with very little furniture except for a huge antique desk that dominated the room. The restaurant, too, had been neat and clean. She'd observed that as she was following the girl to the office. She liked that. The place had a homely atmosphere that made her feel almost comfortable, as if she worked there already and had been doing so for years.

"Ms. Samuels."

Erin turned toward the voice and her eyes widened in surprise. The man was huge, big and brawny but with a friendly face and a wide smile. He reminded her of Yogi Bear.

"Mr. Mason?" she asked as she rose and extended her hand.

"The same," he said with a nod. His hand was like a bear's paw, swallowing hers whole. Then he released her and waved his hand. "Sit, sit. Make yourself comfortable."

Erin sank back into the chair and watched as he ambled around the desk and dropped into the leather chair. Now she understood why the desk was so massive. Mr. Mason would never have been able to fit behind anything smaller.

With his beefy hands he shuffled through the papers on his desk then he grabbed a sheet and held it up. "Here we are. Quite an impressive resume," he said and gave her a smile and a look that made him seem genuinely impressed. " Summa cum laude. Wow. You must be genius material."

Erin blushed, grateful for the compliment but a bit uncomfortable with his praise. "I study hard, that's all."

"And you know what that tells me about you?" Mike said, slamming the paper on the table. "You're a hard worker. You're the kind of person we want here. Now when can you start?"

"Wh...what? That's it? Aren't you going to ask me any questions?" Erin stared at the man, wondering if he'd gone mad. What kind of interview was this?

"Nope. I read your resume, now I've seen you, and I like you. That's it." He shrugged then leaned back in the chair and locked his fingers across his paunch. "So do you want the job or not?"

Erin knitted her brows in confusion. "I...do want the job." She gave him a bright smile. "I can start right away, Mr. Mason."

"Good. We have a party of twenty-two coming in this afternoon and that's in addition to our regular customers so it's going to be busy. Sally will get you a uniform and you'll be good to go." He pulled out a sheet of paper from a folder and slid it across the desk toward her. "Now let's talk money."

Erin didn't bother to hide her smile. She liked the sound of that. A lot.

Her luck had finally turned and now she could breathe again. She'd work hard and tuck away as much money as she could. She guessed she could hide her pregnancy for another three months, tops, and then, God help her, she'd be on her own. Mr. Mason seemed like a nice man but how would he react when he learned of her condition? She could only pray he'd be sympathetic.

But she had to prepare for the worst. As she signed the papers she thought of the tiny life growing inside her. 'Don't you worry, little one," she whispered silently. 'You and me, we'll make it together."

***

"Dare. Are you with me, man?"

Dare dragged his eyes back into focus and stared across his desk at the grinning man.

"You've been out of it lately," his long-time friend and business associate said with a laugh. "If I didn't know you I'd say you were in love."

Dare frowned at him but said nothing. The statement did not warrant an answer. Bart knew him. He had no time for women, least of all the money-hungry kind. There were always plenty of those around. He had his pick. The problem was, he wanted none of them. But there was one woman he could not get off his mind. A slender woman with chestnut hair that curled around her heart-shaped face, a woman with hazel eyes that flashed with the fire of her passion. Bart was right. There was something wrong with him. He was not in love but damn it, he was obsessed. He could not get Erin out of his mind. "Sorry about that," Dare growled then pulled his chair close to the desk. "Let's get back to the business at hand."

"Cool." Bart ran his fingers through his spiky blonde hair then tilted the chair back until it looked dangerously close to tipping over. "It's a sweet deal. You can't pass up on this one. I got a tip on it. Going real cheap, considering."

"You're sure?" Dare admired his friend's ability to find great real estate deals. Bart found the deals and he financed them. That was how he'd acquired resorts on four other islands.

"Trust me, man. You can't lose out on this one." Bart leaned forward, his face earnest. "I can sniff out a deal a hundred miles away. You know I'm good at that."

He was. Dare could not deny it. Working together they'd become billionaires in the real estate business, buying up resorts in the Caribbean and condos in the United States and Canada then renovating and selling them for far more than they'd invested.

"This one's big though, Bart." Dare watched the other man intently. "My biggest investment yet."

"The one you're going to make the most money on," Bart responded.

"But I'm paying almost full price for this one."

"You can buy this resort 'as is'. You'll be filling it with guests in no time. Guaranteed."

"We'll see," Dare said. Then, against his will, his mind drifted to other things like the heat that coursed through him every time he thought of curly-haired Erin. It was no use. He couldn't concentrate. "Let's call it a day," he said and got up. "I've got some other business to take care of."

"Why is my mind telling me it's got something to do with a woman?" Bart was giving him that Cheshire Cat grin again.

"Go home, Bart." Dare walked over to the door and held it open. "This one's got nothing to do with you." He softened his statement with a brief smile.

"All right, my boy. But if you need any advice you know who to call."

It would be a dark day before Dare turned to Bart for advice on women. The man had married and divorced three times already. Still, he chuckled. "I'll bear that in mind."

After Bart left Dare walked over to the large bay window that looked out onto the ocean breaking against the shore. He crossed his arms and as he stared out onto the blue water his mind, as it had done so many times over the past few months, went back to Erin Samuels.

He'd pulled the hotel records and checked her out. Erin Samuels, student at Canucka College in Vancouver, Canada. Her home address was recorded as well as her cell phone number and e-mail address. For emergency contact she'd conspicuously left it blank. She probably didn't want her family being informed of her antics while on spring break. She could have any number of reasons. He'd seen guests leave out that portion before.

So he'd had all her information for the past three and a half months and he'd done absolutely nothing with it.

Wimp. He grimaced as he berated himself inwardly. He wanted to see Erin Samuels again.

Dare gave a bitter laugh. He knew what she was but he'd held out long enough. He had to see her again, if even for the sole purpose of getting her out of his system. First order of business, he'd get his P.I. to check everything out, make sure she was still at the location in the file. Then he'd go there himself.

His mind made up, he went over to the desk and pressed the intercom.

"Yes, Mr. DeSouza." Cool and efficient, the voice of his personal assistant crackled through the speakers.

"Book me on a flight to Vancouver, please. I want to fly in day after tomorrow."

"Very well, Mr. DeSouza. Consider it done." Always discreet, Claudia didn't ask for any further details. She knew he would tell her all she needed to know.

Satisfied, Dare grabbed his keys and headed for the door. Erin Samuels was in for quite a surprise.

CHAPTER FIVE

Erin's first day on the job was a whirlwind of activity. The party of twenty-two showed up at one o'clock and after that there was a steady stream customers so that by the time the restaurant closed at ten o'clock that night she was worn to a near frazzle. How was she going to keep up with this pace, pregnant as she was?

She'd rejoiced at the job offer and she'd appreciated it. Really, she had. But what she hadn't anticipated was to be on her feet for twelve hours at a stretch with only two fifteen minute breaks and a half an hour for lunch.

That night when she got home, despite her best intentions, she was too tired to tackle step two in her plan - look for a cheaper apartment. She needed to move as soon as possible but her search would have to wait one more day.

Day two was almost as busy as the first. Benny's Restaurant was clearly a popular destination for all three meals of the day. From the moment Erin got to the restaurant she was kept running back and forth between the kitchen and the tables. Now she realized why 'Yogi Bear' as she'd come to think of him had hired her on the spot. She'd learned he'd lost a server the day before and clearly he had too much business to be short-staffed.

The work was tiring but her greatest consolation was the tips. She was almost collecting enough in tips as she would from her salary. Yet another perk of working at a restaurant and one she was so grateful for. She was saving every cent of it for the time when she'd need it most.

By nine o'clock that night the ache in Erin's feet turned to numbness and she kept glancing at the clock, willing it to speed up toward closing time. The crowd in the restaurant had thinned out with just a few diners lingering for dessert and coffee. Those, she could handle.

With a sigh she was turning toward a high stool by the counter, intending to rest her feet for a minute, when a man, tall and dark-haired in a dark, immaculately tailored suit, walked in.

Erin frowned, feeling a twinge of recognition, and then her heart lurched as she recognized the man who filled the doorway. She could never forget those steel-gray eyes, eyes that now held her transfixed. It was Dare.

Suddenly feeling faint, Erin grabbed for the counter and held on. What was he doing here? He was from another time, another life. How in the world had he ended up at the very restaurant where she was working, thousands of miles from Santa Marta? He hadn't come looking for her, had he? He was walking toward her now, his eyes never leaving hers, and she stumbled back against the counter then froze. There was nowhere to run.

Why had he come? To insult her again? To throw her wantonness in her face? Her breath caught in her throat, her anxiety rising, knowing that his appearance could only mean trouble.

Dare was right in front of her now, looking down at her as if the two of them were the only people in the place.

"Erin Samuels. We meet again." His lips curled in a sardonic smile as he rested a hand on the counter beside her, trapping her into a corner.

"Dare, what are you doing here?" Her voice was little more than a strained whisper. She was fighting to regain her composure but his nearness, the earthy fragrance of his cologne, were overwhelming her senses. At that moment all she wanted to do was lean into him, feel his hard body against hers, have his arms wrapped around her. But it would not happen, it could not. Not when he despised her so much.

That thought ripped her out of her trance. Dare hated her. He'd used her then thrown her out of his bed. Now he'd strolled back into her life thinking she would do what? Swoon and throw herself at him again? He must be out of his mind. She glared up at him as he towered over her. "Excuse me but I have to get back to work." Her voice was as cool as the steel of his eyes. "I'm sure there is someone else who can assist you." If he thought she was going to serve him he'd better think again.

She stepped around him, intent on putting as much distance as possible between them.

His hand shot out, halting her flight. "Not so fast, honey. We need to talk. When you finish working I'll be waiting. Over there." He jerked his chin toward an empty booth by the window. Without another word he released her and walked away.

For a second Erin could only stare. The nerve of him. We need to talk? About what? Apart from one night of mind-blowing sex there was nothing that existed between them. Absolutely nothing for them to talk about. And then she remembered. The baby. How in the name of heaven had he found out about the baby? That had to be the reason why he'd suddenly stomped back into her life. And what was he planning to do about it?

She gasped as a thought flashed into her mind. Had he come to demand that she terminate her pregnancy?

Blindly, she stumbled into the kitchen and leaned against the counter to catch her breath.

"Hey, are you all right?" Mildred, the sous chef, approached her, a look of concern on her face. "You look like you're about to pass out."

"N...no. I'm fine," she whispered then sucked in a deep breath. *Come on, Erin. You're stronger than this.* She lifted her head and gave Mildred a smile. "It just got a bit too hot out there. I'm okay now. Are any trays ready?"

Mildred pointed to a tray laden with cups and a pot of coffee. "Table sixteen." She shook her head. "Thank God the day is almost over."

Those last thirty minutes of her workday were the hardest of her life. Out of the corner of her eye she could see Dare sitting in the far booth, a glass and a bottle of wine in front of him. She'd moved with feigned ease, serving the customers, chatting with them and laughing where appropriate. But she could feel Dare's eyes burning into her. As discreetly as she could she slipped a paper napkin into her hand and turned away to dab at the perspiration beading her brow. She would never let him see her sweat.

As it neared ten o'clock Erin sidled into the kitchen then headed for the changing room. Moving swiftly, she shed her uniform and donned her street clothes then grabbed her purse. Tonight she would not leave through the front door as she normally did. She almost giggled as she thought of Dare waiting patiently for her return. He'd have a long wait.

She bid her farewell and slipped out the back door that led into a dingy alleyway then she hurried up the path and out to the main road where she took off, walking at a brisk pace.

She heard the purr of an engine and looked up just in time to see an ink-black Mercedes Benz convertible pull up beside her.

"Get in." Dare was scowling at her and his tone brooked no argument.

"I...don't need a ride," she said, clutching her purse tightly to her chest. "I'm fine."

She was backing away when his voice, clipped and cold, stopped her. "Don't make me come get you. I'll lift you up and throw you in here if I have to."

Erin froze. Then she slowly approached the car. He would do it. She could see it in his eyes. This time, she knew, it was best to give in. With a sigh she pulled the door open and slipped into the passenger seat.

She hadn't even settled in before he took off down the road, making her whip around to stare at him. "Where are you taking me?" she demanded.

"Home."

"But…you don't even know where I live."

He didn't even bother to respond. That was all the answer she needed. He did know. Was he having her watched? Had he been spying on her ever since she'd returned to Canada? Erin's heart pounded at the thought. He knew she was pregnant. He knew where she lived. What else did he know about her? Did he know about her past, too?

That thought was sobering, so much so that it left her at a loss for words. She'd meant to blast him with her rage, demand an explanation, but she could not. She was too worried about how much he knew.

Within minutes Dare was pulling into the visitors' parking area in front of Erin's apartment building. He switched off the engine and turned toward her. "Let's go," he said. "We need to talk."

Erin did not even bother to object. Before he could move to get the door she climbed out of the car and marched toward the entrance. If he had to run to catch up with her then it would serve him right.

Unfortunately for her, he didn't need to. Within seconds his long strides had him by her side so that by the time she got to the entrance it was he who held the door open for her. They crossed the lobby then rode the elevator in silence. Deliberately, she kept her eyes averted, breathing slowly, trying her best to calm her nerves. It was not an easy task, not when she was so close she could breathe in the masculine fragrance of his cologne. There was no way on earth she could ignore the fact that he was there, mere inches away from her. The shallowness of her breathing, the tautness of her nipples in her bra, were evidence of the effect he was having on her.

As soon as the elevator door opened Erin was out and away, eager to put distance between them. Her physical attraction was too strong, too disturbing. She had to regain control.

When he strode up behind her she was still at the door fiddling with her keys, her palms slippery with perspiration.

Calmly he reached out and plucked them from her hand, selected the correct one and opened the door. Then with a mocking smile he dropped the keys back into her hand. When they stepped inside the apartment a wave of embarrassment swept over her. Dare was obviously a man of wealth. He'd said something about being a billionaire. She seriously doubted that but she was sure he had some money. He carried himself like a man of means. What would he think of her home, so sparsely furnished that the living room didn't even have a sofa? She'd been meaning to get one since moving in but that had been almost two years ago. Now, under the present circumstances, the chances of acquiring that piece of furniture were slim to nil.

At least she had the essentials - a bed to sleep on and a chest of drawers for her few pieces of clothing. And at least she could offer him a seat. In the living room cum dining room were a small table and two chairs. It wouldn't make for comfortable sitting but maybe that was a good thing. Making him comfortable was the last thing she wanted to do. She wanted him to state his business then get the heck out of her apartment and her life.

Erin could feel her anger return. After Dare had used her and discarded her in the most horrible way, what could he possible want with her now?

Except for the baby, her heart whispered. Apart from the baby there was absolutely no reason why this man would have the slightest interest in her. This was all about the baby.

Erin waved a hand toward the table. "Have a seat. Please."

She could see that he was scrutinizing her home, his eyes roaming the apartment. She could just imagine what was going through his mind. All she needed to see was the expression on his face to know what he was thinking. She wasn't important enough for him. Now he was getting confirmation that he'd made the right decision in throwing her out.

Dare walked over, his height making her apartment seem too small and the ceiling too low. She was glad when he dropped his tall frame onto the chair. Seated, he was a little less intimidating. Just a little.

"Aren't you going to sit?" Dare was looking at her as she stood several feet away, watching him. On his face was an amused smile.

What was there to smile about? "No, I'm fine," she said and released the hand she'd just realized she'd been wringing in agitation. She tucked her hands into the pockets of her skirt. "Dare, what are you doing here? And how did you find me?"

He crossed his legs and leaned back in the chair, somehow managing to look comfortable. "Finding you was easy, honey. We've got all your details at the hotel."

"At the hotel?" Erin's eyes widened in shock. "They let you see my personal information? Who did you bribe?" She couldn't believe the breach to her personal privacy. Sunsational Resort would be getting a letter from her and it would not be pretty.

"Come off it, Erin. Stop playing dumb. It's not becoming." He gave a snort and crossed his arms over his chest. Gone was the look of relaxation. Now he looked exasperated. "Why would I need to bribe my own employees?"

"Your...employees?" What the heck was he talking about? Erin shook her head. The man was making no sense at all. "What employees?" Then, like a light bulb that had just been switched on something in her mind clicked. "You weren't a guest at the resort, were you? You actually work there."

How could she have been so stupid? The man was probably one of the managers at the resort. Now she understood why his villa had looked so grand in comparison to all the others. The man was a big shot at his workplace.

The realization made her all the more angry. "Do you realize I could have you fired?" Her voice was strong now as she realized the power she had over this man. He was an employee of the resort and yet he'd gotten involved with her, a guest, and then he'd had the audacity to show up at her workplace. And now he was in her home.

Now it was her turn to fold her arms across her chest. "You'd better have a darn good reason for being here or else you're going to be in a lot of trouble." Feeling smug at having the upper hand she gave him a smile but it was not a pleasant one. "What would your boss say if I told him that you'd slept with one of the guests? If I complain to your superiors you won't be in your cushy job for long."

Dare's eyes narrowed. Slowly, deliberately, he got up and then he was towering over her. "Are you threatening me?" His voice was hard as the granite of the countertop.

Erin took an involuntary step back. Had she gone too far? She was alone in the apartment with a man who looked just about ready to wring her neck. Goodness, she'd been so stupid. Why hadn't she kept her mouth shut?

"N...no," she managed to whisper. "It wasn't a threat."

A strange look passed over Dare's face and then the anger was gone. His look was almost one of regret. "Look, I'm sorry," he said and expelled his breath. "I didn't mean to scare you. You just annoyed the hell out of me with your pretense."

What pretense, she wanted to ask. Instead, she bit her lip and waited. There was no way she was going to incite his wrath again, not while she was still alone with him. She'd just let him have his say.

"You know I own Sunsational Resort so all this talk about my boss and getting me fired is a waste of my time and yours. Let's just be adults here and-"

"What did you say?" Erin's heart jerked in shock. "You own Sunsational Resort? Are you serious?"

Dare gave her an irritated look then he shook his head. "Here we go again. Will you stop pretending?"

"I'm not pretending," she retorted. "I had no idea you were…are… the owner of the resort."

His eyes narrowed. "You had no idea? So you're telling me that when you spent the night with me you didn't know who I was?"

Eyes wide, Erin shook her head. Now that he'd said it out loud it didn't sound good at all. Sleeping with a total stranger? She cringed inside just thinking about it. How could she blame him for having a low opinion of her?

She could feel the heat of shame rush to her face. He would never respect a woman like her. How could he? She had absolutely no excuse except for the fact that the night he'd taken her to his villa Dare had so captivated her that she hadn't found the power to resist him.

Mortified, Erin could only stare up at Dare and what she saw in his eyes made her wince. Was it scorn or disgust that registered there? Either way Erin knew she was lower than dirt in his eyes.

"Why should I believe you," he grated, "when you all but threw yourself into my arms? Twice. Why would you have done that if you didn't know who I was?"

"I don't need to explain myself," she said with far more bravado than she felt. "You wouldn't believe me, anyway."

"Try me."

She opened her mouth to object but then she breathed a sigh. What was the use? She might as well lay all her cards on the table and then he could do what he wished. "The first time I was just going to ask you out...as a dare, to satisfy my friends. I slipped and that was when I grabbed on to you."

"You weren't trying to kiss me?'

"Absolutely not."

"It sure looked like it."

"Well, I wasn't," she said, glaring at him. He didn't have to look so pleased with the idea. "And the second time, in the bar, it was pure coincidence that I bumped into you. I was trying to get away from a most annoying man and saw you as my means of escape."

"Oh, so that's all I was to you."

"That's all."

"And the third time?"

"What third time?"

"Your going out on the date with me, then to the villa. What's your excuse for that one?"

"I..." She swallowed. She had no idea how to explain that one away. Finally, she said, "You were the one who invited me."

For a long time he stared at her then he spoke, his look enigmatic. "So it was." He nodded slowly. "So it was."

Now what did that mean? Did he believe her or was she still nothing more than a groupie in his eyes?

Well, groupie or not, Dare was here in her apartment, thousands of miles from his resort and his island, and she needed to know why. He'd certainly not come all this way out of love for her.

She was loath to broach the subject but since he seemed intent on skirting around the real reason for his visit Erin decided to take the plunge. She'd always faced her problems head on and she wasn't going to stop now, even if it meant facing off with the lion in her apartment.

"Dare, I've asked you twice and you've not given me an answer. Why are you here?" She lifted her chin and looked him squarely in the eyes. "Is it because of the baby? You want to state your claim?"

Erin never saw someone's expression change so fast. His frown disappeared. In his eyes was a look of shock that was like a slap to her face. He hadn't known. Dare had not had any inkling that she was expecting his child.

"Baby? Are you...pregnant?"

Erin bit her lip and dropped her eyes. Goodness, she'd said quite enough already. Oh, Lord. She'd let the proverbial cat out of the bag and now she would have to face the consequences.

"Erin, are you pregnant?" This time his voice was stern but the shock was replaced by a calm that almost seemed more dangerous. "Tell me."

She swallowed but still she could not speak. Neither could she look in his eyes. She did not want to see the condemnation there. This was her baby, and no matter what she would not feel shame for carrying this life inside of her.

In the end, she just nodded.

He expelled his breath. "And the baby is mine?"

Erin's eyes flew to his and her mouth fell open in shocked anger. "Of course it's yours. What? Do you think

I make it a habit of going around sleeping with different men?"

"How should I know?" His retort was quick and brutal. "You fell into bed with me easily enough."

"Do you know what? Just leave my apartment. Get out before I call the police. I don't need to stand here taking your insults." She marched over to the door and flung it open. "Leave. Now."

Dare gave her a lethal look then strode toward her. As she stepped back he gripped the door and slammed it shut.

Erin gasped. Who did he think he was? "What are you doing? You'd better go."

"Listen to me," he said through clenched teeth, "you can't drop that bombshell and then expect me to walk away simply because you tell me to. I need to know. Are you expecting my child?"

"Yes, Dare, I'm expecting your child as I think you already know." She practically spat the words at him. "But never fear. I don't expect a thing from you. I've already made arrangements for the baby so don't feel you have to contribute anything. And," her voice rose and she pointed an accusing finger at him, "if you came all this way to try to convince me to get rid of my child you can just turn around and go right back to Santa Marta because it's not going to happen."

"Get rid of...what the hell?" Dare raised his hand and she flinched but he simply raked his fingers through his hand. There was a look of confusion on his face. "I don't understand. I used protection every time."

Seeing his bewildered state Erin softened just a little. "They're not one hundred percent guaranteed. You should know that."

"Yeah, I do, but I thought they'd have been good enough for one night." He shook his head. "And you're not on the pill?"

"No."

"But what are the odds..." he began then his voice trailed off and his eyes took on a faraway look as if he was trying to remember something. Then a look of realization crossed his face. "It must have been that third time. When you left and I rolled over there was some dampness on the bed but I didn't think anything of it. The condom must have broken."

"But you would have seen that."

"If it was a small tear, probably not. I don't sit there inspecting the damn things. Once I'm done I just get rid of them."

For a moment there was silence as they both fell into deep thought. Erin had no idea what was going through Dare's mind but her dilemma was coming to terms with the fact that he hadn't known about the baby and yet he was here. What was the explanation for that? Dared she ask?

She sucked in a deep breath. She had to know. Steeling herself against his anger she blurted, "So if you didn't come about the baby why are you here?"

"What?" Dare looked like she'd just pulled him out of a trance.

"Why are you here, Dare? Why did you come looking for me?"

His eyes honed in on hers and for the first time since she'd met him he seemed at a loss for words.

Then his face darkened in a scowl. "I came to take you back to Santa Marta."

CHAPTER SIX

"To take me back?" she spluttered, a look of incredulity on her face. "Are you mad?"

"I'm quite sane, I can assure you," he said, the pace of his heart returning to normal. The girl had turned the tables on him and given him the shock of his life.

"But...why?"

Dare almost felt sorry for her, she looked so confused. He knew he must be driving her round the bend but how could he help that? He couldn't explain it even to himself. One day he'd seen her then spent the following night making sweet love to her and, like the fish in the sea, he was hooked. The funny thing was it seemed Erin hadn't even realized she'd caught the biggest fish in the pond.

"Why, Dare? You threw me out of your bed, remember? Out of your life. So what's this story about coming back to get me?" She threw her hands up in apparent frustration. "For what? Another one night stand?"

She was glaring at him now, her chest heaving with the intensity of her emotions. And who could blame her?

He'd done everything she'd accused him of, and more. Little did she know that he'd seduced her expertly and deliberately into going back to his villa and making love to him. He'd wanted to make her pay for pursuing him so shamelessly. He'd wanted to take what she was offering. And now he would pay the steepest price. His days of philandering were over. He was about to become a father.

He still could not believe it. Dare DeSouza, family man. When he'd left Santa Marta he'd had no idea that the joke would be on him.

But in the end it could all turn out in his favor. Obsessed with the memory of Erin he'd finally given in and come to see her with the intention of convincing her to return to the island. Now, with this development, there was no way she could say no.

"Erin, calm down. Have a seat." He walked over and pulled out a chair. When she hesitated he frowned. "Come and sit before you keel over."

Thankfully, she headed over on shaky legs and sank down on the chair. If she hadn't he would have gone over and lifted her off her feet. He could see that her emotions coupled with her tiredness from work were beginning to take its toll. She was shaking.

He walked into the kitchen and filled a glass with water then brought it to her.

She gulped it thirstily then rested the glass on the table and looked up at him.

It was only then, in the light cast by the chandelier above the table, that he saw how thin and drawn she was. Her eyes were large molten pools in her face. They were circled with shadows of exhaustion.

He pulled the other chair forward and sat beside her. "Erin," he said, drawing her eyes back to his face, "you look terrible."

She looked surprised at his outspokenness then her face broke into a tired smile. "Thanks. You are so kind."

"I mean it," he said, his voice low and grave. "You need to stop this work you're doing. It's too much."

At that she laughed but there was no mirth to the sound. "Stop this work, he says. And then eat what? Air? And how would I pay my rent and my bills?"

"I have the solution for that," he said. "I want you to-"

"Oh yes, come back to Santa Marta," she said, her tone sarcastic. "You forgot. When you came here you expected to take a slender, sexy thing back with you. I'm not any of that. Not anymore."

"Erin," Dare said, trying to keep his voice calm, "listen to me. I want you-"

"No, you don't," she snapped. "Not anymore. Not when I'm going to look like a pumpkin in three-"

Dare had reached his limit. "Woman, will you be quiet and let me speak?" he bellowed. "I want you to marry me."

Erin recoiled as if he'd slapped her. Then her face flushed red and her eyes flashed. "I don't appreciate you laughing at me, Dare. If this is all a joke to you I think you'd better leave."

"It's not a joke," he said quietly. "I'm serious. I want you as my wife."

"But...why?" Her voice was a mere whisper and she looked back at him with huge eyes.

"I would think that's quite obvious. You're the mother of my child."

"Not yet, I'm not."

"Oh, but you are. The youngest of the DeSouza line is now growing inside you."

"DeSouza." She said the name, a look of wonder on her face. "Can you believe I never even knew your last name?" Her cheeks grew red and she dropped her eyes as if in shame.

"There's no need to feel bad, Erin. Just forget the past and look toward the future as my wife."

"As your wife." She repeated the words but there was no enthusiasm there. Then she looked over at him. "You never even asked me the question."

"Of course I did."

"No, you said you want me to marry you. You never asked me." Her mouth was set in a cute pout.

Dare laughed. If a question was what she wanted then a question she would get. He would not be accused of not being romantic.

Just to make it more touching and more likely to be in keeping with her romantic notions Dare slid off the chair and went down on one knee. He took her slim hand in his then looked deep into her eyes. "Erin Samuels," he said, his voice firm and full of meaning, "will you marry me?" Then he lifted her hand to his lips and kissed the back of it.

For a moment she only stared at him then her hazel eyes flashed and she snatched her hand from his grasp. "No," she said, her voice vehement and hard. "Never in a million years."

What the hell? Taken aback, Dare remained on his knees. Then, never taking his eyes off her flushed face he rose to his feet. Only then did he speak. "What the blazes was that all about?"

She lifted her face and gave him a look of defiance. "I said I'd never marry you."

"Then why did you make me ask you?" He could feel the anger rise in him. Did she think she was playing with a damn puppy?

"I wanted you to ask me so I could give you my answer," she said, her tone smug. "And the answer is no."

"Why?"

She gave a toss of her head and one of her brown curls fell across her face. She lifted a delicate hand and brushed it away. "You rejected me so now it's my turn to reject you."

"Oh, being petty are we? So you would reject my offer knowing that you can't support yourself and the child. You would do this just to prove a point."

"I can support my baby and me." She had the audacity to look offended. "We don't need you."

He folded his arms across his chest and glared down at her. "If you think I'm going to let you raise my child in this dump you're out of your mind."

"Dump? You're calling my home a dump?"

"Forgive me. Your humble abode." His voice dripped with sarcasm. "My child will not be living here nor

316

growing up here. My child will be with me in Santa Marta."

She gave a harsh laugh. "I want to see how you're going to accomplish that when I'm not going anywhere."

"You are."

"I'm not."

Dare could feel his nostrils flare in annoyance. Not a good sign. Erin was intent on pushing him to breaking point. He was going to end this before things went too far.

"Now you listen to me. You will come back to Santa Marta with me and you will marry me. If you don't then be prepared to be cut off from the child altogether."

"What do you mean, cut off from the child? You can't do that." Her voice had risen and he heard the fear registered there.

He pressed home his advantage. "Oh, can't I? There's something to be said about having money, Erin. With money comes power. I have a lot of it and you don't."

Erin stared up at him, eyes wide and uncertain. He could see that she was vulnerable now.

"I can hire the best lawyers to present a case that it would be in the best interest of the child to be with me. I can provide everything that he or she would need unlike you who can barely manage to sustain yourself."

She was pale now, and silent. His words were having the impact he'd intended. He decided to drive another nail into the coffin. "There's a good chance you'll lose custody, Erin. Do you want to take that risk?"

"You...wouldn't." Her voice was a broken whisper.

"I would." He would not yield. Not now. He was too close to victory. "Marry me, Erin, and all your problems will be solved. You won't have to worry about money, the care of the baby, anything. But if you choose the other path, know that I will do everything in my power to claim my heir."

For a long time Erin did not respond. Then her lower lip began to tremble and she turned her face away. "You're such a bastard," she said with a sob and covered her face with her hands.

Dare said nothing. He might be a bastard but he was a bastard determined to get what he wanted. He'd come all this way to get Erin Samuels and he was not going home without her.

He could see she was defeated. He softened his stance and went over to take her in his arms, comfort her and let her see she was in good hands.

As soon as his hand touched her shoulder she wrenched away and when she looked up at him her eyes spat fire. "Don't touch me," she said through clenched teeth. "I may have to marry you but I will never be your wife."

Dare sucked in his breath and scowled. So that was the way it was, was it? A marriage in name only.

Well, he'd already won the first battle. She would marry him. Once he got her back to the island he would take on this second hurdle. He was looking forward to the challenge. He smiled to himself. There were ways to make a woman yield and he was an expert at every one of them.

"Get some rest," he said calmly. "I'll be back in the morning to work out the details. Let your boss know you won't be coming back."

He didn't bother to wait for a reply. He knew she was numb from shock and exhaustion. He let himself out of the apartment and headed for the elevator where he gave a satisfied sigh. Erin Samuels was his at last.

***

Within a week of Dare's arrival Erin was in a private jet on the way back to the island of Santa Marta but this

318

time as the wife of one of the richest and most powerful men in that land. So why wasn't she over the moon with joy?

Instead, she felt sick inside. Had she sold her soul to this devil, Dare DeSouza? He'd given her an ultimatum and she'd cracked under the pressure, scared out of her mind that he would follow through on his threat. He could be a ruthless man. She had no doubt about that and she wasn't taking any chances where her child was concerned.

A limousine met them at the airport and they traveled in silence, Erin flipping through a magazine or at least pretending to, and Dare engrossed in whatever it was he was reading on his iPad.

About twenty minutes into their journey the limousine turned off the main road and drove through the stately gates of what looked like a resort. As Erin glanced up she frowned. This was not how she remembered the entrance to Sunsational Resort. She sat up and looked out the window. They were traveling up a palm-lined driveway that climbed a gentle hill and then the limousine turned and there she saw on the crest of the hill a majestic mansion that made her eyes widen. Huge palms graced its courtyard and framed the gleaming ivory walls and red and gold flowers were sprinkled amongst the rich green leaves that formed a soft carpet along its base. It had the look of an opulent tropical paradise.

Was this Dare's home? Erin stole a quick glance at him and saw that he was watching her with hooded eyes. She turned away again. If he'd hoped to impress her he'd certainly done that, and more. She couldn't imagine living in a place like this. The resort had been luxury enough.

The chauffeur slowed the car to a halt then came around to hold the door open for them. As he helped her out of the car Erin continued to stare, admittedly overwhelmed by the grandeur before her.

Then Dare was by her side. He took her hand in his and led her up the steps and into his lavish home. As they passed the threshold they heard the sound of hurried footsteps then a tiny woman with her hair pulled into a bun entered the foyer.

"Welcome, welcome Mrs. DeSouza. We've been expecting you." Her eyes crinkled in a smile so bright Erin had to respond with a smile of her own. The woman had called her Mrs. DeSouza. It had sounded strange to her ears but that was who she was now - the mistress of the house. Sort of. She had to remind herself not to get carried away. Dare had brought her here under duress. This was anything but a fairy-tale marriage.

"Erin, this is Francine Lopez," Dare said with a warm smile that was both surprising and refreshing. It was obvious that he had genuine regard for the woman. "She's my right hand."

"Oh, Senor Dare, you are too kind." The woman smiled back at him then she turned her full attention to Erin. "I am the housekeeper. I have run this house for Senor Dare for the past four years but now that you are here, senora, you will give the orders."

That brought a smile to Erin's face. "I don't think so," she said with a little laugh.

"Oh, yes." The housekeeper nodded emphatically. "The woman, she is in charge of the house. The man, he knows nothing about the house, only about making money."

"Hey," Dare objected with an exaggerated frown. "Are you saying all these years I thought I was in charge I really wasn't?"

"That is so, Senor Dare. That is why you have me."

There was a twinkle in Francine's eyes that bore testament to the comfort she felt with her employer.

Apparently Dare had a pleasant side, one that he reserved for a select few.

"Now come, let me take you upstairs to your suite. You must be tired after your journey." The housekeeper waved her hand and ushered her toward a wide, winding staircase.

Her suite? From the look of the house Erin could just imagine what that looked like. Could she survive more luxury in one day? But she had to admit, she'd loved the sound of the word, not because of the affluence it denoted but because it sounded like she'd be far removed from Dare DeSouza. Of course, he would have a suite of his own.

She glanced back at him and saw that he was still standing there, his gray eyes unreadable as he watched her climb the staircase. She hastened to turn her attention back to Francine and her friendly chatter.

She was now in the lion's den. And she would best be prepared to face what was to come. She would seek refuge in this suite of hers and there she would rest up and then plot her next course of action. At the top of the list would be strategies to stay out of Dare's way. Little did he know it but the man, dastardly though he was, still held a place in her heart. And that, more than anything, made him the most dangerous of foes.

***

Erin was grateful to find that the trials of her pregnancy seemed to be behind her. There were no more bouts of morning sickness, no dizzy spells, and her appetite had returned with a vengeance. She'd been on the island five days now and she and Francine had developed an automatic friendship that surprised her.

She learned that Francine Lopez was in her fifties, the mother of three grown sons who had all left the island for jobs in North America. One was an engineer working in Alaska for a major oil company, another was a professor at a community college in New Jersey, and the third had opened a business in Florida, a chain of dollar-concept stores. They all had families of their own and were doing well and Francine could not have been more proud.

Francine did admit, though, that at times she got lonely and wished that even one of them had remained on the island so that she could have her grandchildren around her. Visits to the United States a few times per year were just not enough. She was glad to have gotten this job with Senor DeSouza because she now came to see him almost as her own son. But she had been hinting - subtly, of course, because he was still her employer and it was not her place - that he might want to consider settling down and starting a family. Secretly she'd harbored the dream of seeing the house full of little ones. What a joy that would be. And now, as she'd told Erin, he had finally made the big step and brought home a wife. Now the house would be filled with the laughter of children.

Erin only smiled at Francine words. If only she knew how close she was to her dream. Well, she would know soon enough. A pregnancy was not something you could hide for long.

Today again, Erin was enjoying Francine's company as she sat at the wrought iron table on the cobbled patio that looked out onto a kidney-shaped pool.

"You used sunscreen today, yes?" The older woman's face showed a hint of concern. "The sun, it is very strong today and your skin looks delicate. You must protect yourself."

Erin chuckled. "Si, mama," she teased and rolled her eyes cheekily. She was having fun with Francine's over protectiveness. The housekeeper was like a fussy mother hen, always making sure she was comfortable and always admonishing her to take care. Erin could only imagine how this mothering would escalate once she learned her condition.

Francine looked as pleased as a kitty with a saucer of milk when she heard Erin's reply. Maybe it was some consolation to her that she now had someone to fuss over.

And Erin did not mind one bit. In fact, Francine was now like the mother she no longer had. She remembered when the older lady asked about her family back in Canada.

"I don't have any," she replied and her breath caught in her throat. It had been nine years but the memory of the tragedy was still raw and painful.

"No family?" Francine asked, her tone incredulous. "How is that?"

"I am...was an only child. My parents were both killed in a car accident when I was twelve."

Francine gasped then her face softened in sympathy. "Oh, nina, how terrible."

"Yes," Erin said with a sigh. "It was hard. It still is. But you deal with what life gives you. What else can you do?"

"And how did you survive without your parents?"

"Foster care." She kept her voice neutral, trying to keep the bitterness from her tone. For her, the experiences had not been pleasant.

"I ended up moving from family to family, each one worse than the one before." She smiled at Francine through misty eyes. "I was relieved when I turned eighteen and could move out and live on my own terms."

"Ah, nina," Francine crooned, "life can be very cruel. *Gracias a dios*, you are here now and you are safe with Senor Dare."

Erin almost laughed at that. Safe with Dare? She doubted it.

So far he had left her to her own devices which was exactly what she wanted. Apparently there'd been some developments with his business which were keeping him busy. Whatever it was, she hoped it would continue for a long time. She could do without his attention. She'd told him she'd wanted the marriage to be in name only and she meant it.

Her ringing cell phone broke into her thoughts. "Excuse me." She hopped up and dashed into the sunroom where she'd left the phone. It was unusual for her cell phone to ring. Since leaving college she hadn't maintained contact with any of her former college mates. She was wondering who it could be when she picked it up and peered at the screen. Robyn O'Riley. Erin's heart sank. If Robyn was calling it could not be good.

She clicked on the answer button and put the phone to her ear. "Hello."

"Erin, you naughty girl, how could you do this to me?" Robyn's words were teasing but her tone gave her away. She was annoyed.

"Do what?" Erin rolled her eyes. Robyn was famous for putting on an act. She was always the wounded woman.

"Don't play with me," Robyn said, the pretense falling and her voice harsh. "You went and got married and didn't even tell me."

Erin stiffened. How in the world had Robyn found out? She had told absolutely no-one.

"You made me have to read about it in the tabloids. How could you?"

The tabloids? Erin's heart sank. So much for keeping all of this a secret. And why hadn't she thought about the possibility of something like that happening?

Dare was a rich man and an eligible bachelor. The paparazzi must have jumped at the chance to break the news of his change in status. Somehow, though, because his business was all the way in Santa Marta she hadn't expected the publicity.

"I almost missed it," Robyn was saying, her tone growing increasingly irritated. "It was a small feature tucked in the corner of the second page. If I hadn't caught sight of it I would never have known. You weren't going to tell me, were you?"

"I…" Erin bit her lip. She hated to lie. It was the truth. She'd had absolutely no intention of telling Robyn anything.

"Still keeping secrets, Erin?" Robyn's voice was low and threatening. Her true nature was showing through. "You know I'm the last person you should keep a secret from."

Erin remained silent. The last thing she wanted was get on Robyn's wrong side. She knew too much and was more than ready to use her knowledge to her own advantage.

"Why didn't you tell me the guy you'd been seeing over spring break was the owner of the resort?" she demanded.

"I had no idea-"

"Do you expect me to believe that? You knew who he was and that was why you spent the night." Robyn's voice was hard with accusation.

Erin knew exactly what her problem was. Robyn should have been the one to snap up the most eligible bachelor on the island, not some poor church mouse of a girl like her. Robyn's parents had money. Not within Dare's range by any means, but she was used to enjoying the trappings of wealth and would have loved the chance to secure an even more prosperous future through marriage with a man like Dare.

It was no use arguing with her, not when her mind was all made up. The best thing would be for this conversation to end without Robyn's feathers being ruffled even more than they already were. Erin decided to change the subject. "How are your parents?"

"Dad's fine." Robyn's response was curt. For some reason, Robyn didn't mention her mother. She was probably on one of her long trips to South America.

"I'm glad to hear your dad's well." Erin didn't have a whole lot more to say to Robyn after that. After all, what would she have to say to the girl who had tormented her for the five months she'd spent in her home under foster care? "I'm glad to hear it."

Mr. and Mrs. O'Riley had been distant but kind, providing more than adequately for her needs while she was under their roof. The first time she met them, when she'd been the insecure age of seventeen, she'd immediately recognized them as people of high social standing. For the life of her she could not figure out why they'd chosen to get involved with foster care. It was not until she'd been there a month that Erin found out that the year before they'd done a tour with a missionary group and had felt obligated to do their part in the community. And so they'd taken her in.

Little did they know that they had a devil among them. Of their three children Robyn was the oldest and bossiest. What made it worse, she was deceitful. Things had started out manageable even though Robyn seemed to think that with the new arrival she'd suddenly acquired a personal servant. Not wanting to put her position in jeopardy, Erin acquiesced most of the time and with each 'favor' she did for Robyn the girl mellowed to her.

Then came the night when, overcome with loneliness and depression, Erin crept into the bathroom to weep in private. That was where Robyn found her, curled up on the bathroom floor, her face buried in a thick bathrobe in an attempt to stifle her sobs.

In that moment of weakness she had shared her secret with Robyn. That was a big mistake. Thereafter the girl used that knowledge to her advantage.

And now she was doing it again. Erin had no idea what Robyn was up to but it could not be good. It never was.

"I'm coming back to Santa Marta. To visit you."

"Excuse me?"

"I want to come for a visit," Robyn said, even more emphatically this time. "We haven't spoken in a while. We need to do some catching up."

The only catching up Robyn wanted to do was to get to know the billionaire ex-bachelor Erin had 'stolen' from under her nose. That was exactly what she was thinking. Erin had no doubt about that.

But Robyn knew too much. And if she felt it would serve her purpose she'd be all too ready to spill those precious beans.

Erin had to think fast. How could she keep Robyn from coming to the island?

"I'm not sure this is a good time."

"Baloney. Now is a great time. I've got to come see you before you get bogged down with marriage. Now let's see…" There was the sound of paper flipping and then Robyn spoke again. "I'm free all of next week. I'll come in on Sunday. I'll e-mail you my flight information so you can pick me up at the airport."

"Robyn, I don't think you should book any flights just yet." Erin's voice was firm. "I need to discuss this with Dare. What if he's not ready for visitors?"

"Nonsense. A girl needs to have her friends around her especially at this sensitive time when she's adjusting to a new life. I have no doubt that you can convince him of that." There was hardness in her tone and Erin knew immediately. Robyn was issuing a not-so-subtle threat.

So that was how it was. Either give in to Robyn's 'self-invitation' or risk the negative repercussions.

She could not take that risk.

Erin sighed. "Okay, I'll speak to him tonight but please don't book any flights till I get back to you."

After Erin hung up she sat for a moment deep in thought. This was not good. She did not like either one of her options. If she tried to keep Robyn away the girl would stir up trouble for sure. And if she came to the island and, even worse, came to stay at the house, Robyn would find some way to make her life miserable. That was Robyn.

Erin drew a deep breath then stood up. She would talk to Dare and then she would start planning. She would have to keep Robyn as busy as possible so she would have no opportunity to be alone with Dare. There was no telling what Robyn would let slip. Erin could see it already. The coming week was going to be a nightmare.

CHAPTER SEVEN

"I don't like it, Dare." Roger's voice was grave. "I don't like it one bit."

At those words Dare's sense of foreboding mushroomed into dread. Roger had been his accountant for over ten years and even when he'd undertaken the riskiest business deals not once had the man expressed such doubt.

But this time was different.

"How bad is it?" Dare almost didn't want to ask but he had to know. He'd never been one to back away from his problems.

"This is your biggest investment so far."

Dare nodded. "Over two hundred and fifty million."

Roger pursed his lips. "I hate to say this, Dare, but it may also be your worst."

The statement was almost a physical blow to Dare. He shoved his chair back and got up. He began to pace the room. Then he stopped and looked over at Roger who was still staring at him, his face morose.

"I don't understand," Dare said with a shake of his head. "Bart told me this was the best deal yet. He's never been wrong before."

"Even so, you should have sent in the experts to check out the property."

"We did. Bart and I discussed it and he made all the arrangements."

"Did he?" Roger's voice was quiet but the look he gave Dare was pointed.

For a moment Dare stared back at him in silence then he raked his fingers through his hair. "I think he did," he said with a heavy sigh. "I hope to God he did."

Roger shook his head. "Couldn't have. Any of the experts could have told you the structures are faulty and irreparable. Any of them could have prevented this. That's what they're there for-"

"All right, I get the point." Dare shoved his hands into his pockets. "I screwed up."

Roger said nothing. He dropped his eyes to peer at the figures on the paper in his hand. Then he looked up. "Did you even see the place?"

"Of course I did. I wouldn't have bought it sight unseen."

"And you didn't see anything to indicate the place was a wreck?"

Dare shrugged. "It looked fine to me. Nothing that some paint wouldn't have put right. Of course, I was relying on professional feedback and that is what I thought I got with those reports."

Roger sighed. "When were you planning on opening this resort?"

"Seeing that all the buildings were in place I was aiming for a Christmas launch. The agency has already started working on the advertising campaign."

"Call it off," Roger said bluntly. "Unless some kind of miracle happens there's no way you'll be ready for a Christmas launch. That's just six months away and the way things look you're going to have to knock down half of those villas and rebuild. A strong gust of wind would knock the damn things off their foundation."

Dare nodded slowly but his mind was miles away. He was thinking about the one man he'd thought he could trust with his life. He'd known Bart Reynolds since college when they'd been roommates and they'd both pursued degrees in engineering. Even while still studying they'd dreamed big dreams and immediately upon graduation they had executed all they'd discussed throughout their junior and senior years. Together they'd found phenomenal success and made a place for themselves among the wealthiest people in the world.

Bart had been there with him every step of the way. So what the hell happened?

Dare raised his head and looked Roger in the eyes. "I'm going to get to the bottom of this and when I do somebody is going to pay."

***

Dare didn't get home till about ten o'clock that night. Even though she was dying to slide into her bed Erin stayed up until she heard the low purr of his car coming up the driveway.

As she heard the front door open she got up from the sofa and pulled the robe tightly around her then tied the sash. She was not cold. She'd deliberately dressed in long pajamas so she was covered from neck to ankles. Feet, if you counted the fuzzy slippers she was wearing. She was making it absolutely clear that she was making no advances.

The door slammed and she heard Dare's footsteps as he began to walk across the foyer and toward his suite. She hurried to catch him before he disappeared.

"Dare," she said, her voice echoing in the dimly lit hallway. He froze then slowly turned to look at her. He'd slipped his jacket off his shoulders and was holding it loosely in one hand. He was in white shirt-sleeves rolled back from his wrists and his tie hung loose around his neck. His face was hidden in shadows so there was no way to determine his expression.

Still, she assumed he was tired so she spoke in a gentle, unassuming voice. "May I talk to you for a minute?"

She was totally unprepared for his response.

"What now?" He snarled then stepped into the light.

And that was when she saw his face - dark and frowning and strained. He'd obviously had a rough day.

"I'm sorry," she said quickly. "It looks like this is a bad time."

He looked annoyed. "You already stopped me so go ahead."

"No, it's fine," she insisted. "It can wait until tomorrow."

"Spill it, Erin. I don't have time for games. You wanted to talk, so talk."

She took a small step back, shocked at his vehemence. What had she done to deserve his anger? And what right did he have to speak to her like that?

"No," she said, her tone firm. "I will not have any discussion with you if that's the attitude you're going to take. We will have this talk tomorrow." Did he feel he was the only one who could have an attitude? He would learn soon enough that she could be just as stubborn as he.

Dare sucked in his breath then let it out in a sigh that told of a world of troubles. "Listen, I'm sorry I barked at you. It's been a long day." He threw his jacket onto a nearby table. "Let's go to the kitchen. I need a drink."

He led the way, his long strides eating up the yards to the kitchen. She padded along behind, discreetly admiring the curve of his muscled shoulders, his narrow waist and a butt that looked delicious in his tailored trousers.

The look of him brought back memories of that night so many months ago, that precious night when she had felt like liquid velvet in his arms. She'd had no power to resist him. And - most horrifying of all - she'd fancied herself to be falling in love with him. She shook her head, clearing that idea fast. If she knew what was good for her she'd get her mind back to earth. The man did not want her. That was clear.

In the kitchen Dare poured himself a drink while Erin pulled out a chair and sat down. He put the glass to his lips and drained it in one gulp then he took a deep breath and walked over to drop his long frame in the chair across from Erin. He cocked an eyebrow. "So what's the problem?"

"I didn't say there was a problem," Erin said and gave him a smile to soften her words. She could see the exhaustion on his face and despite her resolve to feel nothing her heart went out to him. Billionaires could have problems, too. She didn't want to add to those worries so she decided to just state her situation in a matter-of-fact way and let Dare know he would not need to be involved in any way.

"My friend, Robyn, called today and she'd love to come to visit me. We haven't seen each other in a while. We'll be busy catching up on old times so we won't get in your way." Erin threw it all out there, watching him intently the whole time, trying to gauge his reaction.

Dare shrugged then stifled a yawn. "It doesn't matter to me just as long as you don't expect me to be here to do entertaining. Now isn't the time."

"Not at all," Erin said, relieved he had no objections. One less thing to worry about. "You won't even know we're here."

"I doubt that," he said with a crooked smile. Then his eyes settled on her and for the first time that night she felt that he was really seeing her. All week he'd been distant, almost like a visitor in his own home, leaving early and coming in hours after the sun had set. Now, though, he was here in the flesh and all of his attention was on her.

"How are you feeling, Erin?"

"I'm fine," she said, feeling her face redden. It was a reasonable question so why did it make her nervous?

He was silent for a moment, his eyes never leaving hers. Then he reached across the table and took her hand in his.

She jumped. His touch was so unexpected. Surreptitiously, she sucked in some air in an effort to slow her racing pulse. She was dying to pull her hands back but she didn't.

"Are you?" he asked, and the words were more seduction than question. Even as his fingers formed a band of steel around her wrist his thumb was doing a slow, sensual caress in the middle of her palm.

Erin dropped her gaze, trying to hide the effect he was having on her. She struggled to breathe normally but when his thumb left her palm to stroke the throbbing pulse point at her wrist her breath caught in her throat. And she grew moist. Her body was ready and willing even if she wasn't.

"I haven't been treating you very well, have I?" His voice soft and low, he was watching her with hooded eyes. "My brand new wife, home and all alone."

"I wasn't alone. I had Francine," she said, her voice strained, and she tried to pull her hand away. He did not let go.

"Francine," he said with a low chuckle. "Can Francine make your pulse race like it's doing now? Can she steal your breath away like this?"

Before Erin could decipher his cryptic message, Dare was on his feet pulling her into his arms. He dipped his head and captured her mouth with his and kissed her until she swayed and leaned into him. She had no choice. The man had caught her off guard, infiltrated her ranks before she'd had a chance to shore up her defenses. All her well-made plans, all her schemes to resist him were dashed with one fell kiss.

Dare lifted his head and stared into her eyes, his fingers moving quickly. He was untying her sash and loosening the buttons of her top.

Erin gripped his wrist, trying to still his hands. She had to regain her sanity. "Dare, no. We can't-" She gasped, unable to say more.

Dare had sat back down on the chair, leaving her standing, and now he had her nipple between his teeth.

Oh, Lord, how was she going to resist? He was sucking on her nipple now, and her hands that had tried to restrain him fell away, leaving him to do as he pleased. When his heated palms slid up her back, her body shuddered with the feel of his caress and she moaned. Of their own volition her hands went up to cup Dare's head and pull him into her, the better to savor his sweet seduction.

Finally, Dare released her but only long enough to push her pajama top and robe off her shoulders and pull her onto his lap. If she'd had any doubts about the state of his arousal they were dismissed immediately. The hardness that pressed up through the cotton fabric of her pajama bottom was testament to the depth of his desire.

Now totally bare from the waist up, Erin felt a wave of embarrassment wash over her and she turned to bury her face in Dare's neck. She turned her body toward him, clinging to his shirt, trying to hide herself from his gaze.

Her body had changed and her heart faltered as she wondered how he would react. Her breasts had grown fuller, riper and so much more sensitive. The slightest touch sent thrills coursing through her body. But her waist had thickened and she could no longer close the button on her jeans. How would he see her now?

Her face still hidden, Erin could feel Dare's hands roaming over her body. She was not seeing, just feeling - the warmth of his body against hers, his big hands cupping her breasts, his fingers teasing her nipples - and the sensations were so intense that she moaned.

"You're so beautiful."

Dare's hoarse whisper was like a song to her heart and she sighed and relaxed in his arms.

"Come," he said then lifted her into his arms and stood. "It's time I had a real taste of my lovely wife."

At his words Erin's eyes widened and she laid a hand on his chest. "Dare, no. You promised."

He was heading out of the kitchen now, carrying her as if she were nothing but a small child. "Promised what?"

"This marriage. It's in name only," she said as she began to wriggle in his arms. She wanted him to put her down. How firm and businesslike could she be when he was holding her so close she could hear his heart beating in her ear? No, she needed to be on solid footing to have this conversation.

"In name only." He gave a harsh laugh. "You've got to be kidding." He kept on walking, totally ignoring her struggle to get down.

"Put me down." Erin spoke through clenched teeth and gave him a punch on the arm. He didn't even flinch. "I'm not going anywhere with you."

That brought another laugh from Dare. "You seem to be coming along quite nicely."

"Dare, if you don't put me down this instant I'm going to scream and you're not going to like it."

"Go ahead. Scream all you want. Francine is all the way in the far wing of the house and she sleeps like a log."

By this time they were in a part of the house to which Erin had never ventured. They were approaching Dare's suite. She had to do everything in her power to stay out of his room. Once inside, she would be lost. She had to make him stop.

"Dare DeSouza if you don't put me down I'm going to scream bloody murder." She was determined that she would not cross his threshold. He'd rejected her once. She would never, ever give him the opportunity to do it again. She drew for the one thing she knew was guaranteed to make him stop. "Are you so desperate you're resorting to rape?"

If she'd shot him in the chest with a bullet it could not have halted him faster. Dare came to a sudden stop and, his face black as midnight, he stared down at her. "What the hell did you just say?"

Erin dropped her eyes and bit her lower lip. She didn't need to repeat herself. He'd heard her loud and clear. And her plan had worked.

Dare slid his arm from beneath her legs and lowered her to the ground. Once he'd set her on her feet he stepped back and his look was dark with displeasure.

"I want you, Erin. Make no mistake about that. But I'll be damned if I'll be accused of rape." He folded his arms across his chest. "I may want you but I will never force myself on you." His gray eyes turned cold. "Next time, you'll have to be the one to make the first move. I won't lay a finger on you unless you come to me. Begging."

With that, he turned on his heels and walked away, leaving her standing there, her arms still wrapped around her chest.

She'd made her point and he'd gotten the message. Mission accomplished. So why did she feel like her life had just ended?

Slowly she turned and walked back to the kitchen. As she dressed an unexpected tear slid down her cheek.

With a sniff she wiped it away with the back of her hand, disgusted with herself for this display of weakness.

If she was going to survive under Dare DeSouza's roof she'd better develop a backbone.

And if she was going to survive a week with Robyn she'd better return to all she'd learned about suppressing her emotions.

Between Dare and Robyn she was going to have a heck of a time controlling those emotions. Under no circumstances could she afford to crumble in front of either one of them. She would have to call on all her reserves to survive the week. God help her.

CHAPTER EIGHT

After a near sleepless night Dare headed out early the next morning. He'd scheduled a meeting with a private investigator and he was anxious to get an update on the findings.

When the man was ushered into his office at eight thirty that morning he was standing by the desk, ready for the news. He practically paced a trail into the carpet, waiting for him.

They shook hands then he offered Paul Ogilvie a seat. The big man's frame swallowed up the chair.

He began without preamble. "I'm afraid it's not good news, Mr. Desouza."

Dare's lips tightened but he nodded. He'd been hoping for the best, that he'd find some way to redeem his long-time friend and absolve him from any wrongdoing, but it was not to be.

"Bart Reynolds had a serious conflict of interest in this deal." The blond giant leaned over and dropped a large brown envelope in the center of Dare's desk. "It's all there. He was a primary shareholder in that property with full knowledge of its dilapidated state. You did him a favor in taking it off his hands."

The news almost floored Dare. So that was why Bart had pushed him so hard on this deal, giving him all kinds of assurances. The bastard.

Then he thought of something. "Wait a minute. You said the buildings were dilapidated but I didn't see any evidence of that."

"Bart took you on that tour of the property, right?"

Dare nodded.

"Just as I thought." Ogilvie's face was grim. "He deliberately took you to the sections that had been spruced up for your visit. Half of those structures are hollow shells, eaten out by wood termites. He wouldn't have taken you to those."

Dare puffed out his cheeks and blew out his breath. So that was it. He'd put all his trust in Bart and had been taken for a hell of a ride. If he couldn't trust a friend of over ten years who in the world could he trust? "So where is he now?"

"Last information we got he'd left the island for the south of France with a former model on his arm. He set himself up for a pretty sweet life."

"And this is?" Dare jerked his head toward the envelope.

"Photos, bank records, papers showing his connection to the property." The P.I. shrugged. "Nothing I haven't already told you. They're just for your records."

There was nothing more to be said. Nothing more to be done. He probably didn't even have the option of suing. He'd signed in good faith and now he was paying a high price for his trust.

"Thank you for your help."

As Dare held out his hand Paul Ogilvie stood and shook it. "Any time, Mr. DeSouza. If you need any more checks done you know where to find me."

Dare nodded and gave a grunt of acknowledgement. That was as much as he could manage.

Right now his mind was consumed with the issue at hand - how in the blazes to recoup two hundred and fifty million dollars.

***

Erin tapped her rolled-up magazine against her leg as she waited for Robyn to exit the customs and immigration department. The days had flown by much too fast and

340

Sunday had arrived, bold and bright, the day her nemesis would appear. When the flight arrived crowds of people came through the doors, people waving to family members who had come to pick them up and professionals decked out in business wear. This went on for almost an hour and still there was no sign of Robyn. And there was no answer from her cell phone.

Finally, when Erin had paced the airport lobby for the umpteenth time, she heard a squeal.

"Darling. There you are."

She turned to see a bundle of red rushing through the double doors followed by a porter pushing a trolley with bags that looked like they had enough clothes for a year-long stay.

Within seconds Robyn was upon her, kissing her on both cheeks. "You're looking so good," the redhead said with a laugh. "And you've put on weight. Married life agrees with you."

Erin stepped back and adjusted her loose jacket so that it fell away from her body. Robyn didn't know she was pregnant but she would, soon enough. But now was not the time. She'd let the girl gloat, thinking she'd simply grown plump from lack of exercise. She pasted a smile on her lips and looked Robyn up and down, from the red beret on her head to her red suit and matching shoes. She looked almost European in her elegant pencil skirt. She must be going through one of her European phases. At times she considered things European to be en vogue and so she dressed the part and even adopted their accents and expressions.

"You look beautiful, as usual," she told Robyn and watched her face light up even more. She never tired of receiving compliments.

"Thank you," she said and looked around. "So where's that husband of yours?"

"Aah, he's very busy at the moment. Our chauffeur will take us home." As she spoke she dug into her purse for her cell phone. She'd have to call for the car to come around.

Robyn's mouth set in a pout she probably thought was cute. "Aaw, I was looking forward to meeting him."

"You will," Erin said. "Soon." That was what she told Robyn but, in truth, she wished to delay that meeting as long as possible. Robyn was a notorious man stealer and the fact that this was a married man was little consolation. Everyone was fair game on her playing field.

Within minutes the chauffeur was loading the bags, five in all, into the trunk and then they were off, the serpent and the little mouse eyeing each other. Erin almost laughed as the image flashed through her mind. Would there ever come a day when she didn't feel intimidated by Robyn?

That night, and much to Erin's relief, Dare did not make an appearance before bedtime. Robyn's disappointment was palpable. The girl's true colors began to show through her façade when she snapped at Francine during the evening meal.

"Why does she keep hovering around?" she complained as Francine came in to check on them for the third time. "It's so annoying."

"Francine's a lovely woman," Erin said in defense. "She's just a little overprotective, that's all. She's the motherly type."

"Well, she'd better not try to bother me. She's only the hired help, after all." This was followed by a toss of her head.

Erin didn't think Robyn had to worry about more mothering. Francine had been just about to enter the room when she was stopped by Robyn's outburst. The older woman's face fell and she disappeared back down the hallway. Erin could only hope she didn't think she shared Robyn's opinion.

When she finally bid Robyn goodnight and closed the door to the guest quarters she could only sigh in exhaustion and relief. One night down, five more to go.

Another day passed without incident, with Erin taking Robyn shopping at the boutiques scattered around the town's center, and having her walking from store to store until she was beat. By the time they got home Robyn crashed, totally exhausted.

By the third day, though, the visitor was determined that her trip to the island would not be in vain. At least that was how it seemed to Erin. Robyn got up with the rising of the sun and knocked on her door. Not waiting for an answer, she popped her head around the door.

"Wake up, sleepy head," she said, her smile falsely bright and cheerful. "Let's have an early breakfast."

Erin looked at her through eyes still blurry from sleep. "Francine isn't up yet," she said in an attempt to protest.

"Who needs Francine? We'll make our own breakfast."

Erin was not fooled. Robyn hadn't suddenly developed a love for the fresh early morning air. No, her goal was to meet Dare. This time there would be no way to keep them apart.

As per Robyn's plan, both women were sitting at the breakfast table when Dare walked in looking breathtakingly handsome in dark business suit and maroon-colored tie.

"Good morning, ladies." He walked over to Erin and leaned down to give her a peck on the cheek. He smelled of an ocean-breeze aftershave lotion. "How are you today?" He gave her a loving look.

Erin almost laughed. She'd had no idea he was such a good actor. "Just fine, honey," she said, her voice sugary-sweet. Two could play that game. She smiled and looked across at Robyn whose face sported a bright and very false smile. "Dare, I would like you to meet my friend, Robyn."

Dare gave a chivalrous bow and took Robyn's proffered hand. He bent his head and kissed the back of it and she gave a girlish giggle.

Erin almost rolled her eyes. Please.

Dare released her hand then gave her an apologetic look. "You've been here two days and I'm just getting the chance to meet you. My apologies. My work has kept me very busy these last few days."

"Oh, not at all," Robyn said with a wave of her hand. "I know how it is. You have to make the money, right?" She gave a tinkly laugh. "But I hope you'll be here for dinner this evening. After all, you can't work all the time." She cocked her head in her classic Robyn pose, the one where she added a slightly pouty mouth that men thought was cute.

Dare gave a slight nod. "I'll do my best to fulfill my duties as your host."

That got a smile of celebration from Robyn. "I look forward to getting know you." The way she said the words, so low and seductive, left no room for doubt as to her meaning.

Erin felt a slow heat rising from her belly but Dare seemed to take things in stride.

"I'm sorry I won't be able to join you for breakfast." He was reaching for an apple as he spoke. "I'll just munch this on the way. Enjoy your day." With that he was gone, leaving the women alone in the room.

"What was that all about?" Erin hissed.

"What?" Robyn's face was all innocence.

"You know what. You were flirting with Dare. He's supposed to be my husband, remember?"

"Supposed to be?" Robyn lifted an eyebrow. "Sounds to me like you're not sure. Maybe you're in over your head?"

Erin frowned. "What's that supposed to mean?"

"It means, what's a girl like you doing with a man like him? You're not even in the same class."

So there it was. The gloves were off now. No need for pretenses anymore. The fight was out in the open.

"You don't know anything about money," Robyn continued, the veil gone from her face now contorted with spite. "You're out of your league here."

Erin felt her heart tighten. It was true. She was like an alien in this world of riches. But still, Robyn had no right. "He's my husband," she said finally, her voice strong and defiant. "No matter what you may think, he's mine and I'm part of his world."

"We'll see about that." Robyn sat back in her chair, her expression smug.

"Meaning?"

"Meaning we'll just see how long your husband keeps you here once he finds out about the real you."

Erin gasped. "You wouldn't."

"Try me," Robyn smirked.

"You would break up a marriage just to soothe your ego?"

"I just want Dare to know exactly who he married. That's only fair."

Erin took a deep breath. The nightmare had begun and it was far worse than she'd expected. She knew Robyn had not come to the island to be supportive. She'd even expected a little flirtation, but this? To threaten to reveal a secret she'd shared in confidence, a secret that could jeopardize her marriage?

She decided to use her wild card. Her face calm, she looked Robyn in the eyes. "You would break up a marriage even though I'm expecting Dare's child?"

That did the trick. Robyn stared at her, her face frozen in shock. "You're pregnant?"

In answer Erin got up and unbuttoned the loose jacket she'd been using to hide her condition. The bump in her belly was now obvious through the cotton fabric of her blouse.

"My God." Robyn looked at her belly and her face grew red. "How could I have missed that?"

The tension was suddenly too much for Erin. She walked over to the counter as a sudden wave of nausea washed over her. She sucked in a deep breath, willing her churning stomach to settle. She couldn't afford to show weakness. Not now.

She had her head down when she heard Robyn's voice again. It seemed to be coming from far away. "Now I see what happened. You devious little witch. You knew exactly what you were doing, didn't you?"

The venom in the woman's voice was like a knife thrust into Erin's belly. Why did Robyn hate her so much? With shaking hands she reached up and took a glass from the cupboard then filled it from the tap. She took a few sips then drew in her breath and turned around. Now she was ready.

"Robyn, I don't know what I was thinking when I allowed you to come here. Obviously it was a big mistake. I want you to leave." Erin made her voice strong and bold even though she felt almost ready to pass out.

"You...want me to leave?" Robyn spluttered. "You're throwing me out?"

"Yes," Erin said, her voice surprisingly calm. "You came here knowing that you held the handle while I was holding the blade. You planned to use that against me, make me submit to your desires, even if it meant flirting with my husband. Even stealing him. It's not going to happen."

Robyn pushed her chair back, making a long scraping sound on the marble tiles. "Oh, so we're tough now, are we? Don't care about our reputation anymore? One word from me and this doll's house can come tumbling down around your ears."

The nausea was coming back. Beads of perspiration popped out on Erin's brow and again she had to turn away. She couldn't take this, not now, not in her condition. "Robyn," she whispered as she struggled to keep her breakfast down, "please leave."

As Robyn stormed out of the room Erin held on to the counter then made her way back to the table where she sank gratefully into the chair. She sat there for a while gulping in air then she gathered just enough strength to get up and grab a can of ginger ale from the fridge. It was the only thing guaranteed to dispel her nausea.

It took a whole ten minutes for Erin to return to normal. Still, she did not move. She sat there thinking. And thinking.

What was she going to do now? She'd just upset - no, angered - the one person in the world with the power to create a mess of her life. Well, the one person outside of Dare DeSouza. She had created a real enemy.

She clenched her fists in her lap. Whatever Robyn chose to do she would have to deal with it even if it meant that she ended up on the street. But there was no way she would continue to live under that witch's control.

Her mind made up, Erin got up and went to find the chauffeur. Robyn would need the ride back to the airport.

CHAPTER NINE

Dare sank into the seat of the town car and, eyes closed, rested his head against the back. It had been another rough day. They hadn't had any luck in locating Bart Reynolds in Europe. What was the use, anyway? The contract he'd signed was airtight. Two hundred and fifty million. Down the drain, just like that. It was a lot of money to lose.

Dare knew he would recover from this loss. He always did. If there was one thing he knew it was how to fail and keep on coming back. Wasn't that the common factor linking all successful entrepreneurs?

He sighed. Maybe it was a good thing he'd decided to make it an early night. He'd as much as promised Erin's friend that he would have dinner with them and he meant to keep that promise. But God, he was dead tired. He hadn't even bothered to drive himself home. As soon as he called, Carlos had come out to get him. He'd arrived before Dare even had the chance to stuff his papers into his briefcase. Thank God for reliable employees.

Once at home, a brisk shower was all it took to get him back to normal. Dressed in comfortable slacks and a light silk shirt he headed for the dining room where dinner would be served at seven. He was prepared to be pleasant and accommodating, the perfect host. Erin's friend deserved at least that, if even for one evening. He knew Erin would be pleased he'd made the effort.

Erin. As his mind settled on her he shook his head. He could not figure her out. She'd thrown him for a loop when she'd adamantly refused him, even pissing him off by intimating that he would have to force her. He'd never forced himself on a woman in his life and he wasn't planning to start now.

But he would put that incident behind him. Tonight he'd be cool. Tonight it was all about the ladies.

The dining room was softly lit by elegant lamps positioned in the corners. A gold candelabra sat in the center of the table. And there, all alone, sat Erin.

Clearly, she didn't realize that he'd entered the room. Her eyes downcast, she seemed lost in thought. But what made him pause was the slight droop of her shoulders, a posture that spoke of sadness or pain. Even her mouth had lost its feisty pout.

"Erin." He said her name quietly but she jumped and jerked around to stare at him with her liquid amber eyes. Even there, in her eyes, he could see a strain that had not been there before. For some reason a feeling of guilt gripped him. Was he the cause?

"Are you all right?" He walked over and pulled out the chair at the end of the table, the one closest to her. He sat down and was just about to reach out and take her hand when he stopped. An innocent gesture but one she might misconstrue. He wasn't taking any chances.

She gave him a tiny smile and her eyes glittered in the candlelight. Or was that the glitter of tears? Dare could not tell but no matter what he was going through tonight he would be gentle with her. He knew he didn't have exclusive claim to problems. She was probably facing personal challenges of her own. And he could guess that being pregnant was no easy thing.

"I'm fine, Dare," she said, and her voice cracked on his name.

What the deuce had upset her so that she seemed on the verge of tears? "What's wrong, Erin? And where is your friend? Did something happen between the two of you?"

Erin tightened her lips then took a deep breath. "She had to go back to Vancouver earlier than planned. She's all right, though. She's fine."

"It's not her I'm worried about," Dare said, frowning. "I want to know about you. Did she upset you?"

Erin smiled again and shook her head but it was a sad smile and Dare was not fooled.

"Do you want to talk about it?" he asked, watching her intently.

"No, that's okay. Let's just eat." She picked up her napkin and rested it on her lap then looked at him expectantly.

He did the same but he had suddenly lost his appetite. Erin had been upset or hurt by Robyn whatever- her-name-was but obviously she wasn't comfortable talking about it. He would give her some space…for now. But damn if he wasn't going to get some answers. There was a lot about Erin that remained a mystery to him but he was going to get to the bottom of this one sooner rather than later.

They began to dine, in silence at first, and then slowly Erin began to relax in his presence. She popped an olive into her mouth, chewed and then looked over at him. "How did you manage to leave the office early today? You've been so busy with your project I didn't think you'd make it back in time for dinner."

"I promised," he reminded her. "Your friend made me."

At the mention of the recent departee her face clouded over but then it cleared and she was smiling again. "Well, I'm glad you made it."

Dare said nothing but he had to admit he felt good about it, too. Since he'd brought Erin back to the island he'd spent precious little time with her. Hell, they'd hardly exchanged words except for that time he'd tried to carry her off to his bed. And that had ended in disaster.

"And how's it going?" she asked. "Your project, is it almost completed?"

Now it was Dare's turn to look glum. He'd vowed not to even think about the damn thing tonight but now that Erin had brought it up all his anger came flooding back.

"Trust me," he said, "you don't want to know."

"Oh, but I do," she said quickly and reached out to touch his arm.

He dropped his eyes and looked at her hand and it looked so small and defenseless against the muscles of his arm. He was still staring at her hand when she pulled it away and in her eyes was a look of chagrin.

He could see that she was stiffening again and withdrawing into herself. He'd better start talking before she shut him out altogether. "Do you want the short version or the long version?" He said it with a smile, hoping to get her to relax again.

He knew he'd found success when she smiled again and said, "I'm not going anywhere. Let's have the long version."

And so it was that he told her about his two hundred and fifty million dollar dilemma.

"Oh, my God. Dare, you're joking." Her eyes were wide with wonder. "Right?"

He chuckled. "I wish."

"My God," she whispered, her eyes never leaving his face. "I can't even begin to imagine that amount of money. And you lost all that?"

He shrugged. "Pretty much. I still have the property but most of the buildings are only fit to be bulldozed. I guess I'll have to start from scratch with this one."

"Oh, no," she said then she looked back at him with a worried expression. "Does that mean you're bankrupt? Will you lose your house?"

She looked so distressed that Dare burst out laughing. "No need to worry your little head. You won't be put out on the street. I'll still be able to buy you little trinkets."

That got him a glare from Erin. "I'm not worried about me, you idiot. I'm worried about you. I'm used to being poor. You're not."

"So sweet of you, cherie," he said in a teasing tone, hoping to get another rise from her. She was so cute when she was angry. "But I'll be fine. It's a lot of money but it won't make me go broke."

"Wow." The word was filled with awe. "I can't imagine being so rich that I could say words like that."

"Oh, but you are, my dear."

"I'm what?"

"Rich. You're my wife. We didn't sign a prenuptial agreement so you are part owner of the estate." Then he looked at her through narrowed eyes, trying to gauge her reaction. "That's what you wanted, wasn't it?"

For a moment Erin stared at him, a confused look on her face, then as his meaning sank in her face turned red and she shot up from her chair. "Dare DeSouza, you're the one who came looking for me. You're the one who forced me to marry you so don't you accuse me of pursuing you for your money. You've got some nerve-"

"Okay, calm down. I was only joking." He reached out to grasp her wrist and tug gently until she sank back into her chair.

"Your joke was in bad taste."

"Yes, I can see that," he said, trying to look sorry although inside he was grinning. That had certainly put the pink back into her cheeks. He much preferred the passion of her anger to seeing her sad and defeated.

"But seriously," he continued, "do you know the worst part?"

"What? Isn't losing all that money the worst part?"

"No, losing a friend." He hoped she could see that this part was no joke. "I lost someone I've known for years, someone I thought I could trust." He clenched his fists and just stopped short of pounding it on the table. "If you can't rely on someone so close to you, who else can you trust?" He lifted his head and looked at her. "If there's one thing I expect from my friends it's honesty, you know?"

For a second Erin looked nonplussed then she nodded quickly but he could see the blood rising up her neck and to her cheeks. She looked like she wanted to say something but no words came. Instead she carefully placed her napkin beside her empty plate and for the second time that night she stood up. "I'm feeling a bit tired. I think I'll go to bed now."

She didn't even wait for him to reply. She walked away, leaving Dare staring after her in confusion.

Now what had he said to upset her? He shook his head. If he lived a million years he would never understand women.

***

After her dinner with Dare, Erin went back to her old strategy - avoid him as much as possible. That seemed to have been working fine until Robyn came and spoiled everything.

She knew she was being foolish but she still hadn't gotten over the shock of Dare's last statement at the dinner table. It was like he'd been talking about her. The guilt would not let her sit still and she'd had to leave as fast as she could before she broke down and told all.

It was five days since Robyn left the island and she hadn't heard a whisper since then. With each day that passed she breathed a sigh but she could guess that the girl would drop her bombshell at a strategic moment, at that point when it would hurt most. It was only a matter of time.

After a week passed and then two without any word from Robyn, the tension in Erin's belly began to dissipate. The threat still hung over her head but how long could she remain on edge? She willed herself to be calm. She had her baby to think about and she would not let anything - neither high blood pressure nor negative emotions - consume her and jeopardize the health of her unborn child.

She signed up for classes at the local Mommy Yoga Center and fell into a comfortable routine of yoga and birthing classes in the mornings and daily swims in the pool in the cool of the evenings. Eventually she stopped thinking about Robyn and the threat she posed.

With the passing of time Erin grew rounder and rounder until she looked like she had swallowed a basketball. When Dare teased her, calling her his panda bear, Francine came to her defense and laughingly found names for him, too. It didn't help that those names were in Spanish so Erin had no idea what she was talking about. She didn't care, though. It felt good to have another woman on her side. She and Dare fell into a comfortable rhythm that made Erin sometimes forget that her marriage was not quite the norm. From observing them no one would guess that their marriage was in name only.

Their idyllic life on the island hit a snag when it was announced that a hurricane was on the way. At the news Erin became filled with a sense of dread. She tackled Francine in the kitchen.

"What's a hurricane like? Will it destroy the island? Will we be in great danger?" The words shot out in rapid succession, clear evidence of her fright. She was not afraid to admit it. She'd never experienced a hurricane before and she was scared.

She'd heard horror stories of tidal waves taller than ten storey buildings and people getting sucked out to sea. She'd heard of heavy winds flattening houses, people getting electrocuted by downed power lines and people getting sick from contaminated water supplies. Nothing she'd heard about hurricanes was good.

"Ah, nina," Francine sighed, "hurricanes are dangerous but we will survive. And you, in this well built house, you will be safe. I'm happy that you have a strong man to protect you."

"But what about you, Francine? You will stay here with us, right? I want you to be safe." Erin grabbed the older woman's hand. Although Francine spent a lot of time in Dare's house she also had her own home on the island. Erin was worried that she would go back there. She could not explain it but she felt an affinity with Francine that was far more than an employer-employee relationship.

"No, nina. Senor Dare, he arranged for me to go to Atlanta to be with my son. I will leave long before the storm hits."

Erin breathed a sigh of relief. One less person to worry about.

Next day Erin accompanied Francine into the airport where they hugged and shared well wishes. The housekeeper waved goodbye as she stood at the entrance to the international departure lounge and her eyes glistened with tears. Erin, too, felt choked up but she bit her lip and held on. She would not give in to tears. She was not the emotional type and couldn't figure out why tears seemed to come so easily these days. It must be the baby hormones.

Erin spent the rest of the day shopping. Like everyone else she was making sure to have adequate supplies in case the hurricane devastated the island. It was not unheard of that, following a natural disaster such as this, electrical power would be out for weeks. With that in mind she stocked up on flashlights, lanterns and batteries, canned and packaged foods and dozens of cases of drinking water. When the chauffeur bundled her into the car to take her home there was hardly enough room left for her to sit. She didn't mind, though. She'd much rather be over prepared than in need.

That evening when Dare got home he told her he'd arranged for workmen to come in and board up the huge bay windows and French doors. The hurricane winds would easily shatter the panes, sending glass flying. They had to prevent that at all costs. He spoke calmly, almost casually, as if boarding up a house was the most natural thing to do. Meanwhile, Erin was quaking in her shoes.

Dare must have seen her fear because he stepped forward, looking like he was about to take her in his arms. But then he let his hands fall to his sides. Instead, he gave her a gentle smile. "It will be all right. This isn't the first hurricane to hit Santa Marta. We'll pull through just fine."

"But they say this will be the worst one in a decade. And what if we get a tidal wave? We're so close to the ocean." She spoke quietly, her voice steady, but she felt far from it. Her eyes searched his, desperately seeking the reassurance she needed right then. At that moment she would have welcomed his embrace so she could feel the strength and power of his body against hers and revel in the comfort of his arms.

But it was not to be. She'd set her boundary, one he'd vowed never to cross until she made the first move. And she wanted to. Even now as he stood looking down at her she wanted to.

But she could not.

Dare shoved his hands into his pockets and on his face was a look of determination. "We'll beat this, Erin. We just have to prepare the best way we can. I've already taken the necessary precautions at the resort. They're the ones that are close to the ocean, not us. This house is on a hill, remember?"

"You're right," Erin said, frowning. She hadn't thought about the resort at all. "What about the guests? How will they manage?"

"Half of them have already left and a few more will go tomorrow. For the ones who decided to stay we've moved them to the villas farthest from the beach. They'll be on a grade so they should be fine." He gave a sigh. "Thank God for loyal employees. We've got a skeleton staff staying on to serve them. They'll all be paid triple time for staying."

"Because they'll be away from their families?"

"Yes. I want them to know I appreciate the sacrifice they're making." He smiled. "They don't know it yet but I already spoke to the director of finance to factor in an extra bonus for them at the end of the year."

"That's generous of you," she said and her heart warmed to him. He'd been a jerk, no doubt about that, but after seeing this other side of him how could she stay mad?

And how could she stay unaffected by this enticingly sexy man? She'd vowed to keep saying no but with her pregnant hormones raging she seemed to constantly be in a heightened state of arousal. She wanted him so badly she could almost taste it.

But she had to stay strong. For the sake of her heart she could not put herself at risk a second time.

The next day dawned clear and bright. You would never know a hurricane was on the way. It was perfect weather for the workmen to complete their task and within just a few hours they were done.

That evening she and Dare went through their list of supplies, making sure they had everything they needed. At the last minute Dare remembered one critical piece - they hadn't checked the first aid kit. When they found it they realized that all the painkillers had expired and had to be thrown out. Dare made a quick dash to the local drug store, arriving just ten minutes before it closed. After that, with the kit filled with bandages, iodine for cuts and bruises, painkillers, gauze and a splint they were ready.

On the third day Erin and Dare woke to a sky that hung low and gray like an ominous shroud. Everywhere was still. There was no chirping or whistling in the trees this morning. Not a single bird had remained behind. Even the tree frogs seemed to have disappeared. The animals knew what was coming and they, too, had gone to seek shelter from the coming onslaught.

Even the air had stilled. Gone was the usual tropical breeze, the trade winds that would shake the leaves in the trees. It was as if they were in a vacuum-sealed flask.

Then the evening came and with it the first taste of what was to come. The air that had previously been so still now began to stir and within an hour of the first breeze a strong wind began to blow. With each passing hour it grew stronger until by nightfall the force of the wind had the palm trees bending low, practically kissing ground. What had started out as a whistling in the trees had now turned to a deafening howl that was almost human, making the hair on Erin's nape stand on end.

"Come," Dare said and she was grateful when this time he took her hand in his. His strength surged through her and she stepped closer to him.

Dare led her down the hallway and toward his suite and this time she was eager to go. There was a mighty beast outside pummeling the trees and battering the house and she was too frightened to stay alone.

They'd entered the sitting room and Dare was walking over to the table to rest the lantern down when a loud crack rent the air and the lights went out. Erin screamed and reached blindly for Dare.

"It's okay, Erin, it's okay." His voice came to her from across the room and then he was beside her, gathering her trembling body close to his.

"Wh…what was that?"

"Probably a tree uprooted by the wind. It sounded like it crashed into the house." Dare stroked her back as he spoke, soothing her jangling nerves. "I'm guessing it fell on a power line and that's why the lights went out. I'll go check-"

"Oh, no, you won't." Erin clung to him. "You're not leaving me in the dark all by myself."

"You'll be all right. I'll leave you with the lantern and take the flashlight."

"I'm coming with you. I'm not staying here."

"Erin," Dare said with an exasperated sigh, "you're safer here. I don't want you exposed to danger." As he spoke he reached behind his back to pry her fingers open. "I have to go check what's happening at the other end of the house."

He loosened her arms from around his waist and stepped away. Erin almost cried out but she bit down on her bottom lip and swallowed, containing the fright that threatened to creep up from the pit of her stomach. She pulled her robe tighter and went to stand beside Dare who was testing a huge flashlight.

He looked over at her when she came near. "Why don't you lie down for a bit? You have to take it easy, remember? You're in your sixth month now."

"That doesn't mean I'm an invalid," she retorted. "I don't need to lie down."

He reached out and rested a hand on her shoulder. "I want you to. You can have the loveseat or just go into my bedroom. You'll be a lot more comfortable there."

"In the dark? All by myself? I don't think so."

"We've discussed this already, Erin. You'll have the lantern-"

"No, I'm coming with you."

"Jeez." He blew out an exasperated breath. "Talk about stubborn. Okay, come on, but stay behind me at all times. When I open the door any kind of debris can fly in. I don't want you getting hurt."

"And what about you?"

"I can take care of myself."

Erin snorted. He'd spoken like a typical man. And that was why she was making sure to follow him. She'd be there to make sure he didn't do anything rash. He was a man and men did stupid things sometimes, thinking they were strong and brave and therefore near invincible. Well, not this time. She'd be there to save Dare from himself.

And it had absolutely nothing to do with being scared about being left alone with just a lantern as company.

With Dare in the lead Erin padded back down the hallway in her bedroom slippers even as the wind howled outside. The sound had gotten louder now, sounding like a huge freight train rushing by, and Erin's heart pounded harder with each passing minute. When would the assault end? Would the house still be standing when it was over? Would they still be alive?

That didn't even bear thinking about. She shook her head and kept on walking, making sure Dare was just within the reach of her arm.

When they got to the foyer he pulled out a second flashlight, clicked it on and handed it to her.

"I'm going over to the west wing to see what happened. You stay here." With those words he began to turn toward the hallway.

Erin grabbed his arm. "You said I could come with you."

"I know," he said, his face grim. "I changed my mind. There could be broken glass everywhere. The downed power line could have even started a fire. I don't want you anywhere near that." He shook his head. "I should have left you in the suite where you were safe."

"No, you shouldn't," she retorted. "You're not leaving me here so let's go." Before he could object she set off down the hallway, her flashlight on high beam, marching on as if the darkness ahead didn't bother her one bit. She breathed a sigh of relief when, with a grunt of what was probably exasperation, Dare followed her. As they walked Erin could feel a current of wind that flowed stronger and stronger as they went farther into that section of the house.

What she saw when they got to the west wing made her realize the reason for Dare's concern. The huge mango tree that used to stand by the window of Francine's bedroom had toppled over in the wind, smashing through the roof and leaving a gaping hole. The wind rushed through like air blown down a funnel, creating a miniature wind storm inside the room. As the beams from both flashlights lit up the area Erin could see papers, leaves and debris strewn all around and rain streaming in through the damaged roof.

"Jeez, this is bad," Dare murmured and stepped inside to get a better look.

A sudden gust of wind tore a plank from the jagged roof, sending it flying across the room.

"Watch out," Erin yelled.

Dare swiveled round, the light of his flashlight cutting through the air. He never even saw it coming. The plank slammed into Dare's side and smacked him on the head with a crack that echoed around the room. The flashlight was the first to fall. Then, like a hill of flour in a torrent of rain, Dare crumbled and collapsed onto the sodden floor.

"Dare!" Erin screamed but there was no answer. All she could hear was the deafening, diabolical roar of the hurricane winds.

CHAPTER TEN

"Oh, no," Erin cried out and ran to kneel at Dare's side. Her robe was immediately soaked with the water running freely on the floor. She shone the flashlight onto Dare and saw that he had fallen face down on the floor, water only inches from his nose. And he was not moving.

"Oh, God," Erin whispered. "God help me."

Quickly, she propped the flashlight on a pile of cushions nearby then reached for Dare, lifting his face clear of the water. Without hesitation she sat in the water and slid her legs under his head to lay it on her lap. Then, gently but urgently, she patted his face. "Dare, wake up. Please, honey. I need you to get up."

Her desperate pleas fell on deaf ears. Dare had been knocked unconscious.

Erin looked around, her mind racing. They could not stay there with water swirling around them and the shrieking wind threatening to pelt them with more debris. But what could she do? She couldn't possibly lift Dare but she couldn't leave him there either.

Then her eyes flew to the cover on the bed. If she could just roll him onto it then she could drag him out of the room and out of danger. Erin reached for a pillow that had fallen to the floor. Gently, she slid Dare's head from her lap and laid it on the soft support.

Slowly, she pulled her hand away and she almost cried out again. Her hand was smeared with blood. She had to move quickly. Dare was hurt even worse than she'd realized.

Braving the howling winds she half-dashed, half-waded to the bed in the middle of the room. The cover was soaking wet and heavy but she had no choice. She stripped the bed of its cover and dragged it over to where Dare lay. She spread it out on the ground then slowly, gingerly she lifted his head then she heaved and was just barely able to shift his head and torso onto the fabric. His bottom half was easier. When he was stretched out on the cover she propped the flashlight on his chest, angling it so it lit her path. Then she grabbed two handfuls of the cover and pulled. He did not budge. Kicking off her now sodden bedroom slippers she planted her feet on the ground and heaved. And that's when he began to move. Inch by inch she dragged Dare through the door and out into the hallway. Inch by inch she pulled him to safety.

By the time she got him out of the room and at a safe distance away she was panting from the effort. Unable to go further she slid down in a heap beside her prostrate husband.

Drawing up her legs she wrapped her arms around them and dropped her forehead onto her knees. What was she going to do now? Dare needed help but even if she got phone service what ambulance would come running in the middle of a hurricane? But what if he slept himself into a coma? Heavens, what was she to do? She couldn't just sit there all night.

Worn out with worry, a soft sob escaped Erin's lips and then another until she was sobbing in earnest. What made it worse, the harder she tried to stop the faster the tears came. Where had the practical levelheaded Erin gone? Pregnancy had turned her into a mountain of mush and she didn't like it, not one bit. But still she could not stop crying.

"Erin, are you all right?"

The sobs froze in Erin's throat. Her head snapped up and she peered down at Dare who was still stretched out on the cloth but this time his eyes were open. Those wonderful gray eyes were staring back at her.

"Dare," she said, her voice breaking, "you're back."

She scrambled to her knees and reached over to gather him

in her arms. When he flinched she drew back. "I'm sorry. I'll be gentle. I promise."

"It's okay," Dare said in a hoarse whisper. "I'm fine." His eyes roamed the hallway. "How did I get here?"

"I brought you out here," she said gently. "You were about to step into Francine's
  room when a flying board slapped you. It knocked you out cold."

"And you...brought me out here?" He looked around then slowly raised himself on his elbows. "But how?"

Erin shrugged. "I dragged you out. On the blanket."

"You did what?" Dare's eyebrows shot up. He struggled to sit up then swayed and put a hand to the back of his head. "I got clobbered real good," he said with a groan.

"Yes you did, so move slowly. Very slowly." She put out a hand and gently held his chin then turned his head ever so slightly. She shone the flashlight on his head. There was a gash at the back of it but thankfully it was not as bad as she'd expected and the blood had already begun to dry, matting the hair to his scalp. That was good. It would stem the flow.

Erin got up and held out both hands to Dare. "You're soaking wet. We have to get you dry before you fall sick."

"I can get up," he said, ignoring her outstretched hands. He put out a hand and, using the wall as support, slowly and carefully got up from the floor and stood looking down at her.

She could see he was far from steady. Without hesitation she went to stand beside him and pulled his arm across her shoulders. Then step by step they made their way to the safety of Dare's suite. There, Erin stripped him of every article of clothing then helped him into the bathroom where he washed away the grime from his recent repose in the pool of water on the floor.

Erin felt no embarrassment at Dare's nakedness. All such cares were swallowed up in her concern for him. With the dispassion of a nurse she toweled him dry then placed a robe around his shoulders and led him to the bed where she tucked him in.

Dare leaned back into the pillows with a sigh then looked over at her standing by the bed. "Thank you," he said. "You make an excellent nurse." Then he waved his hand toward a huge walk-in closet. "There's another robe hanging on the hook by the door. Why don't you change? You're all wet."

Erin didn't need to be told twice. She'd begun to shiver and she knew it was because of the damp clothes clinging to her body. She got the robe then went back to Dare's bathroom where she shed her garments and took a quick shower. Within a few minutes she was back at Dare's side.

The color had returned to his face and he was looking like his old self again, dark and deliciously sexy as the lantern cast its golden light on his bare chest. He'd pushed the robe away and now lay in the bed, naked from the waist up. And he was watching her. Those gray eyes like molten steel now bored into her, making her blush.

Slowly, suggestively he licked his lips and her nipples tightened in response. She breathed in, her nostrils flaring, and she clenched her hands by her side. What in heaven's name was he doing to her? Even in his wounded state he still had the power to seduce her. Without a word and without a touch he was turning her insides to jelly.

And as the wind wailed its dirge outside Erin knew that at that moment what she wanted most was to be in Dare's arms.

Dare lifted his arms and folded them behind his head, looking very much like an overlord surveying his property.

"What do you want, Erin?" he asked, his voice a bold and confident whisper.

He knew. Heaven help her, he knew how much she wanted him.

"Erin?" As he said her name he cocked an eyebrow, looking very much the rake.

She swallowed. Then she decided to take the plunge. She wanted him. So why should she deny herself?

"I want...you," she said, her voice thick with desire.

"Are you sure?" The look he gave her spoke volumes. She'd rebuffed him before and his look said he wasn't taking any chances.

"I'm sure," she said, her voice a wee bit stronger. Her body was clamoring for him and there was no denying it the release it craved. Not now, when her blood surged with the heat of passion. Certainly not now as the wind swirled outside, making her shiver for want of those muscled arms around her.

"Are you begging?" His eyes, glittering like diamonds in the light, danced with amusement.

She lowered her eyes and bit her bottom lip to keep it from trembling with laughter. Then she lifted her chin and looked him straight in the eyes. "I'm begging," she admitted and she said it without apology.

Dare's lips curled into a smile. He threw back the covers and held out his hands. "Come."

This time when Erin saw Dare's nakedness she felt the heat rush to her face. The Dare she had bathed was very different from the one who now lay bold and bare in front of her, that special part of his anatomy standing straight and proud.

After the trauma that the night had brought she needed him. And so, stifling the caution that would normally keep her in check, she climbed into Dare's bed and into his arms.

This time when they made love it was gentle and sweet. As she lay on her side in front of him he pressed himself against her back and wrapped his arms around her. When he kissed the back of her neck, sending shivers up her spine, she sighed and pushed back against him. When he cupped her breasts, now full and heavy in his hands, she arched her back and moaned until he pinched and rolled the taut nipples with his fingers, making her sweet spot moisten in response.

When he slid inside her, so thick and firm, her body was ready to receive him. Then his hand slid over her belly and down to her center of sensation and he began to stroke so softly like the touch of a feather then faster and faster, until all the colors of the rainbow exploded between her legs and shot like fireworks to every part of her body, making her cry out in release.

And as she reached her peak he pushed deep inside her, one long clean stroke, and then he was emptying his seed deep inside her.

For a long time they lay there, joined as one as they fought to regain control. Then as their harsh breathing died down to the gentle rhythm of satiation Dare gathered her even closer and slid his hand up to stroke the smooth skin of her hip.

And though the wind wailed and the windows rattled, Erin felt if there was one moment in life that defined her heaven, this was it.

But then she remembered. The wind, Francine's room, the plank flying through the air. She gasped and held Dare's wrist, stilling his caress. "Dare, your head. What if I made you worse?"

Dare chuckled into the back of her neck. "By letting me make love to you? You actually did the opposite. I'm cured."

She reached behind and slapped at his bum. "Be serious. You could have a concussion. I don't think making love was a good idea."

"It was an excellent idea," he whispered then kissed her nape, effectively wiping all thought from her mind and leaving her only with the feel of his body and his touch.

Then he turned her to him and dipped his head to confound her even further with a kiss that left her panting.

She lifted her hands and planted them on his chest. "Dare, no. I mean it. No more for tonight. Not in your condition."

He chuckled and leaned back and propped his elbow on the pillow then rested his cheek in his hand. He gave her a boyish grin. "Or in yours." He reached out and rested a big warm hand on her belly. "I hope I didn't disturb little Mr. DeSouza."

"Or Miss," she said, smiling back.

"Or Miss." He stroked her smooth skin then lowered his head to press his ear against her gentle rise. "I wish I could hear it," he said, his voice soft with something akin to wonder.

"Why don't you say something?" she prompted. "The baby can hear, you know."

To her surprise, instead of speaking Dare began to sing, soft and low, his voice a melodic rumble as his lips tickled the skin of her belly. He was singing a lullaby to the baby inside her, a song welcoming the little one into the world.

As the words of the song died away Erin blinked to clear the tears that had gathered in her eyes. It had been so unexpected and so touching. "That was beautiful," she said and raised her hand to stroke Dare's dark curls as he again pressed his ear against her skin. It felt so natural. "I didn't know you could sing."

He lifted his head and chuckled. "I was part of a boy band in college. Bass guitarist and background vocalist."

"Wow," she said with a teasing laugh, "you never cease to amaze me. If you hadn't made it in real estate you would definitely have made it big in the music business."

"Yeah, right." He slid his body up where he could nuzzle her neck. She knew what he wanted and this time she didn't have the heart to stop him. Crack on the head or no, Dare - or more accurately the part of his anatomy now prodding her hip - was ready for another round.

She sighed and stretched languorously then tilted her head up and gave him a peck on the cheek. "Just one more time," she whispered, "but only if you sing me a love song."

"Are you begging?" he said into her ear.

"No, that was an order." She reached up and pulled his head down for a long, searing kiss that would leave him in no doubt as to who was in charge.

CHAPTER ELEVEN

Dare woke to a ray of light streaming in through a crack in the brocade drapes at the window. For the first time in weeks he'd slept through the night. He lifted his head off the pillow to look at his wife as she curled into him. She was still fast asleep and he used the opportunity to explore her body with hands, sliding it over the fullness of her breasts then letting it come to rest in the curve of her waist. She was beautiful in her pregnancy, her skin a delicate rosy hue, her body blooming with his child. What could be lovelier?

If nothing else, the hurricane had accomplished one good thing. Last night they had connected. For the first time since Erin's arrival on the island there had been a harmony between them that he hoped would last. He would do everything in his power to maintain this newfound peace. He'd been a cad but going forward he'd show Erin he could be a loving husband.

Slowly so as not to wake her he slid out of the bed and padded over to the walk-in closet where he grabbed underwear, jeans, a T-shirt and a pair of heavy boots. All kinds of debris would be strewn around after the storm, including broken glass and loose boards with nails sticking out. The last thing he needed was a puncture wound that would send him rushing to the hospital for a tetanus shot.

A quick survey of the grounds revealed that the damage was not as bad as he had expected. Apart from the tree that had fallen onto the west wing of the house everything else was intact. Still, it was going to take a lot of work to clear the mess from the property. He'd have to get a work team on board within the next day or two.

His priority, though, was the resort and the guests who were in his care. A quick call to the resort manager put his mind at ease - all guests present and accounted for and only minor damage to the villas closest to the beach.

He went back to check on Erin and she was up. She'd put on his robe again and it swallowed her up, making her look like a child playing dress up in her parents' clothes.

As soon as she saw him her face lit up and then it clouded over with a look of concern. "How do you feel today?" she asked. She hopped out of the bed and came over to rest a hand on his arm. "Any headaches? Dizziness?"

"I'm fine, nurse," he teased then reached out and pulled her against him. "And how did you rest?"

"Never slept better," she said with a relaxed smile and then her face went pink and he knew she was remembering their lovemaking from the night before.

And she'd soon have a lot more to grow pink about. Tonight he planned to give her even more of the same treatment. But now there was work to do. "You whip up some breakfast while I make some calls and get a work crew organized. It's going to be a busy day."

"Not for you it's not," she said, her eyes flashing. "Your first order of business is to swing by the hospital and have them check out that bump on your head."

"But-"

"Not another word, mister. Go freshen up while I make breakfast. Then it's off to the doctor for you."

Dare could only stare at her in amused surprise. Now where had this bossy spirit come from? There was a lot more to Erin than met the eye.

As much as he wanted to get started on the repairs he realized the wisdom of her words. With a nod and a quick grin he yielded to his new boss and headed off to the bathroom.

Later that morning with the permission of his doctor Dare made his rounds of the resort and ensured that competent staff was on hand to cater to the guests. Then he stopped by his office to make some important phone calls after the storm. He had to connect with his relatives back in Michigan to assure them he was safe and with his insurance company to arrange for an assessment of the damage. It was a good thing he'd included flood insurance and wind damage for all his properties.

When he got back home late that afternoon Erin was nowhere to be found. He called her cell phone.

"There was an announcement on the radio that the shelter got a lot more people than they bargained for. They've run out of blankets so I got Carlos to take me down here to drop some off." There was the sound of static and then her voice came back on the line but weaker than before. "It's really bad, Dare. Lots of damage-" The call dropped, leaving him clutching the phone to his ear.

He tried calling back but only got a busy signal. Obviously the hurricane had not only affected the supply of electricity. It had messed up the phone systems, too.

He just hoped she would hurry back. She was in no condition to be traipsing all over town trying to save the world.

Within an hour Erin was back home looking flushed and eager. "They were so happy for the blankets," she said, beaming. "We should take them some food, too. With all the people who turned up at the shelter I'm sure they'd appreciate it."

"Sure," Dare said, taking her by the shoulder and leading her over to the reclining chair. "But not today. You need to put your feet up and relax. Remember what the doctor said about the swelling in your ankles."

"He said I need exercise, not pampering." But despite her protest she relaxed into the chair and put her feet up, much to his relief.

He could see how much it meant to her to have been able to render assistance. She was obviously a kindhearted soul and he loved her for it.

Dare paused and looked up from where he was kneeling at her feet. Love. Now where had that thought come from? Unbidden, it had popped into his mind, startling him with how easily it had slipped in. Did he love Erin?

If his actions were anything to go by then maybe it was so. Right then he was busy massaging her ankles, helping to stimulate the circulation and prevent swelling. It made him feel...husbandly, if that was a word. But he had to admit, something had changed. He still wanted Erin, that was for sure, but that alone was no longer enough. His feelings for her had blossomed into something far more than just the physical. Now his desire was for an emotional connection.

That evening Dare made his specialty, stir-fried chicken with white rice, and he and Erin sat down to a quiet meal alone. They finished off with a cup of herbal tea for Erin and black coffee for Dare. Then, for the first time since they'd met, he told her about his musical family. He talked about his dad, a country and western singer who had moved to Michigan with his young wife, where they'd performed in nightclubs across the city.

As teenagers Dare and his two brothers often joined their parents on stage. Later, one of his brothers went on to a musical career while the other became a psychiatrist. Dare chose the field of engineering.

"But the entrepreneurial spirit won out, I see." Erin lifted her teacup to him.

Dare nodded. "Never even got the chance to use my engineering degree, but who's complaining?"

They were both having a laugh at that when Dare's cell phone began to buzz. He peered at the screen. "My broker. Calling me now? Weird." He took the call and was on the phone less than two minutes when he hung up. He was all smiles.

"Did you just win the lottery?" Erin asked cheekily. A man like Dare probably never wasted his time or his money on such slim odds.

"Better. That was my insurance broker. He said they'll be going out tomorrow to assess the property damage at that new resort I bought. It's likely they'll cover up to eighty percent of the damage."

"But why not one hundred percent?"

"That would be the ideal but there's that pesky little thing called the deductible they have to take out first." He shrugged. "But the good thing is, Dennis went to look at the place and the bulk of the wind damage was to those villas I was planning to bulldoze anyway. They were too hollow to stand up to the hurricane."

"A blessing in disguise," she murmured.

"You got that right." Then he gave her a naughty look. "To celebrate I'll grant you one wish, anything you want."

"A massage," she said with delight. "I want you to massage me from head to toe. Carrying this weight around is hard on the back and the legs."

He put on a disappointed look. "Nothing else? Just a massage?"

"Yes, Dare," she said, rolling her eyes, "just a massage. We've had enough fun for a while, don't you think?"

He didn't press after that. Erin had been more than generous in that department, considering her condition. He would give her a well-deserved break. He gathered the cups and teapot onto the tray. "Be right back," he said and headed for the kitchen.

Dare had just deposited the tray onto the marble countertop when he heard a yell. It was Erin and she was shouting his name. He jogged back to the sitting room to see what the fuss was about.

What Dare saw made his blood run cold. Erin had collapsed onto the floor. She was clutching her stomach and moaning.

He rushed over to kneel by her side. "What's wrong?"

"Cramps," she gasped, her brow beaded with perspiration. She gritted her teeth and clutched his hand with a strength that rivaled a weight lifter. "I think...I'm going into labor."

"Labor?" he all but shouted. "You're nowhere near due yet."

"Tell that to the baby," she half-laughed half-groaned, then she was clutching his shoulders with both hands, shivering with the pain that shot through her body.

"We're going to the hospital," he said and lifted her into his arms.

"I'm not dressed," she gasped. "My bag. It's not packed."

"Forget all that, Erin. We have to go now." His heart pounded so hard it hurt. What the hell was going on? Erin hadn't even hit her seventh month yet. How could she be having contractions? He placed her in the back seat where she could have more room to stretch out then he jumped into the Jaguar and speed off to the same hospital he'd visited just hours before.

As soon as they rushed into the emergency room Erin was wheeled off to a private room where the doctor on duty did an assessment. That was when they realized that Erin had been spotting.

"What does it mean?" she asked, her eyes wide as she clung to Dare's hand. "Am I going to lose my baby?"

The doctor patted her hand. "We'll run some tests then we'll see what's going on." He waved his hand to a waiting orderly. "Ultrasound department," he said and the man came forward at once to take Erin away in her wheelchair.

Dare was right behind him. "I'm coming, too," he said. There was no way he was going to allow them to take Erin out of his sight. But there was something weighing on his mind, something he just could not shake. As he followed the men he cleared his throat. "Doctor," he said, "if she...exerted herself, could that cause her to lose the baby?"

"These things can happen," the doctor said with a nod. "But what kind of exertion are you speaking of?"

"Exertion of the...sexual kind." Dare could not believe he was feeling embarrassed to speak to the doctor about something as normal as sex between two married people.

"That shouldn't be a problem as long as you're careful," the doctor replied. "Now if she had other kinds of exertion that's a whole different matter. Did she do anything out of the ordinary? Lift anything heavy, perhaps?"

Dare's heart gave a jolt. How could he have forgotten? "Yes," he said as a feeling of guilt washed over him. "Me."

"You?" The doctor looked at him as if he'd gone mad.

"I was knocked unconscious during the hurricane," Dare told him. "She rolled me onto a bedcover and dragged me out of a bedroom and down a hallway."

"Down a..." The look the doctor gave him was one of incredulity. "She didn't."

"I'm sorry to say, she did." Dare's voice was quiet, his thoughts far away. This was his fault. If anything happened to Erin or the baby he would never forgive himself. "And she didn't complain of any pains at the time?"

"No, nothing." Dare shook his head. "We even made love after that."

The doctor let his breath out with a huff and Dare didn't know if it was out of disbelief or disgust. He wouldn't blame him for judging. He was disgusted with himself. What kind of husband was he to put his pregnant wife through all of that?

"She's a strong woman, Mr. DeSouza," the doctor said. "I can see it in her. And we will do all that we can for her and the baby."

All that we can. He hadn't said they'd be fine. He'd given no assurances. That was not what Dare wanted to hear.

When they got to the ultrasound room they wheeled Erin in and Dare went to follow but the doctor put up his hand. "I'm sorry but it's very cramped in here. The technologist needs the limited space to work and I need to be there to see what's going on. Could you wait over there, please?" He pointed to a row of chairs along a nearby wall.

Dare felt like throttling him. It must have shown on his face because the doctor backed away then quickly pushed the door shut. Dare slapped the wall with his open palm. He would have preferred to put his fists through the wall, he was so frustrated. He needed to be there for Erin. He needed to hold her hand, give her his strength, be her support. Suppose she called out for him? And he needed to see what was going on with his baby.

He walked over to the row of chairs but could not sit. Instead, he paced up and down and then stopped in front of the closed door then paced up and down some more. He looked at his watch. He couldn't believe only three minutes had passed. He checked the time on his cell phone, not believing, but yes it was correct. Damn. How long would he have to wait? This waiting was driving him crazy.

He stepped away from the door and paced some more. He was on his sixth trip to the door when it popped open. Erin was back but this time on a stretcher and her eyes were full of tears. Dare went to her and as soon as she saw him the tears began to flow freely.

"The baby is in distress. He can't survive inside me. They have to take him." She began to sob and as she stretched out her hand to him Dare felt powerless. All he could do was take her in his arms and hold her while she cried. A tap on his shoulder jerked him out of his pain. He turned to see the doctor at his side.

"Please. We need to get to the operating room right away. Emergency C-section."

Then before he could do more than plant a kiss on Erin's forehead they were wheeling her away, leaving him standing alone in the middle of the corridor.

Then followed the worst two hours of Dare's life. Other patients were wheeled in to the ultrasound room, other family members came until the chairs lining the walls were filled and still he paced, not caring if he looked like mad man, not giving a damn what they thought of him. He could not rest until he knew his family was safe.

So many thoughts flashed through his mind. What if the doctors had to choose between mother and child? What if he lost one of them? Or both? It didn't bear thinking about. God knew, he would give all his money, every single penny to know that they were both all right.

And if this was what love meant, then he loved them, Godammit. He loved Erin DeSouza and he loved his baby and he was making no apologies for it. He just prayed they'd both make it through so that he could show them how much he loved them.

He was at the point when he felt he would go mad with worry when he saw the doctor in his green scrubs heading down the hallway toward him. He didn't wait for him to get to him. He met him halfway, his eyes searching the doctor's face, trying to read the news that was to come.

"They're…okay?" His voice sounded strained even to his own ears. He could hardly speak. The anxiety was killing him.

The doctor sighed.

Dare almost had a heart attack. Jesus, a doctor sighing. That was not a good sign.

"They're both resting," he said with a small smile.

Dare let his breath out in a whoosh. They were alive. Both of them. That was a start. "Are they okay?" he asked again.

"Mommy is doing well," the doctor said, "but it was a difficult surgery. Baby was in a lot of distress."

Dare glared at the doctor. He was just inches from strangling the man. "What the hell does that mean? Is my baby okay or not?"

"Mr. DeSouza, please," the doctor said, putting up a hand. "There are other people-"

"I don't give a flying fig who else is here. Tell me what's going on with my baby."

"She's been taken to the intensive care unit to be placed in an incubator. She's only two pounds and needs to be placed in a protected environment."

She? Hadn't he heard 'he' somewhere? But it didn't matter either way. He just wanted his baby to be all right.

"Will she survive, doctor?" He kept his voice low, guilty at his previous outburst but still too concerned to worry about an apology.

The doctor pursed his lips. "Her chances are better than fifty percent but I don't want you to get your hopes up, just in case."

Better than fifty percent. It wasn't enough. He wanted to hear that she was perfectly fine, she'd be all right, she'd grow up and graduate from high school and give him all the grief that teenage girls gave their middle aged dads. That was what he wanted to hear. But the doctor was giving him no such assurances so he clung to the only positive word he'd been given. Better. Better than fifty percent. He would hold on to 'better' and make it real.

"Can I see them now?" he asked.

The doctor nodded. "I'll take you to your wife. She's conscious but a bit groggy. You can see the baby afterwards."

Dare nodded and followed him down the hallway. He was taken to a private room where Erin lay in the bed, pale and quiet, her eyes closed. He pulled up a chair beside her and gently touched her arm. Her eyes opened and he could see her trying to focus. "Dare," she said, her voice weak and scratchy, "where's my baby? Is he all right?"

"It's a she, Erin," he said. "We have a daughter. She's in the ICU right now and they're taking good care of her."

"Is she going to be all right?" Erin's eyes searched his face, looking for the same assurance he'd just sought from the doctor.

He took her hand in his and gave it a gentle squeeze. "She's very tiny, Erin. Only two pounds but if she's anything like her mother she'll pull through all right."

"How?" Erin whispered. She looked up at him, her eyes full of distress. "How can she make it?"

"She will," Dare said, his voice firm with conviction. In his heart he knew that his daughter would be all right. They both would. Leaning over he kissed Erin on the forehead. "Just rest for a while. I'm going to check on her." Then he gave her a reassuring smile. "Start thinking of girl names till I get back."

With that Dare left her and headed to the intensive care unit. The nurses there were welcoming but they refused to let him go into the nursery.

"The babies in this section are very delicate," they told him. "Their immune systems aren't developed yet. We have to make it as sterile an environment as possible."

They took him to a wide glass window and it was from there that he got his first view of his daughter, so tiny and pink in her incubator, with a shock of dark brown hair that made him think of her mother. There were strings and tubes leading from her mouth, her nose and her arm and his heart ached at the little one's cold and sterile introduction to the world. He should be able to hold his daughter close right now. She should be lying on the comfort of her mother's breast. But she was all alone and so tiny. How would they even care for her?

But as he stared at her, so small but yet so beautiful in her cocoon of glass, he knew they'd find a way. The baby had done her part by bravely making her way into the world. Now it was time for him and for Erin to play their part.

"You're a fighter, little one," he whispered through the glass, "and we won't let you down."

***

Nearly eight weeks passed before Erin and Dare were allowed to take Soleil Denise DeSouza home from the hospital. By that time she weighed four pounds and had grown another inch. The nurses warned them she was a feisty one, kicking up a windstorm when she was ready to be fed and demanding to be held when it was naptime.

"You have to put your foot down," one of the nurses warned Erin, "or else she'll walk all over you. You need to show her who's in charge."

Erin smiled and thanked the nurse for her advice but when she looked into her daughter's big brown eyes how could she refuse her? She'd already been through so much in her little life that Erin could be excused for spoiling her a little bit, couldn't she?

And Daddy was even worse, jumping up at every cry, checking on the baby every hour of the night. Within a week he'd begun to look so ragged with exhaustion that Erin had to banish him from the nursery for an entire night just so he could get some sleep.

Through it all Francine was a savior. She knew all about babies, having raised three of her own plus a handful of grandkids. She guided Erin every step of the way through the feedings, burpings, bouts of colic and a brief period of jaundice. Finally the whole family settled into a comfortable rhythm - daddy, mommy, baby and adopted grandma - and finally Erin felt that her world was at peace.

Her love for Dare blossomed and she felt she could not love him more than she did right then. Each time she watched him holding Soleil, singing softly to her as she stared up at him with those adorable brown eyes, her heart swelled with pride and she couldn't help smiling. She'd come a long way but so had he. Who would have thought that bad boy billionaire Dare DeSouza could abandon his big shot image to play peek-a-boo and do goo-goo-gaa-gaa speak? She loved it, and in her eyes he was a bigger man for taking the time to amuse his baby.

And on top of all that he'd shown her nothing but love and respect, catering to her every need and going out of his way to make her feel loved. When he wasn't holding Soleil he was holding her, making her feel like the center of his world.

When Dare returned to work after Soleil had completed her second month it took Erin a while to adjust. She'd gotten so used to having him there that she couldn't help missing him. Still, she knew Dare's work was a big part of who he was. He loved what he did and she knew his work made him feel fulfilled. Besides, he had a lot to do on the last resort he'd bought so she needed to give him some space.

One evening as she sat feeding Soleil Dare walked into the sitting room looking handsome as usual in his business wear. He gave her a peck on the cheek then kissed Soleil on the forehead.

"Guess what?" he said as he loosened his tie. "I got a call from your friend. She said she's been trying to reach you on your cell phone but all she keeps getting is your voice mail."

Erin's heart jerked. "My friend?"

"Yes, the one who came to visit. She's been trying to get in touch with you for the longest time. Did you disconnect your cell phone?"

"Ahh, no," she said, which was the truth. But it wasn't the whole truth. The fact was, she'd turned off her cell phone the day Soleil was born and had refused to turn it back on since then. She'd been living in a bubble of her own making. She'd done everything she could to insulate herself from the poison darts that Robyn could throw. But now she could see that her efforts had all been in vain. Robyn was determined to burst her bubble and send her reeling back to reality.

"Did she say what she was calling about?" Erin asked. It took all her effort to keep her face calm and her voice steady.

Dare shook his head. "No, but she left a number where you can reach her." He dug into his pocket and pulled out a slip of paper. He rested it on the table nearby and shifted the vase onto the edge of it to keep it from blowing away. "Give her a call as soon as you can," he said. "It sounds as if it's pretty important."

Erin pursed her lips. She knew exactly what was so important for Robyn. She was intent on ruining her life. But she would not give her the satisfaction of being the one to reveal her secret. She'd run away from her truth long enough and now she was tired of running.

"Dare," she said as she put the baby on her shoulder and gently rubbed her back, "we need to talk."

CHAPTER TWELVE

Dare looked at her, curious. "About what?" he asked. "Something to do with Soleil?" Then he grinned. "Has she been a naughty princess? I know she loves to boss her mommy around."

"No," Erin said, her voice solemn. "It's about me."

Dare frowned. "About you? Is everything all right?"

She shook her head. "No, but let me set the baby down for her nap and then we'll talk." Still rubbing Soleil's back she got up and headed for the nursery.

Dare stood there in the sitting room, confused. Erin had seemed so peaceful when he'd come in but now he could sense her agitation and it bothered him. It had something to do with this Robyn woman, he was sure. Her whole demeanor had changed at the mention of Robyn's name.

He threw off his jacket and dropped on to the sofa to await her return. He didn't have to wait long. Erin approached and her face was serious. Whatever she wanted to talk about was not going to be fun.

She sat in the chair across from him and folded her hands in her lap. She was so beautiful, with her dark hair curling around her face and onto her shoulders, and those hazel eyes that were so expressive. Now, though, they were clouded over with what looked like heartfelt pain. He sat up and reached for her hand but she pulled it back.

"What's going on, Erin? Is something wrong with you?" At her nod his heart jerked inside his chest. "Are you sick?"

She shook her head.

"Then what is it?" he demanded, beginning to lose patience. She had him on pins and needles and was taking her own sweet time in clearing up the mystery. "Just spill it."

She sighed. "All right, I will." She plucked at the fabric of her yellow sundress and then began to twist it with her fingers. Clearly, what she had to say was not easy for her. "I've not been honest with you, Dare. I'm not who you think I am."

His eyes narrowed as he stared at her. "What's that supposed to mean?"

She sucked in a deep breath then let it out slowly. "It means, when I tell you who I really am you'll probably want me out of your life. For good."

That gave him pause. What in the world could Erin have done to let her say something like that? He loved her. Couldn't she see that? There was nothing that could make him want her out of his life.

"Tell me," he said. "Let me be the judge."

She caught her bottom lip between her teeth and for several seconds she worried the lip until finally she opened her mouth to speak. And when she did, her voice was a hoarse whisper. "I know how important honesty is to you," she said. "You said it yourself. You said it was the most important thing to you in a friendship. And that's why I know you'll hate me for this."

"What are you talking about, Erin?"

"My parents died when I was twelve and I grew up in foster care." She'd begun wringing her sundress again. "I was moved from home to home and some of them were…awful." She gave a hiccup up at the last word. She seemed on the verge of tears. "At one of the homes, I had to struggle to survive. I often went without meals. Once, at school, I was so hungry I passed out."

Dare held his breath. He could already guess what she was about to say.

"One day I just cracked. I walked into a supermarket and filled a basket with everything I wanted then I sneaked into the bathroom and filled up my backpack," she whispered then put her fists to her mouth as a sob escaped her lips. "When I came out of the bathroom I tried sneaking out through the back, where the employees worked. I didn't know...I didn't know the alarm would go off. I thought that only worked at the front entrance. I ran. And then...and then they chased me down the alley and onto the main road. I ran and ran but I wasn't fast enough." She dropped her face in her hands and began to cry in earnest. "One of them grabbed me and I couldn't get away. He punched me then he shoved me to the ground. And he kicked me. Many times. And then...the police came."

Dare went over to kneel in front of her then he pulled her into his arms. "Hush, it's okay, honey. It's okay."

"No, it's not okay," she said, wrenching herself out of his arms. "I've lived with the guilt all these years. Before I married you I should have told you but I didn't have the courage. How could I tell you that you were marrying somebody who was charged with a criminal offense?"

"It wasn't your fault, Erin. You were a victim of your circumstances.."

She shook her head violently. "No, it was all my fault. I should never have done that. I...don't know what came over me."

"It's okay, honey. I don't hate you for what you did. We all make mistakes. It was wrong but...understandable under the circumstances." For a long while Dare was silent, just holding Erin, rocking her in his arms. Gradually her trembling ceased and her breathing calmed. Only then did he speak. "Robyn knew about this, didn't she? She used this information against you."

Her head still resting against his shoulder, Erin nodded. "She threatened to tell you everything. I'm guessing that's what today's call was about."

Dare put a finger under Erin's chin and lifted her face to his. "Know this, Erin DeSouza. I love you and there is nothing about you or your past that will make me stop."

Her eyes widened as she stared up at him. "Dare, what are you saying? You've never told me you loved me."

"I know. I was a fool. It was a secret I kept to myself but I'm telling you now. I love you, Erin. You and Soleil are my life. I want you with me forever."

Her face crumpled and he could see she was struggling to hold back the tears . "Do you mean it, Dare? Don't play with me."

"Do I look like I'm joking?" His grip tightened round her. "You're mine and you can keep digging up all the skeletons you want. You'll never scare me off. You're never going to get away from me, Erin. You're trapped with me on this island. I'll hide your passport if I have to."

To his relief that got him his first smile from her. "You won't have to," she said, smiling through her tears. "You have me for life."

And when Dare pulled her close and kissed her she responded with a passion that told him, without a doubt, that every word she said was true.

EPILOGUE

"Thank you so much for coming, Dare." Robyn clasped his hand for a second and her eyes brimmed with tears.

Then she turned to Erin. "And Erin how can I ever thank you?" She took a step forward and wrapped her arms around Erin in a fierce hug. Then she stepped back and dabbed daintily at her eyes with a handkerchief.

"I'm so glad you were able to make it for the funeral. Mom had a special place in her heart for you, Erin. You know that, don't you?" She dabbed at her nose then tucked her hankie into her purse. "That's why I was so distressed when I couldn't reach you. Mom would never have forgiven me." She looked over at Dare. "Did Erin tell you I was always jealous of her?" She gave a little laugh. "Mom was always comparing the two of us. Erin was the angel and I was the devil." She shrugged. "It took me a long time to realize what Mom wanted me to learn from Erin - her strength, her determination." Her eyes took on a faraway look. "During those last days in her battle with cancer we talked...more than we talked all my years growing up in the house. And that's when I began to understand her and how much she wanted the best for me."

She took a deep breath then pasted a brave smile on her lips. "I guess it's time for me to grow up now." She touched Erin on the shoulder then turned and walked across the churchyard to the limousine where the rest of her family waited patiently for her.

After she climbed into the car and they drove off Erin turned to her husband. "Thanks for coming with me," she said.

"I wouldn't have let you come alone," he said with a smile. "Now let's get back to the hotel before Princess Soleil drives poor Francine crazy."

With a chuckle he put his arms around her shoulder and Erin put her arm around his waist knowing that she had the greatest blessing in the world. She was loved.

THE END

DANGEROUS DECEPTION

JUDY ANGELO

The BAD BOY BILLIONAIRES Series
Volume 4

TO CATCH A COMMITTED BACHELOR...

When Dani Swift put on her chauffeur's uniform with her hair tucked under her hat and her face make-up free she looks like a clean-shaven young man. How could she have known her little disguise would lead to a major misunderstanding and even greater deception, one that threatens her heart?

Storm Hunter loves motorcycles and fast cars but now he's got to add one more item to his list of loves - Dani Swift. Bold and independent, she's like no woman he's ever met. But when their little game ends in disaster that's when he knows love can be very dangerous indeed.

CHAPTER ONE

"But Dani…"

"No 'buts'. Just tuck it away for a rainy day." Danielle stuffed the bank notes into her brother's pocket.

"But where'd you get-"

"What did I tell you, Brian?" She shoved him toward the door. "Now go. I'll be right down. I just want to make sure we didn't forget anything."

As Brian exited the door, pulling the large suitcase behind him, Dani turned to look at the boxes still standing in the hallway. She shook her head. She had no idea how all that was going to fit into her Chevy Blazer. She'd warned her brother not to pack too many things but he was taking so much stuff that she almost felt like he was moving out for good and not just leaving Chicago to head out for his first semester at the University of Notre Dame. She went into the living room and then into the kitchen, looking around to see if he had left anything lying about. Finally, she went to his bedroom.

As she opened the door a flood of emotions filled her and she blinked quickly, fighting back the tears. This room had been Brian's haven for the last four years, ever since she had moved them to this apartment when their father died from a heart attack. She had been only eighteen years old but fortunately legally qualified to be Brian's guardian. Her mother succumbed to breast cancer when Brian was only eight and then they lost their dad when he was fourteen. She swore that as long as she had breath he would not lose her, too. He would never be placed in foster care. And she'd kept her promise.

Dani pulled the door closed and went to the living room where she picked up her handbag and slung it over her shoulder. As she went through the door she plastered a brave smile on her face. There was no way she was going to let Brian know how deeply she was affected by his leaving. He was ready to start his new life as a college student and she wanted nothing to distract him. She'd been a mother hen for the last four years but now she would just have to learn to let go.

She took the elevator to the ground floor then went out to the car and hopped into the driver's seat. She turned to her brother. "Ready to go?"

He shrugged. "As ready as I'll ever be."

She reached over and tousled his hair just like she used to do when he was six years old. "Then let's go get 'em, tiger."

******

Dani's first week without Brian was busy, which was a blessing for her. Her new schedule did not allow her the luxury of sitting at home feeling lonely. Each day she rushed home from her teaching job at Applewood Preschool, changed into her uniform for her new night job as chauffeur at Apex Limousine Company, and checked in for work by five o'clock sharp.

She'd been on the job five nights and so far had survived despite some rough spots. Tonight, though, something was different. She'd been summoned to the boss's office and through the glass door she could see Tony Martino, the owner and manager. He was pacing the floor. As she pushed the door open and entered his office he nodded to her.

"We need to talk," he said and jerked his head toward the only chair that did not have papers piled on top of it.

Dani's heart fell. Tony looked none too pleased. What had she done to upset him? She couldn't afford to lose this job, not right now. She'd only been working with the company a week and already had been able to send money to Brian for his books. She was counting on next week's pay to cover the cost of his hockey uniform.

He flopped down in the chair behind his desk then his look softened as he stared at her. "Don't look so worried," he said. "I'm not going to fire you."

Dani let out her breath slowly and cursed herself for having such an expressive face.

"I know you're wondering what this is all about," he said and leaned forward. "I heard about the incident the other night."

She held her breath again, sure she would be reprimanded for literally dumping one of her passengers on his own driveway. The man had been drunk and had tried to grope her as she held the door open to let him out. She'd pushed him off and, unsteady as he was, he'd landed on his behind. Now she was in trouble because of it. She looked back at her boss but remained silent.

Tony's face grew serious. "I heard about the incident through a third party and I'm not pleased. Why didn't you tell me what happened?"

Dani's glance wavered and she looked down at her hands. When she said nothing Tony spoke again, even more sternly. "From the day I interviewed you I could see you were a tough kid but you can't keep things like this a secret. You have to remember that you're a woman and you have to be careful." He leaned back and clasped his hands over his paunch. "And I have to remember that, too. I'm not proud of the fact that I put you in that situation."

Her eyes flew to his face. "But you didn't-"

"Yes, I did." He cut her off. "I should have known better than to give you a random assignment." He steepled his fingers and fixed her with a frown. "From now on you'll be assigned only to reliable customers. I'm going to give you a very important customer of mine. His father was my client for many years and now he uses my services, too." Tony paused as if for effect. "His name is Storm Hunter."

Dani frowned. "*The* Storm Hunter? Of the Hunter's Run clothing line?"

Tony nodded and gave her a satisfied smile. "The one and the same. I've been serving his family for over twenty-three years. I've known Storm since he was a kid." Then his face grew serious. "As I said, he's an important client. The Hunters, they've been good to me. It's not like they need my services that much but they always give me business. That's the kind of people they are."

"I understand and I'll take good care of him," she said, still slightly dazed. Imagine that. She'd be chauffeur to a member of the Hunter family, one of the wealthiest in the Chicago area. They were 'old money' and everyone knew of them. And even with all that money the oldest son, Storm, had branched out of the family's manufacturing business and had started his own clothing line, making himself a billionaire many times over at the ripe old age of twenty-seven.

"And seeing that you've already made some adjustments to your appearance I want you to keep it that way." He gave her a nod of approval. "I can't vouch for all my other customers so I don't necessarily want to broadcast that I have a woman on the team. You don't know who you might attract once that kind of information gets around." He stood up and walked over to check the computer sitting on the desk in the far corner. "Tonight you're going to pick up Mr. Hunter from a party and get him safely home. If he plans to drink he always arranges for us to come get him. You can check the location on your computer in the car."

This was Dani's cue to get going. She stood up and gave her boss a quick nod. "Thank you, sir. I appreciate your looking out for me."

"No problem, Swift. Now just grow some hair on that baby face of yours and look tough." Tony was chuckling as Dani walked out of his office and headed for the garage.

Things had turned out a lot better than she'd thought. There she was, thinking she was about to get fired, and instead she'd been assigned to a man who was probably the limousine company's most prestigious client.

Now if only his tips would be as big as his name, she'd be sweet.

That night Dani arrived on location a whole fifteen minutes before the appointed time. There was no way she would risk being late. And she'd prepared well, too, making sure to pile every last strand of her thick dark hair underneath the rim of the chauffeur's hat. She'd been doing that since the groping incident. She'd ditched the earrings and had left her face devoid of any form of make-up. She'd even practiced her walk, trying to eliminate the feminine sway of her hips and adopt instead the long strides of a man. Thank God she was taller than most of her sex. At five feet seven and a half she could easily pass for a man. Now if only she could grow some hair on her chin. She chuckled at the thought. She was willing to go far but not that far.

At five minutes after ten people started leaving the stately mansion. The cars that rolled out of the driveway included Porsches, Jaguars and a Bentley. Then there were others who chose to depart in limousines. Storm Hunter would be one of them.

Dani recognized him immediately. Over six feet tall and dangerously handsome, he was dressed in a designer suit of midnight black, his dark hair curling deliciously at the collar. He strode down the driveway toward her with an air of supreme confidence that almost took her breath away. He had billionaire stamped all over him.

Realizing she was staring she immediately straightened to her full height and masked her face with a stony expression. The last thing she wanted was for this man to think she was ogling him. Although, if ever there was a man to fit the description of 'eye candy', he was it. But she couldn't be caught staring. She had to remember she was a professional, she was on the job, and on this job she was a man. Sort of.

Storm Hunter was halfway to the car when a tall, willowy blonde ran down the driveway toward him.

"Storm, wait for me," she called in a light, airy voice. "I want to come with you."

For a fraction of a second Storm's brows fell and a look of annoyance passed over his face. Then it went blank and he turned to meet the woman who was now almost upon him. "Lola," he said, his deep voice quiet and cool, "I thought you were heading for home."

"I am," she said with a laugh as she caught his arm and clung to it. "Daddy didn't come for me as he promised so I'm hitching a ride with you." She looked up at him with huge eyes full of adoration then she added the finishing touch when she set her crimson lips in a teasing pout.

Dani almost gagged. Christ, the things some women did to get a man's attention. Then, realizing the direction of her thoughts, she made her face bland. It was not her place to judge or to get involved in the affairs of these people. Best to just focus on doing her job.

"My pleasure," Storm said but his voice was anything but pleasant. He'd spoken with a formality that made it clear that he would have preferred to travel alone.

The woman he'd called Lola didn't seem to notice his reticence. "Thank you so much, darling," she gushed. "Now we can get a chance to talk some more. You know Daddy loves it when we talk." Then she batted her eyes in what she must have thought was an irresistibly seductive manner.

Dani clenched her teeth to keep from uttering a sound. As tempted as she was to give a groan of disgust, that was a luxury she could not afford. But honestly, the woman's simpering was past annoying. She didn't know how Storm Hunter could stand it.

He seemed to be handling it fairly well, though. They'd started walking toward the car and there was a slight smile on his lips, admittedly a somewhat sardonic-looking smile, but a smile nonetheless. The woman slipped a hand into the crook of his arm and he didn't seem to mind. They looked quite comfortable now as they strolled toward her.

But things aren't always as they seem, as Dani soon realized. To her surprise, when the couple got up close she saw the glint of irritation in the man's eyes and then he gave her a knowing look. For that nanosecond Dani's heart froze. Storm Hunter had just exchanged a look with her, a look that said he was pissed and he didn't mind letting her know because she would understand. It was one of those looks shared between men. Except, she wasn't a man.

But he didn't know that.

He was standing right in front of her now. Dani gave a quick nod of greeting, the perfect excuse for her to drop her gaze and break the hold of his stare. "Good evening, Mr. Hunter," she said in a low voice then leaned forward and opened the door of the limousine. Storm helped Lola then he bent his tall frame and climbed in, leaving Dani to close the door behind them. A moment passed before she could move. He'd been so close that the heady fragrance of his cologne filled her nostrils. That, combined with his nearness, had her heart racing like she'd just done a hundred meter sprint. Christ, what in the world was wrong with her?

The man was just a man, after all. True, but this was one handsome piece of man with his thick brows, square jaw and those deep dark eyes that seemed to bore a hole into her soul. He was the first man who'd made her breath catch in her throat. She'd gone through her fair share of romance novels and had read about heroes who stole your breath away but she'd never had that happen to her, had never even believed it. Until now.

She gave her head a quick shake. *Back to reality, Dani. You can't afford to go soft on a guy now. He's the client, remember?* Her emotions again under control, she strode back to the driver's seat and slid behind the wheel. She was calm now, almost able to laugh at herself. And she had a feeling she'd need a sense of humor.

If the last few minutes were anything to go by this was going to be an interesting journey.

CHAPTER TWO

They were less than ten minutes into the journey when Dani heard a tap on the tinted glass separating the driver's cab from the back. As soon as she pressed the button to wind the glass down she heard Lola's petulant voice.

"Chauffeur, don't you have any champagne in this car? I don't like what you have back here. Vodka, gin, they're not my kind of drink."

"You may help yourself to some wine, ma'am," Dani said, never taking her eyes off the road. "We've got white wine and red."

"I don't want any wine," Lola sulked. "I want champagne."

"You've had enough to drink, Lola." Storm's voice was imperious. "You don't need anything but a bed right now."

"Ooh," she purred, "that sounds good."

Dani couldn't decipher Storm's response. It sounded like a cross between a grunt and a snort. She was dying to see the expression on his face. Curiosity got the better of her and she glanced into the rear view mirror. He chose that very moment to look up and their eyes met, his dark brown and mysterious and hers, wide and startled. She dropped her eyes and embarrassment washed over her. Please don't let him keep staring at me. She knew she was probably red as a lobster.

Danielle Swift, keep your eyes on the road and mind your own business. Great advice, except it wasn't so easy to do when you kept hearing whispering behind you, whispers that kept dissolving into girlish giggles and then a gasp. What the heck were they doing back there? *Don't look, Dani, don't look.* She wished she could press the button and put the tinted glass back up. At least she'd be able to block out the sight and sounds. But she knew she couldn't do that. It would be too obvious and besides she couldn't just close the window without their permission. It was not her choice. She was there to serve them, after all.

She breathed a sigh of relief when the giggles died down and she heard the tinkle of liquid being poured into a glass. Apparently Storm had decided to let Lola have a drink, after all. She didn't blame him. At least that would shut her up, which was a great deal more bearable than listening to her irritating giggles the whole time.

The brief silence was broken when Storm spoke. "Make a detour onto Kenilworth Avenue so I can drop Lola off."

Before Dani could respond the woman's voice came out in a wail. "But Storm, I thought we were going to your place."

"No, Lola, *I'm* going to my place." His brusque tone should have been enough to cool any woman's ardor, but apparently not Lola's. Dani heard her shifting on the seat, the fabric of her dress ruffling as if she were sliding closer to her traveling companion.

"Storm, the night's still young and I'm not ready to go home yet. Don't make me go home. Please." She dragged out the last word like a child trying to wheedle a treat from her mother. From her, a grown woman, it sounded desperate.

Dani gritted her teeth. God, she felt like slapping the woman upside the head. All she could think was, *Have some pride, woman. Don't go begging a man for his company.* But again, she had to catch herself. This was absolutely none of her business and she'd better learn to remain unaffected and uninvolved. Just because she'd never be a doormat to any man didn't mean other women didn't enjoy that kind of thing. Although why they would, Dani could never understand.

Storm totally ignored the woman's plea. He gave Dani the address and remained silent even when Lola commenced to sigh heavily and lament how lonely she would be without his company. It was only when she dissolved into soft sobs that he spoke.

"Spare me the dramatics," he said coolly. "I'm tired and I'll be leaving on an early flight tomorrow. You know I have a busy schedule this week so stop acting the victim."

"But I am, I am," she said through her sobs. "You treat me so harshly even though you know I love you. Why do you torture me so much?"

"Save that drivel for somebody who actually believes it," he responded, his tone unapologetic. "You're drunk. Now be quiet and rest your head on my shoulder. I'll wake you when you're home."

"You...you don't hate me do you, Storm?" Lola said, her voice wavering then ending in a hiccup.

He gave a deep, tired-sounding sigh. "I don't hate you, Lola. I just need you to get home safely. Now come."

Dani couldn't resist a glance and this time, thankfully, both her passengers were too preoccupied to look in her direction. She saw Lola curl up close to Storm then he put up a gentle hand and pressed her head to his shoulder. The woman sighed and closed her eyes and seemed to fall asleep in seconds.

Storm's gentleness surprised her. Was this the same man who had been so unmoved just minutes before? She'd thought him a selfish brute and had silently cursed the woman for being so weak. Now, though, his hushed whisper into Lola's ear and his gentle hand supporting her against his shoulder made Dani wonder.

It didn't take long to get to Lola's home. Dani drove up the winding driveway and went around a circular garden to pull up in front of a stately mansion. The place looked and smelled of money. Dani could see that Lola was not a woman to scoff at, which made it all the more bewildering as to why she seemed to have so little self- esteem. Storm Hunter might be rich, sure, but this woman obviously had money dripping out of her pores, too. So why did she act like she had to take anything Storm was dishing out? Okay, so he was cute. Not just cute, breathtakingly handsome with dark, enigmatic looks. But that didn't make him a god on earth, did it?

All Dani knew was that she'd never take that kind of treatment from any man, no matter how rich he was. If that was what it took to satisfy a man, he'd have a heck of a long wait.

She hopped out of the car and went around to open the door for Storm. He rested Lola back against the seat and slid out then without so much as a flex of his muscles he slid his arms under her shoulders and legs and lifted her out like she wasn't the dead weight Dani knew she was in her drunken state.

Storm turned and mounted the steps to the wide porch then reached under her and pressed the doorbell with his thumb. Somebody must have been waiting up cause only seconds passed before the door was flung open and Storm was allowed entrance. He disappeared inside and was gone for a good fifteen minutes, leaving Dani still standing by the limousine, wondering if he'd changed his mind and decided to bed down with Lola.

She'd climbed back into the driver's seat and was just ready to call in and ask permission to leave when she saw him strolling across the porch then down the steps toward the waiting car. Dani rested the cell phone back down and climbed out of the car. She'd better hurry and get the door for His Royal Highness, she thought cheekily, then grinned at her own private joke.

She made it to the door just as Storm stepped up to it and he had to wait for her to grasp the handle and pull it open.

"You seem to be in a good mood," he said dryly then climbed into the limousine.

That was when she realized she still had the silly grin on her face. So much for private jokes. The man must think she'd been hitting the bottle while he'd gone to put Sleeping Beauty to bed. She wiped the smile off her face real fast. The last thing she needed was a report getting back to Tony that he had a weirdo on his staff.

The journey to Storm's place would take another twenty minutes and Dani began to sweat. She'd forgotten to roll up the separating glass while Storm was away and she was dying to do it now but wouldn't that be too obvious? What if he objected? In the meanwhile he had a perfect view of the back of her head and she could feel something tickling the back of her neck. Christ, had a coil of hair slipped out from under her hat and was now hanging down, giving her disguise away? She wanted to put her hand up to check but she couldn't, not while he was watching.

And she could feel him watching. The weight of his eyes was on the back of her neck. He wasn't staring out the window, he wasn't relaxing with his eyes closed. No, he was watching her. She didn't have to glance in any rear view mirror to know that. She could feel it.

Silently, angrily, Dani began to grind her teeth. What did this man find so fascinating about the back of her neck? She wished he would grab a glass of gin and drink himself into oblivion like any normal man would. Then she could drive in peace and not be sweating buckets like a pig in a tanning booth.

She was so deep in her angry thoughts that she jumped when she heard Storm's voice.

"So how long have you been at Tony's? I've never seen you before."

"Uh, only a week or so," she muttered. She had to remember to keep her voice deep and low. She was supposed to be a man, after all.

Although, thinking about it now, it seemed almost silly to be keeping up this pretense. She'd done it to protect herself from weirdos but now that she would have a fairly regular customer in Storm was that still necessary? What if she just told him who she really was?

But then she dismissed the thought as fast as she'd come up with it. Storm Hunter would probably be a regular but he certainly wouldn't be her only customer. And anyway, her boss had told her to keep things secret for her own safety. Better to just leave things as they were.

"So what are you into? Football, baseball, or basketball?"

Don't let him ask me questions about sports. I don't know a darn thing. "Hockey," she blurted out.

"Hockey?" He sounded incredulous. "You're Canadian?"

She gave a little laugh at that but it came out sort of high-pitched and she had to cut it short. "No, but my brother plays hockey. He was recruited for a team at the University of Notre Dame."

"Oh." He sounded unconvinced but Dani was glad that at least, in that, there was no lie.

Another good thing was that Mr. Sports seemed to be out of his element where hockey was concerned. Good. He shouldn't have any questions to ask her about that. Now hopefully he'd just be quiet and let her drive.

"So which teams are you rooting for in hockey?"

Dani groaned. Now why did he have to go and ask a question like that? What did she know about hockey outside of the little she'd picked up from Brian?

She began to pull at straws. "The one Wayne Gretzky's on."

"The one Wayne...hey, isn't he retired?"

Okay, so wrong answer. Time to change the subject, "Nice weather tonight, isn't it? A starry night, too."

"Huh?" Now Storm sounded really confused.

Dani sighed. She wasn't doing such a good job with the male disguise thing. What guy talked about the stars at night? It wasn't exactly the most manly topic of conversation. Thereafter she clamped her mouth shut and, thank God, so did he.

When they finally pulled into the driveway of Storm's palatial home Dani gave a sigh of relief. Freedom at last. She pulled up in front of the mansion and hurried around to get the door.

And just like last time his nearness threw her off. As Storm climbed out of the car he stepped very close to her, so close she wondered if it was deliberate. His invasion of her space made her take an involuntary step backward. She glanced up and, as tall as she was, he stood a good five or six inches taller. And he was staring down at her.

"How old are you, kid?"

"Twenty-two." The question came at her so suddenly she could only blurt out the truth.

"You?" he said with a laugh. "You don't look a day past seventeen. I bet you're still in high school."

She glared up at him. "I am twenty-two and I already finished college. I'm a preschool teacher."

Storm chuckled. "Tell that to your face. It's got a lot of growing up to do. My God, not even fuzz on your chin. You're as smooth as a baby's behind."

That made her step back some more. He was seeing too much. In a minute he'd figure out she wasn't who she seemed.

He was looking at her quizzically now and even though she'd deliberately stepped into the partial shadow his stare was beginning to unnerve her.

"It's weird but there's just something about you..." he began but his voice trailed off. Then he shook his head. "Nah, it's nothing. I must be seeing things." He turned and with the swagger of an uber-confident male he strode away. "Tell Tony I'll need you again next weekend. See you around, kid."

He didn't wait for a response. He took the steps two at a time and then he unlocked the door and was gone, leaving Dani standing there staring after him.

For a moment she just stood there contemplating what he'd just said. Finally, she closed the limo door and walked back around to the driver's seat. As she buckled up then started the engine she shook her head slowly.

She didn't know if seeing him again was such a good idea. All of a sudden the thought made her apprehensive. She was looking forward to it just a little bit too much...and that was really scary.

******

"Time for you to settle down, my boy. You're not getting any younger." Edgar Hunter leaned back in his chair and stared up at his oldest child.

Storm scowled down at his father and shoved his hands deep into his pockets. "Dad, I'm twenty-seven years old. It's not like I'm over the hill. There's plenty of time for that."

The older man nodded. "Yes, you're young but with my heart condition I could check out at anytime. I want to see even one grandkid before I go."

Storm flopped down into the chair across from his father's desk. "You can get grandbabies from Vanessa or Kathy. Why don't you go harass them?"

"Stop talking crap, Storm. You're my only son, the one who'll preserve the Hunter name. It's you I want my grandkids from." Then he shrugged and grinned. "Besides you're the oldest."

Storm could only stare at his father. It was absolutely no use arguing. He'd tried it many times before and the senior Hunter always came back to the same old question - when are you going to settle down?

The problem was, Edgar Hunter had been so busy making money in his younger years he hadn't settled down until he was in his late forties. By the time his first child was born he was already fifty-one. At a time when he should have been looking forward to grandchildren he'd just produced his first offspring. Now that he was in his late seventies he was ever more aware of his mortality. He was determined to see the face of his first grandchild before he left the earth and Storm was the designated deliverer.

"What about Lola?" Edgar asked, his rugged face brightening. "She really likes you. She makes that plain enough. And she's from a good family."

Storm groaned and raked his fingers through his hair. Not the Lola conversation again. He needed to get out of his father's office before the man drove him totally insane. He got up and pulled out his iPhone. "Dad, I've got to go."

"As usual," Edgar snorted. "As soon as we start talking serious business you run off. This is your future we're talking about, Storm. My future. The family's future."

Even as his father raged Storm turned and began walking toward the door.

"You can't keep riding motorcycles across the country and racing cars at the track. You're my only male heir, Storm. Remember that. And you'd better get married and get a child before you try those crazy stunts of yours again." By this time Storm was opening the door, intent on making a hasty exit.

"I'm going to speak to your mother about this. You can't keep refusing-"

"Bye, Dad." Storm pulled the door shut behind him and even as he walked away he could still hear his father ranting about all that he was going to say to his mother.

Storm could only shudder as he headed down the hallway toward the elevator. He knew that strategy well. His father was going to set the bulldog on him. If there was anyone who could wear a person down, it was his mother.

Storm spent the rest of the afternoon at his own office at Hunter's Run headquarters. He was getting ready to launch a new line of fashionable leather jackets for men and women. Italian made, they were of top quality, as were all his product lines. Hunter's Run clothing had a reputation for high style, quality and durability. And they didn't come cheap.

He'd be having a meeting with the advertising agency in two days and he needed to have all the relevant information ready. He was in the middle of working on the briefing when there was a light tap on the door and his executive assistant, Marisol, peeked in.

"You have a special visitor," she said with a bright smile. Marisol only smiled like that when someone from his family came by.

Storm's mood changed immediately. He could guess who was on the other side of the door. His mother.

"Let her in," he said, his voice little more than a grumble. He was not looking forward to the lecture he knew was coming. Why had he stayed in the same city, in the same state, as his parents? He should have moved hundreds of miles away while he'd had the chance. Then they wouldn't be able to just drop in at will. But it was too late now. He'd already bought a home on Earlston Road and he loved it. He wasn't planning to move for a long while.

"Hey, big bro. How're things?" A strawberry-blonde girl bounced into the room, her face all smiles.

"Vanessa," Storm said, and his face broke into a grin. "I thought it was Mom coming to harass me, as usual."

"Only me," she said with a laugh then dropped into the chair across from him. "I've been assigned to do the harassing for today."

"What? Not you, too." Storm frowned at his sister. "I never expected you to turn traitor on me."

She shrugged. "I had no choice. It was either come and pester you or have them bug me all day and night about Buster. It feels good to have the spotlight off me sometimes."

"I can't imagine why," he said dryly. "I mean, with a boyfriend named Buster who seems to have no greater aim in life than to sit around strumming his guitar pretending to be a country and western singer, why wouldn't you want the spotlight on you?"

"For the hundredth time, Buster is not a bum," she shot back.

"I didn't say he was. Those were your words."

"You implied it and that's just as bad." Vanessa was glaring at him now. "When he makes it big in the music business you'll all see."

"Yeah, yeah," Storm said with a wave of his hand. "So what were you instructed to come and harass me about?"

"The usual. Marriage and such stuff. Did Daddy tell you he had a scare the other day?"

Storm frowned at his sister. "What kind of scare?"

"Chest pains, shortness of breath. He thought he was going to die."

Storm felt his heart jerk in his chest. No matter that he was forever arguing with his father, he loved him. The thought that he could have lost him so suddenly filled him with apprehension. "Why didn't anybody call me? What was it?"

"We rushed him to the emergency room but it was just gas." Vanessa gave him a serious look. "We were lucky that time but it could have been worse. Far worse." For a moment she remained silent, just staring at him, the laughter gone from her eyes. "You know what he wants, Storm. You may have to give it to him."

Storm fixed his sister with a sober look of his own. She knew how to jab him right where it would hurt. And this time it did.

"So what's new with Lola these days?" she asked, changing the subject just as abruptly as she'd introduced it. "Are you taking her to the Vanderbilt party on Saturday?"

"No, I'll probably go alone. Or," he said, thinking out loud, "maybe I'll ask Stephanie."

"Why? She's so…unnatural."

"Okay, so she's a bleached blonde. So what? She's still good company."

"I don't know…" Vanessa seemed deep in thought. "Not exactly wife material."

"I'm not looking for a wife," Storm growled. "God, you can get on a man's nerves sometimes."

"That's what sisters are for," she said with a giggle and hopped up from her chair. "Anyway, I have to go. Buster and I are going out tonight."

"And Buster is husband material?" He cocked an eyebrow at her.

"Who said I was looking for a husband? I'm only twenty-three. I've got lots of years before I have to worry about that." She headed for the door then turned to smile at him. "Don't forget what we talked about," she said with a wave of her hand. Then she was gone.

After that Storm totally lost the vibes to concentrate on any advertising campaign. His whole family had ganged up on him. Talk about pressure.

For a long while he sat there at his desk just thinking. He had absolutely no intention of giving in. Like Vanessa he was a long way from being ready to settle down. In the meanwhile, though, he had to do something to get his family, and especially his father, off his back. But what?

With a sigh he got up and grabbed the keys to his custom-made MV motorcycle. He threw on his leather jacket and put on sunglasses. There was only one thing guaranteed to clear his head. He had to go for a ride. He'd hit the road on the back of his motorbike and let off some steam.

******

"Are you being good over there?" Dani chuckled into the phone. "Remember, I'm not there watching over you so I'm depending on you to be responsible."

"Come on, Dani. I'm a grown man. I know what I'm doing." Brian's voice was tinged with amusement. "You can stop being a mother hen now."

"Never will," she retorted. "As long as I'm your big sister you'll have to put up with it. Even when you're married."

Brian groaned then they both laughed.

Ever since he'd gone away to university Dani hadn't let a day pass without speaking to him. She knew she'd have to loosen the reins and let him find his own way but she wasn't ready. Not yet. After being his sole caretaker for the past four years it was hard to let go of her kid brother.

"Thanks for the money you put in my account yesterday," Brian said. "It came just in time for me to pay for my uniform. We have our first game tomorrow."

"Cool. Wish I could be there to watch you cream them."

"Sis, such violence," Brian reprimanded with a laugh.

"That's how I get by in life," she said unapologetically. "You do what you have to do." That had always been Dani's philosophy. She was practical and focused and dealt with life's issues head on.

They chatted for another few minutes then she glanced at her watch. "Listen Brian, I have to go. I've got to be somewhere by five."

"How come you're always running out in the evenings? Do you have another job?" Brian sounded concerned.

"Don't you worry your head about that," she told her brother. "You just focus on getting good grades and being the best hockey player you can be."

"But Dani, I don't-"

"Leave it alone, Brian."

"Okay, but there was one more thing I wanted to tell you."

"Fine, but make it quick." She glanced at her watch again. She could spare him three more minutes.

"I'm getting a part-time job off campus."

"You're what? Why would you want to do that?"

"I heard about a student exchange program and I want to go. I need to get a job to pay the fee. Can you imagine spending a whole year in Europe?" Brian spoke excitedly. "There's this guy who offered me a part-time sales job. I'll start next week."

"No part-time jobs off campus," Dani said in her strongest 'sister in charge' voice. "You're at school to study, not to take on jobs on the side. A few hours of on-campus work is okay but no jobs that will take you away from your studies."

"But the deposit is due next month. I really want to go."

"I'll take care of it," she said with greater confidence than she felt. "Just send me the details."

"Are you sure?"

"I'm sure I don't want you working when you're supposed to be studying. Now you be good. I've got to go."

She hung up the phone and reached for her chauffeur's hat. As she stuffed her thick hair under the crown her mind raced. Another bill for Brian and this one would run in the thousands. Where the heck would she get the money by next month? Every time she thought she finally had things under control something new came along and then she was back in the hole.

There was no time to dwell on that right now, though. She had a pick-up in half an hour and she could not afford to be late. When she got back she'd brainstorm. Her priority - how to make more money. Fast.

CHAPTER THREE

The week flew by too fast for Dani. Maybe it was because her three and four year old charges were particularly rambunctious that week, or maybe it was because Tony had overwhelmed her with pick-ups late into the night. Before she knew it Saturday had come around again and she was on her way to pick up her billionaire, Storm Hunter.

As she drove along the highway her mind went back to her conversation with Brian. It had been four days since they spoke and she was no closer to a money making idea than she'd been then. She couldn't take another job. There were just so many hours in the day and it wasn't like she could go without sleep.

If she couldn't increase her income then she'd have to cut her expenses. She didn't spend much on clothes and even less on entertainment. Who had the time to go out anyway? That only left one thing - housing. As much as she loved her apartment in Hyde Park she'd have to give it up and move to a cheaper place. She grimaced. She was not looking forward to moving farther away from Applewood School. She'd hate having to fight traffic to get to work.

Dani was forced to drag her thoughts back to the present. She was now at the gate of the Vanderbilt residence and would have to identify herself before being allowed onto the estate. She put the car in park, hopped out and went to press the button of the intercom then as the gate swung open she ran back to the car then drove slowly up the driveway. A couple of limos were already ahead of her so she pulled into the parking area alongside them and waited.

And waited.

Dani looked at her watch for what must have been the tenth time then she leaned her head back and groaned. Ten forty-two. She'd been scheduled to pick up Storm Hunter at ten o'clock but he was nowhere in sight. A few more limos had arrived in the last forty-five minutes and they all sat there waiting.

Finally, when it was almost eleven o'clock people began to exit and either head to their cars or their waiting limos. Dani ended up waiting another ten minutes before she spied Storm coming out of the front door, a voluptuous blonde on his arm.

By this time she was not a happy camper. He was almost an hour late which meant she'd end up signing off way past midnight.

As Storm and the woman approached, Dani tried to be professional and put a polite smile on her lips. It didn't work. Her lips stretched across her teeth but it must have looked more like a grimace than a smile. She couldn't help it. She'd never been good at playing the hypocrite.

"Hey, kid. Ready to roll?" Storm was laughing with the woman, probably at some private joke, and he looked like he'd just had the time of his life. Or was just about to.

I've been ready to roll for over an hour, she thought sourly. Still, she didn't give voice to her thought. With a brisk nod she opened the limousine door and held it wide for the smiling couple.

Storm helped the woman inside then just before he got in he looked directly into Dani's eyes. "What's your name? It's getting kind of old to keep calling you kid."

"Dani," she said, averting her eyes from his gaze.

"Danny. Cool. Let's get going then."

He slid in and Dani closed the door with a click.

Let's get going, he said. Not even a word of apology for being late. That was probably one of the perks of being a billionaire - never having to say you're sorry.

For this journey Dani made sure to keep the tinted glass rolled up. She had absolutely no desire to play voyeur or to even hear what her passengers were up to. But, like last time, half way through the journey there was a tap on the glass and she was forced to roll it down.

"Chauffeur," the blonde said, "can you make a detour, please? Storm needs to make a quick stop at the nearest drugstore."

Dani glanced in the rear view mirror. Storm was looking comfortable, his long frame stretched along the seat, and he was stifling a yawn.

"I'm good, Chrystelle," he said through the yawn. "No detours necessary."

The woman turned to him with a frown. "Are you sure? I thought you'd run out-"

"Nope, I've got some. We just need to get home. It's been a long night."

"Okay, whatever you say." She leaned back against the seat with a sigh.

Dani didn't wait to see any more. She jabbed the button to close the window and shut them out of her sight.

What was that all about? Her mind told her it could only be one thing, something she didn't even want to think about. But there it was. The thought crossed her mind and she could not get rid of it. They'd run out of condoms, or at least that was what the woman thought, and she'd wanted Dani to take them to replenish their stock. The nerve of her.

Dani gritted her teeth, angry that the insensitive couple - Storm and the woman both - had dragged her into their private affair. But there was another reason for her anger, a far more frightening one if she dared admit it to herself. She scowled, fighting the thought with every fiber of her being. Then after several minutes berating herself she gave a sigh of resignation. It was no use. Who was she

425

kidding? Storm Hunter was with his date for the night, probably his lover, and she was jealous.

She could have kicked herself, she was so mad. How stupid could she be? She had absolutely no right to be jealous. She was only the chauffeur, for goodness sake, and one who was supposed to be a man. At least in his eyes. What made it worse, even if he'd known she was a woman she knew without a doubt that he'd have absolutely no interest in her. Why would he? He was a playboy billionaire with women falling at his feet and she was nothing more than a struggling schoolteacher with a brother to support. Why would he even give her the time of day?

Stupid to even think about it but that was how the mind worked. Her crazy brain had a mind of its own.

By the time they pulled into Storm's driveway Dani had regained control of her wandering thoughts and had stifled her wild emotions. She was back to her old self - solid, practical and calm. She went and opened the door then stepped back, confident that her face was expressionless and bland.

She had the hard task of staying serene when Storm got out of the car and held out his hand for the woman he'd called Chrystelle. She giggled and leaned into him so that he was forced to put his arm around her to prevent her from falling.

"Oh, Storm," she crooned, "you're such a gentleman."

He only gave her a crooked smile then looked at Dani. "Thanks, kid...Danny. You're on duty next weekend?"

"Every weekend, sir," Dani answered stiffly.

"Hey, no need to be so formal," Storm said with a laugh. "That's what you'd say to my old man, not me." Chrystelle began to sag and he wrapped his arms tighter around her. "Have Tony book you again for my pick-up." He was turning to go when he paused. "In fact, I'm heading to the airport early on Monday. I don't feel like

426

driving so you can take me. I'll have my assistant arrange it." As he turned away he said, "See you then, kid."

Dani did not answer. He'd forgotten her name already. So if she was of so little consequence to him why did he insist on asking for her? It didn't make much sense. All the other drivers had been with the company for years. He probably knew them all, so why not ask for them? There were only two things that made her unique. She was a woman, which he knew nothing about, and she was the youngest on the team. That must be it. He must really enjoy calling her 'kid'.

As soon as she'd slammed the door shut she got into the car and started the engine, studiously keeping her eyes on the roadway ahead. She had no desire to see them go into the house together, no wish to prolong the torture. She'd had enough for one night.

As the wheels crunched on the graveled driveway she breathed a prayer but it was not a happy one. Dear God, why did I have to meet Storm Hunter? Why did I have to be attracted to him, and why does he keep requesting me?

She got no answer except the thought that she'd better get over this crush in quick time or else she would be in a heck of a lot of trouble. She'd been scared that she'd looked forward to meeting Storm again but things were worse now. The fact that she'd admitted to herself that she was actually attracted to the man was positively terrifying.

******

"Here you go, Chrystelle. Just take this and you'll feel better in no time." Storm walked over to the sofa where his guest lay like a daintily withering flower. "You've held up pretty good so far but there's no use torturing yourself any longer."

Chrystelle gave a soft groan and straightened up slowly. "It's so hard to put on a brave face all the time. It's exhausting."

"As long as you're here you don't have to," he said and sat down beside her. "Now here. Take this."

She took the aspirin from his hand and popped it into her mouth. Then she reached out a delicate hand for the glass. When the last drop of water was gone she pushed the glass back into Storm's hand and rested her head against the plush cushions. "Thanks, Storm. I needed that."

"I know," he said and patted her hand. "Now close your eyes and try to get some rest till Jack gets here."

The words had hardly left his mouth before a soft sigh escaped Chrystelle's lips. She'd fallen fast asleep.

Storm smiled and went to the kitchen where he put on a pot of coffee. They'd both had enough to drink for one night. He would just sip a steamy cup of the brew while he waited for his friend to come and pick up his wife.

He'd known Jack and Chrystelle since college and, from freshman year, he'd always known they would be a pair. Where Jack was a spontaneous adventurer Chrystelle was generally level headed and calm. They were the perfect complement to each other. When they told him they were getting married he wasn't the least bit surprised. It was like they'd been made for each other.

Tonight Jack had had to rush off from the party early to do an emergency C-Section at Chicago General, leaving Chrystelle in Storm's care. She was used to this kind of thing. As one of Chicago's top surgeons he was called on at all hours of the day and night. Tonight was just more of the same. Storm had readily agreed for Chrystelle to chill with him knowing that Jack would come by as soon as his magic hands had done their thing. He was quick, he was efficient and he was the best.

As Storm sipped his black coffee his mind wandered to the young chauffeur who'd taken him home for the second time in the space of a week. Danny, he'd said his name was. He frowned as he thought about the kid. There was something about him, something he couldn't put his finger on, that was needling him but what it was he couldn't tell. And that was why he'd asked him to take him to the airport on Monday. He had to get to the bottom of his unexplainable interest in this young man.

As a kid he'd always pestered his parents for a little brother and was more than pissed each time they produced a girl. But that couldn't be it, could it? He was almost thirty years old. He must have gotten over his 'kid brother' obsession by now.

He took another sip of coffee then shrugged. By the time Monday came around he was sure he'd figure it out. With his baby face and huge dark eyes Danny probably reminded him of one of his younger cousins. That had to be it.

Storm nodded in satisfaction. Mystery solved.

******

Today was going to be a great day. Dani was sure of it. How could it not, when she'd received such a wonderful surprise this past weekend?

After leaving Storm Hunter's residence Dani had driven the limousine back to headquarters and she was fuming. Midnight had long gone and now she had to make her way home, another twenty minute drive. She wasn't going to make it to bed until after one o'clock in the morning. Dani groaned just thinking about it. If there was one thing she loved it was her sleep and she was getting less and less of it each day.

She was surprised to see Tony still in the office when she went to drop off her key. She'd expected to see the night manager on duty.

"Ben called in sick," he explained, then he handed her a check.

"What's this?" she asked with a frown. "It's not pay day."

"No, but it's like pay day for you," Tony said with a smile. "That's from Storm Hunter. He told me to charge his account for the amount and write you a check. It's his tip for the two times you dropped him home."

Dani stared at the check then at her boss. She glared at him. "Is this a joke? Because if it is I'm not amused."

"No joke," he said, putting up his hands and backing off in mock fear. "The check is as real as the one you got last pay day."

"Are you serious?" Dani said with a gasp. "This is more than I make for a week."

"I know," Tony said with a grin. "Now aren't you glad I assigned you to a big tipper? Although he seemed to have gone overboard with you. I've never seeing him tip quite so generously." Then his grin disappeared and his eyes narrowed. "Did you tell him you're a woman?"

"Of course I didn't," Dani retorted. "How could you even think that?"

Tony waved his hand. "Forget I said that. Just take the money and be grateful. I'm sure it will come in handy."

"Will it ever," she said with a grin and tucked it into her pocket. This would be the first installment on Brian's trip to Europe.

And that was why this fine Monday, although it was only five o'clock in the morning, she was in a good mood. She was beginning to see light at the end of her tunnel and it was all because of Storm Hunter. Just for that she would ditch her serious face and be especially nice to him. He more than deserved it.

This time when she pulled up in front of his door he was ready. She would deposit him at the airport and he'd probably make his way to an exclusive lounge and then head off on a private jet. Then she would do a quick turnaround, get the limo back to base then dash home to change so she'd be at Applewood school by eight thirty on the dot.

After giving Storm a cheerful good morning which got her a sour look from an obviously still sleepy Storm, she opened the door for him then went to deposit his luggage in the trunk. That took some doing. There were only two full sized suitcases and a carry-on bag but the second suitcase felt like he'd either packed it with lead or had stuffed a dead body in it. While he lounged inside the car she pushed and shoved till she got them in, almost giving herself a hernia in the process. Still, she did it without a murmur of complaint. Whatever this man put her through, overweight bags or no, it was worth it.

Storm seemed to wake up on his way to the airport. With the glass partition down there was nothing to stop him from carrying on a conversation with her and for the first time since they'd met he seemed to take a genuine interest in her.

"So Danny, you're a school teacher, huh?" Storm asked.

She nodded but she didn't turn her head. "Yes. I teach preschool."

"So you teach in the daytime and moonlight as a chauffeur at nights and on weekends." He grunted. "When do you have time for fun? A young kid like you should be out partying with your friends."

Dani almost laughed out loud. What friends? She hardly even had time for herself let alone to socialize with friends. She didn't say any of that, though. "I get by," she said and left it at that.

For some time there was silence and Dani had begun to wonder if Storm had succumbed to his sleepiness when she heard his voice again.

"So, do you have a girlfriend?"

"Um, no…not right now." He'd caught her off guard. Where in the world was he going with this?

"I don't blame you, fellow. It's good to take a break from women sometimes. They're something else, aren't they?" He laughed softly, as if they were co-conspirators of some sort. "They're the most confusing creatures on the planet. Today they love you like you're the only man in the world and tomorrow they can't stand a bone in your body."

"Yeah, I know what you mean," she said, trying to sound like she knew what she was talking about.

"Trust me, don't be fooled by all the glitz and glamour that some of them bring to the table," Storm said with a snort of disgust. "The best thing you can do is find one who's honest and real. If you find a woman like that, hold on to her for dear life. That kind of woman is precious and rare."

Dani didn't have an answer for that one so she said nothing. Thank goodness he didn't press her. He fell back into silence and a glance in the rear view mirror told her that he'd leaned his head back and closed his eyes. To her relief he remained like that for the rest of the journey.

Now what had come over Mr. Billionaire to make him confide in her like that? He'd practically presented his life philosophy on the female sex. She chuckled to herself. If he only knew…

Storm did not open his eyes again until they arrived at the airport. He probably hadn't been sleeping as she'd thought because he knew exactly when to sit up and he seemed fresh and alert. At his instructions she drove through a separate gate and then was directed to a ramp at the end of which sat an impressive private jet. There were a couple of immigration officers in the area ready to process Storm so that he could head out.

He hopped out of the car and while he was speaking to the agents Dani popped open the trunk to get his luggage. The carry-on bag and the smaller of the two suitcases came out easily enough. Then it was time for the one with the dead body. Using all her strength she hauled it toward her then she bent her knees as she'd been taught, grabbed the handles and lifted the massive weight out of the trunk.

And that was when it happened.

The suitcase tumbled out and fell to the ground with a thump, dragging her down with it. She started to pitch forward and only had time to let out a yelp before she was falling, face first, toward the tarmac.

In a microsecond Storm was there grabbing hold of her before her face slammed into the ground. He'd grabbed her by the collar and the back of her jacket and as he hauled her back upright her chauffeur's hat fell off and her mass of dark brown hair tumbled down her back and covered her face, hiding it from view.

"What the-" Storm's hold on her slackened and she almost fell back to the ground. Then his hands tightened on her and he dragged her to her feet.

"Who are you?" His voice was full of outrage.

She pulled out of his grasp and pushed the hair away from her face. And found herself staring into the flashing, dark eyes of a very angry man.

"You're not a guy. You're a girl," he said, his voice incredulous.

"I think I know that," she said, deliberately keeping her voice light. Maybe they could both laugh this off. The situation was actually quite funny.

"Yeah, but I didn't," he bit out as he glared down at her. "Why didn't you tell me? Was this supposed to be some kind of joke on me?"

Now she realized there was no hope that he'd laugh it off. Where was his sense of humor? "Look, I'm sorry I deceived you but it was for a good reason."

"Like?" he demanded then he glanced at the men who were staring at them. Storm grabbed her elbow. "Come over here. You have some explaining to do."

He marched her over to the far end of the limousine where they were partially hidden from view and only then did he let her go. "Now talk."

Okay, so it was like that, was it? He was going to play rough. Well, she could be tough, too. Dani folded her arms across her chest, lifted her face and looked him straight in the eyes. "There's no need for you to fly off the handle. I told you, I had a very good reason to conceal my true identity."

"So spill it," he said tersely.

"I had a scare my first week on the job. One of my passengers tried to grope me. I had to fight him off. I decided right then that I wouldn't put myself at risk again." Her voice was bold and unapologetic. If Storm Hunter didn't get it, then tough. "Ever since that night I've concealed the fact that I'm a woman. It's a whole lot safer, especially during late night pick-ups."

There was a flicker in Storm's eye then the tightness in his jaws slackened - just barely. "Well you could have told me. I wasn't going to grope you. And I talked to you like you were a guy."

So that was it. It wasn't just that she had deceived him, it was that she'd deceived him so well that he'd shared some private thoughts with her, thoughts he'd probably only have shared with a man.

"I know and I'm sorry. But I'd already started being Danny the guy when I met you." She shrugged. "I couldn't very well just abandon that. And anyway, Tony asked me to maintain the disguise. He thought it was safer for me and his business."

Storm was still frowning at her, seeming unconvinced with her line of reasoning. Then he expelled his breath and shook his head. "So what's your real name, anyway?"

"It's Dani."

"Yeah, right."

"No, it is. Really. I'm Dani with an I. It's short for Danielle."

He looked at her through narrowed eyes. "And are you really a school teacher?"

She nodded. "Everything I've said to you is true. Except for the being a guy part, which I never said. You were the one who assumed I was a guy so I never lied to you."

"No, but you let me go on believing a false assumption."

"Listen, I've already apologized to you and I'm not going to do it again. If you can't understand the reason for my disguise then I can't help you." She set her mouth in a rebellious pout and refused to back down. Billionaire or not, she was not about to let any man intimidate her.

That seemed to take him by surprise. He was probably not used to a woman standing up to him. He stared at her for several seconds then slowly, almost imperceptibly, he nodded. "All right, I take your point. But from here on don't even think of deceiving me again."

And with that he turned on his heel and stalked off, leaving Dani staring after him.

CHAPTER FOUR

An hour had passed since the grand revelation and Storm still could not believe it. He'd been duped. Danny, or Dani as he would now have to think of her, had made a sucker out of him. Jeez, was he so easily fooled?

The signs had all been there but he'd been too stupid to see them. Now, in hindsight, he didn't know how he could have missed the clues - the fullness of her lips, the softness of her cheeks, the silky smooth skin of her face. And each time he'd gone near her there'd been that faint fragrance of rose petals.

More than anything, though, he should have known something was wrong when the hair on his arms stood up each time she got close to him. He'd noticed it and thought it strange but then he dismissed it. But now he knew why.

Dani. She was different from any woman he knew. She was bold and confident and she'd actually stood up to him when he tried to intimidate her. He couldn't recall that ever happening to him except for his run-ins with his mother and mothers didn't count.

He began to smile as he thought about Dani and then his smile turned into a chuckle. He was actually beginning to admire her spunk. She'd certainly taken him for a ride and she refused to apologize for it.

Then a thought came to him and he frowned. She was practical, down-to-earth and she did what she had to do to survive. She might actually be the answer to a whole lot of his problems, the primary one being how to get his father off his back.

What would Dani the chauffeur think about ditching that job to come work for him - as his fake fiancée? His smile widened into a grin. He was sure he could convince her to come on board with his plan. She looked like she needed the money. Why else would she have taken on the chauffeur job on top of her teaching career? This could be the solution to both their problems. She needed money and he had lots of it. He needed a female buffer for his annoying family and she looked like the kind of woman who, once the job was over, would cut loose - no strings attached. She didn't strike him as the clinging vine type and that suited him perfectly.

Satisfied, Storm leaned back to enjoy the rest of the plane ride. When he returned Dani would be hearing from him.

What he'd hand her on a silver platter was an offer she would not be able to refuse.

******

"You want me to do what?" Dani stared across the table at Storm, not believing what she'd just heard.

"I want you to be my fiancée for hire." A mischievous grin tickled his lips.

"Are you serious?" she asked, and for some reason her heartbeat accelerated as she awaited his response. "You're joking, right?"

"I'm very serious," he said with a smile. "I find myself in a bit of a dilemma. My father insists that I find a wife and settle down. He's decided that he'll be dead in the very near future and is determined that he should see the face of his grandchild before he departs. My child."

Dani sucked in her breath and glared at him. "You want to pay me to have your child?"

"Hold on, not so fast," he said with a laugh. "I'm not going there. No way. All I want is to give my family the impression that I'm moving in the right direction. You see, he's got them all on his side. I just need a break from all the pressure."

"And you think having a fake fiancée is the answer?"

"It's the perfect solution," he said with a smug grin. "I get them off my back and you - if you agree - get enough money so you won't need to be on the road at all hours of the night." He leaned back in the chair and gave her a look of total confidence, as if she'd be crazy to turn him down.

Dani lifted her glass and took a long sip of her ginger ale. He was certainly full of it, thinking she couldn't refuse him. She had a good mind to give him a flat out no just to wipe that satisfied smile off his face.

To her surprise, on his return to Chicago he'd invited her to lunch, telling her he had a proposal for her, one that would be mutually beneficial. She'd been more than curious and had eagerly accepted his invitation, thinking he was going to offer her a permanent job as his chauffeur. She'd anticipated that he would offer her a salary that would exceed what she was earning with Tony. After all, if he expected her to give up her current employment he'd have to be offering her an increase. A position like that would suit her well, not only for the potential increase in pay, but also for the fact that she wouldn't have to worry about lecherous passengers. She'd looked forward to meeting with him to discuss the new arrangement.

And then he'd gone and sprung this mad hatter plan on her. He wanted to pay her to engage in yet another deception, this one far more dangerous than the first.

But she was nothing if not practical. She'd been racking her brains, trying to find ways to make more money, and here Storm had dumped a solution right in her lap. She would love to turn him down just to have the satisfaction of teaching him not to take her acceptance for granted but she didn't have that luxury. She needed the money.

She gave him a challenging stare. "I want at least double what I'm making with Tony."

He'd been tapping his fingers against his glass but when she spoke he stopped and gave her a nod. "So you're accepting. Wise decision. One you won't regret, I'm sure."

"And you'll pay me what I asked?" she pressed.

Storm gave a laugh. "Honey, your services are worth far more to me than that measly sum. You'd be closer to the mark if you aim for ten times your pay."

Dani's heart hopped in shocked pleasure. Could this really be happening? Then she narrowed her gaze. "You're not pulling my leg, are you?"

He looked amused. "Now why would I do something like that? What? You think I can't afford it?"

Dani remained silent. He had a point. That kind of money was nothing to a man like him.

"I want you to be comfortable when we go out," he was saying. "You'll want to dress nicely. You'll need money to do that."

It was then that she realized he wasn't being overly generous just for the heck of it. He'd clearly calculated her needs and that was how he had come up with his figure.

"I'll take it," she blurted out before she could change her mind. "When do I start?"

"I'd like to announce you to my family in the next few weeks," he said, "so our first order of business is to advise Tony that you won't be coming back and your second," he reached over and took her hand in his, "is to get to know me better."

Dani almost snatched her hand back, she was so surprised. She wasn't on the job yet so why was he holding her?

He must have seen her discomfort because he let her slide her hand from his. "You have to start pretending to like me, Dani. And that means touching sometimes."

She could feel the heat rising in her face. Shoot. She hardly ever blushed so why now? All he'd mentioned was touching and she was turning red. What if he'd mentioned sex? She would have probably looked like a lobster.

Not that she intended to hop into bed with him. Delicious as he looked a girl had to draw the line somewhere.

"We'll spend the next few days in each other's company. I'll show you some of the things I like to do and you can bring me up to speed on your interests. We can't be total strangers when we go to meet my family."

"Okay," she said slowly, "that makes sense."

"And I'll only monopolize your evenings. I know you'll be busy at the preschool until, what, four o'clock?"

"I get off at three," she said, "but you can pick me up at four. I only live five minutes drive from the school."

"That's convenient. Can you be ready by five tomorrow? I'll be free by then and can pick you up."

"Five o'clock is fine," she said with a shrug.

"Wear jeans and a comfortable top. We're not going anywhere fancy."

"Where are we going?" she asked.

He shook his head. "It's a surprise."

Next evening Storm showed up at her apartment right on time. The buzzer sounded at exactly five o'clock.

"I'll be right down," she yelled into the intercom. She was wearing jeans and a white shirt and she grabbed a light jacket on the way out the door. As she exited the elevator and entered the lobby of the apartment building she saw Storm. He had his back to her, his cell phone to his ear. Unobserved, she took the opportunity to admire his strong masculine frame, the breadth of his shoulders in his black leather jacket and the tightness of his butt in faded jeans. Talk about delicious. She would never say this to him but he looked good.

At that moment he turned and when he saw her his lips curled into a crooked smile. He said something into his phone, effectively ending the call, then turned his full attention on her.

"Very nice," he said, his look approving. "This beats you in a chauffeur's uniform any day."

"And...you look good, too." She might as well practice complimenting him. Most likely she'd have to do a lot of that in her future role as fiancée. And it wasn't like she'd be lying. He'd looked handsome each time she'd seen him in formal wear but now in jeans and leather jacket with just a hint of shadow on his chin he looked so much younger and a whole lot sexier.

He seemed to like the compliment because he threw her a boyish grin then gave her his arm. "Let's hit the road."

Dani got the surprise of her life when they walked out into the parking lot and headed toward a big black motorcycle. When they stopped in front of it she looked up at Storm in uncertainty. "Are we going riding on this?"

"Yes, we are. This is my baby," he said, his voice full of pride. "We've been together for three years now and she's never let me down."

"Well you just continue to have good times with your baby. Alone. I'm not going on that thing." Dani folded her arms across her chest.

"Oh, come on, don't tell me you're a scaredy-cat," Storm teased. "You've been such a tough cookie since I met you. Don't tell me you're turning chicken now."

"I'm not chicken," she retorted. "But I'm not stupid, either. Motorcycles are dangerous."

"What if I promise to go real slow and only on the local road, no highways?"

"Still dangerous," she insisted.

He stepped closer to her, so close she could smell the earthy fragrance of his cologne. Her eyes wandered up his torso and the expanse of his chest, over the square jaw with its barely-there stubble and up to his eyes that twinkled with undisguised amusement.

"Would you come if I told you I have two helmets?"

Slowly, she shook her head. "Not even then," she said but this time she was smiling. She'd meant to stand her ground with him but who could resist that crooked smile and the surprising dimple in his left cheek? And the fact that he'd let his hair grow a little longer until it curled at the collar of his jacket did not make things any easier.

She had to admit, the man was gorgeous. Second admission - she wanted to spend the evening with him and if the only way she could do that was on the back of a motorcycle then maybe she'd take the chance. As long as he promised to go really slowly.

"Come on," he wheedled. "You know you want to try it."

She drew in a deep breath then expelled it in a sigh of acquiescence. "All right, you've worn me down. I'll go. But only if you promise to be careful."

Storm put his hand up in a brisk salute. "Scouts honor. You're safe with me."

I'm not so sure about that, she thought, but she didn't say it out loud. She might be safe with him on his motorbike but the closer she got to him, the more her heart was sliding down the slippery slope of attraction. She seriously could not afford to get caught in the mudslide. She was his hired help, not his girlfriend, and she would do well to remember that.

Dani reached out and took the helmet from Storm's hand then she followed his example and pulled the strap under her chin and snapped it closed. Then they were ready to go.

Storm flung his leg over the motorcycle and started the engine with a vroom, making Dani jump. He laughed at her. "Hop on," he yelled over the din, "and hold on tight."

She plopped her bottom on the seat behind him and wrapped her arms around his waist. Even with her fright at being on the back of a motorcycle she could feel and appreciate the taut muscles of his abdomen, and the feel of his strong back against her chest was wickedly delicious.

She didn't even attempt to play modest and maintain some distance between her body and his. She clung to him like he was her lifeline and she planned never to let go.

Storm revved the engine and then they were off, with Dani laughing and screaming all the way out of the parking lot.

If she'd thought being on the back of a motorcycle in a parking lot was scary she got the fright of her life when they hit the road and a car zoomed pass, so close that Dani's heart leaped into her throat and she couldn't even scream. "Please, Storm, please," she whimpered, "This is scary. I want to stop." This wasn't Dani the practical, Dani the brave. This was Dani the wimp but she didn't care if the whole world knew it. She just wanted to get off that motorcycle and on to solid ground. Now.

Storm must not have heard her because he kept on going, slow and steady at first then a little faster until he was keeping up with the rest of the traffic and passing some of the slower cars on the road. To his credit, he did not take the ramp that led to the highway even though that route would have made for a far more exhilarating ride. Instead, he turned off the main road and headed for a side road with just the odd car or van passing by.

They rode for several more miles and with each passing minute Dani's tension eased until she was pressed against Storm, not out of fear, but simply because she was reveling in this one chance she was getting to hold him close. Finally, they arrived at a wide open field with strips of paved road stretching for miles. It looked like an abandoned airport with runways that now lay bare. It was here that Storm let his baby fly.

Dani screamed but this time it was from the thrill of racing down a runway at full speed, feeling like they were in a plane ready to take off. With her adrenalin pumping, her heart racing and her mouth gone dry, all she could do was cling to Storm and shriek.

When he finally slowed the super powerful machine and pulled it off the runway Dani was panting like a dog in need of water. She slid off the back of the motorbike, unbuckled her helmet and staggered over to the grassy bank where she flopped down.

Storm laughed at her dramatic departure then he set the bike to stand, took off his helmet and went to sit beside her in the grass. He looked like he was trying to seem casual but he, too, was breathing hard.

Dani looked up at him as he leaned over her and she burst out in uncontrollable laughter. She had never felt so exhilarated in her life. This man had scared her half to death and then he had dragged her over the edge, past her fear, and into a daredevil realm that had her wanting more. When her laughter finally died down she was still breathless. "That was the greatest," she whispered as she stared up into his laughing dark eyes.

But then as she stared up at him something in his eyes changed. The laughter disappeared and he was looking down at her with an intensity that took her breath away.

As he lowered his head, blocking the sky from view, she closed her eyes and stayed still, afraid to move and break the spell.

And then she felt it, his mouth pressing against hers, firm yet mobile, demanding her response.

And she gave it. She responded with an eagerness that surprised her. She must still be high from the ride because, instead of pulling away in shock, she pressed her lips against his and her hands slid up and around his back.

He must have taken that as license to go farther because his tongue teased then probed and then he was plundering her mouth with a fervor that spoke of pent-up passion.

Dani answered in kind, kissing back boldly, giving in to the raw desire that flooded through her. Then she was clinging to him, pulling him into her, drowning in the feel of his rock-hard chest against her breasts.

When he drew back to look down at her she moaned, wanting more of the same. Her nipples were hard as pebbles and she could feel a trace of moisture between her legs. Even if she were of a different mind there was no denying it. Her body wanted him. But now he was moving away from her, taking his sweet lips and hard body with him.

Storm moved from over her and sat by her side. When he looked down at her, still lying on her back in the grass, there was a rueful expression on his face. "I don't know what came over me," he said, his voice slightly hoarse. "I just had to kiss you."

Dani gave him a soft smile. "I don't mind."

He gave her a real smile then and reached out both hands to her. "Come on, let's ride some more."

They stayed at that abandoned airfield a whole hour more, riding and laughing and enjoying each other's company. There were no more kisses that evening but Dani felt there was a connection between them that was special.

When Storm finally dropped her back at her apartment Dani was exhausted and happy. She couldn't remember when she'd had so much fun. Over the last four years her existence had been dreary, with her main focus being the care of her younger brother. She'd never had time to go out and have fun. She'd been made a parent at the age of eighteen and had lived a life of responsibility since then.

But this evening Storm had given her back the girlhood she'd lost. She'd been free and crazy and she'd had wild fun and for that she was grateful.

Storm walked her into the lobby of the apartment building then shoved his hands in the pockets of his jacket and looked down at her with a grin. "Now it's my turn to get to know a little about you," he said. "Tomorrow evening we'll do something you love. What will it be?"

That took her off guard. What did she love to do? What had she had time to do outside of work? She thought for a moment then an idea flashed into her mind. She grinned up at him. She had the perfect plan. "Let's buy some fabric and make a quilt."

Storm's smile faded and his brows lifted in what looked like horror. "Let's do what?"

"My mom loved to make quilts," Dani gushed, "and I used to help her. I've always loved the peace and serenity of needlework. I haven't done it in years. That's what I want to do tomorrow."

Storm frowned, the look on his face one of doubt. "Somehow you don't strike me as a needlework kind of girl. Roller-skating, maybe. Even bowling. But needlework?'

"You asked me what I want to do and that's it," she said, giving him a look of defiance. "So you get your stitching finger ready, mister, because tomorrow we're going to make a quilt. "

"Well, if you say so," he said, dragging the words as if they were the hardest things for him to say.

Dani gave him a firm nod. "I do say so. I'll see you tomorrow at five. Don't be late."

She waited for him to turn and watched as he crossed the lobby and went through the door, still mumbling in distress and confusion. She laughed to herself as, from the door, she watched him climb on his motor cycle and ride away then she headed back to the elevator, punched the button and headed up to her apartment.

She was still laughing when she went inside. Storm Hunter had forced her to explore a wild side she never knew existed. Now she would force him to explore his softer, more sensitive side.

It was going to be fun watching him squirm.

CHAPTER FIVE

"Lola, calm down. There's no need to be so dramatic." Storm had to grit his teeth to keep his voice calm and under control. The woman was impossible.

"Dramatic?" she shrieked as she clenched her fists and glared at him from tear-filled eyes. "Is that what you call it? No. This is dramatic." She grabbed a stapler from his desk and threw it across the room at him, missing his head by mere inches. He'd had to duck to keep from being brained.

"Lola, stop it," he said in his most imperious voice but it was like talking to a mad woman. She was already reaching for the heavy tape dispenser and he had to dive for it and wrench it out of her grasp.

"How could you do this to me, Storm Hunter? How could you?" Lola's face crumpled and she collapsed into a chair and covered her face with her hands. "I love you. You know I do. Why would you torture me like this?"

"Lola, please. I'm not doing this to hurt you." Storm let out a heavy sigh. He hated to see a woman cry. "You don't love me, Lola. Its just infatuation. It's only because our parents expect-"

"Don't tell me what I feel for you." She lifted her face and spat the words at him, her eyes flashing with a rage that made her look crazed. "For years I've waited for you. Years. And you led me on, making me think you felt the same way."

"But we never-"

"It doesn't matter. I was waiting for you till we were married. I know you had other women, playboy that you are, and I let you have your flings." She sucked in her breath, her nostrils flaring. "I was giving you time to grow up. He'll come around when it's time, I told myself. He'll settle down one day soon and when he does it will be with me, the woman who's loved him faithfully all these years."

Now Storm was getting pissed. What kind of guilt trip was Lola trying to throw on him when he'd never made any commitment, not even a promise, to her? Despite what their parents wished, as far as he was concerned he was not about to be forced into an arranged marriage.

"Get serious, Lola," he said, his voice cold. "We were never going to get married and you know it." He shook his head. "You turned up here suddenly and started with your usual antics, acting like we're lovers...which we're not. I had to tell you because this behavior has to stop. I can't play those games with you anymore."

"So that's all it was to you, a game?" Her voice was a bitter, broken whisper. "All this time I was loving you, you were only playing a game. With my heart."

She stood up then and hugged her purse to her chest like a protective shield. "And now you tell me you've got a fiancée. Where the hell she came from, I don't know. Well, if this is something you cooked up to humiliate me you can give yourself a pat on the back. It worked." With an injured sniff she turned on her heel and walked to the door. This time, instead of her usual 'Love you, darling', she opened the door then turned and said, "Don't think this is over, Storm. We are not going to end like this."

Storm let out his breath and shook his head then he dropped himself onto the leather sofa by the window. He hadn't meant to reveal the engagement - fake though it was - until after he'd announced it to his parents, but Lola had been more annoying than usual. She'd always been expressive with her feelings but today she'd become more physical, throwing her arms around his waist and planting an unexpected kiss on his lips.

It wasn't that he had anything against her. He was just tired of playing her game, a game that their parents wholly endorsed. And that was why he'd seized onto the idea of Dani as his fiancée. She was the perfect solution to getting everybody, including Lola, off his back.

The sad thing was, it looked like he had just created a brand new enemy.

******

Dani dashed around the apartment for the too many-eth time, making sure everything was just right. Her heart was pumping like she was on the edge of a cliff ready to bungee jump.

She could beat herself. She'd invited Storm to join her in making a quilt, not even thinking about where they'd be executing the project. Of course, it ended up that it would be at her apartment. She couldn't very well lay out fabric and put him to work in the lobby of the apartment building. And it wasn't like she had any other place she could take him to do that. It was too bad she had blurted out her idea without thinking about the consequences.

Number one question - what would he think of her modest apartment, with him being a billionaire and all? Number two dilemma - shouldn't she have suggested something that would allow them to be in a neutral place rather than an intimate setting such as her apartment? Number three disaster - now that she'd had a taste of him how was she going to be able to keep her hands of the 'merchandise'?

When the buzzer sounded Dani jumped. She was so tense she had to take two deep breaths before pressing the button to answer. Storm was on his way up to her apartment and she wasn't ready. She felt like she'd never be. She checked the mirror one last time then slid her damp palms down the sides of her jeans.

She heard the elevator door open then footsteps coming down the hallway, the heavy footsteps of a man.

They stopped right in front of her door. She pasted a practiced smile on her face and opened up.

The face that greeted Dani was not the one she'd expected. Instead of a smiling, relaxed Storm she saw a man who looked like he wanted to be anywhere but there. His lips were drawn tight and he was almost scowling.

"Are you all right?" She stared up at him, momentarily taken aback, and then she stepped aside so he could come in.

"Uh, sorry," he said then just like that he seemed to snap out of his trance. It was as if he just realized where he was. The creases on his brow disappeared and his lips relaxed into a smile. "Forgive me. It's been a long day."

She nodded and smiled, accepting the apology, then reached up to take up his jacket. He shrugged out of it and as she went to hang it in the closet he looked around the apartment.

"Neat, " he said as his eyes roamed the living room then the dining room and the kitchen. He could take it all in with one sweep of the eyes.

She came back to stand beside him. "Neat as in organized or neat as in cool?" she asked in a teasing tone, trying to hide her nervousness.

"Both," he said. Typical man. He was playing it safe.

"Nobody says neat to mean cool anymore so I'll take it you mean organized."

"Okay," he said with a drawl then he gave her a quizzical look. "So where's the quilting stuff?"

"My, aren't we eager?" She laughed then directed him to have a seat in the living room. "I'll go get the basket with the supplies."

When she returned to the living room he was lounging in the sofa but as soon as he saw her he sat up and dug into his pocket. He came out with something small and shiny.

"I brought my thimble," he said and held it up proudly for her to see.

Dani had to laugh at that. She set the basket on the coffee table and plucked the thimble off his palm. "Now where did you get that?" She could not imagine a man like Storm having something as domestic as a thimble lying around his house.

"The housekeeper," he said and now he, too, was laughing. "I told her I was going to learn to sew and she said to make sure to use a thimble. Then she gave me this one from her sewing kit. I didn't even know she had a sewing kit. Do people still use those things?"

"Yes, Storm, they do." Dani rolled her eyes at him then she smiled and shook her head. What did billionaires know about such things? She started pulling pieces of fabric from her collection and laid out each colorful section in front of him. "I pre-washed the fabric so they're ready to go."

He picked up a pink polka dot piece. "Why would you do that?"

"It prevents color runs and shrinking once we've completed the quilt. Just some preventative measures."

"Oh," he said then stifled a yawn.

Dani leaned over and gave him a playful punch. "Hey, you could at least pretend to be interested. You didn't see me falling asleep when I was on the back of your motorcycle." She picked up a few of the pieces. "Let's move this over to the dining table. We're going to need a lot of space for this project."

It took a while for them to get organized but soon they were busy following the simple pattern Dani had downloaded from the Internet. She was surprised at how quickly Storm caught on, following her instructions step by step, and even when he had to redo a crooked section she heard no complaint. He was plugging away, so deep in concentration, that after an hour and a half it was Dani who had to call for a break.

"You must be tired," she said. "Let me get you a drink."

"No, I'm good," he said, not looking up from his work. "Let's just keep going till we're all done."

"Let's not," she said and put her hand on her hip. "I'm exhausted. Are you trying to work me into the ground?"

"Hey, I'm enjoying this," he said with a laugh. "It's been a long time since I've had the chance to work with my hands."

"You? Work with your hands?" she asked in disbelief. "When?"

"My dad and I used to tinker around motorcycles when I was growing up. That's why I like the machines so much."

"Your dad? *The* Edgar Hunter? Getting his hands dirty with mechanic work? I find that hard to believe."

He grinned at her. "Billionaires are people, too. Don't think I didn't get my fair share of scolding for not tidying up my room."

"Seriously?" Somehow she'd thought rich kids didn't have to lift a finger. They had maids to do that kind of thing, didn't they?

"My parents didn't play around with us kids," Storm continued. "Sure, we had staff at the house to do the heavy stuff but we had our chores, too." He chuckled. "My mom even taught me how to cook and she's a stickler for perfection in the kitchen. Brrr." Storm gave a shudder.

That made Dani burst out laughing. "Anyway, mama's boy, you deserve a break so drop that quilt."

"Mama's boy?" Storm gasped in mock horror. "You just called me mama's boy? I'm going to get you for that."

Before Dani could move he'd come around the table and was reaching for her. She gave a shriek and dashed around to the other side. She glanced over her shoulder, thinking that he'd given up the silly chase, but he was still coming. With a yell she was off again.

She made it as far as the living room and that was where he caught her, his arms snaking round her waist to pull her back against him. With her back pressed against his torso and his arms a steel band around her she had little chance of breaking loose but still she struggled, her flight instinct kicking in, telling her she had to get away.

He was laughing at her futile efforts as he held her easily but then she turned round in his arms, catching him off guard, and shoved him in the chest. Storm stumbled back, collapsing unceremoniously onto the sofa, but he did not let go of her and she came tumbling down right on top of him.

He immediately seized the advantage. Quick as a cat he rolled over into the softness of the sofa, shifting her so she was pinned underneath him. Then, propping himself on his elbows, he gave her a crooked smile. "Now I've got you exactly where I want you," he whispered wickedly. "You are in my power."

He dipped his head and put his lips close to her ear. "Do you take back what you said about me being a mama's boy?"

Dani turned her lips to his ear but for a second she said nothing, keeping him in suspense. Then her whisper came, strong and bold and defiant. "Never."

"Wrong answer." With a growl he captured both her wrists with one hand and pinned them above her head then he lowered his head, his lips coming closer and closer till they were just a hair's breadth away from hers. "Last chance," he whispered and his warm breath tickled her lips.

"Never," she whispered again and then moaned as his mouth descended on hers, locking her in a passionate kiss from which there was no escape. He was in total control, his lips holding hers prisoner, his tongue tantalizing at first, testing her, teasing her then growing more masterful until she was gasping beneath him.

Still holding her immobile Storm released her mouth to slide his lips down her neck and over her collarbone. There he feathered her skin with butterfly kisses that had her squirming for a different kind of release.

Dani arched her back, wanting more of him. His sweet torture was driving her crazy. Her nipples, now hardened points in her bra, were crying out for their own release, clamoring for his mouth, his lips, his tongue to caress and to soothe them. She sighed when his mouth slipped lower to kiss the tops of her breasts and then he was sliding his free hand down the front of her blouse, loosening buttons until he opened the shirt wide, exposing her lacy bra and bare midriff to his heated gaze.

Only then did Storm release her wrists. "You're so beautiful," he whispered then cupped her breasts in his palms, his thumbs making tantalizing circles over her nipples as they poked through her bra.

Dani was panting now, and he must have decided to take pity on her because he hooked his thumbs in the top of each bra cup and pushed them down below her breasts, exposing them to his view.

Dani almost cried out when he sucked a puckered nipple into his mouth, massaging it with his tongue, rolling it until she writhed in sweet agony. Then he moved his lips to the other and the hands he'd just freed reached up to cradle his head and pull him into her.

When he lifted his head she groaned and reached for him, wanting even more.

With a smile he pulled out of her arms then he began unbuttoning his shirt. As his hands deftly loosened button after button he spoke. "You've got condoms, right?"

The words were like a glass of cold water thrown in her face. Condom? Dear God, what was she doing? It had taken his words to slap sense back into her brain. It was like she'd been in a trance. But now she was herself again and she was not going any farther.

Dani sat up and shoved Storm off then she shot up off the couch.

"What's the matter with you?" His face registered shock and confusion.

"I'm not doing this," she muttered, dragging her bra back in place and quickly doing up the buttons of her shirt. As soon as they were done she lifted her head. "I'm your fake fiancée remember? Fake. That means no sex."

"But we just-"

"I know and I was wrong to let things get that far but you can get your shirt back on. This is were it ends." Dani's voice was cold. She knew she sounded harsh but her words weren't only for Storm, they were for her, too. How the heck had she let things get that far? She, realist that she was, should have known better.

Storm was one of the richest men in the country. He'd hired her to do a job and she'd gone falling in infatuation - because that was all it could be - with him. He was dangerously handsome, with his raven-black hair curling wildly and his dark eyes that seemed to read into your soul. She'd fallen under his spell but now it was time to break free.

She had to remain professional. She could not afford to be used and then discarded once he got tired of her. Because that was what they did, these tycoons. To them, women like her were nothing but toys.

She was glad she'd remembered that before it was too late.

Storm's clothes were back in order now and he was standing there, scowling at her, obviously annoyed by her sudden change of heart. "Do you want me to leave?" he asked through clenched teeth.

Dani sighed then nodded. "I think that would be best."

Without another word Storm turned and walked out of her apartment, closing the door firmly behind him.

Dani felt the fight seep out of her, leaving her trembling and drained. She sank down onto the sofa and put her hands to her mouth as she fell into deep thought. Had she just ruined her opportunity to give her brother the help he needed? Had she just messed up two chances by quitting her job with Tony and then practically ordering Storm to keep his hands off her?

Propping her elbows on her knees, she dropped her chin into her cupped palms. After what had just happened would Storm even call her again?

******

Damn and double damn. Storm slammed his palm against the steering wheel and blew out a frustrated breath. How could he have been so dumb?

He should have known better than to give in to his attraction to Dani. Of course she would be upset. He should probably be grateful she hadn't slapped him for coming on to her like that. He'd hired her, discussed money, and then had gone and practically taken advantage of her. Now she was probably feeling like he'd used her. Jeez, what if she thought he'd assumed he'd bought an all-inclusive package?

He shook his head. He honestly didn't know what had come over him. It was probably because he'd never felt so comfortable in a woman's company as he did in hers.

She'd had him quilting, for Christ's sake, and he'd loved it. He'd probably have enjoyed it just as much if she'd pulled out a basket of old socks and told him to start darning. It wasn't the task that had him on a high, it was the company.

He blew out his breath in a sigh. He wanted Danielle Swift. There was no denying that. The problem was she obviously didn't feel the same way.

He tapped his fingers on the steering wheel and stared through the windshield of his Ferrari. Now he was faced with a nagging question - after what had happened, would she want to go through with his plan? He could easily think of twenty women who would jump at the chance to play this farce with him. But the only one he wanted was her.

It was not an easy task, admitting that to himself, not after she'd thrown him out of her apartment. But it was the truth. Now there was only one thing left to do. He had to apologize.

He dug into his pocket and pulled out his cell phone. For some time he stared at it, fighting the urge to give in to his male ego. What man liked to be rejected? But he had to do what was right. He found her number in the phone and pressed the green button to call.

She picked up on the third ring. "Hello?" Her voice was soft, hesitant, totally unlike the bold Dani he'd come to know.

"It's Storm," he said and started tapping his fingers on the steering wheel again.

"I know," she said then there was silence.

Come on, fool. Your turn. "Dani, I'm sorry about what just happened," he said, his voice strained. "I was out of line to come on to you like that and I apologize."

"I'm sorry, too," she said quietly. "It's not like I was blame-free."

Again there was silence, and for once in his life Storm struggled to find words. Finally he spoke. "So...are we still on for that visit to my parents in the next couple of weeks or...do you want to call it off?"

He heard her sigh into the phone. "I'll still do it, Storm. But you know this is dangerous, right? I mean, deceiving your parents like that? Don't you think they'll see through it?"

"Not if we do it right," he said. "If we just act like a normal couple they'll be sold."

"Normal?"

"Or as close to normal as we can get," he said, trying to clarify.

"All right. I'll...see you in a couple of weeks then," she said, effectively bringing the conversation to an end.

"Right. See you then."

The phone connection went dead and she was gone.

Storm dropped the phone onto the driver's seat then turned the key in the ignition. The engine roared to life.

And that was the end of his evening. Not exactly the one he had envisioned but at least they were back on amicable terms.

He just hoped from here on he'd remember to keep his roaming hands off her. It was definitely not going to be easy.

******

The next two weeks passed far too quickly for Dani's liking. She wasn't ready. Not mentally, anyway. As she went down in the elevator she breathed in deeply then exhaled slowly. Calm down, she told herself, then clutched her purse strap tighter. Just because Storm's parents were super rich there was no reason to be scared. They were human beings, not aliens.

The elevator door opened and she stepped out. The pep talk she'd given herself hadn't really worked but now she had to put on a brave face and a smile. Storm was right there in the lobby and now he was walking toward her. Her fake billionaire fiancé was painfully handsome as usual, in hip-hugging jeans and a close-fitting black shirt that clung to every cut of his muscles. Painfully handsome was the only way she could describe him because he looked so good he made her mouth water...and yet she could not touch him. And it was all because of her own stupid rules. Okay, so maybe the rules actually made sense but she just wasn't liking them right now.

Storm was right in front of her now. He gave her a bow. "Very nice," he said, his voice low and almost seductive. But not quite. He was probably being very careful, making sure not to cross any lines.

"Thank you," she said with a smile and her heart soared. She'd better get a hold of herself. All the man had said were two words, two very simple ones at that, and she was over the moon.

Storm held out his hands. "After you, madam."

She walked ahead of him and when she got to the door the sunshine was so bright she pulled up short as the glare hit her eyes.

Storm ran into her back, nearly knocking her over. His arms shot out to grab her and before she could react she'd been dragged back against his hard body.

Just as suddenly his arms dropped away, leaving her bereft. "Sorry," he said quickly. "Just didn't want you to topple over."

"It's okay," she muttered and stepped out into the sunshine.

He didn't have to draw back from her quite so swiftly, retreating as if she were some kind of leper. She'd wanted his arms around her, wanted the outdoorsy smell of him and the solid feel of him just a moment longer, but he'd dashed away. She was being unreasonable, she knew, but she couldn't help her feelings. Rules or no rules, her body wanted Storm Hunter's touch.

As they stepped out into the sunshine he pulled a pair of sunglasses from his pocket and slid them on. If she'd thought he looked sexy before, that was nothing compared to what he looked like in dark glasses. Now he looked both hot and mysterious, making her nipples peak in futile anticipation.

Oh Lord, this was not working. They hadn't even reached the car yet and her body was preparing for love. She almost laughed out loud. Talk about pathetic.

Storm stopped in front of a fire-red Ferrari convertible with the top down. He reached down to open the passenger door for her.

"Very nice," she said, copying his words as she looked at the car with appreciation. "She looks like a fast one."

"She is," he said proudly. "Clocks zero to a hundred in four seconds."

She slid into the seat then eyed him. "I hope you're not planning to demonstrate."

He laughed. "No, not this time. I'm working hard to stay in your good books."

She could see that. He'd practically run away from her just seconds ago when their bodies touched. If that was what it meant to be in her good books then she'd throw out the darn books. Being a good girl was getting tired.

Storm went around to the driver's side and slid into the seat then they were off, his long-fingered hands holding the steering wheel and handling the car expertly. They were out of the city traffic and onto the highway in less than half the time it would have taken her to get there.

"You drive like a racecar driver." Dani watched in admiration as he handled the gears, revving up and shooting past so many other cars on the highway. She hadn't even seen a stick shift car in years but she remembered when she used to drive one. She'd actually liked the feel of the clutch and the shifting of the gears.

"Used to be one," he said casually, glancing over to give her a mischievous grin.

She looked at him through narrowed eyes. "You're kidding."

"Nope," he said and his smile was so smug she knew he was telling the truth.

"You, the first born of one of the wealthiest families in America, and your parents let you race cars? What were they thinking?"

He laughed out loud. "It's what I love, Dani. Fast cars, fast motorcycles and-"

"Fast women?" She finished the sentence for him.

"Wrong guess," he said with a chuckle. "I was going to say rock music. I love rock music." He reached down and switched on the radio and the music of Hootie and the Blowfish, 'I Only Want To Be With You', blared through the speakers.

That put an end to any further conversation so Dani leaned back and closed her eyes, the better to enjoy the song and the feel of the breeze whipping through her hair.

At that speed, in no time they were pulling off the highway and onto a local road. The closer they got to their destination the tighter Dani gripped the side of her seat. She had no idea what to expect. Would they be snooty and mean, immediately sniffing out her ordinary working class blood? Would they quiz her on things only rich people knew? She could just picture it - a discussion on quality wines, one in which she wouldn't even be able to participate because she didn't have a clue.

Before long they made another turn, this time onto what looked like a country road at the end of which stood a majestic mansion nestled among huge trees which had begun to sport the colors of autumn - yellows, golds and reds among the green leaves. Storm pulled up in front of it and hopped out to come around and open the door for her. Then, as if he knew she needed the support, he took her hand and they walked up the steps together.

Storm pushed the door open and as they entered the foyer he called out, "Mom, we're here."

"Finally. How are you, Storm? You need to come home more often."

Dani turned to see a tiny woman with short-cropped black hair coming down the hallway, her arms open wide. Storm stepped away from her and walked right into his mother's hug. "How are you doing, Mom?" He towered over the petite woman and had to bend over to hug her.

"Always better when I see you. You need to visit more often." She gave him a playfully accusing look. "Are you trying to avoid me for some reason?"

"Aw, come on, Mom," Storm said, looking almost guilty. "I come when I can."

Mrs. Hunter's hrumph told him what she thought of that. She did not respond to her son's defense. Instead she turned to look at Dani. "And who do we have here? Aren't you going to introduce me, Storm?"

"Of course." Storm took Dani's hand and pulled her forward. "Mom, I'd like you to meet Danielle Swift, my best kept secret."

"Secret is right," Mrs. Hunter said softly as she stared up at Dani. "Welcome to Hunter's Lodge, Dani."

"Thank you," Dani replied, almost feeling like she should do a curtsy. Although small, Mrs. Hunter was intimidating with her piercing gray eyes and regal posture. She looked like she should be sitting on a throne in England rather than presiding over a house on American soil.

"Mrs. Johnson has prepared a special meal to celebrate your spending the afternoon with us." She gave Storm a pointed look. "It's been such a long time."

Storms lips tightened but he said nothing. He simply put his hand under Dani's elbow and directed her down the hall after his mother.

Dani was beginning to understand the challenge Storm faced. Just by observing his mother who was obviously a strong woman she could sense that a lot was being demanded of him and he was expected to deliver. She could almost imagine Mrs. Hunter as a matchmaker-mother intent on selecting the perfect bride for him.

As tiny as she was, if Mrs. Hunter was such a powerful force what was her husband like?

Dani found out soon enough. Before she even got to the end of the hallway a booming voice shattered the cool quiet of the house.

"Storm, my boy, what breeze finally blew you our way?"

Edgar Hunter was a big man, both in size and personality, and when he came up to them and wrapped Storm in a huge bear hug Dani almost feared for his safety. As tall and muscled as Storm was, he was about half the size of his father. The man looked like he could easily snap his son's spine with that hug.

When they parted both men were smiling so Dani relaxed and smiled too, then Storm turned to her.

"Dad, this is Dani, the friend I told you about, the woman who's stolen my heart."

"Ah, ha. So this is the special girl you've been hiding all this time." His blue eyes twinkled in his weathered face and he opened his arms wide. "Welcome, my child."

Dani's eyes widened as she stared at the smiling man. There was no way she was going to step into that hug. He'd crush her like a bug.

Unfortunately, that decision was taken out of her hands when he took one step forward and gathered her into his arms. He released her a second later but she could honestly say that for that moment in time he had her fearing for her life. Okay, maybe she was being dramatic but goodness, how did a pixie like Janet Hunter manage with a giant of a husband like him?

"Now come, let's have dinner and get to know one another." Edgar led the way until they came to a majestic dining room with a table that looked large enough to seat forty. The room reminded her of the great halls in the castles of medieval times, it was so huge. Unlike those great halls, though, this room was bright and airy and the table was decorated with vases filled with a variety of flowers that graced the room with their fragrance.

To Dani's surprise dinner was not the elegant fare she was expecting - poached salmon or beef tenderloin in wine, caviar, and other foods of that nature. Instead, and much to her delight, they were served a salad with barbecued chicken, string beans, cornbread and macaroni salad. Dessert was her favorite - strawberry shortcake.

"How did you know?" Dani asked when the dessert tray was brought to the table. She looked over at Janet, as she'd now come to think of her. After the light banter during dinner she was no longer intimidated by the diminutive queen of Hunter's Lodge. "Can you read minds or something?"

Janet laughed. "Not at all, dear. When Storm told us he was bringing a special friend to meet us he demanded that we have strawberry shortcake for dessert."

Dani turned to Storm, still confused. "But how did you-"

"Our quilting session, remember? We talked about our favorite things." He shot her a warning glance.

"Oh, yes, that's right." She reached for her glass and pretended to take a sip of water, but she'd done it to hide her face which might be turning pink right at that very moment. She'd almost given the game away. They were supposed to know each other intimately so her expression of surprise would raise questions, to say the least. Thankfully, the Hunters didn't seem to notice her blunder.

By the time tea and coffee were served Dani was a bit more at ease, feeling like she'd passed the worst. The conversation was flowing and she was actually enjoying the company of Storm's parents. Edgar was so unlike her mental image of a billionaire. Somehow she had expected stuffy and serious, someone who might even look down his nose at her. He was the total opposite of that. Talkative and jovial, at one point he had her laughing so hard there were tears in her eyes. Janet, too, seemed to have softened toward her and they were soon engaged in an animated discussion about quilting techniques. Storm sat watching them, his lips curling in obvious amusement. He must be thinking what she was thinking - who would have known she'd find something in common with his mother?

The tea things cleared away, Storm reached over and took Dani's hand in his. "Mom and Dad, there is something I...Dani and I would like to tell you."

Janet straightened her back and her eyes brightened. Edgar cleared his throat.

"I think you may have already guessed. Dani and I are engaged." He gave her hand a slight squeeze, probably to reassure her.

Dani held his hand tight. He'd probably seen the nervousness in her eyes and felt the slight tremble of her fingers. The moment of reckoning was here. The Hunters had been friendly enough when they thought she and Storm were friends but how would they respond to the announcement that she might become a part of their family? "That's wonderful, honey," Janet said, beaming. She reached over and took Dani's hand. "Congratulations, dear."

They all turned to look at Edgar and he was grinning from ear to ear. "Well, thank God," he said in his booming voice. "Miracles do happen. I'll see Storm wedded and settled in my lifetime." He leaned forward to shake Storm's hand. "Congratulations, son. You're making a big step but it's the right one. A man's got to have a wife to be taken seriously in life and in business. Good move."

Dani released her breath in relief. Well, that had gone well, a lot better than she'd expected. She'd thought Storm would have to defend his choice, get his parents to accept her. She'd expected questions, lots of them - where was she from, what was her family background, what kind of business was she engaged in - but none of those came. Instead, they seemed so open and welcoming that Dani relaxed in her chair as she turned to look at her new husband-to-be.

Storm, however, was another matter. Where she had grown more comfortable with the situation he seemed to have moved in the opposite direction. She was close enough to see the dew of perspiration on his upper lip, and the tightness of his mouth spoke of a tension she'd not seen in him before.

What in the world was going on? Had he changed his mind? Well, if he wanted to back out of this twisted comedy it was too late now.

"Thanks," he said, his tone unusually serious at a time for celebrations. "Thanks for your well wishes and for making Dani feel welcome."

Well, that was a formal sort of way to thank your parents. She gave Storm a sideways glance then squeezed his hand. *Come on, Storm, don't melt down now.*

"And what's the date, son? Make it early. With my heart you know time is of the essence."

"Date…we haven't reached that far yet." By now Storm's face had a slightly pinker hue.

"Well, get cracking," Edgar, said with a laugh. "What ever thou doest, do it quickly. Didn't they say that in the Bible?"

"I agree," Janet said emphatically. "We've been talking to you for the longest time about getting serious about your life and the family business. The sooner you get the wedding out of the way the sooner you can take the reins and give your father a break."

"And start a family," Edgar did not hesitate to add. "I want to spend my retirement years playing with my grandkids."

Dani felt her face grow red at that request. Edgar certainly knew how to ask for what he wanted. Maybe that was why he'd been good at making billions.

"In time, Dad," Storm said distractedly, "in time." Then he looked at Dani, "Hey, do you want to see the tree house I built when I was a kid? It's still there."

Subtle change of subject, Storm, real subtle. Dani almost giggled. He seemed so desperate to get away from any further discussion of their engagement. She kept her face composed, hiding her amusement, and said in her best fiancée voice, "Of course, honey. I'd love to."

"Go ahead, kids," Edgar said with a wave of his hand. "Take her down to the stream, Storm. Nice and peaceful down there. She'll love that."

Storm got up and gave Dani his arm. He looked back to normal now, his face relaxed and smiling. "Are you a good climber? We'll go up and see what animals have taken charge of my old house."

She looked at him askance. "I don't know about that.
"

He was just about to respond when Mrs. Johnson stepped into the dining room. "Excuse me," she said, "but Miss Lola has stopped by for a visit. Should I have her wait in the sitting room or should I send her in?"

Edgar and Janet turned to each other and a look of concern passed between them. Dani looked at Storm. His face had suddenly lost its color. None of those were good signs. And as Dani stood there, looking from one to the other, she could tell that what was coming was not going to be good.

CHAPTER SIX

Edgar was the first to speak. "Please ask her to make herself comfortable in the sitting room. I'll be right there."

Mrs. Johnson nodded and went back through the door.

As soon as she'd left Edgar spoke. "Is Lola aware of this change in your status?' He gave Storm a pointed look.

Janet nodded. "You know how she feels about you. I think she was expecting-" She broke off suddenly and gave Dani a look heavy with guilt. "I'm sorry, Dani. I don't mean to be disrespectful to you. It's just...well, Lola's been in the picture for a while so this could be difficult. You and Storm spoke about her, I assume?"

Dani looked across at Storm, waiting for him to speak. She was the fake fiancée but this was his game. He should be the one giving explanations.

"We were getting to that-"

He didn't get the chance to say another word. At that instant the door to the dining room opened and Lola burst in.

"Janet, Edgar, have you heard? Storm-" She stopped short and her eyes grew round in surprise. "You. So you're the one who's turned him against me." She was staring at Dani, her eyes flashing with violent rage. "You stole him from me."

"Now, Lola," Edgar said, beginning to get up from around the table. "Let's not-"

"No, it's true. She did something to him, bewitched him or something. Didn't he go out with me just weeks ago? He was supposed to be mine." As Lola spoke her voice grew higher with agitation and she began to walk toward the table.

"Okay, that's enough."

Storm's voice must have shocked her back to reality. She halted abruptly and stared at him, her face contorted in her distress.

Storm stepped forward almost blocking Dani from Lola's view and folded his arms across his chest. "Lola, you and I know that there is nothing between us. It's all been a fantasy, a lie you fed yourself for so long you began to believe it. And we did not go out together two weeks ago. We met at the party, remember, then you asked me for a ride home." He released his arms and shoved his hands deep into his pockets. He shook his head. "I'm sorry this has hurt you but you have to get real. You have to give up the pretense."

Dani almost laughed. Give up the pretense, he said. And what were they doing? Creating an even more dangerous lie.

"No." Lola gave a broken sob and reached blindly for the table, looking like she was on the verge of collapsing.

"My child." Edgar was immediately at her side, supporting her and directing her into a nearby chair.

Storm had moved, too, but when his father caught her he froze. He stood back while Edgar patted her hand and spoke soothing words to her.

"I'll get a glass of water." Janet got up and hurried out the door.

For a moment longer Storm hesitated then he approached the now sobbing woman. "Lola, please. Don't cry." His voice was quiet and low and his face dark and serious. It was obvious that he was not enjoying Lola's distress. "I hate it that you're hurting right now and that I'm the cause. If I could have done anything-"

"You could have loved me." Lola lifted her tear-streaked face and looked at him with stricken eyes. "Why couldn't you love me, Storm? What is it about me that you hate so much?"

"Lola." This time Storm's voice was full of frustration. "Let's not go back there."

Lola sniffed then grabbed at the handkerchief Edgar held out to her. She dabbed at her eyes then looked over at Dani. "And who's she? What made her so special that you chose her and not me?" She glared at Dani across the room then her hateful stare turned into a frown. "Where have I seen you before?'

Dani's heart almost reached her throat. What if she was found out? She and Storm would have a lot to answer to. Her eyes went to him but he was scowling at Lola. The woman had the power to blow their cover to the sky.

Suddenly the tears dried up and Lola turned her full attention on Dani. "I know you..." she said, her voice uncertain but then she repeated it, her voice more confident this time. "I know I know you. I just can't say from where." She looked from Dani to Storm then back to Dani.

"There's something fishy going on here," she said, "and I'm going to get to the bottom of it."

Her eyes fixed on Dani, she got up and thrust the now damp handkerchief toward Edgar. Then she turned and her back ramrod straight, she walked out of the room, leaving them all staring after her.

Dani's eyes went back to Storm. Now what?

******

"Well, the good thing is my parents love you." Storm took a swig of his beer then relaxed in his chair and stretched his legs out in front of him. They were at an outdoor café, one she'd never even heard of but he recommended highly. She did not regret his choice. Tucked into a cul-de-sac at the outskirts of an exclusive resort, its clientele included many of the rich and famous of the Chicago area. It had been two days since the drama with Lola, and Storm and Dani were just getting the chance to do a postmortem and discuss their plan of action going forward. After Lola had stormed out they - mostly Storm - ended up fielding a barrage of questions and by the time they left Hunter's Lodge they were both too exhausted to even talk about it further. This evening, though, they would have to plan their next move. Who knew when Lola would strike again and next time she might deliver the killing blow to their pretense.

"You hope your parents love me," came Dani's rejoinder.

"I know they do," Storm said without hesitation. "I could see it in the way my Dad warmed to you. Even my Mom who's a bit more reserved was into you. You could see that she was actually concerned about how you felt when Lola came by."

"I have to admit, they were pretty nice to me," she said as she brushed a stray curl off her forehead and tucked it behind her ear. The light breeze of the outdoors kept blowing wisps of hair across her face. A drawback of dining outdoors but one she could definitely live with. The fresh air and the warbling of the birds in the nearby trees made it all worthwhile. "Still, I don't think they'll be quite so welcoming when they find out who I really am."

"I know my parents, Dani, and they're not snobs. Of course they'll accept you for who you are."

"Not if they find out my role in this farce. They'll hate me for it."

Storm shook his head and there was a look of regret in his eyes. "It's me they'd hate. I'm their son and I'm the one deceiving them." He pushed the beer bottle away and leaned forward. "You know, when my father congratulated me he looked so contented that the guilt slapped me right between the eyes. I almost caved in and told them the truth."

Dani nodded slowly. "I remember. I could see you were uneasy."

"Uneasy is an understatement," Storm said with a grimace. "I felt like a dog to be deceiving them like that." He leaned back in his chair and gave her a rueful smile. "When I first thought of it, it had seemed like a great idea. I didn't know I was going to get soft when it was time to execute."

"So...do you want to call it off?" Dani spoke in a low, quiet voice, not wanting to give away her emotions. At his words her heart had jerked in her chest and it hadn't been a happy feeling. It was as if she could not bear for the bond they had to dissolve.

"Not on your life. We've gone too far to turn back now. And besides," he shrugged and lifted his eyebrows, "you've seen how Lola behaved. If she gets wind that this is all fake she'll be after me again and this time I won't be able to shake her loose."

"I admire your modesty," Dani said, laughing at the way he sat there looking so full of himself. "It must be very trying to have women throwing themselves at you all the time."

"Actually, it is," he said, his look earnest. "Try being a rich, not to mention startlingly handsome, man for a day and you'll see what I'm talking about."

"Oh, you." She laughed and leaned over to give him a playful punch. She was joking around about it but she could understand exactly what he meant. Of course he'd have women after him. He was an eligible and very desirable bachelor.

And that was why it was so important for her to keep her distance, at least from an emotional standpoint. Storm had his pick of women and when he was really ready to settle down he'd select his life partner from his own circle.

She could not afford to start feeling soft toward him. If so, she'd do it at her own peril.

"There's a party coming up in a couple of weeks, one I've got to attend. And I'll need to have my fiancée on my arm." He cocked one eyebrow at her. "Are you game?"

Dani shrugged. "I'm always game," she said casually. "It's my job, remember?"

"Fair warning - Lola might be there."

"Oh." Dani didn't feel quite so confident then. The last thing she needed was the possibility of Lola launching another attack, this time in front of a crowd.

"Oh, is right," Storm said, his face serious. "We'll have to be prepared for just about anything. One thing we can't do is avoid the event. That would just raise suspicions. Lola already started questioning our relationship. We don't want my parents to start wondering, too."

"Oh," Dani said and then fell silent. She knew what he meant. They'd have to stay close to each other's side, hold hands and look like a loving couple. How in the world was she going to deal with that?

"Oh, again?" Storm chuckled. "Don't worry, we got through dinner with my parents and we'll get through this thing together."

She only wished she could be as confident. Needing to ease the tension, she decided to change the subject. "I need to be out of town this weekend. I hope it doesn't clash with any of your plans."

"Not at all," he said with a magnanimous wave of the hand. "You're free to go."

"Thanks," Dani said, more relaxed now. "I haven't been to see Brian since I dropped him off at the university. I want to take him some of his favorite goodies from home."

"You're going on a cross country trip. Sounds like fun." Storm had an eager look on his face. "Mind if I tag along?"

"It's not cross country," she said, bursting his bubble. "It's in Indiana so we'll only be crossing one state line. I'd love it if you could come along." Then, realizing that what she'd said could be interpreted in more ways than one she added, "I'd welcome the company."

"I'll come on one condition."

"What?" she asked, suspicious.

"You let me be your chauffeur."

"You've got it, chauffeur. Just as long as you remember that the highway is not a racetrack."

Storm gave a bow of acquiescence. "Whatever the lady wants."

Dani could only smile at that. She didn't dare divulge what had popped into her mind when he said those words. No, she would keep her mischievous musings to herself.

On Saturday morning when Storm picked her up in his now familiar Ferrari it was a perfect day. The sun, cheerful and bright in an almost cloudless blue sky, put her in an upbeat mood which Storm must have noticed because he gave her a wide smile, a quick hug and even a peck on the cheek then he bundled her into the car and they set off.

Dani grinned. She didn't know what kind of chauffeur he was, greeting his client with hug and kiss, but she wasn't complaining.

Under Storm's expert control the Ferrari ate up the miles in quick time and within less than an hour of leaving Chicago they were pulling onto the university campus. Dani directed him to the parking area then they headed for the student dorms in search of Brian.

"I'll call and let him know we're here." She took out her cell phone and dialed. She didn't even hear it ring before Brian's excited voice was on the line. When she disconnected she gave Storm a wide smile. "He's coming down to meet us."

She knew she probably looked like the Cheshire Cat in Alice in Wonderland but she couldn't help it. She'd missed her kid brother and she was looking forward to seeing him again, even if it was only to wrestle him to the ground and remind him who was boss.

She glanced at Storm then gave a surreptitious giggle. Maybe that wouldn't be a good idea, not in Storm's presence anyway. What would he think of her, a twenty-two year old woman seizing her brother in a headlock? He'd probably want to drop her off at the nearest mental institution.

Within a minute of speaking to Brian he was dashing out of Dillon Hall and down the steps toward them. He grabbed Dani up in a huge hug and spun her round then he grabbed her in a neck hold and tackled her to the ground, laughing the whole time.

Dani was laughing, too, not just at the sheer joy of seeing Brian again but at her futile plan to appear dignified in front of Storm. Brian had totally shattered that dream.

"I got you, Sis." Brian held her down for a second longer.

"Okay, you win, you win," she yelled.

Only then did he let her up. He was grinning as she righted herself and straightened her clothes.

"That was a surprise attack," she scolded and gave him a punch on the arm. "That was the only reason you beat me."

"Yeah, right," Brian scoffed. "I'm in college now, Sis. There's no way a girl can get me now, least of all my sister."

"We'll see," she said softly, making sure her voice reflected a quiet threat. "We'll see."

Then she turned to Storm. "I guess you know who this is."

Storm, who had been smiling at their antics, nodded. "The famous Brian Swift who you've been talking about all morning." He stuck out his hand. "Good to meet you."

Brian took it and they shook hands. "Yeah, same here." He stepped back and looked down at Dani. From his six foot two height that was easy. "Dani told me she'd have a chauffeur on her trip down her." He looked back at Storm. "You don't look like any chauffeur I've ever seen."

Storm laughed at that. "Blame your sister. She's the one who hired me."

The guys were still laughing when Dani clapped her hands together and said, "Okay, let's go. I've got a picnic basket full of goodies in the car but before we loose the human food disposal on it," she gave her brother a knowing look, "I would like a tour of Dillon Hall."

"Sure, I'll show you Big Red. Come on." Brian headed back toward the building with Dani and Storm right behind him. He took them through the lounges, starting with the one in the basement and the two on the main floor then up to the room he shared with one other freshman. As Dani expected, it was a mess.

She sighed. "Couldn't you at least have picked up the clothes from off the floor? You knew we were coming."

"Oh, yeah. I was planning on doing that," Brian said then he shrugged. "I guess I forgot."

Dani rolled her eyes. "God help the woman who becomes your wife."

After that Brian took them to his favorite place on campus, the dining hall which, to his great joy, was right next to the dorm. As he walked ahead of Dani and Storm, talking animatedly about the variety of meals offered, she touched Storm's arm.

"You can see what I had to deal with when he was at home," she whispered. "I was going broke keeping him fed."

"What was that?" Brian yelled back at them.

"Oh, nothing," Dani said but she and Storm exchanged an amused look and a smile.

After the tour they all went for a drive around the campus then they found a quiet grassy knoll with the perfect shady tree all red, green and gold in celebration of fall. There Dani spread out her blanket and laid out disposable plates, cups and flatware. Then, one by one she took out the plastic bowls and lifted the lids to reveal salad, cornbread, corn on the cob, potato salad and the piece-de-resistance, Southern fried chicken.

Brian rubbed his hands together in anticipation. "When did you make all that?" he asked. "This morning?"

"Yup. I was up before the birds. All for you, kid. Enjoy."

Storm shook his head and there was a smile on his lips. "I can see you and my mom have something in common. You're both fans of chicken."

She grinned and reached for a drumstick. "My favorite." That afternoon was one of the most relaxing times Dani had had in a long time. She enjoyed watching the men wolf the food down even though she almost had to fight to get a piece of the corn bread. People always joked about the appetites of growing boys but these were grown men. She'd marveled at how easily they packed away the pounds of food she'd brought.

After lunch she leaned against the tree trunk and listened to them talk animatedly about Notre Dame sports, with Brian giving Storm the low down on the latest wins in hockey, football and basketball. By the time they packed up the dinnerware and headed back to the car it was almost six o'clock.

Dani sighed in contentment, glad for a day well spent with her brother. And, if she were to admit it to herself, the new second-favorite male person in her life, Storm Hunter.

Back at the dorm Storm waited for Dani in the car as she walked up the steps with Brian.

"It was great spending today with you, kid. You look like you're doing good here."

"I am," Brian said with a nod. "I think I made the right choice, Sis. Notre Dame is a great school."

"Here." She dug into the back pocket of her jeans and pulled out a small roll of bills. "It's the money for your trip."

Brian's mouth fell open as he stared at the money. "All of it?"

"It's all here. Take it."

"Sis," he said, his voice soft with wonder, "How did you-"

"Don't worry about that. Just take it." She smiled at her brother, wondering if he knew how very much she loved him. She'd do just about anything to make him happy.

Brian took the money from her hand and tucked it into the front pocket of his jeans. Then he grabbed Dani and hugged her close. "Thanks, Sis. I love you."

"I love you too, Brian," she said and was surprised when her eyes welled up with tears. What was wrong with her these days? Please, she thought, don't let me turning into a softie.

They pulled away and Dani went down the steps and toward the waiting car. She turned and waved to Brian. "Be good," she yelled.

"I will." He waved back.

Storm pushed the door open and Dani slipped in, then they were off. She settled back in her seat, happy to relax and enjoy Storm's company. It had been a wonderful day and she never wanted the feeling of euphoria to end. When Storm switched the radio on and turned it to an easy rock station she smiled to herself. He would have preferred heavy rock music she knew, but he was just being nice. She liked that.

By the time they got to Chicago it was after nine o'clock. Being in no great hurry, they'd made a couple of stops along the way and Storm had cruised back to Illinois. It was like an unspoken agreement between them - let's make this day last as long as possible.

At nine-fourteen Storm pulled the car into the parking lot of Dani's building and switched off the engine. He gave a sigh, whether from tiredness or relief she wasn't sure, then he turned to look at her. "Thank you," he said softly. "I had a great time."

"No. Thank you," Dani countered. "You were the one who gave up your Saturday to drive me all that way."

He gave her a slow smile. "My pleasure."

The way he said it made Dani's breath catch in her throat. Why did he have to look and sound so sexy? He was a tempting dish that she was finding hard to resist.

"Would you like to come up…for a cup of coffee?" Now where had that come from? She hadn't planned to invite him up at all. She would have to blame it on the fact that she never wanted this day to end.

He must have been feeling the same way because his eyes brightened. "I'd love to."

"Great. I want to make sure you're bright-eyed and bushy-tailed for your drive home." She climbed out of the car and waited until he'd walked around to meet her then they walked to the apartment building in companionable silence.

Upstairs she directed him to the living room and gave him the remote control then headed for the kitchen. When she got back with a tray laden with coffee pot and mugs he was still flipping channels. When she approached he put the remote down and looked up at her, his face eager.

Was that look of anticipation for her or for the coffee? She bit her lip, trying hard not to laugh. *Oh please, Dani, let's not get ahead of ourselves. It's the coffee the man wants, not you.*

She rested the tray on the coffee table then sat at the other end of the sofa. She poured Storm's coffee and then hers while he flipped channels some more and finally ended on the Discovery Channel. They sipped coffee as they watched archeologists dig up a body they were convinced was the abominable snowman. When the coffee was done they sat there and watched some more until finally Storm put his hands on his knees and stood up.

"Well, it's been a heck of a day and I enjoyed every minute of it. It's getting late and I don't want to keep you so I'd better go."

"Where are you going?" Dani's voice was bold and imperious.

He stared down at her and his face registered his confusion. "Home?"

She stood up and folded her arms across her chest. "You're forgetting something. You're on my time and you don't leave till I say so."

Storm looked at her as if she'd gone crazy. "What the hell are you talking about?"

"I hired you for the day, remember...Mr. Chauffeur? The day doesn't end until midnight."

Dani didn't know where this bossy persona had come from but she was enjoying it. It was like she was rebelling against her own rules. Darn stupid rules, if she should say so herself. She'd always been the kind of person who went for what she wanted and tonight she wanted Storm Hunter.

She reached out and grasped two handfuls of Storm's polo shirt then plunked down onto the sofa, dragging him down with her. She immediately lay back on the pillows and cupped her hands behind his head then she pulled down so his mouth was pressed against hers.

Dani didn't know who was more surprised, Storm or her. Where had this aggressive Dani come from? Had one day in the outdoors driven her crazy?

Crazy was right. It was almost too outrageous to think about but deep down she knew..she'd gone and fallen stupidly in love with Storm and there was absolutely nothing in the world she could do about it.

He would probably say she'd fallen in infatuation with him, or it was just a crush because of their employer-employee relationship. But she knew. She knew without a doubt that this was love. What else could have her acting insane, doing anything to get this man's attention, to get him to want her?

The day they'd spent together must have been the tipping point for her. The feelings had been welling up but now they burst free from the dam she'd built around her heart and they were flooding her very soul.

Storm got over his shock real fast because, before Dani realized what was happening, she wasn't the one in charge anymore. He took control of that kiss, his mouth moving on hers, commanding then subduing her till she could only gasp then moan. He ignited the fire within her till she was kissing back with ardor that spoke of her need for him. God, how she wanted this man.

She tugged at his shirt till she'd pulled it out of his jeans then she slid trembling fingers over his rippling ab muscles and up to his chest. There she splayed her hands over the hard muscles over his breastbone then took his flat nipples between thumb and forefinger and teased and pinched them till they were hard nubs under her hands. He'd done the same to hers so she knew the effect her caress must have on him. She was rewarded when he stiffened then moaned his ecstasy even as they kissed.

Dani knew that to get what she wanted she needed to be brave and bold. She'd already rejected Storm before and he'd certainly hesitate to go farther than a kiss. If anything was to happen tonight it would all be up to her.

Without hesitation she grabbed the edge of his shirt and began to lift it up, to take it off him.

Storm broke the kiss. "Dani, are you sure?" He asked in a breathless whisper.

She knew what the real question was. Are you going to lead me on then kick me out like last time? She needed to reassure him. "I'm sure," she said and pushed against his chest till he was straight enough for her to push his shirt up and over his head.

Now his muscled chest was exposed in all its glory and it made her mouth water. With her newfound boldness she leaned forward and covered a nipple with her mouth. She sucked that nipple until it peaked in her mouth and she did not stop until he gasped and reached down to cup her head with his hands. He gently pulled her from that nipple and directed her to the other, where she gave it the same caress. He groaned out loud.

Dani knew Storm was ready for her and all that she wanted to offer. He was kneeling over as she lay beneath him and she could feel his arousal pressing into the softness of her belly. She began to unbutton her blouse.

As he looked down at her she stared into his passion-glazed eyes. "I want you so bad," she whispered, her desire for him making her tremble. Her blouse was off now and she started attacking the clasp of her bra. "I'm so sure of this. I want you to be the first and only man for me." The bra was off now and her breasts lay bare before him but she did not flinch. She had no shame, not when it was Storm looking down at her with desired-filled eyes.

Then, inexplicably, something in his eyes changed. "What did you say?" he asked, a frown now marring his face.

"I want you," she whispered. "Please don't let me wait."

"No, that other thing. Did you say...you want me to be the first?' His frown was getting darker which meant something was wrong. Something was terribly wrong.

"Y...yes," she said, hesitant. Could it be possible that this could make him angry?

He hopped up off the sofa so fast Dani literally felt the breeze of his departure. "You're a virgin?" he almost barked.

She sat up, her body going cold. "Yes, is that a problem?"

"What the hell kind of question is that? Of course it's a problem. I'm not into seducing virgins, if that's what you think."

"But...you're not seducing me. I'm seducing you." Dani stared up at him, confused. Then she remembered her bare breasts and crossed her arms over her chest.

"For God's sake, get dressed," Storm spat, his face dark and thunderous. He turned away and picked up his shirt from the floor then put it on and tucked it into his pants. Then he looked at her.

"Let's not do this again. I don't have time for games."

And that was when he killed her. His words, so full of venom, were like a poisoned arrow to her heart. She lifted her eyes to him, her heart pleading, but she could not say a word. She could not even move.

He stared at her for a moment longer and she thought she saw a flash of...regret? Too soon, it disappeared and his face became impassive and cool.

"Goodnight, Dani." His voice was quiet, emotionless. To her it was even worse than his anger.

When Storm left, closing the door behind him, Dani was still on the sofa, shirtless, her arms crossed over her breasts. She was staring straight ahead, her eyes unseeing, her heart feeling like it had died inside her.

In this very apartment she had rejected Storm and now he had rejected her. She'd been assertive, she'd been bold...and she'd been so foolish. Storm was her employer, not her fiancé. She'd begun to live the lie. But today it had seemed so real.

And so Dani sat there, the hurt holding her immobile. She wanted to cry, so badly, but she would not give in. She was Dani Swift and she never cried. She felt the sob rise but she refused to let it escape.

And so she sat there, staring at nothing, while the tears streamed down her face.

CHAPTER SEVEN

For the first time in his life Storm was watching an NBA game and could not focus. If anybody were to ask him what two teams were playing he'd probably get it wrong, he was so distracted. Asking him the score at that point was futile. He was still seething. Why had Dani come on to him, knowing she was a virgin? He knew that a woman's first time was usually a significant milestone in her life, one she would not take lightly. She'd remember it for the rest of her life. And she'd remember him. How then could he casually have sex with her? And that was all he'd wanted, just sex. Nothing more. But she would want 'forever after'.

And there was no way he was going to commit to 'forever after'. Not now, anyway. Maybe when he was forty. Maybe even thirty-five. But now? Not happening.

Okay, so he was a coward. He didn't want to commit to anyone but that was why he had hired her, wasn't it? She was supposed to be there to keep women off his back and his parents out of his business. But she'd betrayed him. She was trying to complicate his life even more than it already was. Talk about a turn of events.

He rubbed his hands across his eyes and gave a sigh of frustration. He didn't need this kind of stress on a Sunday afternoon.

His cell phone rang and he gave it a suspicious glance. He didn't want to talk to anyone right now, least of all his mother or father. But it was neither one of them. It was Lola.

God, what now? Another drama? Against his better judgment Storm reached out and pressed the answer button. This had better be quick. He put the phone to his ear. "Yes?"

"Storm, I'm so glad I got you. I need your help. We need your help."

"We?"

"My friend Charlene, she's starting a new business and we desperately need your advice."

"We?'

"Well, *she* needs your advice. Not we, she. But I was wondering, can we come see you and discuss her business plan? We just need to know if it makes sense."

"Not now."

"Of course not, Storm. We weren't planning to come now. What about one day this week? What about on Wednesday?"

For a long while Storm did not speak. He was in no mood to deal with Lola or her friend. He was a busy man and on top of that he had a lot on his mind. But he knew Lola. If she didn't get what she wanted she was like an alarm clock that never shut up - the kind that kept moving and hiding till you'd chased it all over the room. As much as he hated the idea the only way he'd be able to get rid of her would be to see her.

"Come by the office at four o'clock," he said, his voice impassive.

"Four o'clock. That's a little too early for us. What about six?'

"I leave the office at five. It's four o'clock or nothing."

"I'll take it. I'll see you then, Storm," she said in a sing-song voice.

"I? I thought it was 'we'."

"Oh, yes. We'll see you then. *Au revoir.*"

When Storm hung up the phone he gave up on the game, snapped off the TV and went to bed. It was the first time since the age of three or four that he'd be heading to bed while the sun was still in the sky but he just didn't have the energy to stay up any longer. He felt drained.

But in the bedroom sleep would not come. He lay on his back and stared up at the ceiling. What was happening to him? In his mind he kept reliving the previous day -the journey to Indiana, meeting Dani's brother, the fun they'd had on the way back…and then that disastrous night when she'd almost trapped him in her virginal dream. She was looking for a Prince Charming, not him. Not the man who hated the very thought of being tied down.

Storm had no idea when he finally drifted off to sleep but obviously he had, because the next time he opened his eyes it was Monday morning. And he felt lousy. And all he could think was, *Danielle Swift, stop screwing with my head.*

Wednesday came around but at four o'clock neither Lola nor her friend showed up at Storm's office for the meeting. He didn't bother to call to find out why. There was one thing he knew, though. They'd never get a slot on his calendar again.

That evening Storm was reading the day's news on his iPad when he heard a car pull up outside. He went to the door just as Lola hopped out of her silver sports car. She skipped up the steps, all smiles.

"Storm, you look so gloomy. Aren't you happy to see me?" She walked up to him and gave him a peck on the cheek.

"Lola. What are you doing here?" This woman was becoming an annoyance.

"The business plan, remember? We were supposed to discuss it today."

"At four o'clock."

"Oh, that. We got stuck at an event downtown. Couldn't make it."

He didn't bother to argue. What would be the use? "So where's the 'we' you've been talking about? All I see is you."

"Oh, Charlene couldn't make it," she said with a flippant wave of her hand. "It doesn't matter. I know all about the business. I can discuss the plan with you."

Storm seriously doubted she could, or if there was any plan at all, but he left it alone. He'd not been himself lately and he was not up to knocking heads with a woman as stubborn as Lola.

Once inside the house Lola seemed to have totally forgotten about the business plan. She made herself comfortable on the sofa in the den then found a way to cross her legs so that the slit in her skirt revealed a long length of thigh.

So she'd come to his house to flirt. Without being rude he'd have to find a way to extricate himself from this mess.

"Storm, honey, could you get me a drink? I'm so thirsty," she said, fanning herself with her hand.

"Water?"

"Chilled white wine will do nicely," she said. "Thank you so much."

It took all his willpower not to throw her out of his house. *Gently, Storm. Just give her the wine then tell her to go.* He left her lounging on the sofa and went to the kitchen. As soon as she'd had her drink she'd be gone. She'd already worn out her welcome.

******

To call him or not to call him, that was the question. Dani stared at her cell phone yet again, trying to shore up the courage and take the plunge.

Three whole days had passed since she'd last seen or heard from Storm and today, Wednesday, would make it four days. Since agreeing to play the role of his pretend fiancée this was the longest she'd gone without speaking to him and she felt as if she'd lost a limb. Was this what it meant to be in love? To be so consumed by another person that you couldn't eat, you couldn't sleep, from thinking about them? If so, this love thing was nothing but a nuisance. She'd been happy before she met Storm and now she was miserable. This kind of problem, she could do without.

She needed to talk to Storm, though. She had to tell him she would not be attending the party with him on Saturday night.

She was still staring at the phone, trying to work up the courage to make the call when it rang, making her jump. It was Storm. Ready or not, it was time to start talking.

She pressed the green button. Before he could even speak she blurted out, "Storm, I can't go through with this. I can't go to the party with you on Saturday night."

The response she got was surprising. Complete and utter silence. "Storm, are you there?" she asked.

The voice that came back to her was not Storm's at all. It was the high-pitched voice of a woman. A voice she knew. Lola's.

"Oh, please. Why would Storm take you to the party when he's got me?" She gave a mocking laugh. "In fact, we're all tied up right now. Aren't we, honey?" There was more laughter then the line went dead.

Dani took the phone from her ear and stared at it, not believing what had just happened. Storm had actually dialed her number and given his cell phone to Lola so the woman could insult her? How could he have sunk so low? With trembling fingers she laid the cell phone on the coffee table, her heart sinking to her toes. Storm must really hate her to do something like this. If only she'd never met him.

******

Dani's eyes welled up with tears and as they spilled over onto her cheeks she dabbed at them with a tissue. It was so sad, oh so sad. Why did they even make movies like this?

And yet, Steel Magnolias was one of her favorite movies. Each time she'd watched it she'd felt sad but she'd never actually cried until now. What was wrong with her? It was as if now she could cry at the drop of a hat.

What a way to spend your Saturday - watching old movies and bawling. She was reaching for another tissue when she heard the buzzer. Now who could that be, buzzing her at seven o'clock on a Saturday night?

Then she froze. Surely it wasn't Storm Hunter? She prayed someone had simply pressed her buzzer by mistake. She got up and pressed the button on the intercom. "Hello."

"Are you ready?" Storm's voice boomed back at her.

Her heart fluttered in her chest. "Ready for what?"

"For the party. I'll wait for you in the lobby."

"But...I'm not going."

That was greeted by silence. She'd thought he would shout, she'd thought he would rage. But when he spoke it was in a voice that was quiet, firm and ice-cold. "I'll give you until seven-thirty. If you're not down here by then you can go your own way and I'll go mine. But just remember, you'll have to pay me back every cent I've given you under this contract." He didn't wait for a reply and Dani was left clutching the phone to her ear, her body frozen in shock. Then she sagged in defeat.

She'd wanted to defy Storm. She'd wanted to hurt him as badly as he'd hurt her. But it was no use. He was too strong. He knew she couldn't pay him back and that was why he'd played that card.

She glanced at the clock. Two minutes after seven. No time to stand there pondering. She had exactly twenty-eight minutes.

Dani moved at the speed of light. She grabbed a dress of burnt gold from the closet, slipped on gold sandals then ran to the bathroom where she brushed the curls from her hair and fixed it into a sleek chignon. Then she applied make-up. Luckily she'd never been too heavy in this department so she was done in minutes. Then she dug in a box in her closet and pulled out her one elegant purse, a gift from an old family friend. Now she was ready and the clock read seven twenty-five. Just in time.

When Dani stepped out of the elevator she knew she looked composed and elegant. No one would have guessed she'd just been frantically dashing around the apartment. When Storm came forward to greet her she gave him a frosty look and a tight-lipped smile that would leave him in no doubt as to how she felt. She did not appreciate being bullied.

His greeting was just as cool. "Dani," he said with a nod then gave her his arm.

"Storm," she replied just as coolly, and slipped her hand into the crook of his arm.

They turned together and walked out of the lobby and toward Storm's waiting limousine, saying not a word until they were seated in the luxurious car.

Dani had thought that things couldn't have gotten any worse than that. But they did.

In the car there was no need for her to hide her true feelings. At the party, it was another matter. There, Dani was introduced to friend after friend of Storm's and each time she'd had to smile brightly and act happy and in love.

When they saw his parents the experience was even more trying. Whereas the friends merely greeted her, Edgar and Janet questioned them at length, even on matters that should have been personal. When were they going to start a family? If there were issues would they consider fertility drugs? They weren't married, hadn't even made the engagement public, and already they were getting the third degree.

Dani could see that Storm was not comfortable with the line of questioning. She was not surprised when he took her hand and asked her to dance. She knew exactly how he was feeling. Like him, she just wanted to get away.

They excused themselves and walked out onto the dance floor. Unfortunately, right at that moment the DJ decided to switch from the party beat of Rihanna's 'Love In A Hopeless place'," to the slow and sultry 'Crazy Love' by Brian McKnight. When Storm reached out to gather her in his arms she could hardly resist, not in front of all these people. As much as she wanted to stay far away from him she had to do her job and play the part of loving fiancée. He'd made it clear that shirking her duty was not an option and she planned on fulfilling her obligations to the letter.

Dani melted against Storm and gave him a look of love that she was sure could have won her an Academy Award. His look of surprise was enough to tell her the act was believable. And that was all it was - an act. Because from here on that was as far as she was going with Storm and not one step farther.

And so they danced in close embrace like any loving couple would, and no one could doubt their love.

The song had almost come to an end when they heard a clapping of hands and Dani, Storm and everyone else turned to see Edgar, looking grand in his beige suit with gold tie, calling for their attention. The DJ lowered the music and Edgar stepped forward, looking flushed and eager.

"Friends, I'd like to make an announcement."

There was a hush over the crowd as they all paused to listen.

"I have happy news," he said with a broad smile. "I don't think it's a secret that I've been hounding my son to settle down for the last couple of years. Well, folks, I'm happy to tell you that he has finally selected his bride-to-be and she is right there by his side tonight, Miss Danielle Swift."

A murmur went through the crowd and everyone turned to stare at the couple who stood frozen on the dance floor.

No one was more surprised than Dani. What had Edgar done? This was supposed to have been a game, nothing more, just something to keep the overly-eager parents happy for a while. Now Edgar had gone and made the whole thing public...without their permission.

Edgar and Janet were beaming proudly at them while Dani's heart was sinking into her shoes. She was not engaged to their son and never would be, not in this lifetime or ever. Even if she'd once held out hope of his ever loving her, she knew now that it was a hopeless dream. The man had engaged in the worst deception of all - at the same time he was playing games with her he was still leading Lola on. Obviously, he'd made the woman think she was still in the picture. What kind of man would do that? Unless he really did want Lola?

She had no chance to ponder that question because at that moment Storm put a firm finger under her chin and lifted her face to his and before she could react he was kissing her in front of the now cheering crowd.

It was too much. The betrayal, the shattered hope, the pain...and now having him kiss her like he was in love with her when they both knew it was a lie.

Distraught and furious, Dani pulled out of his arms, stepped back and slapped him across the cheek. Then she whirled, hot with humiliation, and ran across the dance floor and out the door.

CHAPTER EIGHT

Dani had nowhere to run. She had no car and because she'd stormed out of the place she had no purse. She wanted to leave. She wanted to get away from the reach of Storm and his friends and family. But how could she escape?

She hurried down the driveway, walking as fast as her high heels would take her. She would walk all the way home if she had to.

She heard footsteps and she didn't need to turn around to know who was following. She could sense Storm's presence from a hundred yards away.

He caught up to her in seconds and grabbed her arm. "What kind of stunt was that you pulled in there? You embarrassed me in front of everybody."

Dani jerked her arm away and turned on him. Even if she had no right to be furious, she was. "You deserve it, you beast. How dare you kiss me like you mean it when you have Lola waiting in the sidelines? Why didn't you hire her to be your fake fiancée?"

He frowned. "Lola? What the hell does Lola have to do with any of this?"

"Oh, don't play dumb with me, Storm. I'd respect you more if you'd just come clean."

"Come clean with what?" he almost shouted. "Will you stop talking in riddles and tell me what you mean?"

"Well, if you insist," she said sarcastically. "You called me Wednesday night and gave Lola the phone. What did you expect us to talk about? You?" She put her hands on her hips. "Or were you just trying to make a point, that if I didn't want to play the part you still had Lola to fall back on? What kind of a sick-"

"Hey, stop. You just stop right there." He put up a hand, silencing her. "First of all, I did not call you on

Wednesday. Since last Saturday the first time I reached out to you was tonight." He folded his arms across his chest. "And secondly, there is nothing going on between Lola and me and there never will be."

He sighed and released his arms. He looked like he wanted to hold her but instead he shoved his hands into his pockets. "I think I know what happened. Lola dropped by my place uninvited Wednesday night. I left for maybe five minutes and went to the kitchen. She must have used the opportunity to find your number in my cell phone and call you." He shook his head. "You have to understand, Dani. Even though there was never anything between us, Lola sees herself as a woman scorned. She would do anything to destroy what we have."

Dani's heart lurched. "What we have?" she whispered, almost afraid to repeat it. "But...we have nothing."

Slowly, Storm shook his head and a smile softened his lips. "That's where you're wrong, Dani. We have everything. I was just too stubborn to admit it."

Dani stared up at him, confused. "I...don't understand."

"I don't blame you," he said enigmatically. "The truth is, I didn't understand either, until tonight." He took her hands in his. "Do you know why I got so angry last Saturday when you told me you were a virgin?"

"No," she said, frowning. She was still lost about that one.

"I was a coward, Dani, afraid of commitment, afraid of losing my bachelor lifestyle. When you told me you'd never made love before I realized that I couldn't be with you and walk away. You'd want more. And I was afraid of that." He gave a bitter laugh. "I was so darned stupid. It took the time I spent away from you, time I spent in misery, for me to realize how much I want you in my life."

Then he gave her a look so open and honest that she could not doubt his words. "I'm tired of running, Dani. I want to commit and I want that commitment to be with you."

"And...Lola?" she whispered, holding her breath.

He laughed out loud. "And Lola. This is my commitment to Lola - to stay as far away from her as I can, so help me God."

"Oh, Storm," she said, her voice cracking, "I love you so much."

"And I love you, my sweet Dani," he replied, and put a finger under her chin to lift her face to his just as he had done before. He put his lips to her cheek, kissing away the tears that ran down her face. "I thought you said you never cry," he whispered.

"This time," she said with a sniff, "it's because I'm the happiest girl in the world."

He kissed her then, full on the lips, and she kissed him back with all the love she'd stored up in her heart.

It was several minutes before they stepped back and out of each other's arms. "Come," Storm said finally, "let's go back inside before they send the police to hunt us down."

She chuckled, took his hand and walked proudly by his side. There was nothing anyone could do or say that would make her feel embarrassed, not as long as she had Storm, her man, by her side.

As they entered the room everyone turned toward them but they must have seen something special on their faces because first one person started to clap, then another, until the entire room was clapping, welcoming them back.

Then, as if she hadn't had enough shock for one day, Storm led her to the center of the room and the crowd backed away, clearing a space for them.

Her heart leaped into her throat when right there, in front of his friends and family, he went down on one knee and took her hand in his.

"Danielle Swift," he said, looking up into her face with an expression of such devotion that her heart trembled, "will you be my wife?"

"Yes," she whispered, "a million times, yes."

The crowd erupted in whoops and cheers and as the whistles and yells filled the room Storm got up, gathered her in his arms and gave her a kiss that made up for all the other kisses she'd denied herself.

And Dani knew that this new job he was giving her, the job of being his wife, was one that would last a lifetime. She could hardly wait to start.

EPILOGUE

"Do you know you're crazy?" The words were said in a soft, almost sleepy whisper as Dani lay in Storm's arms and stroked the taut, smooth skin of his chest.

"Hmm?" He sounded just as sleepy and contented as she did.

That was what happened to you after round after round...after round...of love-making. They were both too exhausted to do anything but drift off to sleep.

"I said you're weird." She chuckled softly as her cheek rested above his heart. She loved hearing the steady thump. It was a solid sound, a sound that made her feel that their love was solid and sure and would last forever.

They'd been married three days now and it felt like they couldn't get enough of each other. At least that was how it felt to her and, based on Stone's enthusiasm, she would say he felt the same way. She wished this honeymoon would never end.

'Why?" This was followed by a stifled yawn.

Dani smiled and slid her hand up and over his tight stomach to caress his broad chest. "Because you're probably the only man in the world who would follow a smack with a marriage proposal."

She heard a rumble in Storm's chest and then he was chuckling. He wrapped his arms around her and pulled her close.

"What else could I do? I had to save face somehow, didn't I?" He was still laughing softly as he stroked her arm but then his laughter died away and he drew in a deep breath. "But seriously, Dani, there was absolutely nothing else I could have done. Call me crazy, but no matter what, I was not going to let you go." He pulled her even closer. "Once I admitted to myself that I'd fallen in love with you,

there   was
hardly anything you could have done to get rid of me."

He leaned down and kissed the top of her head. "Sorry, but you're stuck with me for life."

She turned her face up to his. "Bad boy," she whispered, "you're not sorry at all. And neither am I. I love you, Storm."

"And I love you." He bent his head to kiss her ever so softly on the lips.

Dani smiled and rested her cheek back in its special place above his heart. And as she listened to the steady thump-thump, and as she slowly drifted into slumber, she sighed softly, happy that the man she loved with all her heart would share her life...from this day forward.

THE END

Thank you for reading the BAD BOY BILLIONAIRES Collection I, Volumes 1 - 4. I sincerely appreciate your support. If you enjoyed reading these stories, please drop by my book page on Amazon to leave your review. That's the best support any author could ask for. Thank you in advance.

BAD BOY BILLIONAIRES
Judy Angelo

Volume 1 – Tamed by the Billionaire
Volume 2 – Maid in the USA
Volume 3 - Billionaire's Island Bride
Volume 4 - Dangerous Deception
Volume 5 - To Tame a Tycoon
Volume 6 - Sweet Seduction
Volume 7 - Daddy by December
Volume 8 - To Catch a Man (in 30 Days or Less)
Volume 9 - Bedding Her Billionaire Boss
Volume 10 - Her Indecent Proposal
Volume 11 - So Much Trouble When She Walked In
Volume 12 - Married by Midnight
Volume 13 - The Billionaire Next Door
Novella - Rome for the Holidays
Volume 14 - Rome for Always
Volume 15 - Babies for the Billionaire
BAD BOY BILLIONAIRES, Coll. I - Vols. 1 - 4
BAD BOY BILLIONAIRES, Coll. II - Vols. 5 - 8
BAD BOY BILLIONAIRES, Coll. III - Vols. 9 - 12

The NAUGHTY AND NICE Series
Volume 1 - Naughty by Nature

MEET THE BAD BOY BILLIONAIRES
FROM COLLECTION II
VOLS. 5 - 8

TO TAME A TYCOON - Vol. 5
Enrico Megalos - A shipping tycoon with a big problem but one which 'lion tamer', Asia Miller, is determined to fix.

SWEET SEDUCTION - Vol. 6
Jake McKoy - Billionaire author, philanthropist and recluse - a man with a past that is tearing him apart. Will Samantha Fox be the woman to pull him out of his shell?

DADDY BY DECEMBER - Vol. 7
Drake Duncan - Billionaire investor and a man determined to win the love of his life: a woman who is just as determined...to stay the heck out of his way.

TO CATCH A MAN (IN 30 DAYS OR LESS) - Vol. 8
Stone Hudson - Owner of Hudson Broadcasting Corporation, Stone is thrown for a loop when he meets a woman gutsy enough to laugh at him. And then she turns into a temptress. How can he resist?

Alpha males at their best - which one will you fall in love with?

(One free story in this collection)

MEET THE BAD BOY BILLIONAIRES FROM COLLECTION III VOLUMES 9 - 12

BEDDING HER BILLIONAIRE BOSS - Vol. 9
Rockford St. Stephens - The owner of a newly acquired luxury vacation business who finds himself boss to an executive assistant who can't stand him...but who he finds impossible to resist.

HER INDECENT PROPOSAL -Vol. 10
Sloane Quest - The media mogul who's rocked back on his heels when his top competitor, the lovely Melanie Parker, makes him an offer he can't refuse.

SO MUCH TROUBLE WHEN SHE WALKED IN - Vol. 11
Maximillian Davidoff - The cosmetics giant turned NASCAR entrepreneur who's bowled over by the most ornery woman he's ever met.

MARRIED BY MIDNIGHT – Vol. 12
Reed Davidoff – The fashion mogul who gets caught up in a fairy tale romance that makes him wish he could reverse his past. After the mistakes he's made, can he win the hand of the princess?

(One free story in this collection)

VOLUME 5 - TO TAME A TYCOON

HOW DO YOU TAME A TYCOON?

Enrico Megalos is bold, brash and a big problem...at least for his staff in the Miami office of Megalos Shipping. And that's where the lion tamer comes in.

Asia Miller, personality coach, is hired to tame the big boss. She takes on the challenge, not realizing until it is too late that while taming him she is also losing her heart...to the one man it doesn't pay to love.

Sun, sea and a steamy affair - a thrilling ride on the sensual side.

VOLUME 6 - SWEET SEDUCTION

SEDUCTION SO SWEET...

Jake McKoy moves to a tiny town in upstate New York to escape a painful past. He has no idea that it is here that he will find healing and strength and a new start in life. And that healing comes in the form of a fresh-faced woman who steals his heart.

Samantha Fox was only a month away from her wedding day when her fiance broke the engagement. He'd found a more 'suitable' bride. Haunted by the constant fear that she's not 'good enough', Sam finds it hard to give her heart to another man. And when that man happens to be a billionaire who can't let go of his past, things become complicated indeed.

Can Jake and Samantha overcome their difficult pasts to forge a bright future together?

VOLUME 7 - DADDY BY DECEMBER

A DADDY IN THE MAKING...

A little girl, a wish, and a woman determined to stay out of his reach. How to reconcile the three?

Billionaire investor, Drake Duncan, is at the top of his game. He decides to hire a ghostwriter to work on his memoir. Little does he know that the writer who will answer the call is truly a ghost - from his past.

Meg Gracey is the proverbial 'starving artist', a writer down on her luck. When she is offered a contract as ghostwriter she jumps at the chance, only to later realize that the job will throw her directly in the path of the man she vowed never to 'touch with a long stick'. Caught between starvation and emotional torture she is forced to choose.

Does she follow reason or give in to the desires of her heart?

VOLUME 8 - TO CATCH A MAN (IN 30 DAYS OR LESS)

HOW DO YOU CATCH A MAN...IN 30 DAYS?

Indiana Lane is in a pickle. She must find a man, fall in love and get married...all within the space of thirty days. How in the world can she pull this off? And then she runs into Stone Hudson - or, more accurately, he runs into her - and that's when the adventure begins.

Stone Hudson has met his match. He is used to women fawning over him and then he meets Indie, a woman who tells it like it is. And worse, she dares to tease him wherever and whenever she desires. Stone is intrigued, to say the least, but then his heart is snagged on a wire from which there is no escape.

Will the wedding bells ring for Indie, and will they ring in time? Thirty days is not a lot of time...

VOLUME 9 – BEDDING HER BILLIONAIRE BOSS

SLEEPING WITH YOUR BOSS – CAN ANY GOOD EVER COME OF THAT?

Dana Daniels considers herself to be the consummate professional and she would never, under any circumstances, mix work with pleasure. She's got the reputation of being the 'office bulldog' and has killed the hopes of many an interested male co-worker. But when her kindly boss is replaced by a rigid block of stone, that's when she knows that she's in trouble. Because the man who now runs the show, a man she would love to hate, is the only one who has ever made her want to forget the rules and partake of forbidden fruit. But how can she give in to her desires? The man is her boss, after all.

From the first day he lays eyes on her, Rockford St. Stephens is blown away by his executive assistant. Much good that will do him, though. The woman hates him from day one…and she says so. But although he knows how she feels, he can't resist the pull of attraction. Boss or not, he wants Dana Daniels. And if ever there were a situation that could lead to trouble, this is it. Can he afford to go down that road?

Conflict meets passion – a heady combination…

VOLUME 10 - HER INDECENT PROPOSAL

GIVE ME A BABY...NO STRINGS ATTACHED

Melanie Parker is at the top of her game. Thirty-three years old, owner and CEO of Parker Broadcasting Corporation, with assets totaling over a billion dollars. There are many who would die to be in her shoes. But there's one thing Melanie feels is missing from her life. A child. She's always dreamed of one day being a mother but just never found the time to fall in love. And now time is running out. So she seeks out the one man who she knows can give her what she wants and will demand nothing in return, a man who's a billionaire himself.

Sloane Quest can't believe it when the owner of Parker Broadcasting Corporation – his biggest competitor in the media business – makes him the craziest of all proposals. The decision he makes is quick, and it probably defies all reason, but he has an ulterior motive which will not be denied.

Complications, intrigue and a baby bargain in the middle. Can love conquer all?

VOLUME 11
So Much TROUBLE WHEN SHE WALKED IN

TROUBLE TO THE 'NTH DEGREE.

When Maximillian Davidoff meets Silken McCullen little does he know how much trouble will follow in her wake. The woman practically gets him thrown out of an establishment he could have purchased without a thought. And then, as if that weren't bad enough, she bulldozes her way into his life and proceeds to act like she's in charge. He soon finds out that there's a whole lot of woman packed into that petite bundle.

Silken McCullen has always had a feisty streak but no matter how she tries to curb her fiery nature it's forever getting her in trouble. When she first meets Maximillian Davidoff it is under less than ideal circumstances...particularly because her temper clouds her judgment and she ends up cursing him out. It is only after she has given him a good piece of her mind that she finds out that he is innocent of her charges. Now it falls on her to track him down and apologize. But apologies come hard for Silken and, before you know it, she's in a new kind of trouble with Max...but this time it's oh, so sweet.

With Silken McCullen, trouble is always just around the corner.

VOLUME 12 - MARRIED BY MIDNIGHT
A modern-day Cinderella Story

A PRINCE TO THE RESCUE?

Golden Browne is the victim of a fate that, while not worse than death, is almost more than a girl can bear. Having no way out, she resigns herself to her sad fate. And then she meets a man who is like a prince from a fairy tale, her knight in shining armor who will rescue her from the wicked wizard, A.K.A. Dunstan Manchester, the stepfather she just can't stand. But just when Golden thinks her story will have a happy ending, fate takes a nasty turn and she finds out that the man she'd hoped would be her savior is not the man she thought he was.

Reed Davidoff is entranced when a girl with hair like sunset runs out of his fashion show leaving behind a golden slipper, his only clue to who she is. He is determined to find this enchanting creature but when he does he realizes he has bitten off more than he can chew. Because, after all, how can he give Golden what she wants when he's in a prison of his own?

Will this fairy tale have a happy ending?

VOLUME 13 - THE BILLIONAIRE NEXT DOOR

NEVER PIT AN ALPHA MAN AGAINST A FEISTY FEMALE

Soledad Felix doesn't take guff from anyone, not even if that someone is the tall, dark and gorgeous hunk who moves in next door. Since the day he moves in he's a royal 0pain in the rear, going out of his way to make himself a nuisance. But then, as fate would have it, her big, bad and bossy neighbor falls right into her hands. And with him at her mercy, it's time to make him pay...

Ransom Kent likes to mind his own business and lead a quiet life but tell that to his crazy neighbor next door. From the first day they meet it's like she's got this thing against him, a crazy vendetta of her own making. And it doesn't help that she's both beautiful and bewitching, with a whole lot of hot sauce on top. It's an alluring combination that he just can't resist. But when he gives in to the temptation and hands her his heart on a platter, that's when he realizes she's nothing like the woman he thought she was.

The epic battle of fire and ice, and only one can be the victor...

NOVELLA - ROME FOR THE HOLIDAYS

Talk about sexy as sin...

Arie Angelis is floored when she lays eyes on the handsome hunk seated at the head table at the holiday event she's catering. She literally can't take her eyes off him. She's always prided herself on being the consummate professional, but not this time. But, attracted or not, when she finds out who he is she realizes he's way out of her reach. But you can't stop a girl from dreaming...

Rome Milano is used to getting what he wants but when he meets the hot and heavenly Arie Angelis he learns that he can't always have his way. He's used to calling the shots but, if the lady has her way, not this time...

'

(This story has a sequel - Volume 14 - Rome for Always. Read on to learn more)

VOLUME 14 - ROME FOR ALWAYS
(sequel to 'Rome for the Holidays)

SHE HAD ROME FOR THE HOLIDAYS, BUT WOULD
SHE HAVE HIM FOR ALWAYS?

Arie Angelis is on top of the world. She's engaged to the
man of her dreams, the super-handsome and successful
CEO of Belitalia, Rome Milano. She could not believe it
when he proposed on Christmas Day. Of course, she said
yes! But then, only a month into their engagement there's a
turn of events that threatens to steal her newfound
happiness. In the past she'd made a life-altering choice.
Now it's time to stand by that decision. The only question
is, will Rome stand with her or will it send him running?

Rome Milano knows a good thing when he sees it and
when he meets Arie he has no doubt that she's the one for
him. He falls so swiftly in love with her that within weeks
of meeting her he's proposing. He can't be any happier
when she accepts.
But there's just one problem - how to convince the
important people in his life that this is for real. Now that
he's found happiness will he be forced to choose between
love and loyalty?

It's decision time on both sides. Through it all, will love
prevail?

The NAUGHTY AND NICE Series

VOLUME 1 – NAUGHTY

THE NAUGHTIER THE BETTER...

Tessa Tyndale is known for her naughty nature. Although she's a high school teacher she's no angel. She's been guilty of a prank or two. And then she meets Wolf Spencer, gloomy and serious, the very opposite of Tessa's idea of the ideal mate. But, strangely enough, this is the man who makes her heart race. Now if only she can change him from grumpy to fun-loving...it's a challenge that she's willing to take on. With Tessa, anything is possible.

Wolf Spencer is intrigued by the petite blonde pixie he meets at his friend's wedding. But when he tries to make friends he's surprised to find that she's not at all interested in him. And then he realizes that she's nothing like what he'd thought. Far from being demure, this woman is daring and bold and not at all afraid of playing tricks on him.

Wolf soon finds out that around Tessa nobody is safe, especially not him...

If you would like notification when I have new books out just drop me an e-mail me with the simple subject line: 'Yes'.

I'll keep you posted!

judyangelotreasure@gmail.com

Happy reading!

Made in the USA
Coppell, TX
14 September 2020